TO SLIP THE SURLY BONDS OF EARTH

TO SLIP THE SURLY BONDS OF EARTH

BOOK THREE

THE CLOUDS OF WAR

HUGH CAMERON

Rev. date: 08/10/2020

To order additional copies of this book, contact:
Xlibris
1-888-795-4274
www.Xlibris.com
Orders@Xlibris.com
813509

CONTENTS

To Slip the Surly Bonds of Earth

Book 3
The Clouds of War

Hugh Cameronbstract

The West continues its precipitous decline. The ancient, magnificent, awe-inspiring Christian churches, which had taken centuries to build, are burning all over Europe; and that tragedy and violence on the streets are becoming so commonplace that it barely is mentioned by the media. Even the most egregious terrorist outbreaks are passed over by politicians as something that occurs in big cities and the indigenous population should simply get used to it.

Policing in most of the West has sunk to an all-time low. Rape of women and children has reached unprecedented levels. Crimes against property and person are largely ignored. Breaking and entering now no longer even merits a police inspection. Horrifying acid attacks—where acid is thrown on a young woman, destroying her face—never before seen in Europe, are barely mentioned. Any vestige of free speech has become a thing of the past, and there is a return to the thought police of the Communist era.

The Prometheus Group, a disparate collection of people who fear for the future of civilization, especially the unlikely enlightenment concept of intrinsic individual human worth, have established small colonies on Mars and the moon. They continue to fly under the radar of public attention as much as they can while quickly expanding these colonies. The economic collapse of countries, such as Greece, had long been anticipated. Unsurprisingly, the economic situation in Canada suddenly deteriorates, and the US president is forced to step in to prevent complete anarchy, which would threaten the undefended US northern border. Unwilling to involve the United States government directly, she asks the Prometheus Group for personnel to help oversee and assist the economic rescue of Canada, which the group agrees to with exceeding reluctance.

More of the exceptional children continue to be sought by the Prometheus Group and continue to be found in the most unlikely places.

As before, they are mainly seeking girls whose genius would otherwise be missed. These children are enlisted into the effort to produce the science that will get as many people as possible into space and speed the terraforming of Mars before the cataclysm of civil war, which is now inevitable in Europe and will likely spread to involve the world. Any extension of war outside Europe will inevitably result in a nuclear exchange with unimaginable destruction, as a single nuclear airburst could produce such an electromagnetic pulse to wipe out all computers within the blast area. This disaster, multiplied many times over and almost certainly aided by biological warfare, would produce a possible reversion to primitivism, tribalism, and savagery or the establishment of a dystopian rigid, unchangeable medieval philosophy.

About the Author

Hugh Cameron is an internationally known orthopedic surgeon, born in Scotland, who lives and works in Toronto and who was at the forefront of modern joint-replacement surgery. He was the codeveloper of the modern method of fixing artificial joints to bone on which most people with artificial hips walk. He has designed numerous artificial joints, some of which continue to be implanted. For more than thirty years, he, with a small band of largely North American colleagues, traveled the world teaching modern joint-replacement surgery. He has published more than two hundred scientific articles and is the author of six books, two being technical, one entitled *The Technique of Total Hip Replacement*. This novel is the third in the series To Slip the Surly Bonds of Earth, which follows the fortunes, lives, and loves of the Prometheus Group, set against a realistic view of the ominous future, with ideas about escaping the oncoming tragedy.

INTRODUCTION

The Prometheus Group is a disparate collection of farsighted people who came together years before to look for exceptional children, particularly girls, whose genius would likely otherwise have been missed. The search continues. Initially based in Luxembourg, the rising tide of terrorist violence in Europe and the realization that the only safe harbor eventually will be space, forced them to relocate their headquarters to the US.

The group, now consisting mainly of strong, opinionated women, have reached the conclusion that the US would stand as a bastion of freedom when the rest of the world crumbled into despotism, collectivism, or anarchy. The deserts of the southwest were the only realistic places to establish an earth base, where shuttle rockets could be launched to take emigrants to the new colonies on the moon and Mars.

They were exceedingly pessimistic about the place of women in the looming new, degenerate medieval-type world and the long-term survival on Earth of that strange enlightenment concept of the intrinsic value of each human, a belief that had arisen nowhere else in the world's history. It was that belief, and that belief alone, that had mankind reaching for the stars.

The group was constantly concerned about government takeover of their organization, with consequent smothering of new ideas under futile burgeoning rules and regulations. In consequence, they preferred as much as possible to fly under the media and political radar.

CHAPTER 1

Sheila

Sheila MacDonald was found in what was euphemistically called a new city in Scotland. Glasgow—and in particular, an area called the Gorbals—was at one time notorious as the worst slum in Europe. It was famous for its gang fights with the favorite weapons being open razors and bicycle chains. A new city was built many miles outside Glasgow, and the slum population, most of whom were on welfare anyway, were moved out of the inner city into their new residence. Little in the way of public transit was made available for the inhabitants of this new city to visit Glasgow, which was reasonable as very few of these people were employed in any case. The results were of course predictable, but no one cared; out of sight, out of mind. A similar tactic of shifting the problem populations to an isolated suburb was adopted in several other cities in Scotland.

Sheila, like all the children who joined the Munro Foundation, came to the attention of a teacher through her extraordinary mathematical ability at an early age. The teacher was vaguely aware of the Munro Foundation and its search for children with just this ability and the possibility of remuneration for the finder. He sought more information and applied in her name, and a psychologist showed up. IQ and personality testing showed that the child fulfilled the criteria they were looking for—specifically, a hard-driving genius, low in empathy, high in conscientiousness, and with an astounding IQ of 175.

Manon, one of the founders of the Munro Foundation based in Luxembourg, had by now established an extensive economic empire across

Europe. One of her people, a young woman who now oversaw one of her businesses in England came up to Scotland to interview the parent, as the girl lived with her father, her mother long since having disappeared. The girl was nine years old. As it was late morning, the father, who was an unemployed alcoholic, was still sober. He actually was very clever himself and had insight into his own wasted life. All he saw most days was the bottom of a bottle and an early death, which, like many alcoholics, he was resigned to and quite welcomed.

He was hungover and remorseful. He had no illusions and knew in his heart that if his child stayed with him, she would end up as a single mother, working a dead-end job, if she worked at all, and that her child would be the same, an endless cycle of hopelessness and despair.

When the Foundation program of a residential scholarship was explained to him, he realized immediately that this was a chance for his daughter to break out, to be something he never was and never would be. This was the one and only chance she would ever get. He signed the papers, hastily packed her few things, and saw her to the door with the young woman. He knelt and embraced his daughter. There were tears in his eyes, his voice hoarse with emotion.

"Dinna come back, Sheila. There is nothing for ye here, no hope and no future. Work hard at your lessons now, lass, and make me proud o' ye."

He saw his child enter the limo and remained watching until the vehicle disappeared. He went back into his house and closed the door behind her with an empty sense of relief. He felt he had done one good thing in his life. In a fashion eerily similar to Takes Away Clouds Woman's father in Alaska, he drank very heavily that night and fell asleep, wishing that he would not wake in the morning like so many alcoholics. He got his wish. The body was not discovered for several days. No one knew where she had gone, so it was several weeks later before Sheila found out that her father was dead. She mourned for him, for his bright talent, for what might have been, for his goodness when he was sober, and for his tearful regrets. She was forever grateful to him for forcing her to leave and telling her not to come back.

When Sheila joined the Prometheus Group, they were still based in Luxembourg. She was one of these extraordinarily pale-skinned, green-eyed redheads who needed a little cosmetic dentistry only. The other genius children already there were far ahead of her. Once she caught up, which with tutors she did rapidly, she came to love the fierce academic competition among the children and the grind of the study program. She also found the vigorous physical training that everyone undertook strange at first but then accepted as fact of life. They were also encouraged in some form of the arts, such as dance and music, if they wished. When the group went to Arizona, she learned to ride and shoot, like the other hothouse plants.

Neil Munro, another Scot and a former boxer and Luxembourg politician, was, among other duties, the nominal leader of the Foundation academy and oversaw the education of these children. To compete for Munro's attention, which Sheila craved, she taught herself a little Gaelic, the old language of Scotland, of which Munro himself knew barely anything. She spoke to him in Gaelic, and he did learn a few words just to please the earnest little girl, although she kept chiding him that he knew more Irish than Scottish Gaelic.

She learned the Scottish dancing, especially the sword dance, where they dance over the crossed swords, and she always pushed him to dance with her. Munro had learned to do so on the recommendation of his American publicity agent when he was a professional fighter. The big man and the little redhead dancing side by side drew some smiles, but both took it seriously. When the policewomen from Japan began to come for further training at the ranch in Arizona with a view to become Praetorian Guards, they also liked it. Some learned the dance, as did Tomiko, the famous Japanese Olympic pistol shooter and head of the Praetorian Guard organization, who were closely allied to the Munro Foundation.

Sheila raced through the education program, and by seventeen, she had a double degree in engineering, which Munro saw as a basic degree for everyone, no matter what they decided to do subsequently, and accounting, as she had no interest in pure science. At fifteen, she had spent some time working with Manon, who had remained behind in Luxembourg, overseeing her ever-expanding business conglomerate when the rest of the group moved to the US. Sheila adored that elegant, hard, cynical woman.

Sheila enjoyed that experience so much that after she came back to America, as soon as she graduated and could decide her own future—as could all the children in the program—she returned to Europe to work for Manon. In preparation for her departure, she relearned French and some German, and of course, living in Arizona, she knew Spanish; and from contact with the visiting Japanese, she had a working knowledge of that language. Very quickly, her genius enabled her to become one of

Manon's senior analysts. Manon, ever conscious that looks can smooth the way, encouraged cosmetic surgery with a minor nip and tuck here and there. When Sheila initially looked askance at that suggestion, Manon pointed out that she spent money on her hair, so why not on other physical attributes?

As her empire continued to expand, Manon sought to vertically integrate companies so that they could function semiautonomously internationally and automated as much as possible, as she saw automation and robotics as the future. She wanted to build factories to build machines to build machines, as she put it.

The man sent originally from Japan to protect Munro's first wife, Kodama, had for years served as Manon's enforcer, providing necessary muscle when it was required. When Kodama went back to Japan, he had remained behind to protect her children and subsequently the Foundation children. They called him the Ninja although he kept pointing out he was not that. Since the ninja had gone to Arizona with the children he protected, and to whom he taught martial arts, Manon did not have a regular enforcer. He would return only if necessary. All the Praetorian Japanese shooters knew the ninja. He spent time training them and therefore got to know them reasonably well.

He found that a couple of the young Japanese shooters particularly relished the thrill of the hunt. Realizing that they seemed a little different, he had them sent north to Alaska where, with Running Bear—the head of an Athabascan Indian tribe who was also associated with the Prometheus Group—they could hunt deer and moose. As they liked that experience and wanted more, he obliquely broached with them the topic of the ultimate hunt: eliminating really bad people.

These two young women were intrigued, so he quietly had them take a course of defensive driving and, at the gun range, taught them to use more lethal weapons than the pistols most of the Praetorians used. He then took them on one of his corrections. This was a particularly awful group who had come to Western Europe after the Berlin Wall came down. Having operated in the Soviet East, there was nothing so evil that they would not do. This group was threatening one of Manon's enterprises.

After careful planning and surveillance, one night, the three attacked the house in France where the gang were headquartered. One girl drove. The other, leaning out of the car door with an assault rifle, hosed down the guards stationed out front and then the windows of the house, while the ninja, leaning out of the moon roof of the limo, put several shoulder-mounted missiles into the house. The chief and the majority of the gang leaders died in the conflagration.

They drove quietly off. The three independently made their escape from Europe without incident. As the female Praetorians acted as unassuming Asian tourists, they drew little attention. Thereafter, when necessary, the ninja used one or the other as his helper. Eventually for a time, they became independent enforcers for Manon's organization. Sometimes one or the other would do what was necessary, but they preferred to work as a team. They made it clear that this was short term only, and they did not plan on doing it for long.

Manon did not want Tomiko, who was one of the nominal leaders of the Praetorians, to be compromised and therefore kept her out of this particular loop. Tomiko probably knew or suspected, as little got by her, but "don't ask, don't tell" seemed the best approach. Occasionally, one of the other Japanese women Praetorians would hint that they, too, wanted to take part, almost like an initiation or a secret rite of passage, especially for the younger ones. Such activities remained very secret.

Sheila, when much younger, had brought up the question of the use of force at one of the evening sessions that Munro held with the children. She had been told by someone or had read somewhere that force solved nothing. This seemed to her one of these idealistic and foolish statements. When she mentioned it to Munro, he laughed and quoted Cicero, "There is nothing so absurd that some philosopher has not said it." Turning serious, he quoted Hobbes, "'Covenants without the sword are but words,' and there is an old poem,

> 'That presently word would come,
> That a tribe had been wiped off its icefield,
> Or the lights had gone out in Rome.'"

She realized immediately from that quotation that all things in life could not be solved by goodwill, and sometimes naked force, or the threat of naked force, was required. Understanding and believing that, Sheila, who shot at the range with the other children and had trained for years in self-defense with the ninja, did some hunting in Alaska. She wanted to become comfortable with the idea of weapons, as it was becoming obvious that anyone who wished to live in Europe would need to protect themselves, as the police there had become totally ineffectual and no longer could or would stop terrorist activity.

As in the future, she would probably become one of Manon's senior analysts, she wondered about going along with one of the girls on a comparatively small exercise to eliminate a man who was physically threatening one of Manon's newly acquired enterprises. His threat was that he would bring in one of the numerous criminal gangs who existed within the new migrants. She discussed it quietly with Manon.

"I have hunted animals, but I have never killed a human. I can see that if I am to help you run things, I will be required, from time to time, to order the elimination of some of these monsters walking on two legs that are present in the world. I am not sure if I could or should give that order if I have not myself done it."

"It is never pleasant, as there are always very significant risks, which are worse every year, as there are more and more CCTV cameras and everyone has a camera on their phone. I really wish that it were not necessary, but the police are so useless, and even if they somehow catch a criminal, these awful excuses for European judges let them off with a slap on the wrist. I killed one really bad man once myself a long, long time ago, as I had no one else to turn to. I suppose you should do it, Sheila, but only once. These Japanese girls use fake passports and can disappear if anyone looks for them, but I would hate to lose you to the wilds of South America, or into space, if you are identified and have to escape. I mean, look at yourself. These Praetorian girls blend into the background as just another anonymous Asian woman touring Europe. But with your pale skin and red hair, you will really need a disguise."

Manon pointed out that the assassin's gun, the 22 mm, was easily carried in a purse, but the job was getting harder with the universal adoption of CCTV and facial recognition technology. Long-range shooting was always fraught with danger as open, seemingly empty countryside always had an unseen observer. They really did not want to introduce the Russian techniques with ricin or radioactive polonium. The brush past, with a small gun in the ear and three 22 mm soft-nosed slugs in the head, remained the usual modus operandi.

Sheila, her skin colored with brown makeup and with a black wig and mouth guard to fool any CCTV cameras, was taken along by two of the Japanese girls for a planned elimination. They walked by as the object arrived at his office. The two Japanese girls distracted the bodyguard as he was looking around after getting out of the limo ahead of his employer. Sheila, simply walking past, put a silenced gun, which never left her purse, under the subject's chin as he was starting to get out of his limo and put three bullets in his head and, without stopping, walked away. He fell back inside the vehicle. The bodyguard, rushing to his aid, was shot in the back of the head by one of the Japanese girls as he leaned inside the vehicle over his boss. She pushed him into the car, and the two girls walked off in the other direction. All three were lost in the confusion. The execution had taken place in France. The two Japanese girls separated, one taking the train to Paris and the other to Brussels, and then separately, they flew back to the US. Sheila, with the wig and makeup gone and the gun dropped in the river, took the train back to Luxembourg.

Manon was relieved to find that Sheila was unaffected by the experience. As she had told her prior to the execution, it was impossible to predict how anyone would react. The immediate dopamine hit was always the same, but the letdown afterward affected different people differently. She had not thought it likely but was a little nervous of the possibility of the Raskolnikov effect, as described in Dostoevsky's *Crime and Punishment*.

"Well, you did it. How do you feel?"

"Surprisingly, I feel nothing—no shame, no sorrow, no regret. He was a thief and a murderer. The world is better with him gone. I have no particular wish to do it again, but I can see that sometimes it may be necessary."

Shortly after she finished her studies and returned to Europe, Manon began to use Sheila's wide-ranging brilliance as a troubleshooter. When a business seemed to be underperforming, Sheila would audit the books to see where the problem lay, and she and Manon would discuss options and develop plans accordingly, which Sheila—initially with the help of Teresa, an American who had been with Manon for a very long time and who was Manon's senior assistant—would implement. Sheila was constantly on the move and had her growing staff scanning the journals looking for new small businesses or startups in which they liked to invest or buy.

Manon told Munro that in Sheila, she had found a possible successor to her long-term deputy head, Teresa, when she moved up, but Manon wanted Sheila to get some international experience in running a government department. She hoped that Munro would give her part of the state of Texas to run, under his supervision as governor, but instead, a sudden opening occurred, and he gave her the province of Ontario in Canada.

CHAPTER 2

The Banana Republic

Having been in the mining business for years, Elizabeth, who was the current sitting US president, of course had long known Canada, or at least Northern Canada. She had a couple of mines there and found their legal system cumbersome and difficult. She had looked at the so-called Ring of Fire in Ontario as the potentially most lucrative mining area in the world, but she found that development impossible due to problems with the surrounding Indian bands and the lack of any help in resolving apparent insurmountable issues by successive provincial and federal governments.

The fact that native tribes were all on welfare, although they called it something else, with no financial transparency of where the government money went to and had no clear chain of command, with a constant war going on between hereditary chiefs and elected chiefs, made it difficult to negotiate with them. Even if they did not own the land where the mining concession had been obtained and had no legal right to do so, they could block access roads and railways; and the police, for no clear reason, would not enforce court orders to remove them, even when such could be obtained. These bands could appeal to successive levels of Canadian courts without spending a penny of their own money. The Canadian judges seemed to have the ability to completely ignore the actual written law. Their Supreme Court was answerable to no one and created laws at will, often seemingly without any serious thought about the implications of their judgments.

Running Bear, the Athabascan chief from Alaska, who for years now had done Elizabeth's necessary negotiations with the Indigenous Peoples—or First Nations, as some of them liked to be called—had told her of some of the hilarious laws the Canadian Supreme Court had passed. In one case, they had allowed Indigenous People to hunt and fish out of season. Of course, the outcome was that Indigenous People would then act as guides for unscrupulous hunters from all over the world who would hunt and fish at any time of the year. If caught by the authorities, the native would claim that he had killed the dead animal or caught the fish, and therefore, everything was legal. Running Bear could give numerous other examples of equally poorly thought-out laws with unintended consequences.

In pillow talk with her husband, Munro, as they lay comfortably propped up on pillows, side by side in the afterglow of lovemaking, Elizabeth had wondered to him why so many leaders in the Western world seemed so crazy. Perhaps *crazy* was not the correct word. Perhaps it was simply silly. People like Boudreau in Canada and the various European leaders, like the idiot who ran France, who felt he could spend his way out of debt, the classic Keynesian folly. She had always had difficulty deciding if they were fools or traitors, but if traitors, why and to whom? Munro had no clear idea why the political class seemed to share this visceral hatred, not only of their own nation, but of Western civilization as a whole. Quite what they thought it should be replaced by was never clear to him and certainly never was made clear by anyone other than the obvious Marxists.

Elizabeth felt that Marx's desire to destroy the West was probably simply the failure's hatred of what he had failed at, as witnessed by some of the appalling poetry of his younger years, which clearly indicated his underlying psychopathology. Maybe Lenin's pathological hatred of everything was also based purely on psychopathology, like Pol Pot. But equally, it was hard to believe that some, like Mao, were not simply evil to the core, the devil in human form come straight from hell. Idiots like Boudreau and Mitterrand made no sense, so maybe they were just idiots.

Canada refused to protect its fishing industry by failure to enforce a two-hundred-mile exclusionary zone for no clear reason, other than possibly virtue signaling. In consequence, that collapsed due to overfishing. The endless trawling destroyed the fishing grounds until the cod fishery was decimated and ceased to exist, effectively throwing a whole province out of work.

In Canada, there were also these weird government-sponsored environmental and cultural evaluations of this and that, which took forever and none of which had any internal logic, as ultimately the decisions were made by bureaucrats who knew nothing at all about the actual mechanics of the project. One judge running such a commission had blocked a pipeline to transmit oil coming down from the north for so long that, rather than run through Canada, it had been run through Alaska, and the Canadian leg was no longer required, with huge job and opportunity loss. Since Sandra, who was peripherally associated with the Prometheus Group, had taken over as governor of Alaska, she had cleaned up the corruption.

That state now appeared open for business, which Canada was definitely not. The Canadian government and law courts seemed to have the racism of low expectations that natives were better in a state of nature, in poverty, illiteracy, disease, and despair, rather than joining the modern world.

After the first prime minister, Sir John A. MacDonald, their prime ministers seemed to be a strange lot. Their only consistent policy appeared to be anti-Americanism. They had finally elected, with great acclaim, a French Canadian named Boudreau. As far as Elizabeth could make out, this man's father or grandfather had made money, but Boudreau had never actually had a job. He had some sort of law degree from somewhere and had lectured on something inconsequential in some college or other. He seemed to be some sort of extreme socialist or Marxist. After he was elected, he had done a Mao, destroying the main Canadian resources, the oil and gas industry, and in the process, had bankrupted Alberta, the powerhouse province of Canada. Just why he had done so, no one knew, and he could never quite explain it himself.

He had produced an incredible debt in a very short period of time, which would put any decent banana republic to shame, with nothing to show where and on what the money had gone. He had introduced bilingualism into Canada, whereas before French had existed only in one and a half provinces. This increased the cost of everything, as everything had to be labelled in French, and labels cost money. The number of bureaucrats skyrocketed as duplicate civil servants had to be hired on the sole grounds that they could speak Quebec French. There was also this peculiar monopoly on dairy products, eggs, pork, and a host of other things, which made the prices Canadians paid for these products almost twice or three times as much as the Americans. Quite where this came from, no one seemed to know, but in some strange fashion, these monopolies openly paid off political parties in bloc votes or money, or both.

Boudreau had introduced some sort of constitution that was incomprehensibly foolish. In English Common Law rights were assumed. In this new constitution, rights were not inalienable but were given and specified by the government. This would result in giving ultimate authority to a handful of unelected, unrecallable, politically appointed judges. This suicidal constitution—which, by the way it was written, could effectively not be changed except by seemingly every politician in Canada agreeing—made no sense to any uninvolved observer. It seemed to have been accepted with great joy by the Canadian media, who did not actually appear to have read the document and who themselves seemed to be increasingly and unapologetically socialist collectivists. His greatest friend, with whom he and his family spent considerable time, seemed to be the murderous Fidel Castro in Cuba, of whose policies Boudreau appeared to approve, as if they were reading from the same manifesto or play book, and would implement if he dared.

He had changed the immigration policies, now making it very difficult for Europeans to immigrate, instead bringing in people from the Third World countries, many with no training or education, including their elderly and disabled relatives, who could never contribute in any way to the Canadian economy. Elizabeth had been told that the reason was political. Very few Europeans, escaping from the tyranny of socialism, were likely to vote for Boudreau, with his socialist policies. Whereas a permanently unemployed immigrant underclass, who would likely never integrate and remain forever dependent on government largess, likely would. California, after all, was attempting to do exactly the same thing, quite successfully.

The Canadian government had blocked the development or multiplication of pipelines to transport oil to either coast or in bulk to the US, again for no clear reason. These maneuvers forced Canadians to buy oil imported from the Middle East, rather than use their own. Elizabeth could think of no reason for this absolutely lunatic decision, unless someone was being paid off with huge bribes from the Middle East. Not that she cared or even thought much about it. The corruption in other countries was their problem, not hers. With no other buyer, and limited pipeline access, any Canadian company who wished to sell to the US had to accept prices at 40 percent below market value. The result of that was that almost all major oil producers left Canada.

In consequence, Canada was not a major player in American life, so when Elizabeth became president of America, other than cancelling the previous free trade deals that did not help America, she watched the approaching economic train wreck with amusement. She knew that if she could see the train wreck coming, other more financially savvy people could see it also, and she assumed the raiders like George Soros and her eldest son, the Buccaneer, who lived and whose hedge funds were based in Luxembourg, would be preparing for an assault.

As she expected the Canadian dollar to end up worthless, she made sure that all US government debt to Canada was in US dollars. She knew that when the run began, the Canadians would turn to the US for help. In view of Boudreau's repeated silly and gratuitous insults over the years—not only to herself in particular, but to America in general—she had no intention of helping and quietly put in place a block to the US banks helping. She did not see why American taxpayers should pay for the stupidity of others.

It was in the dying days of Elizabeth's second term when the raiders struck. Canadians went to bed one night and awoke the next morning to find themselves under siege and, by the end of the day, effectively bankrupt. This was worse than the raid on the Bank of England or on Thailand. Everything went into free fall, and overnight, the Canadian dollar plummeted. Boudreau, being an economic moron, having been told that the raid had been organized by international financiers, whom he hated, tried to defend the dollar; and when that collapsed, he did the standard socialist thing and made the problem worse by continuing to print worthless money by the carload. It was the Weimar Republic and the Venezuelan, the Chilean, and the Argentinian hyperinflation all over again. Elizabeth blocked the central bank from providing emergency loans.

Within a few weeks, they were beginning to run out of food. As Boudreau had destroyed Alberta, one of the world's potentially biggest oil producer, the country began to run out of energy, which being winter, Canada really needed. It had to be imported, largely from the Middle East, and that had to be paid for at true market value, so the cost of gasoline at the pump and the cost of heating soared. To pay for this energy, they had to borrow at astronomical rates in US dollars, backed by collateral of all the government monopolies, including airlines, railroads, national parks, and Boudreaux's instrument for destroying Alberta, Petro-Can. With hyperinflation, there was no possible way of paying off these loans. As they had been signed offshore, foreclosure transferred the assets to private hands very quickly.

Within a short time, the raiders had come and gone, and Boudreau's reaction had left Canada a smoldering ruin. It slowly became obvious even to the most besotted media socialist that Boudreau had to go. He was forced out of office, and a man, whom Boudreau had himself previously forced out of office due to his opposition to the destruction of Alberta, ended up in charge. This new prime minister looked around and really did not know what to do.

He called Elizabeth, who was still president. During the crisis, she had refused to talk to Boudreau, having been insulted by him often enough in the past and utterly despising him. Boudreau, she said, could talk to Sandra, the incoming president. The only problem was that Boudreau and the Canadian media had insulted Sandra also, implying she was an Alaskan backwoods buffoon, so she, too, had no wish to speak to him. The contact person therefore by default was Sweet Wolf, the acting assistant secretary of state. She, in turn, did not like anyone who would insult America, and she loathed Canadian bureaucrats, who had treated her adoptive father, Running Bear, with disdain when he had been negotiating in Canada on behalf of Elizabeth and other international oil and mining companies. She knew that in Boudreau, she was dealing with a doctrinaire socialist who had never had a real job and whose grasp of economics was childlike. She also knew he saw himself as a Don Juan, a great lady's man.

Both Elizabeth, the outgoing president, and Sandra, the incoming one, knew Sweet Wolf's character, but they did not see any reason to restrain her. That name had been given to her by her by Running Bear. She therefore lived up to her name. She took great delight in meeting Boudreau in private, wearing very provocative short skirts that had Boudreau in very short order, trying to get his hands under. Unseen cameras recorded the event. While he was fondling her, she got him to sign all sorts of agreements as she convinced him that he was so clever and knew so much more than his advisors.

He ended up borrowing money from the US and proxies such as the Buccaneer's fund. She ensured that a large part of that money immediately went to paying off old loans from the US, which had tiny interest payments, in exchange for new, very high interest loans. She also convinced him that as a quid pro quo, given the low Canadian dollar, now was the time to buy new US fighter planes and helicopters, which he did, barely looking at the contracts and not understanding the huge penalty clauses for cancellation. To celebrate this piece of monumental folly, she let him have her on her own desk. As she was not sure where, and with whom he had been before, she insisted he use a condom. *Every country gets the government it deserves,* she thought.

She could barely contain her laughter as he dutifully plunged away. *Lie back and think of England,* came to her mind. *Munro must know where that quotation comes from. It really is time for me to get married and have a kid or two, and then divorce and head back to Japan. I don't feel like being a babysitter, so maybe I will ask Tomiko to loan Munro to me for a year or two so he can look after my kids and leave me free. Tomiko is so busy she does not have the time for anything in any case, and I know that she is extremely disappointed that Munro is still in love with Elizabeth. Elizabeth won't care as she wants a divorce from him as soon as she leaves office.* Boudreau did not notice that she seemed rather distracted.

Sweet Wolf thought Boudreau was an utter fool but continued to charm him, although she never let him touch her again. The only ones she told about how she had managed her incredible financial coup were Munro and Running Bear. Munro thought it was hilarious, as he said, "It could not happen to a nicer chap. That must be the most expensive sex in the history of the world." Even Running Bear, who disapproved of her behavior in principle, could not help smiling at her infectious grin. Sandra, as incoming president, did not want to know any of the details.

After Boudreau was maneuvered out of office, the new prime minister went to Washington. Elizabeth spoke to him but pointed out that within a few days, she would be leaving office and Sandra would be taking over. She suggested he speak to her. The Canadian press had treated Sandra very badly, making her out to be a bigoted, gun-toting, ill-educated moron from the backwoods of Alaska. Sandra therefore was in no hurry to see him and refused to do so until after she had become president, by which time the situation in Canada was getting desperate, almost like the Weimar Republic. People in border towns were trading whatever they had, such as paintings, jewelry, and anything portable into the US for food and fuel. Prostitution, the world's oldest currency, became rife, with Americans coming across the border for a cheap thrill. Toronto was perhaps not quite as wide open as Berlin in the early twenties but was certainly getting there.

After inauguration, Sandra saw the new prime minister in a private room with Sweet Wolf. One of Jacques's photojournalists was there, quietly recording. No other people were present.

"We are bankrupt. The money Boudreau borrowed has gone."

"I know."

"The only way out is a very large loan."

"And then you default. I don't think the US can give you that loan."

"No Western country has ever defaulted."

"Oh? How about Germany and the Weimar Republic or Argentina or communist Russia? I can only lend you money if I control the money."

"What do you mean?"

"I mean my people will have to control it. Your government bureaucrats and politicians are obviously completely incompetent or are such doctrinaire socialists that they simply do not understand economics. But having an economic basket case on our northern border, especially one with a large number of unscreened migrants, is not in our interest. It would be very expensive to defend that border. We may have to do it someday, but I would rather not. You will have to allow the people I choose to have control of your central bank and the ability to make decisions affecting the economy. They will absolutely not be people associated with my government. We do not, under any circumstances, want political control or political involvement. I want my government to be completely at arm's length. You will have to come to your own relationship with these people."

Sweet Wolf interjected, "You will have to get rid of all your government monopolies, including Western Grain, Quebec Dairy, Forestry Stumpage, and other irritants." Sandra pointed out that these were political decisions. "Do you have enough votes to make them go away?"

"I think I do."

"If you do not, then we are wasting our time."

"I have enough votes for that. For sure, however, that will be my political death sentence, but the next general election is three years away."

"I respect your integrity, Mr. Prime Minister. I am sure that there will be a place in Canadian history for a man of honor. But that is not the only bad news. You may not know this, but your province Ontario has been driven so deeply into debt by the socialists who have been running it that it is effectively bankrupt. The only way out that I can see is also to cede economic and financial control to external advisors. You will have to lean on these silly politicians, and also, I think the idiots who are running your main city, Toronto. Effectively, they need what I suppose are bankruptcy trustees to run it. If you cut off federal funds to these people, it could be done, and they will have to declare bankruptcy."

"I suppose, but it will be extremely difficult."

"A little hunger helps concentrate the mind wonderfully. I hear the average Canadian is beginning to lose weight and the world media is starting to call it the Boudreau diet. Now, Sweet Wolf, who would you suggest being our adviser in Canada?"

"How about Governor Munro? He is recently divorced again, as Elizabeth wanted her freedom, so he has a little more time. He is also originally European, so the Canadians are likely to resent him less than a native-born American."

"Munro? Well, he certainly could, as he has no problems being the governor of three states, but would he? Why would he want to go to Canada?"

"He would not need to. He can run it the same way he runs the states he controls. He has more than enough of these very bright kids from his Foundation."

"He won't do it. Why should he? He is not crazy."

"Let me ask him. I have a business and personal proposal for him. If I might ask everybody just keep quiet. Just keep the camera on me and no one else."

She phoned and contacted Munro on a video link she had prepared ahead of time, as she knew what outcome she had been looking for. She had also spoken to Maria Martens, Munro's assistant, about having him available for a face to face talk. Munro was in his office. The connection was made without difficulty.

"Ryoko, how nice to hear from you."

"And you, Governor."

"What can I do for you?"

"You can run Canada."

"What? That bankrupt place? No, thanks. You don't know enough English literature, Sweet Wolf. Nashe wrote about five hundred years ago, 'From winter, plague and pestilence, good Lord deliver us.' That's current Canada."

"Come on, Munro, just think about it."

"Think about it? Why? It is cold. It snows. Half the people do not speak English, and the French they speak, I have some difficulty with. It is a divided country, which has deliberately destroyed its own economic base. They completely depend on the American auto industry, but their only foreign policy is anti-Americanism. They elected, with a majority, an unbelievably doctrinaire socialist who thinks that that monster Castro is a great man. Why would anyone want to run a country like that?"

"You know you could do it. Think of it as a challenge."

"Ah, don't sweet talk me, Sweet Wolf."

"But your people could run it. Maria could do it in her spare time."

"Of course she could, but why would any of my people want to do that?"

"Hinchcliffe wants to run something. If you don't give her something soon, she will take her paramilitary Legion and take over one of the moons of Mars."

"Well, yes, Hinchcliffe is an idea. Letting her loose would be instructive and a very good experience for her. She could run the feds, but that still leaves that disaster state of Ontario.

"They call them provinces in Canada, Governor, and Sheila MacDonald needs something to do, and you could get Isis to run Toronto. She is always boasting she can do anything. Be interesting to see her run a city."

"Isis? Isis! Are you crazy? The best brain in the world, and I am going to let her go into harm's way. Didn't that Boudreau fellow fill Canada with unassimilated migrants? And I am going to let an apostate near them? Anyway, why ask me?"

"I want to get married."

Sandra raised her eyebrows and made a face but said nothing.

"That is quite a jump. Then talk to my kids."

"You have not been looking. They are all married or too young. Don't you want me?"

"Sweet Wolf, any man who is not a frozen corpse would want you."

"Well, good. Propose to me."

"But I can't. Elizabeth."

"She says OK, within limits."

"Yes, but you know what the limits are. She waves her hand, I come running."

"That's OK."

"What about Tomiko?"

"She says if she is going to get married, she wants the whole loaf, not half, so she says it's OK for a couple of years because she is very busy, and before you ask, Manon says if I don't marry you, you will be over in Europe, taking up time she does not have."

"Well, that is true."

"Then make me an offer."

"Jesus, Ryoko, this is so sudden. Why now?"

"I want a couple of kids now, and society insists I be married to do so, and I want a man to look after them for me."

"But if you marry a gaijin, the people of Japan will not want you back."

"Let me worry about that, OK? Since you have no other excuses, propose to me now, please."

"Are you serious?"

"Yes, I am."

"OK, OK, this is all so sudden, but if you insist. But I will not live in Canada. Let me do this properly and get down on one knee to propose. Here is my offer: I, Neil Munro, citizen of the UK, Luxembourg, and the United States, former Heavyweight Champion of the World, formerly prime minister of Luxembourg, currently governor of Arizona, Texas, and New Mexico, do solemnly ask for the hand of Ryoko Tanaka in marriage. I promise to cherish and honor her forever and to look after her children."

"Now me—I, Ryoko Tanaka, daughter of Japan, with Japanese and US citizenship, currently a resident of the US, do accept your offer of marriage. I promise to bear your children, to honor you forever, and to stay with you as long as we mutually agree. The usual contract is acceptable."

"Governor, this is Sandra. I overheard your offer of marriage. You seem to have left out the love bit, but I guess the rest is OK."

"Madame President, you set me up."

"Well, yes, but someone has to take care of our northern neighbor."

Sweet Wolf flew to Arizona to talk to him about the arrangements for overseeing the disaster that Canada had become. Until then, he had not been entirely sure that she was completely serious about either of her requests.

"I don't want to be one of these bitter old women who forgot to have kids. Make me pregnant now, Munro. If I get pregnant, we can quickly get married. I want to see what it is like to feel a new life inside me."

"If that is indeed what you want, Ryoko. What sort of a wedding?"

"Small and discreet. I don't want it to be trumpeted in Japan, as I will be going back someday, and I don't want Tomiko to be seen as a loser."

"In Europe then? Or maybe a small affair with La Contessa in Mexico? A secluded hacienda. The old ninja priest, or do you want Shinto?"

"Not Shinto. Too obvious. One of La Contessa's haciendas would be good."

When pregnancy was confirmed, they were married quietly in Mexico, with no publicity at all. The former bodyguard of Munro's first wife, who was now an official high in the Catholic Church in Japan, came over to marry them. The wedding party was just a few close friends.

She continued to work for Sandra in her job as assistant secretary of state. After delivery, which she had by C-section, Sweet Wolf stayed at the ranch for six weeks, during which time she breastfed the baby. By then, she was chafing at her relative inactivity, although she had been working steadily by phone, fax, and email. After six weeks, she talked to Munro as he had been expecting that she would.

"This is driving me crazy. I have to get back to Washington, to the center of power. I cannot drag a baby behind me. You have more than enough people here and experience looking after children."

"If that is what you truly want, Sweet Wolf."

"With my current hormone flux, I don't know what I want. I will have a better idea in a couple of months. Do you blame me, Munro, for my lack of maternal feelings?"

"No, Sweet Wolf. We both knew that being barefoot in the kitchen was never going to be your style. We will cope. You can follow your dreams. Ulysses Ryoko, 'You will become a name for always roaming with a hungry heart.'"

"*Hai*! A hungry heart. I love you for your understanding." She grinned at him. "Maybe I should keep you, Munro."

He smiled down at her. "That was not part of the deal. You will want to be the ruler of Japan and probably the world. You need to be free. Kipling wrote,

'Down to Gehenna or up to the throne
She travels fastest who travels alone.'

Listening to a gaijin who burdens you with his fears, his concerns, and complaints won't help your journey."

"And you think Tomiko will willingly listen?"

19

"It is almost Sakura time. I would like to walk under the Sakura, arm in arm with her. Even if it is only for a few moments."

"You are talking again?"

"You know I have loved her from the moment I saw her. It is too long since I have been with her. My heart is hungry in me for her companionship."

"People! Love! I don't understand. Maybe someday I will."

"The child will be here anytime you want to see her."

"And you, Munro?"

"I will always be here, your safe haven. Until then, Ryoko. Godspeed! Vaya con Dios."

After fairly simple negotiations with the Canadian government, it was agreed that Munro would temporarily supervise the economic recovery of Canada. Hinchcliffe, one of the more senior of the first Prometheus genius girls, went to Ottawa to help sort out the Canadian federal finances, backed by US money. The first thing she wanted to do was offer Quebec, the French province, its independence. She made it absolutely clear from an economic perspective that that was the only thing that made sense. Czechoslovakia had split up successfully, and she saw no reason not to do the same thing in Canada. She pointed out that this was a political decision and, as a financial adviser, not hers to make, but if Quebec decided to remain within Canada, the rules would have to change.

A referendum was hastily called. Faced with the very real prospect of becoming independent, as this was actually being promoted as being essential by the economic czar, Quebec decided overwhelmingly to remain as part of Canada. Hinchcliffe pointed out that it was not a pure French Canadian vote and questioned its validity, but that was political and outside her area of command. She wanted countrywide bilingualism abolished, but the government refused. She did get significant economic reforms. It was a simple matter to get rid of the so-called supply management, the strange crony capitalistic government collective monopoly that suited a few key voters in Quebec to the detriment of the rest of the country. They simply compensated the farmers involved and dismantled the whole edifice. All other supply management systems were also terminated, with appropriate reduction in government employees.

She wanted the abolishment of so-called equalization payments, a strange system where a great deal of money was sent to the federal government in Ottawa by the provinces. This was divided up and sent back. She did not succeed in completely eliminating it but did so substantially.

She pointed out that if there were no jobs in one province, then move to another. Having the government pay people to sit and do nothing for their whole lives was destructively insane. She had all sorts of other demands, most of which she got. As she always pointed out, what she wanted was for rules, regulations, and laws to be abolished, not passed.

She wanted 90 percent of the embassies closed. She pointed out that the telephone had been invented, which made ambassadors obsolete. She got that.

She wanted to leave the UN and completely defund it. She got that.

She sold off all state enterprises, including the Canadian Broadcasting Corporation and the post office.

She defunded all arts programs and all environmental groups and social activist groups.

She pushed for the legalization or at least the decriminalization of all drugs. In that, she was partially successful, which hugely cut court and prison costs. She had pardons issued for previous minor drug offences.

She eliminated the Canadian Health Protection overview and similar boards, simply relying on US and European regulations, which brought very significant cost savings and again substantial reductions in numbers of civil servants.

She abolished the federal minimum wage and reduced so-called unemployment insurance substantially, but not as much as she wanted. She privatized everything that could be monetized. She reduced federal funding to all liberal arts colleges and universities. She had junior lawyers and accountants go through the statute books, rapidly repealing ancient and irrelevant laws. Every law repealed allowed a reduction in the number of bureaucrats employed, with consequent significant spending reductions.

She wanted to do a lot more things, including huge tax credits for traditional families with children so that women who wanted could afford to stay at home and raise their own children as opposed to impersonal daycares. People felt it strange that a young single woman should think that this was important. She ran into all sorts of vested political opposition for that viewpoint. She shrugged her shoulders and pointed out that she was not Canadian and would not be staying so that it was their choice. As this was more political than economic, she did not push the issue hard.

All this took time and a huge amount of wailing and gnashing of teeth. The interim prime minister, whom Hinchcliffe had come to admire as he stoutly protected her, slowly lost his majority due to attrition and anger with the new policies whipped up by the media. She wanted immigration to stop until the financial situation had stabilized. In spite of pointing out that there was no money for new resettlement and that bringing in people with no skills to an economy that had no place for unskilled workers made absolutely no sense, that bill was defeated.

Hinchcliffe had developed into an attractive young woman, which was a product of vigorous exercise since childhood and a little surgical nip and tuck here and there, as Munro saw no reason that cosmetic surgery should not be available to the girls in the Prometheus Group. She had a classically beautiful face, again with just a little cosmetic dentistry and some knife work. She dressed exquisitely, thanks to Edith in Luxemburg, where she bought her clothes, so there was no place for her to keep her handgun, which she carried with her constantly. She had to keep it in her handbag. She had been a trained shooter since childhood but had never had any desire to compete. Like Munro, she had been watching the rise of terrorist violence in Europe and was well aware of its increasing occurrence in Canada. Hinchcliffe knew she would be a target sooner or later as she was inevitably and unashamedly polarizing.

The first homegrown Canadian assassin announced his presence by shooting a couple of ceremonial guards who carried rifles that had no bullet in them, for reasons Hinchcliffe could never understand. He then charged across the plaza to the government building where she was working. He ran in the main door and shot another couple of guards with his assault rifle. The remaining guards who heard the commotion locked the office doors while the bureaucrats and politicians hid under desks and in closets and toilets.

The gunman ran up the stairs to the second floor. Hinchcliffe had heard and recognized the shots. She heard the feet running up the stairs, stepped out behind a half open door, gun in hand, and shot him twice in the face so that he fell back down the stairs.

She walked down the stairs, her gun pointed at the assassin. She put another bullet in his head to make sure he was dead and picked up his weapon.

"Pick him up," she said to two guards, who appeared when silence fell. "Come with me."

They carried the dead body out of the building and stood at the top of the steps.

"Throw him down."

"We can't do that."

"Do it, or I will have you dismissed, and you will never work in this city again."

They were holding the would-be assassin by his arms and legs. They swung to get some momentum and tossed him down the front steps of the building onto the plaza. Hinchcliffe, who had been carrying the terrorist's rifle, was caught on camera as she stood at the top of the steps. She removed the magazine, threw the gun on top of the corpse, and went back inside. She walked calmly to central communications, where she announced on the overhead speakers that the assassin was dead and that they should all return to work immediately. She reminded them, "I have a committee meeting in the second-floor boardroom in five minutes. I expect everyone who is supposed to be there to be there unless they have soiled themselves."

That last remark did not make her popular with the bureaucrats, and the media were not happy about the body being tossed out of the building like a used Kleenex. When interviewed by the media, she simply said, "He was a murderer. He is dead. We need to work in that building without any police interference. Whatever investigations they want to do is now outside the building. What more is there to say?"

The police, of course, dismissed the episode as an attack by a mentally deranged man, as almost all such events in the Western world were now classified, whether or not there was any evidence to the contrary. As usual, no substantive further investigations as to his associates or source of funding was carried out.

There was another so-called lone wolf attack a month later. This man managed to penetrate the building before he began firing, so there were more casualties than the first assault. Again, Hinchcliffe heard him coming, stood behind a pillar, and shot him twice in the head as he passed. The bureaucrats, mindful of the previous media criticism, refused to touch the body, so she herself threw him down the inside stairs, grabbed a foot with one hand, dragged the corpse to the top of the outside steps, kicked the body over, and threw his rifle after him. This exploit was also caught on video and went viral.

After that, she decided that if she were going to be a frequent target, she needed a mechanism whereby a well-dressed lady could carry a gun on her person. A hip holster was wearable but did not look good with a lady's dress. Shoulder holsters were made for men. On women, the breasts got in the way. If she stuck it in the back of her skirt, it was uncomfortable to sit. It did not take much thought for her to come up with a couple of designs that she felt might work.

She took a few days off and flew to the ranch. She flew commercial. Knowing she was coming, the ninja, now back from protecting La Contessa in Mexico, met her as she came out of the tunnel, disembarking from the plane. He bowed low before her. She was still his favorite child, whom he remembered as a fierce little girl, and he was very proud of her. She bowed to him, her sensei. She then took him in her arms and hugged him, a very un-Japanese thing to do. Everyone at the ranch knew of her exploits and were very excited. The younger children followed her about like the hero she was.

In Europe recently, there had been an upsurge in terrorist attacks using knives. The existing body armor material, Kevlar, would certainly stop that, but in adequate thickness, it was stiff and therefore of limited use. One of the girls, who had come through the Foundation program, was a chemical engineer and had been working with some male students from the newly established Space Academy on a new material that was relatively soft and conforming. This could be made into body armor that could stop a knife cut or thrust and yet was reasonably flexible and could be woven to be semipermeable. The prototype could therefore be worn like a body sock or a sleeve. Patents had been obtained, and Manon had set up a small factory in Arizona to begin manufacturing.

Manon and Munro felt that the financial ramifications were huge, as indeed they subsequently turned out to be. The costs of custom fit were initially prohibitive, but once the initial manufacturing process was debugged and simplified, anticipating a large demand, she also set up a factory in Ireland because of its low corporate tax structure. Universal, as opposed to custom-fit manufacture, was now feasible, although for those who could afford it, custom was clearly preferable. Once the process had been adequately automated, a further factory was opened in Texas.

An advertising blitz was begun, headed by Raoul, who was Manon's head of advertising and now also ran the video journalism school originally established years ago by Jacques in Japan. The product sold extremely well to police forces all over the world. Manon was sure that some of the knife gangs in London and other criminals also bought the armor, and kept the data, but European, and especially British police, seemed uninterested in any details about potential criminals.

Hinchcliffe took her holster concepts to this materials group, who made some prototypes, which girls around the ranch wore as a trial. Two types of holster design for women were eventually decided on and made from this new material. The shoulder holster was a bra, with a pocket hanging from the left side, below and to the left of the breast, which lay along the rib cage, secured by a slightly wider bra band. The material of the holster itself was slightly stiffer so that the gun could easily be withdrawn and replaced without catching. The forward-facing handle was accommodated with a slot cut in the blouse or dress so that the butt of the pistol was exposed and could easily be reached.

The thigh holster was part of the panties, which extended down the leg on that side. The holster was again slightly stiffer to hold the gun to the thigh. The dress it was designed to be used with had either a long slit or was like a Chinese Chong Sang skirt, with a split coming high on the thigh to allow the pistol to be grasped easily. This was meant only for women who were happy to display their legs. Hinchcliffe, Raoul, and Tomiko, who were their consultants, also had great fun with Smith and Wesson, who advertised that they could make a custom pistol with a curve on the butt to match the contour of the thigh or chest of the wearer.

Hinchcliffe was happy with either model, although she knew that most men preferred it when she used the thigh holster. Some of the other girls were happy to model these devices, and the advertising campaign was orchestrated by Raoul. In a parody of the Victoria's Secret parade, he had some models strutting the catwalk with the new holsters, wearing a variety of handguns. The makers of pistols were quite happy to pay for it. The patents they obtained were hardly defensible, but even so, the market was so specialized that few of the major lingerie companies bothered; so Hinchcliffe, Edith, and the engineers developed their own line of ladies underwear, which Manon manufactured for them, which made a very reasonable financial return over the years.

The fighting women, such as police and security, all over the world bought in large numbers as the first piece of equipment ever made specifically for them. Edith was consulted on the appropriate design of clothes to go with the new holsters, and a range of different types were manufactured, from work clothes to evening wear, which again sold well.

Hinchcliffe initially refused a bodyguard, but after the second attempt on her life, Munro insisted and dispatched two of the Japanese Praetorian Guard shooters to accompany her. She also asked for and got Carmenlita, the little jungle girl from South America whom the ninja had trained into a fearsome fighter with guns, knives, or anything else. There were no further attacks on her. She was not sure if it was because she was a known killer or if it was because of the reputation the Praetorian Guard was establishing. A Japanese woman in a kimono was now treated with considerable respect in the West, especially if she was wearing a white obi with purple lightning bolts, in case she was one of the famous or infamous shooters.

The Canadian prime minister did his best to honor his commitment to the US president, but he watched his majority slowly slip away, and after a little over two years, he finally was reduced to a minority government. He struggled on for another six months but could get no new bills passed in the legislature. His term of office would be up in a few months, so he decided to dissolve Parliament. Hinchcliffe felt that he was an honorable man who had done what he could, and under her guidance, Canada was definitely rapidly pulling out of the economic collapse.

For some strange reason, some quirk of chance, the opposition Conservative Party managed to select a leader no one had heard of. He was Joe something or other, so the public called him Joe Who. He was so inept that, despite the unpopularity of the existing government, he just squeezed in with a minority. Given the fact that he had almost no mandate, one would have expected a little caution. His reign was characterized by pomposity and stupidity. He therefore did not interfere with Hinchcliffe. Indeed, he succeeded in doing nothing, which Hinchcliffe felt was very good. Unfortunately, one day, he decided to have a vote of confidence. Obviously, someone forgot to tell him that the chance of winning a vote of confidence with a minority government was close to zero. As predicted, his government fell, and after nine months, a new election had to be called. Hinchcliffe could see the writing on the wall and prepared to leave.

Chapter 3

Isis in Toronto

With Hinchcliffe effectively financially running Canada, advising the interim prime minister, whom she quite liked, two major problems remained. One was Toronto, the main city in Canada. A bunch of feckless ideological socialist benchwarmers had effectively destroyed the financial powerhouse of Canada.

Everything was unionized with aggressive public service unions used to getting their own way so that strikes and threats of public service strikes were a frequent occurrence. These unions provided significant political funds, as by law, payment of union dues was mandatory. They also provided a solid block vote, as were assiduously cultivated by politicians. This influence extended to the incredible fact that only companies employing favored unions could bid for city construction business.

The state schools were a shadow of their former selves, and the private schools were not much better. The state schools made little attempt at functional education, with the continuation of ludicrous concepts such as Whole-Word English, which had been shown one hundred years ago to be ineffective and worthless. As a result, many children were functionally illiterate and, with new math, also innumerate.

No one seemed to know or care that 'Whole Word' English was developed one hundred years before to teach congenitally deaf children, for whom phonetics could not work. It was introduced in Boston, and it was found that it was completely ineffective for normal children. Nonetheless, for reasons no sane person could understand, it kept being reintroduced, perhaps by those who did not know its history.

The children were fed postmodernist ideology, combined with open, unapologetic Marxism and whatever other *ism* was in favor. No world history was taught at all, nothing. Nothing at all about the horrors of the Marxist/Leninist Soviet Union and Holodomor, with its 7 million dead and the 30 million killed in the gulags, or the Chinese communists Great Leap Forward when 60 million or more people starved to death. No Canadian child had ever heard of the Killing Fields of Cambodia, where one-third of the population were beaten to death by Pol Pot's socialist goons. The various socialist-induced starvations in Africa were never mentioned. Instead, socialism was praised. T-shirts were sold to ignorant university students celebrating the psychopathic murderer Che Guevara.

Isis was shocked to find this out when she first went to Canada. Not just a little history was taught, but effectively none at all. There was a brief mention of some totally unimportant events in Canadian history, but that was that. Even science was becoming increasingly corrupt, as it had to be seen through an ideological lens, and some of the science taught was completely contrary, not only to accepted science, but to common sense. The numerous school trustees, whose actual function was not at all clear, were largely ideologues pushing progressive agendas. Departments of education were really the true Orwellian opposite: departments of disinformation.

The taxes and more important regulations were raised so high that businesses were leaving the city in droves, taking employment with them. Public housing was full of drug dealers and quasi-illegal immigrants, and amazingly, there was no mechanism to evict the more troublesome ones. It was also so poorly maintained that almost half the public housing stock was virtually unusable. The public transit system had not been significantly upgraded for thirty years, apart from three new stations only, and even there, the architects forgot to install toilet facilities. The traffic was said to be the worst in North America. No attempt had ever been made to coordinate the traffic lights due to the ideological war on cars.

The debt level had come to a crisis. The current mayor, who had absolutely no interest in balanced budgets, had taken on huge loans at ruining interest rates. He did not particularly care that his children and his children's children would have to pay the debt, as long as the media sang his praises during his term of office. "After all," he pointed out, "many utterly hopeless leaders in the past were looked back upon with fondness," and twisting history was not difficult. All one had to do was look at how widely accepted it was that Roosevelt's New Deal had saved America, whereas in reality, the opposite was true. The New Deal did not fix the Great Depression, it prolonged it. As collateral for his loans, this mayor had put up just about everything in Toronto, including public transit.

He and his lawyers seemed not to have read these contracts or more likely they did not care that many of them were signed in US law and were answerable to courts there. The city finally ran out of money. When the federal government effectively went bankrupt, Toronto was unable to borrow more money so one lender foreclosed on the Toronto Transit Commission, who ran the subways and buses, and threatened to close it down, which would have brought Toronto to a grinding halt. They wanted to get rid of the mayor and his cronies.

The province, who had undergone a similar shake-up and was now being run essentially by Sheila Macdonald, one of the Prometheus Group's prodigies, agreed, as did the federal government. The city was taken over by the provincial government and turned over to a small band of bankruptcy trustees. The question was who would run the city for the next few years to get it back on track and bring it out of bankruptcy?

Isis, a young physicist who had been found as a child in Egypt and had come through the Prometheus education system, pushed Munro, the nominal head of Prometheus Group, very hard for the job, as she wanted to demonstrate that she was capable of anything. This was the last thing Munro wanted. This utterly brilliant, if a little erratic, girl could clearly do it, as indeed she could do anything, but to what end? To expose this mind of the century, as Munro thought of her, to a bankrupt, occasionally violent so-called Sanctuary City, full of unscreened migrants, made no sense to him. Isis, however, was not to be denied.

She promised that if given the chance to show that she could revitalize this city, in a couple of years, she would work seriously with the Prometheus Group's two most brilliant scientists, Little Sister and Helga, on solving the problem of developing sustained fusion power. She also promised to continue working on Musha space drive, which she thought was realistic, and start to actively look for wormholes in space, for which she thought she had a theoretical basis. As Little Sister was still having difficulties trying to maintain fusion in any economic sense, Munro reluctantly agreed.

The immediate changes she made were similar to those instituted by Hinchcliffe. The city council had been reduced by Sheila MacDonald to half a dozen people only, who met when Isis wanted something officially passed. She would listen to advice but not windy debates. She hugely downsized the city staff as she could not find out what many of them were actually supposed to be doing.

One union went on strike. Isis fired them. They went to court. Isis had her own lawyers tie up proceedings indefinitely. She hired replacement workers, and life went on. She told the strikers that they could stay on strike forever as far as she was concerned. When the employees tried to return to work, they were told that their jobs had gone. As Hinchcliffe by that time had significantly cut welfare, some of the strikers found themselves in a difficult situation.

The other unions, seeing this, tried to settle quickly, but found that in many cases, Isis was in the process of privatizing their jobs. There were new contracts that they could sign or not sign, but with the companies who were now doing the job, not with the city. In doing this, she cut expenses to a level never thought possible. While everything was in turmoil, she began to move against the police, whose budget was crippling. The practice of having police officers stand around building sites, acting like traffic wardens and acting as security at courts and the like, seemed a ridiculous waste of manpower. She privatized a multitude of their previously mandated duties, which significantly cut their required numbers and therefore the budget. She suggested they concentrate on crime. Parking enforcement she privatized. City parks and unused schools and a host of buildings, which for no clear reason the city owned, were sold off.

As Munro had done and as Sheila MacDonald was doing, she brought in graduate students in forensic accounting and senior law students to go through the books and check expenditures, contracts, and expense accounts. To encourage this, she offered substantial prizes for conviction of criminal activities or admission of guilt, which she announced weekly with great fanfare. She took particular satisfaction in seeing long-standing city councilors in the dock, as they were the ones responsible for the slow-moving disaster Toronto had become.

She moved with such speed that, while the courts would be tied up for years and doubtless many of the guilty would walk free, the level of "snobbery, jobbery, ignorance, and incompetence," as she called it, would be reduced for at least a few years. She made sure that those accused did not remain for years on the public payroll while the grossly inefficient courts dawdled along.

With a substantial reduction in entitlements and the dismissal of large numbers of city employees, she was able to reduce taxation such that businesses began to come back into the city and unemployment dropped and money began to flow again. Myriads of ridiculous regulations were identified and subsequently repealed via her newly created Department of Silly Regulations. The debt load due to the loans run up by the last administration would be a millstone round the necks of the populace for the next twenty years. She calculated the interest due to these particular loans and separated it out so that it stood separately in the value added tax, where possible under the previous mayor's name, on every receipt for every major purchase, so everyone knew who was responsible.

Underground transit was a terrible mess. There was some for the West End of the city, which was now private and, therefore, after the initial unpleasantness and mass firing of a myriad of unnecessary bureaucrats, was functioning much better, but almost none for the East End. She simply decided to set up a parallel system east and west. Some overlap was inevitable, but the businesses could sort that out themselves. The contract she let for new transport was huge but cost her virtually nothing, as it would remain private. With the help of Sheila MacDonald, who was in effect running the province, she blocked these ridiculous environmental assessments, which enabled activists to hold up any project for years. By repealing noise legislation, she ensured that any work undertaken would go on round the clock to get it finished as quickly as possible.

Following the example of Margaret Thatcher, she sold off public housing to the occupiers. In conjunction with the province, she removed rent control, so adequate housing immediately became available. Many regulations on rental properties were abolished. The disbanding of these ludicrous Human Rights courts had immediately increased the number of people prepared to rent. Previously, the threat of these ideological quasi-judicial tribunals, who did not use English Common Law, but preponderance of evidence, had people so afraid of their insane rulings that it was safer not to offer rental in case of a complaint. This lunatic ideologically driven kangaroo courts had almost always found for the complainant. Justice or even truth, it was acknowledged, was no defense.

Combining with the province, contracts for new high-speed rail lines from peripheral hubs were begun so that in the future, it would be feasible to commute to the center of the city from towns where land and therefore housing would be cheaper.

Don Pedro, the owner of the huge Spanish construction company, had already bought at auction the major highways from the province and was busy double-decking the busiest parts of them. He also secured the Eastern Transit contract. In consequence, he had established a large work camp just outside the city, staffed largely by his own men from Spain. He hired some locals, but only if they were prepared to work. Unions were not considered.

Isis, who saw transportation as a major problem for the future, was particularly interested in tunneling. She had always thought that vacuum tunnel transportation, pioneered by Isambard Kingdom Brunel in the late 1880s, was feasible certainly on the moon and probably Mars, where she was sure she would eventually make her home. She therefore spent a fair amount of time with the men in the tunnels, wearing a hard hat. The fact that she could speak to them in Spanish, which she had learned while growing up in the Prometheus ranch in Arizona, endeared her to them. Applying her agile mind to the issues, she made some very significant improvements to the moles, or tunneling machines. These changes were patented and implemented as rapidly as possible, which considerably improved their efficiency. Francisco Gonzalez was Don Pedro's local manager, and Isis maintained a close liaison with him. The Spanish-speaking workforce was so large that she made a point of visiting their camps when they were celebrating their own cultural days.

When Isis first took over Toronto, she was appalled when she walked around to see how many road-work sites simply appeared to be obstructing traffic, with no one actually working. Furious, she pulled in those responsible and if private companies tried to ensure that they never worked for the city again. She put a stop to the rule that they had in place—that work could only be done during daylight hours. She wanted small jobs started after evening rush hour and finished before morning rush hour.

As the companies that previously had done most of the city work seemed so incompetent and full of feather bedding, Isis encouraged more and more for any other companies, especially Francisco Gonzales, to bid for even small jobs. She introduced real penalties for late completion. When she was driven around, she noted that at almost every intersection in residential areas, there were four-way stops. She had that changed to European-style roundabouts, which vastly decreased the number of accidents, increased the efficiency of traffic, and reduced emissions by preventing unnecessary idling.

Privatization of parks, where possible, helped considerably, not only with reduced costs, but also with increased public use due to innovative projects, which reduced rules allowed. The privatized parks were actually supervised, such that people who let their dogs off leash and refused to pick up after them had to pay the existing fines, which people had simply ignored previously. As parks were no longer dog toilets where unsupervised animals and drug addicts ran free, children came back to play in them. She saw no reason why the larger parks could not have beer gardens and food trucks and mini festivals, including plays, shows, and music, for whomever wanted to use them, and that these amenities also be available at outdoor skating rinks during the winter.

When Isis would do her walkabout on the city streets to see what was happening, if she came across a small project being done by Gonzales men, she and her bodyguard would frequently get the men coffee and a pastry from a local coffee shop. After doing so, she would encourage them to work hard to get the job finished; otherwise, she would say Francisco Gonzales would blame her for wasting their time. The men looked forward to her visits as she would sit with them and ask them about home and their children. There are very few men in this world, far from home, who do not love it when a beautiful woman brings them coffee and talks to them in their own language.

Isis had no objections to buskers, especially one young man who would sing grand opera at one of the busiest street corners in Toronto. She would reward him generously when she passed and encouraged others to follow his example. She loathed beggars in a country with extremely generous welfare benefits and had old bylaws reactivated. She found that in fact, most so-called beggars were simply scam artists and had them charged under existing but never enforced laws. Genuine Skid Row alcoholics were encouraged to enter residential rehab.

She also saw the need to establish a power base somewhere if she was to control the city. She accepted that the existing lib/left base, including most of the media, would of course hate her due to the ideology taught to them in schools, especially journalist school, which had been dominated by Marxist teachers for more than a couple of generations. The existing power base would try to block anything she proposed, knowing that as a contract employee, her time in office would be limited, and all they had to do was wait it out until she left. She did note that there were a fair number of Spanish speakers in the city, so she set out to cultivate them. The easiest way was through local schools in ethnic areas, which she started to visit, talking to the children in Spanish and encouraging these schools to offer Spanish classes. She encouraged dance and cultural events.

She also emphasized Christianity as the basis for Canadian identity, which surprised people as it had become such a secular city. At Christmas, she had a traditional tree put up with lights and decorations, and she made sure that the greeting was the traditional "Happy Christmas," not that ludicrous politically correct "Happy Holiday."

Since she had observed, somewhat to her surprise, the comfort that faith in something transcendental had brought the dying Kodama, Munro's first wife, Isis had slowly become interested in the obvious relationship between quantum physics and theology, especially the similarities of ancient stories of all old religions. The old gods of Egypt seemed as reasonable as any, and given her background, she saw no reason not to revive them. She bought an old building in a little-used side street with a view to establishing a temple for her favored gods Osiris, Horus, and Isis. People were somewhat tolerantly bemused about this, but others, especially many newer migrants, were not so happy; and her prospective place of worship was firebombed. Anticipating this, she had had steel shutters installed over the windows, so only the facade burned, which she in part left as a visual testament to intolerance. She did insert a large bas-relief of the phoenix in the center of the burned area. That event created quite a media stir.

Growing up mostly in Flagstaff, Arizona, and Japan, she had never personally been exposed to violence, having been knowingly or unknowingly surrounded by layers of security. While therefore she knew intellectually that she would be a target for her presumed apostasy, the thought did not really trouble her, as she still had the youthful sense of invincibility. She accepted a Praetorian bodyguard, but otherwise, she really did not think much about it.

When leaving city hall late one afternoon, however, she was attacked by a knife-wielding assailant. Munro had insisted that she be accompanied at all times by one of Japanese policewomen who were Olympic-class shooters acting as Praetorians. Dressed in a modified kimono with the white obi with purple lightning bolts, they were very visible and were very expensive, but considering the vast sums of money Isis was saving the city, that cost was insignificant.

As was happening so frequently now in Europe, a bearded man suddenly burst from the crowds milling around outside city hall. Isis usually passed through the crowds on the way to her limo without any special precautions. The use of cars as weapons by immigrants to kill the locals had forced the use of concrete bollards to keep cars away for the entrance to city hall.

Clearly, she was the target, as shouting the customary death slogan, the man ran rapidly from the right with his butcher's knife raised, pushing people out of the way. The terrorist got to Isis, grasping her with his left hand, spinning her toward him. She shrank back in terror. Just as he was about to plunge in the knife, the Praetorian, as ever when crowds were present, with her hand inside the opening in her obi resting on the gun she carried, got her pistol up and shot him three times in the face.

Isis, looking at the body on the ground, was shaken and trembling from her narrow escape.

"My god, he almost killed me. Why are people like this in Canada? What should we do now?"

The bodyguard, a Japanese police lieutenant, was looking around intently, hoping to identify and get a shot at the terrorist's handler, but she could not identify him in the shifting crowd. She frowned, poked the body with her foot to make sure he was dead, shrugged her shoulders, and put her gun back in the holster in her obi.

"Let's go. There is no sense in waiting around for the police, as they are useless."

She felt that waiting for the local police was a waste of time, as the hope that they would do any useful investigation was slim. Their previous history of handling numerous such terrorist attacks was simply to dismiss or completely fail to find or even look for any evidence of collusion with anyone or any chain of command and excuse the attack as being mental illness on the part of the assassin. In no terrorist case in Canadian history had the police ever found the handler.

"What should we do about the body?"

The Japanese girl shrugged. "That's not our problem. There will be a garbage truck around sooner or later. Let's go."

They walked to the waiting limo without looking back. The Praetorian saw a shaken Isis home and then, without delay, took the limo across the border into the US so she would not have to face the inevitable gun-related charges by the local Toronto police. As self-protection was interpreted as being against the law in Canada by all police forces and most courts, she knew she would inevitably have been charged with some crime and vigorously prosecuted.

On the way to the border, she changed out of her Praetorian's uniform, and once across the border, using a different passport, she simply disappeared. From the US, she returned to Japan. As such legal problems had long been anticipated, her name and photograph on her Canadian employment records and her Panamanian passport bore no resemblance to reality.

After the assault upon her, realizing that Munro's warnings had to be taken seriously, Isis contacted the engineers who had been working on this new experimental body armor and had an outfit constructed for herself, which she thought was quite stylish and dashing. This armor would stop a knife, but not a bullet. Anything to stop a bullet would be too rigid for daily use. This armor was quite flexible and, being form fitting, initially had to be customized for the wearer. It was semipermeable so it was not ridiculously hot. Isis was happy to find that it could be made in a variety of colors.

One of the senior foremen, with whom Isis had spent some time in the transit construction tunnels, thought she resembled his granddaughter and was appalled at the attempted assassination and the inaction of the police. He spoke to some of his men, and they began to offer their services to her as bodyguards, with different men depending on which shift they were working, as the construction was going on around the clock. Isis encouraged this with little gifts and compliments. She would turn up at outdoor events and at the Spanish-speaking schools with three or four burly workmen carrying pickaxe handles. She found it comforting to have them around her, so after a few outings, she had them taken to a tailor and had custom suits made for them. She would bring them with her when she went to restaurants, especially Spanish and Portuguese ones that she occasionally attended, where they would eat and dance as a group. It became well-known inside the community that she was being protected by the working men from Spain. Some of the younger local Hispanic men also began to offer their services, which Isis accepted with pleasure when she was out on the town.

The Spanish restaurateurs loved that, as the young men brought the young women. Some of them converted part of their space to a small dance floor and the back and front of their buildings to outdoor patios. Normally obtaining permission to do so was difficult due to the labyrinthine city hall rules, but Isis simply repealed these silly rules when her attention was drawn to them. Her new Department of Silly Regulations were repealing these rules by the hundreds. She set up an additional competition, open to everyone, with cash prizes for identification of the Silly Rule of the Week, which she would then repeal; and she did not limit it to one rule, as there were literally thousands of them.

She also encouraged the boys and girls at school to learn some musical instruments, guitar, voice, and dance; and she encouraged the restaurateurs to use the older school children to perform at their establishments, which again needed rule elimination, and also encouraged events and competitions. She went further than that. She encouraged improved academics in these schools, insisting especially that Spanish history be taught and offering visiting scholarships to Mexico and Spain for the very brightest students. She also encouraged the young men to approach Francisco Gonzales to explore job opportunities. In fairly short order, she became a favorite of the Hispanic community.

When asked why she appeared to be favoring that group, she simply said that these were men, and she liked being with men who were men. She pointed out that as far as history was concerned, if other groups, including native-born Canadians, had no interest in their own history and that of the West, it would lead inevitably to a loss of cohesion and a deterioration of society and would eventually be their downfall. She quoted Cicero to them, "That those who do not know the past remain children forever."

In the little temple she was slowly building, she put in a copy of Munro's favorite painting of Salvador Dali's the *Christ of Saint John of the Cross*. She put a large crucifix below it so that when the Spanish workmen accompanied her to her temple, they would have something of their own to which they could bend the knee. She had statues created of copies from Egypt of the ancient gods. One different thing she did was to use holograms, which were turned on when the church was open. It was basically simply a large room with a background projected on the back wall of the desert, the night sky with moving stars, the pyramids, and the Sphinx. Little alcoves contained statues of the gods, along with quiet audios describing them and their admonitions and their wisdom. Shimmering curtains hanging from the ceiling absorbed the ambient sound, giving it a cathedral hush, but she had a large gong that could be struck. It was, she emphasized, a concept in development. It began to attract some interest, and she advertised it among the Egyptians living locally, although she recognized that most were in fact Coptic Christians fleeing from persecution.

Isis, well aware of the difficulties governing Egypt, had never once been critical of the general currently in charge. The general, in turn, had always been proud of Isis and her accomplishments, as by now, she was already one of the most famous theoretical physicists in the world. He looked on her endeavors with considerable interest. When she communicated some of her tentative ideas about religion to him, he took her seriously and began to think thoughts of his own and thus began to refurbish some of the millennia old temples and pay tribute to their old gods. It was good for tourism if nothing else. He anticipated extreme difficulty, but felt if he moved slowly, he could overcome some of the current religious concepts, which Isis pointed out to him were but a blink of an eye in time compared with the old gods. Any trouble around his newly refurbished temples was put down with vigor, and any attacks on tourists were not tolerated. He also saw that attacks on Coptic churches and Aramaic churches within Egypt were significantly harming tourism. That ceased after he adopted the tactic of mass jailings of all family members, no matter how remote, of those involved in the violence. Encouragement to sectarian violence was not initially cracked down on, but when the more vocal players in Egypt revealed themselves, they and their associates slowly disappeared.

Isis largely ignored the local Toronto media, and indeed Canadian media in general, but it did not take long to see who was prepared to give her the benefit of the doubt, and she would speak to these few people. She never gave press conferences, as all that ever consisted of was a bunch of unruly, ill-informed shouters whose ideological beliefs and prejudices were already well-known.

She avoided official functions where possible but felt she did have to attend one a couple of months after the attempted assassination. She was sitting on a raised dais with the meeting chairman and others. A microphone was in front of her as she was due to give a speech after dinner. Five of the Spanish workmen stood behind her, including the senior foreman. They were resting on pickaxe handles they carried. A Japanese woman guard wearing her Praetorian kimono stood with the men, who all knew and liked her because she also spoke some Spanish, as she had done training at the ranch in Arizona where Spanish was frequently spoken.

The dining room was large with numerous separate round tables with a number of people at each table. The second course had just been served when a curious couple entered and made their way to the head table. The leader was a small Japanese woman in a gorgeous kimono with a white obi with a purple lightning bolt motif, similar to that worn by Isis's bodyguard. With her was a tall man with long, black hair held back by a headband with a single eagle feather. He was wearing an old-fashioned long, black frock coat.

They made their way onto the dais and came up beside Isis. The room quieted, looking to see what was going to happen. The Japanese woman looked at the workmen, dressed in their best, leaning on their clubs. She spoke in a voice that could clearly be heard, as the man turned on the microphone that had been in front of Isis.

"Who are these men?" she asked Isis.

"These are men of Spain who work for Don Pedro and are here to protect me."

The woman bowed to them and said, "I thank you for being gallant gentlemen of Spain for protecting this young girl. The people of Spain would be proud of you, and I will make sure Don Pedro knows of this. Muchas Gracias."

She bowed to them again and turned to look at Isis and saw the body armor under her dress.

"Tall Bear, rip that dress off."

He did, taking the neck of the dress with both hands and tearing it open, exposing her upper body and left arm. The audience saw for the first time the new strange blue shimmering upper-body armor she was wearing, which extended down her left arm to the elbow.

The Japanese woman said in a loud voice, "Dear god, body armor, in North America. A girl has to wear body armor to keep assassins at bay and is protected by foreign workmen. It is obviously true what they say, that north of the border, the men are mice. This is intolerable. You will come with us. You can return when we have organized full protection. Come now."

The tall man bent and whispered to her, reminding her of the reputation of the Canadian Special Forces unit, that they were the best snipers in the world.

"I misspoke," the woman said and bowed to the audience. "I apologize to the men of Joint Task Force Two. My people and I respect and admire the men of the JTF2."

Isis rose, and the man took off his jacket and draped it around her shoulders. The audience could see he had a gun strapped to his thigh. They moved off as a group, the Spanish workmen coming with them. The man opened the door to leave. There were shouts and whistles from a crowd of demonstrators standing just outside the main door. The Japanese woman said loudly to the police, who were standing by looking on, making no effort at crowd control.

"Officers, remove these people."

"Can't do that, miss. Legitimate demonstration. If you ask nicely, maybe they will let you through. Otherwise, you will have to wait until they allow it."

The group retreated inside the hall.

"Tall Bear, clear that trash out of the way."

"*Hai!* Form a wedge. I will be the *schwerpunkt*, the point. Tomiko on my right. You," he said, pointing to the other Japanese girl, "on my left. Isis in the middle behind me. You men, form up behind us."

The two Japanese women took clubs out of their modified obis and clicked them open to extend them to their full length. The man picked up a wooden chair and smashed it on the floor, breaking off a leg, which he picked up and brandished. He told the men in Spanish that there was a black stretch limo parked across the street, waiting for them. They were not to stop for anything and should club and run over whoever got in the way.

"I feel like the Cid," he said in English, brandishing his club above his head, and in a loud voice, continued, "I ask nothing more of life than to ride into battle beside my queen." He looked down at Tomiko, who smiled back up at him. Then in Spanish, he said, "Get ready for the charge. We go out on the run. Do not stop. Are you ready?"

"*Sí.*"

"On my word, we will advance at the run. Are you ready?"

"*Sí.*"

He raised his great voice and shouted, "Viva Hispania, Domino Gloria. Charge!"

And they left on the run. The guest heard the shouts of the demonstrators turn to curses and screams, as for the first time, these soft silly demonstrators, who had so often promised violence, met people who were not afraid of violence. The noise trailed away, apart from some weeping. The nearest person closed the door.

"What was that all about?" asked the meeting chairman sitting on the dais, who had been silent during this strange interlude. "Who were these people?"

One of the newspaper women, who had known Isis, stood up. "The woman, I think, was Tomiko-san, the Japanese policewoman who is a movie star and the Olympic shooting champion. The man, I think, is Tall Bear, who is former president Munro's partner in Munro Mines."

"But they can't just come in here and beat people up."

"They just did. The demonstrators were that noisy, violent group who call themselves the Poverty Coalition, who frequently close down city hall and whom the police do not seem able or willing to control. They keep threatening violence. I think that they have just come across two of the most violent people in the world. I wonder where they took Isis"

The police desperately wanted to arrest Tomiko and Tall Bear, but they were long gone and had no interest in responding to any Canadian enquiries. When the police came snooping around the Spanish work camp, amazingly, no one could be found who spoke English, and no one knew who had been with Isis that night.

CHAPTER 4

More Trouble in Toronto

The affair of the brawl at city hall, as the media called it, occurred on a Friday. Tomiko and Tall Bear got out ahead of any police reaction. After dropping off the Spanish workmen, they flew out from the downtown Toronto island airport where, unbeknown to the police authorities, their plane had been waiting for them. They had been on their way from Japan, where Tall Bear now lived. Tomiko had accompanied him, planning to see her children who lived with Munro at the ranch in Arizona. Tall Bear had had some business with a mine in Alaska, so they had stopped briefly there. Munro, knowing of their plans, had asked them on their way south to call in on Toronto to see how Isis was coping after the assassination attempt.

On their arrival at the ranch, it was reemphasized to Munro just how potentially dangerous Toronto had become because of all the poorly screened migrants brought in by Boudreau, the former prime minister, presumably in exchange for their votes. He had virtually stopped European immigration because those escaping from the socialist tyrannies in Eastern Europe were unlikely to vote for another socialist. Munro really did not want Isis to go back to an environment like that, but she insisted, as after she recovered from the shock of the attempted assassination, she had decided she was having fun living on the edge. Munro reluctantly let her return, but only if she would accept proper protection, and she eventually agreed.

On the following Monday morning, at 8:00 a.m. a stretch limo drew up across the plaza from city hall. As with most cities in the Western world, depressingly ugly concrete blocks had been placed around the plaza to prevent migrants from driving cars into crowds in open places. Isis and her Praetorian got out, followed by four kilt-wearing soldiers carrying rifles. A bagpipe player followed them. The piper played as they marched up to city hall. Two of the soldiers took up position on either side of the main door, and the piper stood in the middle. He played the old scornful rebel rant "Hey, Johnnie Cope, Are Ye Waking Yet."

Two of the jocks then followed Isis up the stairs to her office. One sat at the end of the corridor so that he had a free field of fire at the elevators, and the other sat outside her office. The men rotated positions throughout the day and left with her after she finished her day's work.

The soldiers were from Hinchcliffe's Legion, who had been brought over from Europe to protect Isis. They found that staying in what they called Fort MacDonald was of interest because everyone was studying something. Sheila MacDonald and Isis were constantly busy, one with European business and the other with a mixture of theoretical physics and practical tunneling. The Japanese Praetorians were studying for their university courses, which they were eligible to take as part of Tomiko's police shooting squad.

The men of the Legion were also encouraged to study by Sheila MacDonald. As they were currently based in Spain, they had to improve their Spanish as part of being in the Legion. Most of the men now guarding Isis also learned a little Japanese to be able to speak to the Praetorians, who were all young women.

The Legionnaires were a mixed bunch from various militaries. Two of the men, Jock and Colin, were Scottish and were old friends, having been together in the SAS, the British equivalent of the US Special Forces. They had been tested, as all the prospective Legionaries were, and their dossier, which Isis had seen, showed that they were both highly intelligent but had very little education. She pointed this out to them and encouraged them to learn something, at least Hinchcliffe's books on war, if nothing else. The school system they had grown up with had, like all public education in the West, deteriorated to the extent that they had never actually ever been encouraged to study anything and found the suggestion that they both could and should quite novel. Isis was fairly forceful in her suggestion.

Alcohol was certainly available at the fort, but they noticed that few people overindulged, and while nothing was said, clearly the females, who made up the bulk of the live in personnel, did not like it when anyone drank too much. Raoul, having taken over when Jacques—who had originally set up a photojournalist school in Japan—passed on, had provided his library of videos. After the attack on Isis, one of his photojournalists had been stationed with the group to cover any interesting events since the local media, as was now true all over the Western world, were simply so indoctrinated in journalism schools, which had been taken over by adherents to the Frankfurt school, that they could not be trusted to report events accurately.

There were in fact so few trustworthy members of the local media that those who were soon became known by name, and if there was any event that Isis or Sheila MacDonald had to attend, they were invited, even occasionally, to the fort. Some of them had never shot a weapon before and had an interesting experience at the firing range, including firing a variety of weapons as the guards, and especially the Praetorians, all of whom were competitive shooters, practiced regularly.

Some of the Legion men, especially Jock and Colin, developed a surprising taste for knowledge, which they had never known they had. They spent long hours on guard duty. As it did not seem likely that anyone could easily get near her office, Isis provided desks and chairs for her upstairs guards so they could study, with their weapons lying on the desk beside them. Isis pointed out to them that they could not really be soldiers without knowing military history and encouraged them to study that. Hinchcliffe had produced a manual of subjects to be mastered, if the soldiers were looking for additional income, as every examination passed led to a slight increase in salary.

The men, being men, could not stay in the fort all the time and had to get out occasionally, looking for female companionship. Isis took them with her when she visited the Spanish-speaking schools. The fact that they could speak a little Spanish was met with enthusiasm, which encouraged them to learn more. There was a violent rape of a Hispanic girl by a non-Hispanic refugee, which was barely reported in the mainstream media. Isis was not happy about this suppression of news, as she called it. She called publicly on all young Hispanic men to protect their women and organized a fiesta at one of the schools, encouraging the parents to come. She welcomed all comers but indicated the proceedings would be in Spanish. It was a great success, so she did it on a rotating basis. She suggested the schools teach the girls to dance and encourage the Spanish guitar.

The press suggested that she was encouraging divergence in the communities, but she ignored them and, after that claim was made, organized the occasional potluck at the main largely Hispanic school, with Flamenco dancers from one of the upscale restaurants. She made sure that these fiestas had license to serve alcohol, which before she came, was very difficult to obtain.

In view of the increasing violence in some parts of the city, probably mostly related to illegal drugs, which Hinchcliffe had not been able to get completely decriminalized, Isis announced at one of the fiestas that she had asked her Legionnaires, when they were out on the town, to stay in the Hispanic areas. The men were warmly welcomed into these bars and nightclubs as, by now, their Spanish was quite understandable.

Living in close proximity, they got to know each other. Sweet talk did occur and occasionally pillow talk with the Japanese girls, who were cycled in and out, as they had to maintain their hours in their permanent job in the police force in Japan. The soldiers got to know a little about the ranch and the Foundation, as occasionally, one of the Foundation girls would come up to Toronto for a specific problem in theoretical physics they wanted to discuss with Isis or to take a temporary internship with Sheila. The videos available at the fort were interesting, as they showed the soldiers things they had never seen before, like Tomiko's triumph at the Olympics and some of Munro's professional fights. Jock was intrigued when he found out that Munro, a former world champion boxer, and one of the Japanese shooters had published a book of collected love poems in two languages. He was also told that they were putting together a second book of Haikus, which Munro had been collecting for years.

Isis made a point of regularly walking on the streets with a few of her people to show the world that, unlike Europe, no-go areas did not exist in her Toronto. She wanted to demonstrate publicly that when she was in charge, it was possible to walk the streets in peace—any streets. Her guards were extremely vigilant during these walkabouts.

An assassin who is prepared to die, however, can almost always get through, a fact known since the Old Man of the Mountain and his gang of Hashashim. These international assassins based in the Middle East had terrified the medieval world until the Mongols, led by Subotai and Jebe Noyan, climbed up, killed his followers, and literally threw the Old Man off his mountain.

One afternoon, when Isis was walking past a group of young men standing outside one of the migrant meeting places, which she insisted on doing, violence suddenly erupted. The group recognized her and were clearly unhappy and were muttering. Some were shouting and waving their fists at her, being egged on by traditionally dressed agitators.

One young man, holding a knife, dashed out of the crowd. He was so quick he almost got her, knifing one of the soldiers, pushing him out of the way to get at Isis. Colin hit the assassin with his shoulder, which spun him a little and gave Jock just enough time to smash his rifle butt into the man's face. As the assassin staggered back, Jock spun his rifle and put four bullets into the man's face, blowing out the back of his head.

Incensed at how close the man had come to killing Isis, Jock proceeded to kick the corpse in what was left of its face. Some of the crowd were very unhappy at that and, encouraged by the agitators, began to shout louder and were threatening to advance on the group. Jock, Colin, and the other Legionnaire menaced the mob with their rifles. Isis was on her knees, looking after the wounded soldier. Fortunately, it was a defensive arm cut only, but was bleeding profusely, so Isis was applying pressure. Her Praetorian had called for their armored limo, which was on the way. Isis did not like it to shadow them too closely. A couple of police cars came screeching in. Two policemen got out with their guns drawn.

"Drop your weapons!" they shouted to the Legionnaires and the Praetorian.

"I'm not dropping my gun on the street. Why don't you go and arrest some of those murderers?" said an angry Jock, gesturing to the noisy crowd who looked and sounded threatening.

"Drop your gun! You have committed murder."

"Don't be daft. I was protecting the lady."

"Unnecessary use of force. You are under arrest."

"Ach, go away, ye silly wee man."

But more police arrived, and Jock was surrounded and stripped of his gun. He was handcuffed and hustled into a police cruiser. Isis was livid, screaming and shouting at them. They took no notice, glad to get back at her for her very significant financial curbs on the police force, as she had hugely cut the budget by eliminating what she regarded as inappropriate use of police.

Isis found out which police station they were taking him and, as soon as the paramedics turned up to look after the wounded Legionnaire, ran to her own armored stretch limo, which had just arrived. She phoned the chief of police, who had tangled with her at many police services board meetings and did not like her at all. He told her he would look into it but did nothing for a while.

"Let her stew a little," he said to his assistant with a laugh. "She is such a goddamn pain in the ass."

Jock was booked and thrown into a cell, which already contained four migrant criminals who were just waiting to get some revenge on the people who were guarding Isis the apostate. They looked on Jock with pleasure and attacked. Jock was ex-SAS and killed one with a fist to the throat, breaking his voice box, and he dislocated the kneecap of another. He fought them off with blows and kicks for some time, but there were too many, and he went down. One of the prisoners had a prison shank, a sharpened toothbrush. Jock had his shirt ripped up, and the man stabbed him repeatedly in the chest. Jock was still trying to fight them off when the prison guards finally opened the door and dragged him out, bruised and bleeding.

In the meantime, Isis had found the police station holding Jock and was in the booking area. She was getting increasingly frantic.

"I want him out, and I want him out now."

The booking sergeant ignored her. She was shouting at them when the door to the jail cells opened, and Jock was dragged out with his shirt torn off and bleeding from chest wounds.

"Call an ambulance now!" the prison guard shouted to the front desk. "He's been shanked."

"You give him to me now, you bastards. Look what you've done to him! I need to take him to the hospital, and I am going to sue each and every one of you," hissed an enraged Isis. The police put up a token resistance only, realizing that they might have problems, and Isis and her people dragged Jock to the stretch limo and got him in. The driver clipped his lights and siren onto the roof, and they set off for the Toronto Central, the closest hospital, at high speed with the siren blaring. By the time they got there, Isis had opened the medical bag, which all their vehicles carried, and had an IV going and was running in saline from a drip bottle. She also had a blood pressure cuff on. Jock was maintaining his pressure. The driver pulled up at the door of the emergency department. They put him on a waiting stretcher and ran him in.

Isis shouted at the triage nurse, "I need a chest surgeon right now!"

"Calm down, calm down, we will have a look in a minute."

"I want a chest surgeon right now."

"Don't be silly. Sit down and be quiet."

Jock, who had been lying quiet, semiconscious, suddenly lifted his head off the stretcher and gripped Isis, who was bending over him.

"Isis. Pharaoh. I canna breath. I am dying, Pharaoh, hold me."

She knew immediately what was happening. Most of the Foundation children spent time in Miami with the thoracic surgeon they called Chest Doc and in the emergency rooms in Miami and Flagstaff in preparation for spending some time in the mining camps, which was felt to be a useful adjunct to their education. They knew that there were very few real medical emergencies. Jock had been stabbed repeatedly in the right side of his chest, so it was unlikely that his heart had been injured. The most likely thing causing shortness of breath was that the air was leaking into his chest cavity, and the pressure of that was compressing the rest of the lung and progressively the other side as well. They all had seen the videos of Elizabeth Munro, who had had the same condition, which was not uncommon with chest wounds, when she had been shot in her first South American gunfight.

"Tension pneumothorax," said Isis. "Don't you dare die on me, Jock MacGregor."

They all knew what that meant. They had brought their own emergency medical bag into the emergency room with them. Isis grabbed a scalpel, ripped the cover off it, and stuck it into the right side of his chest. She did not have time to count, but thought she was about the seventh rib. Someone put a loaded chest tube in her hands, and she jammed it into his chest and pulled out the metal spike, which acted as an introducer. There was an immediate rush of air, and Jock took a deep breath. Isis almost fainted with relief. Someone attached a flutter valve to the chest tube to prevent air reentry into the chest and gave her a big handheld needle. She put in a suture and tied it to the chest tube. Jock only grunted as the needle went in.

This whole affair had been recorded on video, as they had a video journalist with them. The situation then degenerated into a farce. Seeing the flurry of activity, the triage nurse had come over to see what they were doing. She saw three women bending over the patient, who now had a chest tube in. One was in fancy Japanese dress and another was operating a video camera. There were two men dressed in kilts looking like Scottish Highlanders. She saw they were carrying rifles. She had no idea what was happening, so she pressed the emergency silent alarm to summon the police. Isis saw the nurse and shouted at her, "Get me a chest surgeon and a vascular surgeon right now!"

"What is going on here? Step back from that man."

"You moron. Get me a doc."

"There is no need to use language like that. The doctor will be here soon."

Isis had grown up listening to Munro and knew his favorite oath. "Sweet suffering Jesus Christ, get me someone in authority."

One of the emergency room doctors appeared, drawn to the commotion in the waiting room. Isis saw the white coat. "You, get me a chest surgeon."

"Now, now, wait a minute."

"Get me a chest doc." She noticed the saline bottle was almost empty. "Get me more saline."

The Praetorian hooked up another bottle from their own emergency kit. The doctor leaned over Jock.

"What is going on here?"

Jock was by now feeling a lot better, "Ach, just a wee scratch."

The doctor looked up. "Call x-ray for a chest."

"What do you mean call x-ray?" said Isis. "Take him there."

"Now, young lady, let me do my job."

"Oh, sweet Jesus. Phone Chest Doc and get me Sheila and Hinchcliffe."

Chest Doc, who fortunately was in his office in Miami, answered their dedicated line immediately. Isis gave him a short history, and the camera showed him the situation. She read off Jock's pulse and blood pressure. One of the residents who had been in the emergency department showed up.

"What is going on here?"

"Who are you?"

"I am the surgical resident on call."

"Then talk to Chest Doc." She offered him the phone.

"To whom?" he said, not touching it.

"This is a Miami chest surgeon. He will tell you what to do."

"Yeah, yeah, and I am the fairy godmother."

At this point, the x-ray technician arrived with her machine. An x-ray plate was slipped under Jock's chest, and they all stepped back until the x-ray was done.

Isis thrust the phone at the resident. "Talk to the doc. He will tell you what to do."

"Don't be silly, go away."

By this time, Hinchcliffe had been contacted and knew what was going on and had got through to the prime minister on a private line and had told him that one of Isis soldiers had been stabbed almost fatally and that Toronto Central was not taking it seriously, and Isis had put in a chest tube herself in the emergency department and asked if he could help to get some action. He phoned the hospital and asked to speak to the chief administrator of the hospital. He said he was the prime minister. The switchboard operator put him on hold while she tried to contact the administrator, who was out of his office. She did not believe he was the prime minister and asked him to call back later and disconnected him.

In the emergency department, the technician called to say that the x-ray was up. Isis pushed the resident aside so that the camera could show Chest Doc the image. The resident tried to push her aside, but she forced the phone on him.

"Take that phone, you moron, and speak to the man."

Reluctantly, the resident listened to it. Chest Doc, who had been listening to all this commotion, was not pleased when the resident asked who he was.

"I am the senior chest surgeon in the Miami General. Listen, sonny, I want you to get your goddamn chest surgeon or senior resident down here, stat, immediately! Do you understand? And I want a CT of that chest now. Do you understand? I also want a vascular surgeon here just in case. Now jump to it."

At this point, Sheila MacDonald and her entourage arrived. She did not trust the chief of police at all and had herself driven from the nearby Ontario government building. She blew through the emergency room doors at a dead run, shouting for Isis. She saw the crowd and bulled her way through and took the situation in at a glance. Isis took the phone from the bemused resident and gave it to Sheila, telling her that Chest Doc was on the line.

"Good. Chest Doc, this is Sheila MacDonald, what do we need to do?"

"Get a chest surgeon and a CT of his chest."

Sheila looked at the resident and said very slowly, with great emphasis, "You-get-me- your-superior-right-now. I-am-running-this-goddamn-province. Do-you-understand-English? Now-means-now!"

Just then the police, who had been summoned by the triage nurse, arrived. They saw the rifles and drew their sidearms. "Drop the weapons!"

A furious Sheila turned on them. "You fucking idiots, do you not recognize me? I am Sheila MacDonald, and I run this useless province, and this is your mayor. Shut the fuck up and get the hell out of here."

All this noise and confusion had drawn a large crowd of curious onlookers, of which there were many, as the waiting room was absolutely full of patients waiting to be seen. Everyone looked at everyone else, and nothing was happening, all being carefully recorded on film. It was driving Sheila and Isis mad.

Fortunately, the prime minister had finally got through to the hospital administrator. Several of his aides had had to call the hospital before the operator finally believed who it was and connected him. The prime minister was not happy about the delay.

"What sort of a cluster fuck are you running there? In two minutes, I am going to have the president of the United States on the line asking me what sort of a joke Canadian hospitals are. There is a wounded soldier in your emergency department, and your people seem to be screwing around. I am told he needs a chest surgeon and a vascular surgeon immediately. I assume you have one. Please go yourself to the emergency department and take charge. Call me back at this number when you get there and tell me what is happening and what you're doing about it."

The administrator, who knew a career-ending crisis when he saw it, had a chest surgeon and a vascular surgeon paged on the overhead, asking them to report to the emergency department immediately. This sent the two of them at a run to emergency. He himself also ran for the first time in years. When he got there, he found his chest surgeon talking on the phone to their chest surgeon. He phoned the prime minister back and told his surgeon who it was and gave him the phone. The prime minister asked the surgeon if, as a special favor to him, he would look after the patient immediately and let him know later what was happening.

The administrator stayed with Sheila and Isis until Jock was in a bed in the ICU. It was not a fun experience for him, as both were furious. He had never been with two such angry ladies before. His misery was relieved when the chief of police arrived. The chief endured a cold, quiet tongue-lashing about his force's inadequacies, incompetence, and culpability. He had thought about having a police officer stay with Jock, who was, after all, charged with a serious crime. But then he thought the better of it. They wanted a written report on their desks by morning, with the names of those who had, as they put it, conspired to have Jock MacGregor murdered. They wanted criminal charges laid against all involved. Isis also wanted the logs from his office, which would indicate when she had called him and when he had done something about it. He claimed to have no such telephone logs in his office. Both women looked at him in utter silence for a very, very long minute and then advised him that he could leave.

After investigations, it was decided that the chest tube put in by Isis was in adequate position and could be left, at least until the following morning. He was transferred to the ICU. When it was apparent that he would live and everything under control, Sheila went home. Isis sat down to stay the night.

"You can't stay here," said the ICU nurse.

"Get me the surgeon."

The surgeon came, not all that happily. He had had about enough of these people. The Florida chest surgeon had done his best to control his irritation, but it had still shown. The hospital administrator had asked him to bend over backward to be nice to them. He had pointed out that these two women controlled his hospital budget. Isis told the surgeon that this man had been wounded saving her life, and she and her Praetorian would be staying with him. The surgeon shrugged his shoulders and acquiesced.

Throughout the night, Jock slept intermittently. When he was awake, Isis, who had never really been close to death before—other than the fleeting, surreal experience when the Praetorian shot her attempted assassin—held his hand and talked to him. She told something about her childhood as a peasant girl in Egypt, which she had told no one except Munro. While he slept, she phoned Chest Doc, who knew what was going on, having been in contact with the Toronto surgeon. He knew that Jock would probably be OK. Isis was not happy. She wanted him out of this ship of fools, as she called it, and into a good hospital. She had been looking at a map, and the closest one she could see was in Buffalo by ambulance or the Mayo by flight. Chest Doc ruled out flying with a bad chest.

He spoke to his counterpart in the Buffalo General and explained the situation. He told the surgeon of his personal interest, that he was a paid consultant for Munro Mines, and that the former US president was now back leading that company, and she could speak to him if necessary. He also pointed out that he knew Sandra, the current president, and if necessary, he would get her to speak to him. The situation, as he saw it, was that Isis had no confidence at all in the Toronto Central.

"She can be difficult, but she is absolutely brilliant. I know her as she spent four weeks with me a few years ago. They tell me she is maybe going to be the next Nobel Prize winner in physics. She is already a full professor in Arizona and Tokyo, so what she's doing running a bankrupt Canadian city, I do not know. I know the guys in Toronto are perfectly competent, but she is convinced that they are village idiots. This is your big chance. These people video record everything. You will be splashed all over the news networks as the go-to chest surgeon in your neck of the woods. I am going to fly up there first thing tomorrow because Isis wants me there. As soon as he is safe to travel, I would like to transfer him to your care in Buffalo. Florida is too far away to take him with a chest wound. It would look really good on TV if you yourself, wearing operating room greens and carrying a stethoscope, came up in the ambulance to pick him up. Then you and I and Isis can take him back to your hospital. Be safer to bring an anesthetist also."

He thought for a minute, then added, "You could get your own publicity people to arrange something. Maybe get the hospital administrator on board. We could unload the patient from the ambulance on a stretcher and run him up to the operating room. All the TV people will see is us running with the stretcher and the OR doors banging open."

"A three-ring circus, eh?"

"Put that way, yes. But that will surely help your reputation and the hospital's—that an injured European is rushed from a major hospital in Canada to the Buffalo General because they do not have the skill to look after him."

"I wonder if I could get the chief of police to hustle him across the border and give him a full police escort, with sirens and all."

"That would certainly add to the drama. Jesus, I had better phone the assistant secretary of state, Sweet Wolf, to make sure there is no holdup at the border. Maybe she should speak to your highway patrol and your police chief to stir things up."

"You know her also?"

"Not well, but I do know the president, so I don't expect problems."

"Sounds like Hollywood. Like the movies. Call me when you need me, and I will come."

It worked out just like a soap opera. The concerned American chest surgeons in OR greens, one already at the Canadian hospital, having flown in from Miami, and another coming up from Buffalo with an ambulance, to transport a desperately ill patient. The strikingly beautiful mayor in a very short skirt accompanied the wounded man who had saved her life; the sirens and the lights and the high-speed border transit, with an American police escort; the anxious hospital staff standing by at the hospital entrance; the hospital administrator opening the ambulance doors, running the stretcher along a corridor; and the doors of the operating room closing. Isis was happy to play along. Her palpable relief at having Jock in a US hospital came through very clearly on the videos, and she expressed deep gratitude to the Buffalo General Hospital, the doctors, and the Buffalo chief of police.

A few days later, when Jock was let out of hospital, he was sent to the ranch in Arizona for rehabilitation at Isis's request. Initially, he could barely walk the jogging track up in the foothills, but he slowly improved. The first morning he tried to run in his combat boots, with a 25 lb. pack, and carrying a rifle; he made it about halfway round, then had to stop. A big teenage boy ran past, stopped, took the pack, put it on his own shoulders, and ran on. A little girl stopped, took his rifle, and encouraged him to run with her.

"Come on, Soldier Jock. I'll carry your gun."

In later life, he always told that tale. With the exercise, the food, the air, and the constant encouragement, it did not take long for him to feel he was ready to resume his duties in Canada. The criminal charges against him had been dropped. Isis was looking at civil charges against the police as the crown prosecutor had decided there was no prospect of a criminal conviction of those responsible for allowing the attack on Jock.

Isis put on a show to welcome the wounded hero home. She waited in the foyer of city hall. He got out of the limo in full Highland dress and marched across the plaza, with a single drum beating. When he reached her, he went down on one knee before her, looking up into her eyes.

"You saved my life, Isis, so my life is yours to do with as you wish."

Isis stood regally erect, like a queen. "You do me honor. I accept the offer of your life."

"One more thing, Isis, I would be your ghillie, your man, forever."

The audience did not know how to take that, but Isis did. She knew the legend of Gilgamesh. She put her hands on his shoulders.

"I accept your offer with pride and humility that you will be the shield on my shoulder, the sword at my hip, and the axe in my hand, until I let you go."

She bent over and kissed his forehead with tears in her eyes, her voice breaking as she said, "Oh, Jock." She choked up and simply put her arms around his head and pulled him into her body.

For Munro, that was enough. The craziness of letting the genius of Isis be put at risk where she could be killed by some worthless nameless jackass was utter madness. He was finally able to convince her to return to either Japan or Arizona—he didn't care where. He just wanted her in a place where she could be surrounded by layers of security.

Finding a replacement for Isis was not difficult. There were more than enough of the Prometheus girls who had spent time with Maria Martens or Manon and who would enjoy running Toronto. Hinchcliffe was delighted as she had already moved Colin back to serve as one of her commanders in her growing organization and wanted Jock to oversee other operations, which were rapidly multiplying.

CHAPTER 5

Sheila in Canada

Sheila arrived from France to find a disaster. Once the engine of Canadian prosperity based on manufacture and commerce, after years of socialist rule, Ontario had become one of the most indebted subcountries in the world. Nothing worked anymore. Ludicrous "green" policies with wind and solar and the closing of coal-fired and nuclear plants had raised energy costs to extremely high levels. Because the alternative energy output of wind and solar could not be controlled or stored, it often had to be given away to the US just across the border at far less than cost, and sometimes for nothing.

Manon, based in Luxembourg, who had people who kept an eye on these things, had actually made a great deal of money in Canada from these futile, often corrupt, green energy policies, just as she had in Germany, Denmark, and the UK. She never expected such foolishness to last, so she got in and out, running sales up then selling her companies to those who thought the gravy train would last forever. Rules and regulations made this business extremely difficult, both to start and maintain, requiring significant political and bureaucratic influence, which came at a price, sometimes deposited quietly in offshore banks in tax havens. Because these affairs might be investigated some day for the corruption that was so often present, she made sure that her involvement was so circuitous and so hidden that even if such dealings came to light, the discovery of her connection was very unlikely.

Sheila did not have absolute authority and was more or less only a highly placed economics adviser. An election had been called and given the disastrous state of the economy and soaring energy bills, the previous ideologically driven spendthrift government had not only been voted out of office but had virtually ceased to exist. The new premier of the province was still a local politician, but unlike the previous doctrinaire socialist disasters, he was and remained a businessman. He knew that hugely unpopular measures would have to be taken to pull Ontario out of the financial swamp. He knew if he instigated these reforms himself, he would never be reelected, so he preferred to let them be instigated by Sheila, in her name. Sheila made no secret of the fact that she wished to return to Europe as soon as she could. Her popularity, or lack of it, with the people of Ontario was of supreme indifference to her, and she was not particularly troubled by being made the scapegoat.

She anticipated that she would have to stay for several years. There had been an increasing number of terrorist attacks all over the world, including Toronto where the provincial government was based. As usual, these had all been passed off with little or no investigation by the police and media as having been carried out by mentally disturbed people, the standard laughable claim, which only the most gullible continued to believe.

All that ever happened officially following such an attack was a call for further restrictions on gun ownership, leaving people even less able to defend themselves against future attacks. Having previously assisted in the elimination of a criminal, Sheila was aware of her vulnerabilities and saw no reason to expose herself any more than necessary. She therefore bought property on the outskirts of the city, brought one of Manon's architects over from Europe, and built, using one of Don Pedro's companies, a structure that came to be called Fort MacDonald.

She knew that when she pulled Ontario out of its economic slump, Toronto would grow into a world-class city, and expansion would inevitably come, unless blocked by idiot politicians. She therefore bought a large acreage, anticipating substantial gains at some stage in the future.

The bankrupt city of Toronto itself was to be taken over by Isis, of all people. Why Isis, she did not know. Isis was a theoretical physicist, fond of 'blue-sky thinking, not a practical woman of business. Sheila did know, however, that Isis had made a great deal of money as a teenager by upgrading some car parts and other activities for a Keiretsu in Japan and also on some work in automation for Manon, so maybe she was becoming more practical. Nonetheless, she felt Isis should be in a lab somewhere with Little Sister and poor Helga, who remained trapped in her Asperger's prison despite every effort to socialize her. Sheila knew that Munro felt Isis had the brain to change the world, and therefore, what she was doing, wasting her time in a bankrupt dangerous city like Toronto, was beyond her comprehension. Baghdad North, she felt, was not the place for a delicate hothouse plant, especially one from the Middle East, who would be viewed as an apostate by the myriad of so-called refugees brought in by Boudreau.

She and the architect designed for the future. Like the ranch in Arizona, she wanted a building that could be expanded, not only on each side but also vertically. She had at least three levels of basement dug, as going underground was the only sensible thing to do in a winter city like Toronto. The design was much the same as the ranch, but the finish was hardly done at all. To her, it was simply a barracks and should be left as undecorated as that. After all, what ages a building is not the building but the finishing. The architect left several options that could easily be followed. When they sold the place, which Sheila hoped would not be too far in the future, the new buyer could finish it as he wished.

It was not planned that anyone would stay long. She and Isis were contract workers and would leave immediately after the work was done. She brought with her a couple of Japanese policewomen Praetorian bodyguards. These girls were expensive and rotated back to their regular police jobs in Japan every two to three months. Sheila didn't care about the expense, as she knew she could save Ontario more in five minutes than the cost of her whole security for a year. Even her limo driver was security, who had been trained in such arcane driving skills like the famous Moonshiner's Turn, where he could spin a car 180 degrees. He also was a trained shooter. Munro Mines had several such drivers, mostly ex-Special Forces men.

When Hinchcliffe's Legionnaires arrived to protect Isis, Sheila thought that there were enough people to make it worthwhile, so she put a sprung floor into the gymnasium, an indoor-outdoor swimming pool and hot tub. The cook and the cleaners lived out, and they were restricted to the public rooms only. When the building was built, it was surrounded by a serious security fence, with up-to-date surveillance, which was overseen by a couple of ex-Special Forces personnel, who also manned the gatehouse. When Isis came, she, too, had been provided with a bulletproof limo and driver.

Sheila simply followed Hinchcliffe's economic protocol and modified for local conditions. She wanted a return to Thomas Jefferson's doctrines of minimal government. She had always found the concept that a bureaucrat knows best absolutely ludicrous. Her main problems of course were political. The premier did his best, but the opposition was relentless, not only from the opposition politicians, but also the media and the public service unions.

As Munro had done in other jurisdictions, she brought in forensic accounting and law students to examine the books of the previous administration. After they had put cases together on the most egregious examples of influence peddling, she managed to get a number of them charged with bribery and corruption, which reduced the opposition noise a little. The courts were so desperately inefficient she had little hope of a trial any time soon, let alone a conviction. A significant reduction in revenues from government advertising muted the media complaints a little, and the situation improved considerably when Hinchcliffe sold off the national broadcaster and most federal advertising ceased also.

Her most visible improvement was in transportation. She auctioned off the main highways, which were bought by Don Pedro's outfit from Spain. They recognized what everyone else knew and simply built a new road on top of the existing highway where it was most congested, a simple double-decker technique used frequently in Japan for decades. Removal of these bottlenecks vastly improved the flow of traffic. She also removed speed limits on the main highways, like the German autobahns. When the weather was bad, speed limits were imposed, and if a surveillance camera caught a speeder under these conditions, the fine was very heavy.

The other thing she did, in conjunction with Hinchcliffe and Sweet Wolf, the assistant US Secretary of State, was to have a new superhighway built into the US with a new border bridge. She completely ignored the usual environmental assessments, which used to hold up construction for years. Sweet Wolf ran roughshod over the protesters on the American side. A customs preclearance system for trucks vastly improved border transit times for industry.

Sheila and Hinchcliffe did their best to solve the drug problem. They could not get legalization of all drugs passed, but they did manage to decriminalize them to a large extent. The police and the courts continued to obstruct, deny, and delay. She dramatically reduced the size and scope of the provincial police. Everything that could be privatized was. The cost savings were huge.

Like Isis, she concentrated on reducing taxes. She paid off some of the old debt, but the debts run up by the spendthrift socialist government of the last decade could not easily be paid off due to the crazy ironclad contracts they had signed. Like Isis, she separated the interest on the debt from the last government and tried to ensure it showed up by name on each and every significant purchase. She knew of Milton Friedman's teaching that the first thing to do was to get rid of all taxes possible, as eliminating the debt simply allowed the next government to borrow more.

Health care was such a contentious issue she preferred to leave it alone, as the responsibilities were shared with the feds. If Hinchcliffe could get the laws changed, then she could move, but not before. After the Jock-stabbing debacle, she cultivated good relationships with her equivalents across the border in the US, as she saw that if trouble came to her group in Canada, it would be the escape hatch. She made friends with the Buffalo chief of police and attended some of their functions. She saw to it that she and her staff had US medical coverage and made it clear that the US was where they would be seeking treatment if necessary, until such time as the Canadian state system could be cleaned up, which would not be any time soon. On Munro's suggestion, she did delist from state coverage or privatized numerous minor inconsequential surgical procedures, which by their very number, always clogged state waiting lists. This resulted in a significant reduction in overall wait times for serious conditions.

On the unlikely chance that really bad things would happen, she made contact with the various US major military units close to the border. To cement relationships, she asked Tomiko, the Japanese policewoman who was wildly popular with the US troops and had been stationed in Okinawa, to make a visit to address some of them when she was in the US for other reasons.

Sheila, being a stranger in a hostile land, as she saw it, was always security conscious, but as time passed and she herself had not been attacked, she became a little lax. If she had any time off, she chose not to spend it in Canada, but to be with her friends and business interests in Europe, especially France, the country she had fallen in love with long ago. She owned an apartment in Paris, which was where she preferred to live. Because she flew frequently to Europe, she got into the habit of flying commercial, taking Air Canada, rather than waiting for the Munro company jet to take her there. The cost of chartering a private jet for her own use, she felt she could not justify.

She also felt, because of all the existing security, a single Praetorian was enough at the airport. She would be dropped off at security outgoing and be met at the passenger egress after passport control on reentering Canada. In France, she had her own security. She also got accustomed to having an Air Canada official hustle her through passport control. She would phone her own security when she landed in Toronto so that they would be waiting for her at the exit door.

On one flight back from Paris, an Air Canada official she did not recognize led her to an egress door she had not used before. She was assured that her security had been informed. He opened the door and ushered her out. When she exited, he stepped back in and closed the door behind himself.

She was immediately attacked. Her own Praetorian, who was waiting for her at a gate fifty or so meters away was expecting her and was looking around and saw this happening. Sheila and her assailant had grappled and were too close together for her to get a shot off safely. The Praetorian started sprinting, gun in hand, blasting through the passengers who got in her way.

The heavily bearded attacker towered over Sheila and struck with a long knife. She threw herself backward and was just able to get her left arm up. The knife opened her arm from elbow to shoulder. He fell on her, his weight forcing her to the ground, and lying on her, he held her down with his left hand. He raised the knife for the killing strike at her throat. She should have died then.

But this was Sheila MacDonald, a tigress, a daughter of Angus Og, the Lord of the Isles, a daughter of the Makolquito, MacDonald of the Left Hand. As a child, like all the Foundation girls, she had endlessly practiced with a true killer, the ninja. With her wounded, weakened left hand, she caught the attacker's wrist as the knife came down and was able to force it to the left while she jerked her head to the right. The knife opened her neck, but only the skin and muscle.

With her right hand, she clawed his face. She got her nails into his eyes. With the strength of desperation, she forced her long manicured nails behind his eyeballs and ripped one of them out. The man screamed and let go of the knife. She twisted, pushing him slightly off her, and reached over, grabbed the knife, and drove it up under his jaw into his brain. As she did so, the head above her exploded, covering her with blood, brains, and bone fragments.

The Praetorian, who had stopped to shoot, jammed the gun back in her obi and took off running again. The door behind Sheila opened, and the man the Praetorian thought of as Judas, the Air Canada official, put his head out to see what was happening. The Praetorian pulled her club out, flicked it open, and as she ran past, hit the man square on the side of his face, swinging as hard as she could. She heard and felt the bones crunch, and the man screamed.

She dropped to her knees beside Sheila and rolled the dead attacker off her. Some passing passengers began to scream in horror when they saw the dead face with the knife protruding from his beard and the eyeball hanging down the cheek. She assessed the neck injury. It was bleeding profusely but seemed to be superficial. She used the knife to open Sheila's dress to see the extent of the arm wound. She could see bone in the base of the cut, but no major arterial pumping.

She applied pressure to the wound using Sheila's ripped-off sleeve, but it was too small. She looked around for help. People simply stood there. She saw a flight crew from JAL, Japanese Airlines, leave the door behind her and shouted at them in Japanese. They looked around and ran over.

"I am Captain Iwasaki of the Tokyo police force. I need your help. Give me a blouse to pack this cut."

Without any hesitation, one of the stewardesses dropped her jacket, pulled off her blouse and gave it to the Praetorian, who packed it in the wound. She demanded a second blouse.

"Help me wrap the wound."

The stewardess knelt and held Sheila's arm as she used the second blouse to wrap the arm to force the first blouse in place to apply pressure to stop the bleeding.

"Lean on this and give me your scarves to wrap the neck wound."

She pulled out her phone and contacted the driver, who was waiting just outside. He leapt out of his limo, grabbed the medical bag, which they all carried, and ran in through the terminal and to the passenger egress. The Praetorian, with the driver and the stewardesses, quickly got an IV going in Sheila's good arm and began to run in saline from a bag, which one of the stewardesses held. She took her blood pressure and pulse and felt they were stable. She used a tensor bandage to wrap the arm again to apply more pressure to the blouses crammed into the wound. With the help of the others, she got Sheila more or less to her feet and dragged her out to the limo, which fortunately was a stretch, and laid her down.

She directed the stewardesses who had donated their blouses to come with them in the limo. The driver clipped on the siren and lights and pulled out, straight into a traffic jam.

The Praetorian phoned Toronto Central, thinking that, in view of the last debacle, they would have cleaned up their act, but she was mistaken.

"I am Mineko Iwasaki, a captain in the Tokyo police force. I have Sheila MacDonald here who has been wounded. We are on the way from the airport. Clear an operating room and have a surgeon standing by. And connect me to the emergency department."

The switchboard operator simply attempted to put her through to emergency. The line was busy. She knew that no emergency was going to take orders from anyone and simply said, "The line is busy. Just go to emergency. They will look after you," and disconnected.

Mineko called her back immediately. The switchboard operator tried emergency again. It was still busy, so she said the same thing in exasperation, "Just go there. They will look after you," and disconnected again. Mineko called back again. The operator recognized her voice and told her to stop calling and disconnected her.

Mineko was furious and at wit's end. She had no idea how long it would take to clear the traffic jam going into Toronto. She knew that an hour or two was not unusual at that time of day, as the traffic in Toronto was reputed to be the worst in North America. The double-decking of the highways was under construction but not yet completed. She had no idea how to get a helicopter or even if one could approach a busy airport. At high speed, Buffalo was probably about two hours away. Sheila seemed stable and could probably survive the journey, as the bleeding seemed under control with the pressure bandages, and her vital signs, being taken by one of the airline stewardesses, were stable.

She told the driver to change course and bull through, no matter what the cost. With lights flashing and siren screaming, going up on the shoulder and pushing other cars aside with his reinforced and heavily armored vehicle, regardless of the damage, the driver broke through the jam, which was headed toward Toronto. The traffic going the other way was much lighter. He floored the accelerator, and with the siren and lights going, he started his run for the border.

Mineko phoned Chest Doc in Florida on his emergency line and got through immediately. Using her phone, she showed him the makeshift bandages on Sheila's arm and neck. Pulse and blood pressure were stable, so he thought the run to Buffalo was not foolhardy. He would contact Buffalo General and Munro if she would call the Buffalo chief of police. Mineko called on Sheila's phone. The chief of police recognized the number and picked up. Mineko explained the situation, that they had left Toronto and were on the highway. She asked if there was anything he could do to speed up things, perhaps find a helicopter to pick them up on the highway and if his office could also alert the border guards and the hospital.

The police chief rose to the occasion magnificently. He knew Sheila and liked her, and being asked to effectively save her life, he called in all his favors. Being begged by a Tokyo police captain also helped. He knew that Tomiko had given a talk recently to a nearby military unit because he himself had driven her there. He phoned the camp commandant and explained the situation. He begged for a helicopter to cross the border and pick up Sheila. The commandant said under no circumstances could he authorize a border crossing. Mineko had called Munro, who in turn had called Sweet Wolf, who called Sandra and called the chief of police while Sandra was on the line. She got through to him while he was on the phone to the military. He connected the two. Sandra was in no mood to argue.

"Go get that girl. To hell with Canadian air space. I will take care of that. Send your fastest pickup helicopter to get her on the highway and get her to the Buffalo General."

With a direct order from the commander in chief, he scrambled a couple of the fastest helicopters he had. Thirty minutes later, they picked up the speeding stretch limo on the Highway 401 heading toward the border with its lights flashing. Mineko was alerted to their approach, and when they were overhead, the driver pulled onto the shoulder with the siren and lights still going. One of the helicopters landed on the highway in front of the car. The driver had parked at an angle to protect the helicopter from any inattentive driver. They hustled Sheila and Mineko on board and lifted off.

Mineko had told the stewardesses to stay with the driver, who would take them back to their hotel. She noted their names and told them to charge any clothing they needed to Sheila's account, and they needed a lot, because they and Mineko were covered in blood by that time. She gave them her number and told them to get the clothing store to call her cell phone for authorization. Any additional requirements were also to be charged.

Meanwhile, Chest Doc had called Buffalo General. The administrator, remembering who Chest Doc was and the priceless publicity they had had after the Jock affair, said he would certainly have a staffed OR available with an anesthetist. Chest Doc told him he wanted a plastic surgeon immediately available, with a vascular surgeon and a peripheral nerve surgeon on standby, although based on what Mineko had told him, it did not seem likely that any serious nerve or vessel damage had occurred. He asked to speak to the plastic surgeon on call and was put through.

He explained the situation to the plastic surgeon, who was a young man who had recently joined the hospital. He told him who he was and what he did and what the injuries were, as they had been described to him. The young surgeon did not see what the fuss was about. Chest Doc told him that this was one of the famous Munro Foundation girls who had been brought in to pull Ontario out of its financial mess, and if a woman in her early twenties was doing this, she was clearly destined for the big time, and there would be lots of publicity. If he was in any doubt, he only needed to ask his colleague the chest surgeon who had looked after Jock, the wounded man who had been guarding Isis. Managed properly, this would hugely enhance a young surgeon's reputation.

Chest Doc suggested that the plastic surgeon meet her in his OR greens, with a stretcher and an OR tech, hold her hand and tell her he would look after her, and rush off with her into the OR. When talking to the press, he should emphasize that this was a serious injury, which the Canadians apparently could not handle, so the patient had been rushed to his care at Buffalo General, and so on. Chest Doc pointed out that the media were rather credulous.

The hospital administrator, who had been through this before, had organized the hospital photographer to be ready to take stills and videos. When he heard she was coming in by military helicopter, he had them all at the rooftop helipad and notified his favorite press people, who raced to get there. They began to film as soon as they heard the helicopter.

The helicopter landed, and the military men jumped out to help unload Sheila. Mineko, assisting in a blood-stained kimono, was caught on video. The plastic surgeon and the hospital administrator rushed to assist. Sheila was awake, but groggy. The administrator seized her uninjured hand and told her that they and the plastic surgeon at his elbow would take good care of her. She was put on a stretcher, and they left at a run. As the stretcher disappeared through the doors, Mineko sagged with relief, and in a touching scene, the chief of police, who was also present, caught her in his arms, all carefully recorded.

Amazingly, the huge gash in her arm had only injured the radial nerve, the main nerve going down the back of the arm. As it was a clean knife cut, the peripheral nerve surgeon did an immediate repair. As it was largely a motor nerve, he hoped that there would be a good return of function over the next year or as otherwise, she would have permanent weakness of the wrist and hand and would conceivably require muscle transfers. The plastic surgeon repaired the damaged muscles and closed the skin. He also closed the neck wound, which fortunately was only through the superficial neck muscles. She had lost a lot of blood, but as she was young and fit, they deferred transfusion to see what she would be like the next day.

After surgery, he had her put in a private room with monitors. The Praetorian insisted on staying the night with her. They let Mineko shower to wash off the blood and gave her hospital greens to wear. It made an interesting tableau, this little Japanese woman sitting at the bedside with her two guns and club on the table beside her. The plastic surgeon, being a man wise beyond his years, also decided that he should stay the night in the hospital to keep an eye on the patient, which he did several times that night. His colleagues derided that as overkill, but he simply said to wait and see.

The story of the attempted assassination, the miraculous escape, and the heroic American rescue of course made headlines around the world. Sheila remained incommunicado for the first day. The plastic surgeon, with her permission, gave the media updates. He had been anticipating that she would be the usual celebrity jackass, with whines and complaints and impossible demands. Sheila, however, was a pro. Having spent a few months working in Elizabeth's northern mining camps and having been Manon's assistant, she had had hard men eating out of her hand for years. There were no complaints. Everything was wonderful. Everyone, including the floor cleaner, was wonderful. What impressed the floor cleaner even more was that Sheila spoke to her in Spanish.

On day 2, there were photographs of her smiling bravely up at the surgeon as he held her hand. There were photographs of her with the chief of police, the air force general who had sent the helicopter, and the hospital administrator. On the third day, it was felt safe to allow her to go home. The air force general elected to send her home in a military helicopter with another as an escort. As a special request from Sheila, they were equipped with loudspeakers to play the "Ride of the Valkyrie," as seen in *Apocalypse Now,* the famous movie about Vietnam.

As the helicopter landed on the roof, Sheila was brought out in a wheelchair, pushed by the plastic surgeon himself, dressed in his operating room greens. Sheila had her left arm in a sling and a brace on her wrist to compensate for the partial paralysis. There was a prominent bandage around her neck. She stood and shook hands with the air force general and the hospital administrator. She embraced the chief of police, to his intense pleasure, as she regarded him as her chief rescuer. She made to shake hands with the plastic surgeon, but to everyone's surprise, including his own, he raised her hand, bowed, and kissed it. When later asked why, he said he did not know. It was not as if he did not know any women, but he said he felt he had been privileged to meet a great lady. He would be going to Toronto in about a week or so to check on her wounds and remove the sutures.

She entered the helicopter with the Praetorian at her back. Mineko usually avoided publicity, but she had been interviewed by one of Raoul's video journalists, who had come with some assistants to video the proceedings. The Praetorian had been livid with rage. She called the Air Canada official Judas Iscariot and wanted to know who had given him the thirty pieces of silver to arrange Sheila's death. She had broken his orbit and upper jaw when she hit him with her club, and he had required surgery. She promised to do a lot more to him when she got back to Toronto. She wanted him charged with accessory to attempted murder, but the crown prosecutor indicated that the police had not found enough evidence for him to lay charges. The Praetorian seethed with anger at what seemed to her a miscarriage of justice.

As the helicopter took off, the pilot turned on the music, and the "Ride of the Valkyrie" blasted out over Buffalo. They had had their flight path cleared because Sheila insisted on coming in off Lake Ontario over Toronto, with the music blaring over the *whop-whop* of the helicopter. They flew to the north end of the city where the helicopter flared and landed at the helipad of Fort MacDonald.

Sheila, her arm in a sling, was the first person out. Munro, in full Highland dress, had come up from Arizona to meet her. Tomiko, dressed in a kimono, had been visiting and had come with him. They stood motionless and unsmiling as she walked toward them. She stopped a little way away.

"Ye have come home, daughter of Og?" asked Munro.

She recognized the words. "It is Sheila. Am I welcome in this house?"

"If ye had a murdered man's head under your armpit, you were still my child." He held his arms open, and she came to him. "*Neach-gaoil*, beloved, ye have been sore wounded, but you are home."

"Ard Riache."

"Nay, not Ard Riache, more likely Brudarach, the dreamer. But here, Tomiko waits."

He turned and presented her to Tomiko, who put an arm around her and looked straight at the camera held by the video journalist.

"I thank all those who took part in the rescue and saved the life of Sheila MacDonald. I thank the Americans for their help. Their legendary efficiency we have come to expect, from the helicopter pickup on the highway to the speed and skill with which she was taken care of. But it is the kindness and generosity of the American people that stands out. They took in a poor wounded girl from a foreign land, who was not their responsibility, and cared for her. It is for this reason that I thank you and will never forget." And she bowed to the camera.

A couple of Hinchcliffe's Legionaries in full uniform pulled a cart into view. It was laden with cases of single malt Scotch from one of Manon's distilleries. They proceeded to load them onto the helicopter. One of the pilots who had dismounted said to Tomiko, "Ma'am, we can't take this back across the border. We will be bootleggers."

"Well, if you don't tell anyone, I won't. And don't open a bottle until you get back to base and keep a bottle for the general."

"Yes, ma'am." And they took off and disappeared into the distance, blaring the "Ride of the Valkyrie."

Ten days later, the plastic surgeon drove up to Toronto to check the incision and remove the sutures. This was again recorded and released to the media. Sheila was happy with his services and approached Elizabeth to sign him on as a plastic surgeon consultant for Munro Mines.

The JAL hostesses were not forgotten. Back in Tokyo, Tomiko contacted the head of JAL and gave him their names. She wanted to make sure that the girls were publicly rewarded for helping in Toronto when no one else would. One of the video journalists interviewed them and filmed them receiving an award from the head of JAL. Tomiko herself also thanked the girls in her capacity as chief of police and was seen giving them an award.

CHAPTER 6

I am Samurai

After the fall of the hapless Prime Minister Joe Who, who did not realize that a minority government should not call for a confidence vote, another election was called in Canada. By this time, the ultraleft wing of the Liberal Party, which had been seething for the last three years, managed to push out the former prime minister and replace him with a silk stocking ultrasocialist who espoused globalism, multiculturalism, post-nationalism, and any other *ism* that was currently in favor. Sandra, the current US president, and Munro were grimly horrified, but not surprised, when he won a majority.

"Here we go again," said Munro, who was visiting Sandra in Washington for an official function. "I wonder how long it will take this one and his party to bankrupt Canada again."

"I don't know," sighed Sandra. "We have built a wall on the southern border. It looks like we will have to build a wall on the northern border too, if he does what he says he is going to do and fills his country with even more potential terrorists. How could they be so stupid as to go down that disastrous road again? Do these people have a death wish?"

"God alone knows, but Hinchcliffe's days in Ottawa with that clown are certainly numbered. I am sure she will be happy to move on."

"What will be next for her?"

"I don't know, but she has certainly grown her Legion substantially. There is lots of work for private armies and logistics companies like hers

---

in some of the more troubled countries in the world like Nigeria and the Middle East."

As Munro had predicted, the new prime minister's first move was to inform Hinchcliffe that her days as adviser to the Canadian government were numbered and that she should report to his office at 2:00 p.m. the next day. Hinchcliffe, who had been expecting this, phoned Munro, who flew up for the meeting. He very seldom left the US, other than the odd visit to Europe, and when he did so, Elizabeth, his former wife, would send him her own jet and her own pilots.

Maria Martens, who effectively ran things for him, especially his government duties, had an armored stretch limo, which was used by his people in Toronto, driven up to meet them at the Ottawa airport, as he was accompanied by two visiting Japanese shooters he had brought with him as bodyguards. Outside of his own states, he liked to have at least one female bodyguard with him to forestall any unpleasantness.

"After all," he would say, "if I kicked a protester's ass, it would be brutality, but if a woman did it, everyone would laugh." A Japanese video journalist came up from Toronto with the limo driver. Munro anticipated that Hinchcliffe would leave with him and return to Arizona.

Hinchcliffe met them at the front door of the building where the new leader had his office; otherwise, they would not have been allowed in. All members of the group, including Munro, were carrying guns, as terrorism had become a real issue worldwide. The metal detectors now installed at the doors after the attempts to assassinate Hinchcliffe by the lone wolf shooters would have picked them up. She briefed Munro on the situation as they went to the new prime minister's office. He was a French Canadian but had an apartment in Paris where he seemed to have spent most of his time. He had lectured on something at some sort of college in Quebec and occasionally in France but had never really had a job of any significance.

He disliked Americans on general principles, and particularly disliked Sandra, more because she hunted animals than for anything else. He disliked Munro, whom he had never met, but saw simply as Sandra's lapdog. Munro was frequently attacked on Canadian television, but he cared so little about the international media's opinion that he rarely consented to an interview by any media.

On the prime minister's orders, Munro was excluded from the meeting and only Hinchcliffe was allowed into his office. She had to leave her gun with Munro, as the new PM would not allow her to wear one in his presence. Part of his election platform was that he planned to ban all private ownership of guns in Canada. Munro and the others waited outside. The PM was unhappy about these people sitting outside his office.

"Have them marched out," he said to his private aide. "They can wait outside the building."

"I would not order that, sir," said Hinchcliffe.

"No one asked you. You are dismissed as of now. Leave this building immediately."

"Yes, sir, if you would just sign this document saying I am terminated."

Beaupre, the prime minister, glanced at it briefly. It was in English with no French translation, but it seemed like a boilerplate statement of dismissal, so he signed it. There was a commotion outside his office. Hinchcliffe pocketed the paper and opened the door. Munro remained seated in a corner, holding Carmenlita in his arms. She appeared to be struggling to get free. The three Japanese women Praetorians had formed a ring around him, holding off the security people who had become threatening and belligerent, trying to physically throw them out, as ordered by Beaupre's aide.

As she came out of the office, one of the security men, exasperated by the women, punched one of the girls in the face, knocking her to the ground. He in turn was levelled by a blow from the club one of the Praetorians withdrew from her modified obi. Hinchcliffe pushed through the melee, took her gun back from Munro, and put a couple of shots into the ceiling.

"I will shoot the next man who moves. Stop this stupidity. You," she said, pointing to the security people, "line up against the wall."

In the shocked silence following the gunshots, the security people lined up. The prime minister came raging out of his office and shouted to them to eject the Americans. Hinchcliffe turned the gun on him.

"Be quiet, sir. We just want to leave. There will be no further trouble."

Beaupre, who had never seen a gun up close before, let alone looked down the barrel of one, went white and hurriedly backed off into his office. Inside his office, he slammed the door. Then, thinking about what had just happened, he became livid.

"These goddamn Americans. They come to my office and make trouble. Have them arrested."

His aide, who had been upset at the treatment of one of the lone wolf assassins, whose dead body had been thrown down the steps by

Hinchcliffe, had alerted some acquaintances. He knew they were furious with Hinchcliffe, who had not only escaped the ordered assassination, but had disrespected the assassin's body. He had informed them that she and some of her equally hated American companions would be leaving the building at about 2:00 p.m. that afternoon, so a reception committee of a large number of ideologically driven demonstrators had been organized by their leaders and were there outside the building, waiting for Hinchcliffe and her party to leave. The aide immediately alerted the protest group that the targets were on their way. He did not know or care that some were armed.

Munro and his group left the building and were halfway across the plaza, making their way to their limo, which was waiting for them at the far side, because concrete blocks had been placed there to prevent suicide car bombers from approaching. A large group of protesters, many in traditional dress, had assembled and had been ordered to spread out in a semicircle and, on command, began screaming and shouting slogans and then on the urging of their organizers, some of whom had bullhorns, began to run toward Munro's group.

Knives were seen and shots rang out from the rapidly approaching mob. Bullets whistled overhead, and several of the group were hit. One of the Japanese Praetorians went down. Hinchcliffe had her gun out, but before she could fire, she was hit in the leg and fell. She was back up in an instant on one knee, firing at the crowd. All the group, including Carmenlita and Munro now had their guns out and were also shooting. One of the other girls was hit in the arm, and she dropped her gun.

The waiting limo driver had seen what was happening. He was ex-Special Forces and so was ready for anything. As usual, he had an assault rifle concealed within his vehicle. He seized that, leaped out, and leaning on the hood of the car, opened up and put a full clip into the mob, which now saw it was being attacked on two sides, so they turned tail and ran. One of the Praetorians, an Olympic champion shot, saw one of the organizers in traditional dress at the back of the crowd with a bullhorn trying to rally the mob. She took careful aim and shot him in the head. Hinchcliffe looked at her in admiration.

"That has to be some sort of record kill."

Seeing the wounded Praetorian lying on the ground, the driver grabbed the medical bag and, still carrying the assault rifle, sprinted to the group surrounding her. Munro was down on his knees beside the girl and had unclipped her artificial obi and pulled open her kimono to expose her chest wound. The clothes the Praetorians wore looked like the classic kimono but were modified for physical action.

"Kill all that scum," he said, pointing to the bodies on the ground, remembering Tomiko's advice from a previous encounter. The shooters were happy to oblige. Most of the assailants were dead anyway, as the professional shooters mostly used head shots. Munro knew that if any lived, there would be constant lawsuits stirred up by this new idiot prime minister. There would be much less sympathy for a dead terrorist than a wounded one.

The driver opened the medical bag, and Munro, with the help of one of the shooters, started an IV on the fallen Praetorian. She had a bullet wound in her upper thigh, which was bleeding, but not arterial. One of the shooters simply applied a pressure dressing. He turned to the chest wound.

"I am samurai," said the girl. "Let me up. I am OK."

"You may be samurai, but to me, you are just a brave wee lassie with some bullets in her. Lie still there while I take care of things."

Munro, a former orthopedic surgeon, put a stethoscope in his ears to listen to her chest, but the roar of the gunfire had temporarily deafened him. She had been shot on the right side of the chest. He felt he could definitely hear breath sounds on the left but did not feel he could hear much on the right. He asked one of the girls to phone Chest Doc in Florida. The video journalist had had her camera going and had documented the whole assault. She now concentrated on the wounded woman, who had had her kimono, underclothes, and bra stripped off and was naked, except for her panties. She lay on her back on her kimono.

"Can you breathe, sweetheart?"

"It is a little difficult."

He listened again. His ears were rapidly improving, and he was certain the chest sounds were much less on the injured side. He was sure he would have to put in a chest tube to relieve the pressure so that she could breathe. He knew that this was one of the few true emergencies, so he unpacked the preassembled apparatus. The girl was having increasing difficulty breathing. He listened again and was certain. By this time, Chest Doc was on the line from Florida and he could look at the girl via the camera. He agreed that a tube should be put in. Her blood pressure remained reasonable. Munro put in some local anesthetic but was unwilling to wait for it to take full effect.

"Hold her down. This is going to hurt."

"I am samurai. You do not need to hold me."

He took a scalpel and cut her. He then introduced a thick, pointed metal spike with a plastic tube over it and pushed it into her chest. The girl tensed and grimaced, but not a sound escaped her lips.

"Aye, lassie, you are indeed samurai," said Munro. He pulled out the metal spike, leaving the plastic tube behind. A rush of air followed. He quickly connected it to a one-way valve to stop any air from reentering. He used a large handheld needle to sew the tube in place. Her blood pressure remained good.

When Hinchcliffe saw that her help was not needed, she had Carmelita plug the bullet wound in her thigh and apply a pressure dressing. The other wounded Praetorian also had a pressure dressing applied to her arm.

"Let's get out of here," said Munro, and they carried the girl with the chest tube to the limousine. No one had approached them during the whole episode. The government security and the bureaucrats stood at the open doors of the building now that there was no further shooting but made no effort to help. The prime minister looked down from his window with some satisfaction. They got her to the stretch limo and laid her inside. Hinchcliffe was the last one to board the vehicle. The camera caught the look of disdain and disgust as, with her head high, she looked back at the building where she had worked for the last few years. She hawked and spat on the ground, entered the car, and never went back.

"Where do I drive to?"

Munro was torn between two realities. "If we take her to a hospital, that silly vindictive man will have us all charged with murder, and we will be held in jail and will have real difficulty getting out. But if we fly out, she may die on the plane. But I don't really have a choice. Take her to the hospital and drop her off. I will stay with her, and you others head for the plane and get out of here, or if that is too difficult, drive to the US border and alert Sweet Wolf for clearance.

Kuniko, the wounded Praetorian, whose command of English was reasonable, was listening to the discussion. "I will be fine, sir. I can breathe perfectly well. Please take me on the plane. I insist."

Munro looked doubtful, but the prospect of a Canadian jail was uninviting, not only for himself, but also for all the others, as the jail population in Canada was becoming like the jail population of Europe, largely migrants. The risk of their assault by migrants and death in jail was real.

"OK, let's head for the plane. Driver put on the lights and siren. Do not stop at any roadblock."

From his office window, the prime minister watched the limo leave the plaza. He turned to his aide and said with a smile of satisfaction, "Excellent. Call the police. We will have these arrogant Americans in jail for a very long time, and then we will see their president crawl to get them out. I wonder how that crowd knew to be waiting for them."

"I arranged for it, sir, as I knew how much you disliked them. We got them good," said his aide as he began to dial.

"Stop! What do you mean, you arranged it?"

"Yes, sir. I did not know some of the guys would be carrying guns, but that is so much better as we can have the Americans charged with murder and have real bargaining power with the US."

"Dear god in heaven. Do not make that call to the police. You arranged it? You had that mob waiting? Then you are responsible for these dead people out there and that injured American."

"No one will know. We have a huge advantage if we conceal the weapons the protesters were carrying and accuse these Americans of shooting unarmed people. That scenario works just fine in Gaza."

"Eh! What? This is Canada, you cannot hide that. There are people out there with cameras. There will be videos. They will trace it back to my office."

"No one will say anything, sir. You know the media. They will pretend to believe anything we tell them. The police will say nothing. We can simply call any other videos fake news."

"No, that will not work. No one believes the media anymore. We simply will say nothing. The incident occurred after they left my office. It was unfortunate. We make the main issue that we need tighter gun control. Make sure that there is to be no further comment from my office. What happened, happened, and had nothing to do with us."

The limo driver turned on the siren and the flashing lights, which he had clamped to the top of the car. He set off at high speed toward the airport. The police did not intervene on the journey. Why, Munro was not certain. He had contemplated calling President Sandra, but given the absence of police, he decided not to involve her. Carmenlita placed the rifle the driver had used back in its concealing bag as they planned to take that with them on the plane to leave as little evidence as possible.

Hinchcliffe contacted the pilot and explained the situation, that they wanted an immediate departure, unauthorized if necessary. The pilot had the plane ready at the private terminal as they drove up. They abandoned the limo and hustled straight through the terminal. Munro and the driver carried the wounded Praetorian on a collapsible stretcher they always carried in the limo. They brought the medical bag with them. The shouts of the officials were ignored, and they bulled and stiff-armed through those who tried to stop them and ran directly out onto the private plane apron. Munro had checked the wounded girl's vital signs just before they arrived at the airport and, in consultation with Chest Doc, felt that she could make it to at least Buffalo, the closest American hospital.

Ignoring shouts to stop, they all boarded the plane, including the driver, as he had also been a shooter, and was therefore at risk of prosecution. As soon as they were all on board, as they were closing the plane door, the pilot taxied to take off. The copilot told the control tower, "We have a medical emergency. We are leaving now. Mayday, mayday, clear the runway. We are leaving."

Ottawa was not a busy airport, so the pilot pulled his plane in front of one, which was waiting to take off, and seeing no planes approaching, he gunned the engine, and they took off, pulling hard to the side to get out of the flight path as soon as he was off the ground.

Munro got through to Sweet Wolf to get permission to land at the Buffalo airport. She took care of that and called the chief of police, who knew the Munro group very well. He arranged to have a police escort on the runway, waiting for the plane to land. He also contacted a couple of reporters he was friendly with and gave them the bare bones of the story, as far as he knew it.

Chest Doc, who had had dealings with Buffalo General in the past, contacted the chest surgeon he knew at that institution and also the plastic surgeon they had on a retainer. The hospital administrator was informed. He remembered the wave of excellent publicity the hospital had received the last time they had an encounter with the Prometheus Group. He also fondly remembered Sheila MacDonald, who had charmed everyone, so he rushed to get everything set up, including their own publicity department.

The plane belonged to Munro Mines, so it was not a normal business jet, and the pilots were Elizabeth's own people. The pilot put on his afterburners, and in a very short time, they saw the Buffalo airport come up. Munro was thankful. He had been deeply concerned that the wounded girl might deteriorate quickly due to decreased pressure while they were in the air, so the plane had stayed low, and she had been given supplemental oxygen. He had been very worried that she might die because he did not want to do jail time. Fortunately, she did not deteriorate and was still stable when they arrived in Buffalo. The two surgeons contacted by Chest Doc were there to greet the plane, dressed in greens for the operating room. They hustled the patients off, the Japanese shooter with the chest tube, and Munro in one ambulance and Hinchcliffe and the other wounded Praetorian in another.

Investigations were rapidly undertaken, and the situation seemed under control. Other than changing the chest tube, no further surgery was required. The additional bullet wounds were treated simply by cleansing and closing them. The wounded girl was kept in ICU for a couple of days and then kept under close observation in a private room for several days before she was felt fit to travel. Hinchcliffe and the other girl were looked at briefly but were not felt to be seriously injured.

Hinchcliffe and Carmenlita decided to take a few days of R and R in Arizona before returning to Europe and the men of the Legion. Her only question to Munro was why he had been holding Carmenlita back from the fight. He smiled and pointed out that Carmenlita was different. She was a girl they had found in the South American jungle and was devoted to Hinchcliffe. She was not a policewoman and likely would have killed the unsuspecting security men. Hinchcliffe agreed that it was certainly a possibility and took Carmenlita with her.

When Sweet Wolf informed the president about the debacle in Ottawa, which she felt was likely an arranged attempted murder by the mob of migrants, Sandra was exceedingly unhappy with the conduct of the new Canadian prime minister. She blamed him for the whole fiasco. She told him in private that any attempt at prosecution of any of the people involved would result in severance of all diplomatic ties with Canada and immediate expulsion of Canadians from the US. She unleashed Sweet Wolf on him.

"No holds barred," she said. "Take that clown for all he is worth. Just keep me and the US government out of it, plausible deniability."

As her name implied, she was all sweetness and light, happy to sweet talk Beaupre and praise extravagantly his nice hair, his good looks, his colorful socks, and his masterful intelligence, and to arrange huge loans at astronomical interest. This prime minister, after all, was quoted as saying that "budgets balance themselves." His minister of finance was no better, having been the figurehead for a financial company set up by his daddy. Like his leader, the minister of finance's grasp of economics was minimal. In fairly short order, Sweet Wolf set the scene for another Canadian financial meltdown. Hinchcliffe shrugged her shoulders in resignation, as she watched Beaupre fritter away all that she had achieved in bringing that country's finances back to normal.

Raoul, coordinating the publicity surrounding the affair, which he used to boost the public awareness of the Praetorian protection agency, had released the complete video of the carnage in the plaza outside the Canadian parliament buildings. The video of the wounded girl went viral, as she lay there exposed. She was so beautiful and brave, telling them that they did not have to hold her down and grimacing only as the fearsome-looking chest tube went into her.

In Buffalo General, Kuniko experienced a chest infection, which cleared with antibiotics. After a couple of days in the intensive care unit, the chest tube was removed. When she felt strong enough, she was interviewed by the media and told them that she was a Japanese policewoman who, in her off-duty time, was employed by the Praetorians to do a protection job that, in view of the events that had transpired, clearly was necessary. She was simply doing her duty, as any Japanese policewoman would. That last statement went over very well in Japan, not only with the other policewomen, but with the populace as a whole, where she became an instant heroine. They also learned that she was one of the best 25 m pistol shots in the world. Tomiko felt that she had generated so much good publicity for Japan that she promoted her one level up—to lieutenant. She was offered a return to Japan to recuperate there. However, Kuniko preferred to go to the ranch in Arizona.

She had been there previously and had found horseback riding in the foothills both novel and enjoyable. She had become a deputy member of the Border Patrol, as did most of the Praetorians, and liked the troopers. She had found herself attracted to Pedro Morales, who was obviously climbing the ranks quickly when she first met him. When she returned to Japan after they first met, they had remained in contact.

As a boy, Pedro had fallen in love with Hinchcliffe, and to some extent, he still was. He thought he probably would be forever. Even as a young girl, she had a preternatural calm. She laughed and smiled, but that all seemed relatively superficial. He never asked about her background, and she never told him. All he knew was that she was one of the brilliant Foundation girls and had originally come from Britain. They both liked riding and shooting and other physical activities. He knew she had a special relationship with the Japanese man they called the ninja, who taught martial arts. Pedro managed to get himself into some of these classes, learning a little Japanese to do so, as when they were together, Hinchcliffe and the ninja only spoke Japanese.

They were both young, healthy, good-looking people, so of course, they had sex. They were not supposed to do so until she was older, but they simply hid it. One of the other girls gave Hinchcliffe the pill to avoid any unexpected consequences. She encouraged Morales to take his studies seriously, and they would study together on occasion. She also encouraged him to apply to the Border Patrol as soon as he could. She thought he had a future there. When she was a little older, Hinchcliffe went off to Europe for a few months. When she came back, she seemed to have changed subtly. For one thing, she knew a lot more about sex, which she taught him. No one had ever done these things to him before, and she taught him what she herself liked.

She clearly liked his attention, but unlike the other girls he had known, there was never any talk of love or marriage. It seemed to him that Hinchcliffe would rather spend time with Munro if she could, and they would talk about old wars, battles, and retreats and tease each other over names and dates and poems. This mutual attraction Morales was sure did not include sex, as Munro seemed interested only in the Queen of Hearts, as he called Elizabeth, and Tomiko-san, the Japanese policewoman whose children were being brought up at the ranch.

When Hinchcliffe moved back to Europe to work for a woman called Manon, whom he had never met, he tried to maintain contact, but relations became distant, especially when she came back to run Canada. She seldom returned to the ranch, as she seemed extremely busy. She was now also running a logistics and paramilitary organization called the Legion, based in Europe. He asked her about joining it, but she told him he would be able to help her more if he became head of the Border Patrol and perhaps eventually of all the US borders.

She gave him the book she had published on the military history of Mexico and her recently finished book on the military history of South America. He looked through these books, and it became obvious that other than Cortes and Pizarro, the only other military man she admired in South America was Thomas, Lord Cochrane, the admiral who effectively had been the main instrument in the defeat of Spain, having largely singlehandedly beaten all other local navies.

Apart from Hinchcliffe, with whom it became obvious he would never have a permanent relationship, Morales had also been with several other women, as he was lean, dark, and handsome. He had also cultivated the thin mustache that Mexicans wear in Western movies. *Might as well look the part*, he thought, and dressed accordingly. If Miguel, when he was a champion boxer, could walk around looking like a movie Mexican, he saw no reason why he should not when he was off duty. He liked the black-eyed, voluptuous Mexican beauties and also the blond, blue-eyed gringas. He particularly liked the young Japanese shooters who frequented the ranch, either training or on their way to an assignment or a competition. His favorite was the Olympic shooter, Kuniko, who naturally shot much better than he did and whom he had helped teach how to ride. She had liked him and had remained in contact with him when she returned to Japan.

As a group, all the shooters seemed similar. Perhaps they had been picked for that, or perhaps it had been drilled into them. While generally friendly, they did not speak to outsiders about their assignments or exploits, but he had a suspicion that when they were working in Europe, violence was sometimes involved. He did not know that for sure, but when he interrupted them when they were with the cadre of American Olympic shooters who had formed the original Praetorians, with whom they laughed and told stories, the conversation stopped abruptly or changed into something innocuous or occasionally Japanese.

These girls were always calm and controlled, even when doing gymnastic antics with the strong boys from school, who often came to the ranch to work out, as there were free weights not only in the gym but also lying about in stations all along the jogging trail. Being professional shooters, all the girls had strong arms. One of the favorite tricks that Kuniko could do was to do a handstand onto the hands of a strong boy, on his back on a weightlifting bench. The boy would bench press her, and she would do a push up at the same time, demonstrating incredible balance. He had occasionally seen some of the girls after assignments with a split lip or missing tooth and a bruised face, about which nothing was ever said.

When the wounded Kuniko returned to Arizona after the shootout in Canada, she found that Morales was now the assistant head of the Border

Patrol. She was the first of the Japanese women he had seen who had been seriously injured. He felt immensely protective of this little wounded bird. Seeing the video of her lying there not moving as the chest tube went in produced a flutter in his heart, a peculiar sense of longing to be with her, which he supposed was love. During her rehabilitation, he spent as much time as he could with her. She initially seemed a little lost and frightened, but as she was treated by the Foundation children as an object of pride, she appeared to rapidly recover.

Morales had worked for several years at improving his Japanese, speaking when he could to the others who already knew the language. *There are,* he thought, *likely potential long-term advantages to that.* After Kuniko's injuries, he got into the habit of arriving at the ranch early in the morning and joining her as she ran over the jogging track. Initially, she had to stop many times, holding her wounded chest, but she gradually improved. As she did, she wished to increase her physical fitness and saw dancing as one way to do so. He had never danced in his life but realized that this was a way to be closer to her, and so he learned Latin American dance. He also learned flamenco, as so many of the women at the ranch loved that dance.

One night, she told him somewhat shamefacedly that she had a fear of being shot again. She felt that this admission was wrong and that Tomoe Gozen, the famous twelfth-century female samurai would be turning over in her grave hearing such an admission. She wept. Morales did not know what to say. He simply held her in his arms until her sobs subsided. Perhaps in gratitude, she undressed him, and they made love. He was very gentle with her initially.

Over the ensuing few weeks, their love life became more passionate, and he became sure that gratitude was no longer her main motivating factor. Other than Hinchcliffe, whom he knew was unattainable, this was the first woman with whom he truly felt he wanted to spend the rest of his life. When he told her that while he was embracing her, she arched her back and looked up at him.

"Do you really mean that?"

"I mean that."

"Then I would be happy to share my life with you."

He was all for marrying immediately, but she was only twenty-five, and Tomiko wanted her girls to be active policewomen until age thirty. After that, she felt they could get married and take a leave of absence from the police force. As long as they continued to contribute to their pension plan until age sixty-five, they could ultimately collect full police pension and benefits and full health-care coverage. They could, if they wished, rejoin the Japanese police force at any time, simply dropping one or two ranks from their highest attainment.

Tomiko felt it would be unfair to others if Kuniko were given the same plan. After consultation with her police chiefs, they made a consensus decision that if Kuniko contributed another ten years of pension contributions as a lump sum, she could enter that system. She did need to serve a little longer, however. Kuniko returned to Japan and worked for another six months. Tomiko promoted her to captain. She then took a leave of absence, returned to America, and made arrangements to marry Morales.

They had a Shinto celebration in Japan so that her parents and her Japanese friends could attend, as well as her superiors in the police force. Later, they were married in the Catholic faith in Arizona, well attended by the Border Patrol officers and the people from the ranch. Tomiko was Kuniko's bridesmaid and Munro, Morales's best man. The marriage proved very successful, and they had three children. She became an American citizen and actually shot for the US in the 25 m pistol competition. She also, although Morales was not too happy about it, continued work as a Praetorian. While she never entirely got over her fear, she was samurai enough to conceal it from him.

She continued however to mull over the problem. As she saw it, the only way to nullify her fear, which she knew was a post-traumatic stress reaction, was to face gunfire again. Avoiding it simply made the problem worse. The protection jobs she did as a Praetorian Guard almost never involved any exchange of fire, so while the assignments helped, she remained troubled. Finally, tired of concealing her fear, she spoke to the ninja. "You have no fear."

"Perhaps."

"You have killed many times."

"Perhaps."

"I have fear, and I wish to overcome that fear to make it go away. Some of my friends have killed. Tomiko-san has killed many times. I have never done that."

"Kill and fear are different."

"To you maybe, but how can I be a proper *Onna-bugeisha*, a female samurai, if I have not killed where there is risk involved? I have tried hunting in Alaska with Running Bear and here in Arizona with my husband but killing during hunting does not help."

"Killing is killing. It will not help."

"It may help me."

He sighed. "I am an old man. You call me ninja. I am not ninja. The gaijin call me ninja. Ninjas are hereditary. My father was not ninja."

"I do not care. You are more of a ninja than anyone else I will ever meet. Help me, please."

"If you really want to do this, it will have to be in Europe, for the daimyo Manon of Luxemburg. There are risks. They have facial recognition technology. I might be recognized. And you, these Canadians cannot be trusted. Perhaps they have analyzed your face and sent your data to Interpol."

"There are always risks. I do not want to live in fear."

"Killing will not help."

"I must try. Help me, please."

He sighed again. "*Hai!*" he said sadly. "If you wish." Then he proceeded to contact Manon. They were exceedingly careful, as surveillance now was so incredibly sophisticated. He made a telephone call on a throwaway phone with voice-altering technology. Several weeks went by. A telephone call came on a landline with a date and a hotel name. The date corresponded to Munro having to fly to Luxembourg for a business meeting with Manon and Don Pedro. The ninja asked if he could take Kuniko as a passenger. Munro did not ask why, and they were not on the list of passengers. The ninja had not been on a passenger list of any private flight to Europe for years.

They entered Luxembourg with false passports but avoided any official recognition and went to the hotel, which turned out to be a large American chain. They sat in the lobby coffee shop and waited. A woman walked by, made a finger gesture, and slowly made her way to the elevator. They got up and followed her. They followed her off the elevator and into a room she opened. It was Manon wearing a wig, dark glasses, and a hat, with dental rolls to alter her facial contour. She also knew where the CCTV cameras were in the lobby of the hotel. She told them that two groups were pressuring one of her numerous businesses. She wanted that stopped, preferably by starting a gang war between the two gangs, one French and one Italian. She had had the leaders spied on for some time so knew their habits. Detailed information was passed over. Kuniko and the ninja changed into new clothes and left.

After the meeting, they went to the central railroad station, where a key they had been given opened a locker. Inside the locker, they found a package that contained four 22 mm pistols and some extra clips. Kuniko already knew about 22 mm pistols, how the bullet would stay inside the skull and bounce around—the perfect assassin's gun. Even without a silencer, it was not very noisy. The Praetorians used guns like that when they were functioning as Sky Marshals. Short silencers were available. They took the train to Paris.

They walked past the address that Manon had given them and went to a nondescript cafe to eat and pass the time until evening. They had already purchased tickets for a sleeper train to Rome, leaving late that evening. They sauntered by again, with some clothing alterations, just before 7:00 p.m. The streets were crowded, and they did not stand out. Both wore dark glasses in spite of the fact that it was evening. So many people did that now that it did not look silly. Both wore hats. Carefully timing it, they stopped at the door of an elegant townhouse and looked at a map of the city. They put it away as the front door opened, and a man came out looking all around. He obviously saw nothing of significance, so he gestured, and a second man came out. The girl walked past the bodyguard, bumping him slightly. He glanced down at her. She smiled up, placed the gun with the silencer she had inside her handbag under his chin, put three bullets in his brain, and walked on without breaking stride, the gun never having left her bag. There were noises, but no one really noticed. The second man, the real target, saw his bodyguard begin to go down. While he was momentarily distracted, the ninja put the 22 mm in his ear and fired three bullets. Again, the gun and silencer never left the bag he carried. He likewise did not stop and simply kept walking. The crowd was looking at the first fallen man, so they did not immediately notice what happened.

The ninja and Kuniko were swallowed in the crowd. The two men falling on the sidewalk created a furor, and a dense crowd gathered. This enabled the two to step away. In an alleyway, the girl hastily pulled off the dress she had been wearing, revealing shorts and a T-shirt. The ninja was wearing a reversible jacket. They bundled these clothes, along with the dark glasses and the hats, into a bag, from which they donned new ones. After walking quietly across the Seine, they noticed a large industrial trash container at the side of the road. The bag was thrown in there. As they walked along the Seine River, they dropped their guns into the water and stuffed the gloves they had been wearing into another trash container. They walked to the central train station, where they stood quietly in the shadows until shortly before departure, then boarded the train to Italy.

Posing as father and daughter, they shared a sleeping compartment. They washed their hands repeatedly, but having worn gloves, they were probably safe from powder residue anyway. They woke up the next morning in Rome. Again, they wore hats and dark glasses, wigs, and mouth guards to attempt to fool the facial recognition cameras. They used another key to open another deposit box in the Rome station. This was a bulky package. When examined later, it was found to contain a sniper rifle and an assault rifle with a considerable amount of ammunition. There were also pistols. The package also contained room keys for a couple of hotels. Also included was a map detailing the position of the CCTV cameras in the region of the hotels.

Two hotel rooms had been booked and paid for with cash in advance, so they had the room keys, and there was no need to check in. They examined the rooms and saw that the windows, which could be opened, had a good field of fire, looking down on a building opposite. They had something to eat, carefully avoiding the CCTV cameras, which had been marked on the map given to them. They later returned to the rooms. They opened the windows and set up a firing position, staying well back so that they could not be seen, and waited.

Midafternoon, a group of men came out of the building opposite. Two came first to look around, and then a group of six, surrounding a man in the middle. Kuniko, who was above and to the left facing them, opened fire on the group on fully automatic with the assault rifle. The ninja, on the right with the sniper rifle, got a clear shot of the protected man's head, and watched a spray of blood as the top of his head came off. He fired another quick two shots into the mass of men surrounding their chief, left the weapon on the table, ran down the stairs, and walked out of a previously scouted rear exit. Kuniko, who had also left her rifle, walked out of her own hotel. They made their separate ways to the central train station. On the way, the hats and outer wear were dumped in garbage receptacles.

They had left behind some evidence from Paris, including a week-old movie ticket stub and some other casual debris to suggest that that was where they normally lived. At the station, they boarded the first train leaving, which happened to be for Milan. They took the train from there to Luxembourg and rendezvoused with Munro, who was flying back the next day. The ninja told Munro he had been introducing Kuniko to some old friends. Munro did not inquire further. Again, there was no official recognition, and neither the ninja nor Kunika appeared on the passenger manifest.

They were never identified and were successful in instigating something of an international gang war, and Manon felt no further pressure for a while. Kuniko was never entirely sure what she had accomplished for herself, other than fattening her bank balance. There was, of course, the huge immediate dopamine rush from the kills, but she was uncertain as to whether or not there was any long-term effect. She felt no regret for those she had killed, as they were definitely not good people and the world was a much better place without them.

The ninja told her that his days of contract kills were over, and he did not intend to do it again. He told her that it would be a major mistake on her part to take his place. Clearly, she could do it, but he felt the necessary secrecy would destroy her marriage, which he saw as her only hope for real happiness. She initially agreed with him, and there were no further executions, at least for some time, when her children were small.

She did continue in the Praetorians, as there was no secrecy about that—rather the reverse—and where she enjoyed the camaraderie and the extra income. When her children got older, she returned to carrying out the occasional execution, either on her own or with the help of another couple of Praetorians, who did most of the wet work. Some of the younger women saw these affairs almost as a rite of passage and looked forward to it.

Pedro Morales, her husband, suspected what was happening, given her absences, when she said she was on secret Praetorian business. He discussed his fears privately with Munro, who understood his concern. He pointed out, however, that if that was what it took to overcome or contain Kuniko's PTSD, then so be it.

"Clearly, she never recovered completely from being shot in Ottawa, but she makes a brave face to show the world. If this is the therapy she needs, better that than an invalid," he said.

Munro also pointed out that someone had to be the mailed fist protecting Earth Base One and the Space Academy from those who inevitably would wish to do harm. As the organization grew bigger and more successful, he expected the attacks and attempts at infiltration to worsen.

"I wish I had someone a bit more ready to bend rules." He sighed. "Maybe someday Sweet Wolf, but I think she wants to run Japan."

CHAPTER 7

Hinchcliffe

Hinchcliffe was glad to leave Canada. She had shown that she could run a country within fairly tight parameters. When she first went to Canada, she thought it would not take long to turn that economic basket case around and show the world her capabilities. To her, the guiding principles of a functioning democracy were always simple and clear: don't hit anyone, don't steal anyone's stuff, and keep your promises. It was as brutally simple as that. She saw that it was the sole role of government, nothing else.

For some time, she had thought that, having sorted out Canada, she might then enter British politics and clean up their mess—drain the swamp, as someone had said. One of her goals since childhood was to jail all those police and politicians who stood by and allowed the sexual enslavement and trafficking of thousands of little English girls, a horrific decades-old scandal. The world knew of this ongoing horror being perpetrated on these little girls, and yet no one in power in Britain seemed to have the slightest interest in resolving it.

However, the political games, the hoops that had to be jumped through, and the greasy compromises with slimy power-hungry people had sickened her. The constant contact with these puffed-up little bureaucrats running their own tiny kingdoms, the Adolf Eichmann's, and the utter banality of evil seemed an unchanged fact of politics. The Canadian prime minister had sheltered her from the worst of it as much as he could, for which she was most grateful. But in consequence, there was no longer any desire to be a political leader.

After being dismissed by Beaupre, the new Canadian prime minister, and leaving Ottawa, she had planned on accompanying Munro to the ranch for a few days of R and R and then returning to her Legion, currently headquartered in Spain. While she had been in Canada, the numbers had grown, and the assignments had grown. The job she had done in revitalizing Canada had by no means absorbed her complete attention or even a small part of it. Throughout her time there, she had been building her organization.

The Legion was now a recognizable body, one of several mercenary forces, really private armies, such as the Academi, the descendent of Blackwater. Hinchcliffe had watched the career of Erik Prince, the founder of Blackwater, with interest. Not being US-based, she had seen and often taken the opportunities denied to him by the US State Department. The Legion was by no means the largest of these burgeoning organizations, some of which numbered in the thousands.

Some of her more lucrative contracts were now training various national militaries for specific roles and supplying some US forces overseas. There were also true hot work roles protecting the oil rigs off Nigeria, providing armed protection, including snipers, for the ships sailing past the Horn of Africa, at risk of being taken by the Somalian pirates, who had started up again after having been wiped out by Erik Prince and his group and even providing protection from some pirates now operating again in the South China Sea. That had stopped when Western naval forces hung the pirates, but the relative impunity with which the Somalis had returned to the business had encouraged the revival of piracy elsewhere. Of course, there was always work in the Middle East protecting the various UN and humanitarian contingents from shaheeds and other fanatics.

She still found that the provision of gaudily dressed soldiers to protect high-end jewelry and other stores in major cities, a reasonable source of income and a welcome relief for her men after some of their more hair-raising duties elsewhere.

Hinchcliffe was looking forward to expanding her force further, as the opportunities seemed endless. The US State Department made it difficult for US-based companies to compete, but she was under no such restrictions. With so many nations, especially European, having only a token army, all generals with very few actual soldiers and little combat-ready equipment, and the military in other countries simply being undisciplined thugs, it really was a return to the condottiere of the Middle Ages. The private mercenary forces like the Great Company of Werner von Urslingen and Hawkins White Company were back in business.

While Hinchcliffe was in Arizona, La Contessa, the first genius child found by the Prometheus Group, called her and asked her to visit her in the province in Mexico, which she was now running. She indicated that there might be a job for the Legion. Hinchcliffe and her shadow, Carmenlita, flew in for the meeting. La Contessa laid out her problem and possible solutions. Criminal gangs were out of control. When Elizabeth was president of the US, she had managed to decriminalize marijuana, and several states had legalized its use. Since entering politics years before in Luxembourg, Munro had been pushing to legalize, or at least decriminalize, all recreational drugs. His feeling always had been that downers like opiates were less likely to cause mayhem than alcohol. If someone became addicted, that was a tragedy, but it was a personal tragedy and had nothing to do with the state.

Munro pointed out to anyone who would listen that the war on drugs had been tried before. It had failed then as it was failing now. The Chinese Mandarins, who wielded extreme power, including the death penalty, could not stop the opium smugglers. He knew that two of the most notorious smugglers—or in modern terms, drug lords—had been a couple of wild boys from Scotland, Matheson, and Jardine, one being a medical doctor. Munro could never get over a sneaking admiration for these hard men, sailing up the Pearl River, guns out, fighting off the Mandarins. They had ended up running one of the biggest trading houses in Hong Kong.

He also pointed out that Portugal had decriminalized recreational drugs, which meant in that country, almost no one was in jail for drug offenses. The money that had been spent interdicting drugs now went to providing treatment, with a consequent reduction in the number of helpless addicts.

When running the US, Presidents Elizabeth and Sandra had both felt the same way about recreational drugs but had to deal with fractious houses with dubious loyalties, which made progress slow. Enough had been done to significantly reduce the jail population in the US and the amount of money flowing to the drug lords of South America and the Middle East terrorist groups, who sourced mainly in Afghanistan and China. This reduced money supply had weakened the drug gangs and made it possible for La Contessa to at least consider their elimination.

Her problem, as she saw it, was the basic structure of South American Hispanic culture, which was the culture of the family. Protestant Northern European culture had, since the Reformation spearheaded by Martin Luther, and in particular, John Calvin in Geneva, emphasized that hard work was holy and that the community was in the final analysis, more important than the family. In South America, the family was paramount, hence nepotism and the cover-up of criminality. Corruption was inevitable under such circumstances.

Ideally, conversion to Protestantism would be the answer, but that version of Judeo-Christianity seemed to have lost its allure and power. Its leaders, especially in Europe, seemed not to believe in anything, let alone God. She was aware of one ridiculous case in Britain where an official, high in the Church of England, famously did not believe in the existence of God. All she could conceive of doing was to try to ensure that it would be culturally acceptable that when corruption was found, the whole family would suffer, not just the malefactor, which was the basis for English common law.

As corruption was so endemic—including politicians, judges, the army, and the police—getting a start was difficult. The only way La Contessa could see to do it was to bring in outsiders. Argument and reason were not likely to be of much value. Force would be needed—and ruthless force at that, especially initially—until a cadre of honest people could were established, preferably from the bottom up, but in reality from the top down, leading eventually into vertical integration or the cleansing of the whole society.

General Pinochet in Chile had managed to do that, at least to some extent, by controlling the criminals and inviting in the economists from the Chicago School, who completely turned around their economy to effectively become the most productive in the region. He was reviled in the mainstream media outside Chile, so she was under no illusion that she would be seen or portrayed as an evil person if she was to bring the country kicking and screaming into modernity to fulfil its full potential.

Changes would have to be made, and they would initially not be pleasant at any rate and would be looked on by the populace she was trying to help. As Munro and his inevitable quotation would say,

The cry of those you humor
Ah, slowly to the light.
Why brought you us from bondage
Our loved Egyptian night.

As someone had once said, "You cannot clean a pigsty with a toothbrush," or something like that. She could see no alternative, so she called in Hinchcliffe, whom she had known for years.

Hinchcliffe knew history, and she knew all these factors she would be struggling against and felt that the problem was almost insurmountable, that she was being asked to change a culture. She knew that if it all went wrong, or even if it went right, she would be pilloried and called a monster. Likely, her only escape would be to literally fall on her sword or go into space in exile. The only comfort she could find was that others had been there before. As Winston Churchill once said, "I felt as if all my past life had been but a preparation for this hour and for this trial."

She flew to Spain to put La Contessa's proposal to the Legion. She pulled in Jock and Colin from their current duties leading her organization in other countries. By now, they were two of her senior men. She sat down for a serious discussion with them. Carmenlita, as ever at her shoulder, was present but quiet. She outlined the problems.

"So what are we supposed to do? What are our objectives? Are we there simply to guard La Contessa, which is easy, or are we nation building?" asked Jock.

Hinchcliffe looked at him. She thought that he had come a long way in a short time, from an uneducated, wild young man to someone who could think and plan calmly and logically. If she could do that with him, she thought there must be thousands out there who were functioning nowhere near their potential.

"From what you say, I think La Contessa plans to root out corruption," said Colin, "but I am not sure she understands that that would ultimately be or necessitate nation building."

"I have known La Contessa for years. She was one of the first of the Foundation children, and I do not think that there is anything she has not thought through. She has worked all over the world and did build a financial empire in that corrupt country, so she will be under no illusion."

"If we are going to build as opposed to protect, it will be brutal work. These criminal Mexicans are macho. Putting them in jail is pointless. The judges and the police are afraid of them. They will have to be eliminated, killed."

"Publicly or privately?"

"If we kill them publicly, hanging them from lamp posts, it will frighten off some of them, but the downside would be the hysterical disapproval of the international media. Look at the furor about the Philippines where the president is trying to clean house by getting rid of some bad guys. They would bring serious pressure on Sandra, the president of the US, to act to stop us."

"You think none of the mainstream media would support us?"

"Support the vigorous suppression of corruption? Not even one. They all sing the same song. These are the people who supported that murderous MS13 gang in the US. Simply disappearing the bad guys would avoid the worst of the criticism."

"The media will come looking."

"Perhaps some media people could get accidentally shot by the bad guys."

"That might back them off a little. Maybe photo evidence of underage sex and a well-publicized trial of a few of their doyens might help."

"Yes, using the media's own favorite dirty tricks against them might be fun. But the Mexican bad guys who need to go down, how many?"

"Thousands. But shooting the actual criminals will not be enough. La Contessa points out that the family is what matters in that culture. The whole family or extended family would have to be impoverished. If they are left with money, they will hire people to hurt my boys, who will be at risk of a bullet in the back. So the whole family will have to lose all their money, their jobs, and their houses and all possessions. I don't see any other way. Do you think the boys are up to it? Are you up to it? Am I?"

"That is asking an awful lot."

"I know. But if we don't go in full bore, there is no point in going in at all. It would mean simply that our boys get killed and nothing changes. If we are not serious, then when we leave, it will be as if we had never been there. I will not let my men be sacrificed for nothing."

"But we will have to offer the populace something other than fear."

"Optimally, we would like to introduce the Protestant ethic, but Protestantism seems to have lost its way and its dream and its power. But we had better give the Legion something."

"You mean a religion?"

"Yes. The Roman legions had Mithras, but that would be too difficult. Perhaps just a more austere Calvinism. We will certainly need a song or a hymn for the guys to sing for unit cohesion."

"Nothing better than the American 'Battle Hymn of the Republic.'"

"Yes, I like that. 'For mine eyes have seen the glory of the coming of the Lord, / he is trampling out the vintage where the grapes of wrath are stored.' That would certainly do. Isis is thinking about religion. I don't fully understand it. No one does, but she says something about religion and theoretical physics or quantum mechanics, that somehow, they are interrelated. Perhaps I will talk to her. I don't think the guys would accept Horus or Amon Ra."

"We will have to expand and accept Mexicans. We will have to indoctrinate and integrate them into a fighting force."

"The soldiers of the Spanish Empire, the *terciers* were plenty tough, and so were conquistadors, so there is a history to be told."

"The Legion. We are already paramilitary and are going to have to have ranks as it expands. How about Roman? I would like to be a centurion and carry and march under an eagle. You could be the legate."

"Nice idea, but I think we should use regular army terms. An emblem is a good idea. Not the eagle of Rome, but Christ on the cross. With Christ on the cross leading, we become his vanguard."

"Like the Templars?"

"Exactly. We become the soldiers of Christ. That will make it harder for the Marxists media to attack us. We may even have some defenders."

"How about enlisting some women? Daughters of Christ sounds pretty catchy too."

"It certainly does, but women could be a problem. Mixed units are always a disaster. The men protect the women at risk of their own lives, and then they fight over them. Maybe a separate unit, the Amazon division. When it eventually becomes a clash of civilizations, which it will in a few years, an all-female combat unit would help deflect criticism."

"Put the women into combat first. If they run into serious opposition, the men would come in behind them like berserkers, like devils from hell."

"Half of them will be bull dykes. How would you protect the femmes from them?"

"I don't know. But you are right. Bull dykes can be plenty tough. Carmenlita," said Hinchcliffe, turning to her, "you will have to think about that problem."

"OK. So we are the Legion, the Soldiers of Christ Crucified. Uniforms? Standard US battle rattle?"

"Yes. But dress uniforms? I don't know. I like the kilt, but tunics? Maybe white with a red cross or red with a white cross? Follow the knights of St John or the Templars?"

"We can't use that. They still exist in Portugal, I think. We can't have black on white. That is the Teutonic Knights. Maybe blue on white. With Christ Crucified at the center, certainly of the flag."

"OK. Then we have to decide. Are we in? Commander Hinchcliffe, with all due respect, this is not what I signed up for."

"I know Jock. We can still walk away and be meaningless little toy soldiers and lead meaningless pleasant little lives while Rome eventually burns down around us."

"I gave my word to serve Isis, and I know that she hates the creeping corruption and foul ideologies that are infecting and taking over the West. She thinks that the only hope is the new colonies on Mars because this world is doomed. But I am stuck on Earth as I will never have the qualifications to go into space. Colin, what do you think?"

"There is an old poem I read about men like us:

'Their shoulders held the sky suspended.
They stood, and earth's foundations stay.
What God abandoned, these defended,
And saved the sum of things, for pay.'

I am in. 'Better to die on your feet than live on your knees,' as I think someone said."

"Then Colin and I will serve you, Commander, as you will. It is a bitter road I see before me, but as a man, I see no other choice. I will speak to the men. I think they will mostly come. No, I think they will all come with us."

"Then I will tell La Contessa that we will come."

Hinchcliffe initially brought into Mexico only a limited number of her Legion. They were initially given the title of the New Federales, with special anticorruption duties. They answered to La Contessa only. She wanted the brightest, as she wanted information. The families of all the officials in La Contessa's state were to be trashed one at a time. She had La Contessa adopt Munro's techniques of "catch a politician" and jail him. Once the rout began, they all incriminated one another. Corruption was so widespread that the first thing to do was to suborn some judges and prosecutors to actually do the job they were supposed to do. She enlisted a team of hackers to break into bank accounts.

Some judges were brought in for questioning. One somehow had a heart attack, and investigations subsequently revealed that he and his family had hidden wealth, a considerable amount of which was located offshore. This enabled the whole family to be accused as a criminal enterprise, and as many as possible were jailed as flight risks long before any word of a trial. Confessions were readily extracted. A second judge was offered a heart attack or cooperation. If he cooperated, his immediate family of wife and son could disappear into Spain and be safe. Money would not be a problem in terms of housing, education, and future job opportunities. The alternative was that he would have a heart attack, and all his extended family would be sent to jail immediately while awaiting trial, which might take a very long time to materialize, like the family of the first judge, who were still in jail with no prospect of a trial any time soon. He chose to cooperate, and all subsequent cases came before this crusading judge.

The jails were gradually cleaned out. All gang members were taken quietly away, executed, and buried in mass graves deep in the desert. They simply disappeared. Any family member who complained had their bank accounts examined, the money repatriated to pay for the Legion, and senior male members had heart attacks. The next step was the police. Among the senior police ranks, an amazing number had heart attacks while being questioned. Eventually, some agreed to cooperate. Hinchcliffe found some younger members of the police force who were not totally corrupt, and La Contessa promoted them so that in six months, there was a small cadre of at least reasonably honest people in charge.

The jailed families found, to their surprise, that often the monies they had counted on to buy their way out of jail had strangely disappeared, even from overseas accounts. This money was used to pay the increasing number of the Legion who were being brought across to Mexico. They also set up local recruitment and training camps, because eventually, Mexicans would have to save and run Mexico.

Schools were established for the families of men who enlisted. The education—or as some would put it, indoctrination—was based on material written for that purpose, inculcating true history, and describing in detail the horrors of socialism, with its inevitable corruption and the fall of empires and cultures. Teachers who stepped outside the guidelines were let go. Any attempts to threaten the families of the enlisted men were pursued with extreme prejudice. The men were warned that Legion had its own secrets, not to be shared with anyone, even their immediate family.

When a sufficient cadre had formed, La Contessa moved against the first drug lord. He had his hideout well away from the towns, staffed by large numbers of gang members. In a coordinated attack, his bank accounts were looted, along with those of all his known accomplices, including lawyers and government officials. To keep the information about the attack secret, only the Legion was used. The walls were breached in several places, and they swept through the compound. These ex-Special Forces and SAS men had no problems overrunning the gang members. The leaders were interrogated, and when all useful information had been extracted, they joined their men in an unmarked hole in the desert. The families of the gang members had all their money confiscated, and they all lost any government position they had. Their properties were also confiscated and sold.

There was no official publicity about the taking down of the first gang. The information extracted was shared with the few Americans who understood the objectives. Some rogue states, like California, received no information, as it was felt they would have immediately shared it with their residual gang members. The states who believed in the rule of law had the gang members living in that state charged. They were offered a deal. If they voluntarily revoked their US citizenship, they were free to be deported. If they did not, they would stand trial with no bail. If not convicted, they would be charged with some other offence and again could wait in jail for a trial sometime in the future; and that cycle, pioneered initially by the corrupt Washington deep state against Elizabeth's supporters, could be repeated endlessly. Many chose to renounce their American citizenship and go home, where the data on them was transferred to the Mexican authorities, but also remained on file. Any subsequent criminal activity was not tolerated.

Attacks on other drug lords and their enablers continued. Jail sentences were not part of the plan. It was felt that the gates of death were nearer and surer. Elizabeth, when she was US president, had effectively closed the border to illegals coming up from the south, so criminals fleeing Mexico went south rather than north. At this stage, La Contessa did not care where they went, as long as they left her state.

Local recruits for the Legion grew rapidly, as the pay was good, and the safety of the men's families guaranteed and their children were educated. The family of one recruit was taken by criminals, the women and children raped, and the males tortured and killed.

The Legion swept into the village where the atrocity had taken place and whose inhabitants claimed they had seen nothing of what had happened in the village square. They hanged the mayor and the chief of police on a tree outside the jail. Half the village admitted under interrogation to having taken part or facilitated the murders. These men disappeared, and their houses were torn down. The families, stripped of everything, were trucked to the slums of a major city. The underworld was warned that if the family of a Legionnaire were harmed, retribution would be swift and brutal.

Gradually, young men and women, only lightly touched by corruption, were promoted, and crime levels dropped. The police were warned that La Mordidita, the little bite, was a thing of the past. Protection money ceased. Anyone found or accused was interrogated and, if found guilty, simply disappeared.

When corruption, especially government corruption, vanished—or at least came down to reasonable proportions—businesses began to open. No one from outside previously would have considered doing business in this dangerous, lawless state, so there was pent-up demand. New roads were built, and schools became active, schools with a useful curriculum. Trade schools to teach the skilled trades were established. Property rights and the rule of law produced its magic, as always.

La Contessa had always been coy about what was happening in the state she was running, but the improvement was so dramatic that everyone knew something good was going on. She moved gradually to consolidate her power within the existing political structure, and with the unexplained disappearance of some of her more vocal rivals, she was finally elected president of Mexico. By this time, the Legion amounted to several thousand troops. Eliminating corruption in a country, as opposed to a state was much more difficult, and had to be done in a much slower and more secretive fashion. Once the process began however, it gathered speed. When it became obvious the way the wind was blowing, many left Mexico, running for cover.

The states were brought under control, one at a time, starting with the northern border and working south. The same techniques used in the original state were practiced, leaving La Contessa's people in control. Some pitched battles were fought with the extreme criminal gangs. Hinchcliffe, knowing history, always used overwhelming force, and there was no attempt to limit casualties to the actual gang members. Word slowly got around that if caught, not only would they disappear, but there would be consequences for the extended family. When other jobs appeared, criminal life seemed a lot less appealing, and a large number hung up their guns.

Visiting media were not encouraged. Some got caught in a crossfire or were injured during a robbery. One of the most vociferous social-justice types was caught and filmed having sex with what turned out to be, or was reported to be, a ten-year-old girl. He received a long prison sentence. President Sandra was called to intervene. She refused.

"The man has been convicted of pedophilia. How many unreported cases are there in the US? He should serve time for his crime. He was raped in prison. Oh well, bad things happen. I don't think our jails are any better."

In one of the last drug lord battles, they were likely betrayed. To date, the Legion's losses had been fairly minimal, as Hinchcliffe, a student of Carl von Clausewitz, always believed in concentration of force. On this occasion, the attacking group ran into unexpected resistance. Colin was leading, introducing some of his new all-female Amazon Legion into battle. The first wave into the compound, after the gates and walls were blown, was decimated by a 50 mm machine gun. Ten of the attackers, all women, died, and Colin almost did, as his left arm was blown off at the elbow. His life was saved by a tourniquet applied by one of the second wave. The women of the second wave were so furious that no living thing in the compound survived.

The sergeant major, the senior surviving officer, a hard young African American woman, wept for her dead; and with a samurai sword she liked to carry with her into battle, she took the heads off all the defenders. She made a pile of the heads and photographed it, totally against orders. That photograph was shown surreptitiously to others and got out into the media. As it was a pile of heads only, with no other identifying features, the Legion always denied that it had anything to do with them.

After emergency surgery, Colin was flown initially to the Legion headquarters in Spain for rehab. After he stabilized, he was sent to the ranch, where the children were very impressed alternatively with his empty sleeve pinned to his shirt or with his Terminator-type of prosthesis.

While he was recovering, he realized his days of battle were over, so he began to study logistics and even went to work for Manon and Sheila MacDonald for a while to get practical experience. When he was sure he was proficient, he returned to the Legion as their quartermaster general. Napoleon had always said that an army marches on its stomach, and Colin made sure that the stomach of the Legion was never short of supplies for eating or fighting.

It was obvious to the triumvirate of Jock, Colin, and Hinchcliffe, and increasingly Carmenlita, that La Contessa could not or would not stop at the boundaries of Mexico. Venezuela, with its crazed socialist dictator, Chavez, would have to be taken out some day. This would require an amphibious wing and an air wing. The regular Mexican army forces would have to be gradually disbanded or, better still, gradually transferred to the Legion. Colin made plans to accommodate this. The Mexican border with the rest of Central America was tightened so that the people would have to remain in their own filthy countries and thus realize that they would need internal revolution or reformation for them to join the prosperous world.

With Mexico coming under control, La Contessa recognized what a disaster most of Central and South America was. She recognized that a first-world country, which Mexico was rapidly becoming, could not live easily with a failed state next door. The country, which most obviously needed liberation, was Nicaragua. As a step along the way, Guatemala was overrun in a lightning attack, which simply carried on into Nicaragua. The people there were so disgusted with the excesses of the Sandinista dictator that they cheered when he and his kleptocratic government were hung from the lampposts outside the presidential palace. The army and the police, which had been completely taken over by the Sandinistas, had their corrupt leadership decapitated by a surgical, or not-so-surgical, strikes. All the high-tech weapons, on which the dictator had spent Nicaragua's wealth, were taken over by the Legion, whose ranks were swelled by Nicaraguan recruits.

Governors were appointed. Nicaragua and Guatemala remained sovereign states but fell within the sphere of influence of Mexico. La Contessa was not prepared to spend Mexico's treasure on funding an empire. If there was to be a commonwealth, it would have to be self-sufficient.

Having liberated Nicaragua, the adjacent states of Belize, Honduras, and El Salvador were taken over one after another, and corruption weeded out. The curtailing of corruption, enforcement of property rights, and the rule of law produced its magical effect on their economies almost overnight.

Mexico, corruption finally under control, underwent its long-anticipated entry into the developed world. It boomed. Now that the country was safe, tourism was fully exploited. Manufacturing flooded in. Desalination plants—redesigned by some of the Foundation children and built with the money from the drug lords and the taxes, which were now being collected at a 15 percent flat rate—provided irrigation, which opened up large, formerly dry areas of Mexico for agriculture, initially for domestic consumption, but soon for export.

Criminals who tried cross-border raids were pursued. Running back to hide in their own country did not help them. The Legion ignored borders in their pursuit, and as always, the criminal's family was made responsible. The various hellholes were cleaned up, and Hinchcliffe and La Contessa set their sights on the disaster that was Venezuela. It took some time to clean up and consolidate the liberated countries in Central America. Before that could be completed, Venezuela had descended into the usual inevitable socialist paradise of open corruption, widespread jailing, and starvation.

US President Sandra was informed of the impending invasion by Munro personally and very unofficially, as La Contessa kept him in the loop. The president kept the information to herself to give absolute deniability. She herself had no interest and did not see that the US had any interest in who ran what in South America. As far as she was concerned, if La Contessa wanted to run it all, that was fine with her. The huge flood of illegal migrants coming in through Mexico had stopped, and South American criminals were being stripped of their citizenship and deported. If no other country would take them, then Mexico would, for a consideration. What happened to them after that was of no concern to Sandra. If a criminal disappeared, too bad, but that had nothing to do with her. The mainstream media had increasing reservations about visiting the countries controlled by La Contessa after some further unfortunate accidents and accusations of criminality occurred to the most vocal of their number.

The invasion of Venezuela took place with a surgical strike at the presidential palace and the main government buildings using daisy cutters, these massive fuel/air bombs. This was coordinated with sea and air landings, and Hinchcliffe took over the seaports and airports, starting by immobilizing their air force. As in Nicaragua, the Venezuelan army gave surprisingly little resistance. They had looked invincible beating up crowds of unarmed protesters but dying for the dictator who had taken over from Chavez was not exactly high on their list of things to do. The dictator had extinguished any concept of Venezuela as a country. It was simply his personal fiefdom, and as far as most people were concerned, he and his cronies could defend themselves. How could any foreign invader be worse than what they had?

With some semblance of a rule of law reestablished, initially with military courts and a new peso issued to stabilize the currency, the country rapidly began to revive. Food and toilet paper flooded in. Why toilet paper should be the first commodity to disappear and reappear has never ever been explained. The dictator's family and his cronies were stripped of their funds, which had been largely hidden abroad. The nationalized companies were returned to their original owners and commerce returned. Again, with the twin terrors of socialism and corruption removed and with privatization, the petrodollars began to flow, which not only led to an economic recovery but helped defray the cost of the Legion.

Hinchcliffe was not sure when the next murderous socialist dictator would appear, but she was certain he would. She thought that Bolivia or Paraguay would be next, as they were landlocked. She agreed with Colin and increased her air force capacity, especially heavy air transport, which she could rent out when not in military use. She was certain that she would never face a First World country in combat, so she saw no need to spend huge sums of money on the newest planes or fighting vehicles. The equipment she had liberated from Venezuela and Nicaragua was quite sufficient.

She saw, however, that any further liberation of South America would have to be put on hold, as Sandra's presidency was coming to an end. The likely next president would be a far-left wing man who had never been anything but a politician and was therefore not only naive beyond belief but would not look kindly on the Legion and its activities. Going to war with the US was not something Hinchcliffe planned. She would have to hunker down, be quiet, and wait him out until sanity would be restored north of the Mexican border. She and her commanders would have to avoid US-controlled territory in case some deep state operative tried to have them arrested on some spurious charge. Four years—and worst case, eight years—of lunacy loomed.

CHAPTER 8

Ash

"We have a live one here."

"Her IQ is outstanding. Yes, sure, but look at her background. She is way outside our parameters. She is from a very wealthy background. She will have had everything money can buy. She will have gone to the best private schools in the US northeast, so she will have been indoctrinated with identity politics. She will be a tiny, brainwashed, useful idiot Marxist waving a placard, mouthing slogans."

"That is not what her personality shows. This is one tough little cookie."

"She simply will not put up with the brutal program the little peasant girls go through here. She has known nothing but privilege, and they have known nothing but poverty and misery."

"Can't you give her a try? If you don't, it will be such a waste of human potential."

"I think we are wasting our time, but if you feel so strongly, I will speak to Munro. I am sure he will not be in the least interested."

Teresa was now, among her myriad of other duties running Manon's empire, the head of the Munro Foundation enrolment program. She phoned Munro, who ran the residential end of the program and discussed the issue with him. He pointed out, as she already knew, that the guidelines had been established long ago and were successful to date. The scions of the wealthy, no matter how clever, would have no interest in the academic grind necessary to take them to the top of the scientific or business tree.

The cliché, clogs to clogs or shirtsleeves to shirtsleeves, in three generations was real. There was nearly always a reversion to the norm of average, and they had no interest in good average children or even very good average.

Those who had already suffered the indoctrination of Marxist/postmodernist teaching, which began as soon as children entered any school in the West, were likely damaged for life; and any reeducation was at best likely to be very incomplete. Teresa pointed out that the girl's test scores were over 180 IQ, and she scored low on compassion and empathy and high on conscientiousness, which was one of the patterns they were looking for.

"Jeez, Teresa, if only she came from a trailer park."

"Like me!"

"Yes, like you, exactly like you. I wish we could find more like you." He sighed. "Well, I suppose we could try, just this once."

"Do you want me to interview her?"

"Yes, if you have the time, but given her father's status, I suppose I should come too. We had both better to talk to the girl and her parents. Elizabeth has some reception she wants me to attend in Washington in a couple of weeks. Is that convenient for you?"

"I have a meeting in New York, followed by another in Japan, so we can get our staffs to coordinate times."

The girl in question was eleven years old. Her father had started a company that had brought him considerable wealth at an early age. His daughter, who was the template blond American beauty, had grown up an only child in a wealthy neighborhood, surrounded by semi-servants and wealthy friends. She swam competitively when she was younger but had lost interest. She played tennis quite well but had no interest in undertaking the training required to reach the ranks of those considered even possibly good. She voiced no particular ambition and seemed no different from the numerous girls who surrounded her.

Teresa made an appointment for Munro and herself to interview both the parents and the child. Home was the easiest place, as evening was the only time they were both free. When arranging the meeting, she told the father that the girl had scored very well in an intelligence test, and they wished to interview her with a view to perhaps an offer of a scholarship at their establishment. The father, when he heard about the Foundation, was intrigued, even more so when he heard that Munro himself would come to see the child. Munro was already reasonably well-known as the silent husband of the current US president.

Munro and Teresa turned up at the appointed hour and were introduced. Munro also had with him a young Japanese woman wearing a kimono. She was introduced as Munro's security. The father thought that was improbable. He had heard, however, that the president did have a Japanese bodyguard who had protected her during one attempted assassination.

"This young lady is your security? You look like you would be protecting her."

"What are you, Keiko, the third or fourth best shot in the world?"

"*Hai.* Third in 25 m pistol rapid fire at the last Alaska shootout."

"What, is she armed?"

The Japanese girl pulled out a pistol from the holster concealed inside her modified obi, which was chalk white decorated with purple lightning bolts.

"Oh yes. Her full-time job is with the Japanese police. A captain, I think?" he said, turning to the girl. She nodded.

They sat around a coffee table, and Teresa pulled a sheaf of papers out of her briefcase.

"How did my girl come to your attention?"

"One of her teachers picked her out as being exceptional and had her tested. She scored so high that they did a personality scan on her. The teacher had heard of our program and contacted us."

"She did that, and we weren't told?"

"Schools do that all the time. Sometimes they want to stream children, and sometimes they just want to know what they are dealing with."

"And my daughter?"

Teresa fanned out the papers on the table. They were clearly marked with the girl's name.

"How did you get these? That's private. This surely can't be legal."

"The teacher contacted our organization."

"She can't do that without contacting us!"

Munro glanced at Teresa, rolled his eyes, and sighed.

"I am sure it is perfectly legal. As far as I know, these are the only copies of her test scores. I leave them with you."

He again looked again at Teresa, shrugged, and got up, leaving the test results on the table. She raised both hands palm up in the universal gesture of resignation and got up herself. "Well, nice to have met you," she said, and they headed toward the door.

"Where are you going?"

"Home. Sorry to have bothered you."

"Just wait a minute."

"No, no. We were mistaken. Sorry to have bothered you."

They left the room where they had been sitting and made for the front door. The father ran to intercept them at the door.

"Just a minute, please. You came to offer my daughter some sort of scholarship?"

"Yes, but obviously, it would not suit her. Goodbye."

"Wait a minute, wait a minute." He stood in front of the door, blocking it. "Can we just talk for a minute? Please sit down. I am sorry if I inadvertently offended you."

"It is not a question of offence. It is a question of suitability. Look, I have to get back to Arizona, and Teresa has to go to New York. Maybe some other time."

The father recognized a brush off if there ever was one. Some other time meant never.

"Please, please sit down. My wife and I would really like to hear what you had thought to offer my little girl."

Munro looked at his watch, sighed, and then looked at Teresa, raised his eyebrows, and shrugged. "Well, OK."

They sat down again. Munro was silent. Teresa was the one who took up the conversation. She briskly explained that the girl had a very high IQ, and her personality testing indicated that she would potentially fit their program. It was an enhanced school program concentrating mainly on STEM. The children were pushed as quickly as possible through the system. There were three streams, including the genius stream, like Little Sister, the Nobel Prize winner in physics, of whom they might have heard. There were of course almost no children like that, and given her scores, it was possible, but not likely, their child would be in that class. The regular stream of children, where their daughter would be, were pushed very hard in academics, really hard, hours per day. They wanted them to do university-level science by the time they were teenagers.

"Why push them so hard?"

"The really good mathematicians are usually at their best in their early twenties, so to make maximum use of them, we need to have them absolutely on top of their game as teenagers."

She went on to explain that there were arrangements with various universities in the southwest, Luxembourg, Japan, and soon Madrid. A lot of these children would complete a basic engineering degree by the time they are fifteen, and then they could look around and see what they wanted to specialize in. They could take a second degree in another field or a PhD or start working."

"Working at fifteen?"

"Yes. If the kid is a computer whiz, the sooner he or she starts real work, the better. Little Sister was a full professor at age fourteen."

"The third stream are the kids who can't stand the pressure. Some go home, although very few, because most come from a terrible background. These kids are all very clever, so they go to a local charter school and go to university sooner than most kids, but the pressure is much less. We do not like that because it means we picked wrong, in the sense that we are squandering our scarce resources. But it would be totally unfair to send them back. Once they have spent a year or so with us, they would never fit back into the hellhole they came from."

"And my little girl?"

"We don't know. We have never taken a rich girl before. She has had a life of privilege, unlike the other kids, who largely have known nothing but poverty and misery. They are, to some extent, a tabula rasa, a blank slate, and have a huge incentive to work, but does a rich girl? When the pressure comes on, she will probably fold and just want to go home. If she does that, she is wasting our time, which is why we have never before made an offer to a rich girl. That's it! That's the program."

She shrugged and made the palms up gesture again. She turned to the girl, "What do you think?"

"So I have to study hard. Is there anything else?"

"You will be living in Arizona, so many people speak Spanish, and we have contacts with Japan," she said, gesturing to Keiko, "so most learn a little Japanese. If you want to go to Europe, then French also. We expect you to become a southwest girl, so you ride, shoot, dance, and cook."

"Shoot?" said the father. "We don't like guns."

"There seems to be some sort of connection with math. You know how piano playing and math seem to be in the same part of the brain, so the one helps the other. We are not sure, but we think that shooting is the same."

"You mean you shoot too?"

"We all shoot, and we all exercise, and we regard the discipline of dance as part of that exercise."

The father looked at his child. "What do you think?"

"I think it sounds like fun. Learning and studying are easy, riding horses and shooting a gun. It sounds like Western movie. I think I would like that."

Munro spoke to her. "It will not be easy. If it were easy, we would accept many people. In reality, we accept about three or four per year worldwide, often less. You have had an easy life so far. The children you know are bright average. The children you are going to meet are the best in the world, and they are really driven, extremely competitive. They would work twenty-four hours per day if we let them. They plan on being the best in the world as soon as possible. Just to keep up with them, you will have to work harder than you have ever worked in your life. If you are not sure, don't do it."

"I want to try."

"If you really, really want. Now we will have to explain to your parents how it works. Teresa will tell you."

"This is extremely expensive. None of the other children have any money at all. We rely on donors to support us. You have money. My accountants estimate that you should pay $100,000 per year. That will help to fund another couple of kids. You will pay until she gets her primary or secondary degree and starts work. She can leave at any time, but if she does, she cannot come back. She can start work whenever she likes. She will pay 25 percent of her income to the Foundation until age thirty and 25 percent of any patents she develops. After age thirty, she can stay with the Foundation or go on her own."

"Steep terms. She will be an indentured servant."

"Yes, but if she stays with you and the rest of her little friends, how much money is she going to make in the standard make-believe job most rich little girls do?"

"That is still a pretty steep price."

Munro stood up again and shrugged. "Whatever. We are not interested in negotiating. I really have to fly back to Arizona now. If you decide that is what your girl wants, the papers are there. Read them. Keiko here," he said, gesturing to the Japanese woman, "will stay in town overnight and will contact you tomorrow. Tell her if you want to sign them. If you do, she will witness them. You keep a copy, she keeps a copy. She will escort the girl to the ranch in Arizona. To be frank, I think this is a mistake. I don't think your girl is going to like it, and I think she will come home to you very soon."

The three left, boarding the waiting limo. The parents and the girl talked that evening. The mother was not impressed.

"I don't want my little girl to go with these people. It sounds terrible, like modern slavery. It sounds like all the students they have are stolen from poor people. I don't want my daughter to grow up with people like that."

"To be the best in the world, I would like to try. You know that I learn nothing in school here. It is all so easy I don't have to think. I have to be careful not to show up my friends, who are so much slower. I have never met anyone who is as clever as me. It will be interesting."

"He did say that scientist with the ridiculous name, Little Sister, came through their program. I hear that she is not the standard poor scientist. She has made money out of her discoveries and is independently very wealthy, so they don't keep all the money for themselves."

"But at the place she is going to live, they have all sorts of undesirable people. I saw on the news the world champion boxer lives there. That is no place for a girl. And some sort of Japanese policewoman with a gun is going to take her there. I don't think so."

"I want to go," said the girl. "It sounds exciting. I can always come back if I don't like it."

They talked long into the night. The girl became more and more adamant that she was wasting her time in her own school, along with a bunch of dummies. Her parents had never heard her talk that way before about her friends. She explained that she had not known there was any alternative, and she thought that she would have to spend her life with people like that, and she had better not stand out too much in case she was excluded from the in group. Her parents finally, reluctantly, agreed to let her go.

Keiko showed up the next morning with a limo. They were surprised to see that she was still wearing a kimono, which would certainly stand out in the US. The parents signed the papers, which they had carefully examined the night before. She asked the girl if she was ready to leave.

"Leave now?"

"Yes. I have to get back to Arizona, and I have a flight booked for both of us."

"What should I take with me?"

"Gym clothes for sure. Anything you like, but hurry. You can always send for anything you need and have it shipped."

Keiko told the parents that it was not necessary for them to go to the airport with her, but they insisted. At the airport, the girl hugged her parents, who were intrigued when an official met them and escorted Keiko and their daughter through, bypassing security. What they did not know was that the Praetorians had an agreement with most of the US airlines, that when they were flying, they would be official Sky Marshals. Keiko could hardly go through normal security with a couple of handguns in her obi, along with an extendable club and a can of bear spray.

The commuter flight was uneventful, but the girl did notice that Keiko seemed to know the air hostesses, talking with them in the galley and walking the full length of the plane twice. She was very noticeable in her flowered kimono and her broad, white belt with the purple lightning bolts. In Chicago, they changed planes. Again, they joined the air crew as they boarded. The girl asked why they were so privileged. Keiko showed her an identity badge hanging around her neck, which she now took from under her kimono so that it could clearly be seen. It said Sky Marshal.

"What does that mean?"

"It means I am sort of an airline policeman."

"I thought that you were a Japanese policewoman?"

"I am, but we have an agreement with some airlines."

She settled the girl in first class and went back to the gangway, where she could observe the boarding passengers. When all had boarded, she came in and walked the length of the plane.

"What are you doing?"

"I am observing the passengers, looking for anything abnormal."

The flight departed uneventfully. An hour later, the trouble began. One man at the rear of the plane had obviously had too much to drink. How he had managed to get into that state in the early afternoon was not clear. They later suspected he had had liquor with him and had inadvertently drunk too much in the toilets. The stewardess did not immediately recognize the situation and brought him a drink, but refused to give him any more. He became belligerent. The stewardess came for Keiko, who went to confront him. The flight was not full, so the passengers close to him had moved away, sensing trouble. Keiko sat down beside him.

"Who are you?"

"I am Keiko, a Sky Marshal," she said, and she showed him her badge.

"You are joking. If you work for these people, get me another drink."

"No, sir. You have had too much to drink already. Can I get you some coffee and a sandwich?"

"I don't want coffee. I want a drink," he growled and he made to get up.

"Please sit down, sir."

"Or what?"

"Or I will have to arrest you, sir, and think of what that will mean. Taken off the aircraft in handcuffs. Taken to jail. Photographs of you in handcuffs all over the local newspapers. Questions asked about why your employer would hire a drunk. You will be jailed, and your boss will fire you. Your neighbors will think you are a total moron. You will embarrass your wife and kids. This is potentially really serious for you. It could ruin your life. Now just be quiet, sir, or I will have to restrain you."

"Restrain me? You and what army?"

"I am a captain in the Tokyo police. I have my handcuffs with me. If you want a face full of bear spray, just keep acting up. If you calm down, I will take you up to first class and get you something to eat."

The threat of jail time, job loss, and bear spray got through to him; and he calmed down. She took him up to first class where there were empty seats. She put him in a window seat and made sure he was seat-belted in. She then got him a spare meal from the galley, along with coffee and sparkling mineral water. She checked the girl she was supposed to be guarding, who was very interested in the whole proceedings, and then sat down beside him.

There are very few men who will not calm down when a beautiful woman sits beside him and asks him questions about himself. She asked him about his job, his life, his hopes, and his dreams. She found out that he was single and had recently broken up with his girlfriend. He had been feeling sorry for himself, which he used as an excuse to explain his overindulgence in alcohol. He had a good job, which did involve a lot of travel, and was climbing the corporate ladder quickly.

She took his tray away, and he fell asleep. Keiko patrolled the plane once more, then sat beside the girl.

"What was that about?"

"Oh, just some poor guy who drank too much. He will be OK."

"And is that a Sky Marshal's job?"

"Yes, mostly. Just some poor guy who forgot to eat and drank too quickly. They just need a bit of food, sleep, and coffee."

"Does it get worse?"

"Occasionally, not for me yet. The number of terrorists who make it onto a flight is vanishingly small. Usually, we catch them as they board."

"How can you tell?"

"The Israelis have worked out a system that we follow, called profiling."

She noticed the man had woken up. She got him more coffee and mineral water. She sat beside him and told him that he had given the three air hostesses a hard time, and he should do something for them.

"Like what?"

"How much money have you got on you?"

He checked his wallet and found $300. She suggested he give each one $50.

"Just like that?"

"Just like that. Here is an envelope. Give it to the head stewardess as you leave and apologize."

"I will give them that if I can have your telephone number."

"Yes, you can, if you wish. Here is my card. This is my office number for the Praetorians, who are the security outfit I work for part time. This is my number in Japan, if you are ever there.

"I would like to see you again."

"I think you are a nice man. I will be on duty in Tokyo for the next six months. If you are there, call me."

"I think I may be. I will call if I may."

"See you then."

It actually happened. After a few months of correspondence, he was in Japan on business and met with her. Six months later, he flew back again, and in a beautiful garden in Kyoto, he declared his love for her and his desire to be with her forever. She was already a captain in the police force and thirty years of age, so she was looking for a man. She took permanent leave of absence and flew to America and married him. She remained an active Praetorian.

There were some trouble, as there are in all marriages, but they weathered the storms, and had three children. Keiko stayed in touch with the little girl, whom she regarded as the one who brought her luck. In later years, her husband ended up working for the girl, so their lives remained intertwined due to the unlikely event of one drink too many.

The little girl fitted quickly into her new environment. She found that while before, she always had to conceal her blazing intelligence from her "friends," here, all the children and many of the adults were of equal or greater intelligence and proud of it. She found initially to her consternation that she required tutors. Later, the fact that she actually had to struggle to keep up gave her pleasure. She began to enjoy the physicality of it, the early morning runs, the exercise classes, the dance, the shooting, and the horseback riding.

She got to know the fighters. There were very few, as Munro was simply too busy to run a fight school, although the more advanced students, especially Maria Martens, took most of the administrative load off his shoulders. Archie Moore, the current world heavyweight champion, lived at the ranch and was in full training. The bigger children thought it an honor to do some road work with him and to be in the same gym. She would see him slamming punches into the heavy bag or watch him in the ring with sparring partners. Eventually, she would greet him, as did all the other children.

"Good morning, Archie."

"Good morning, miss."

The competitive shooters, mainly the visiting Japanese policewomen, spent endless hours dry-firing. All the children learned to shoot. The girl was physically strong and soon passed her NRA tests so that when she was old enough, she could carry a gun on her hip, just like a Western cowboy or like some of the local children with whom she shared some school classes. There was no conflict with these local children, some of whom would come to the ranch after school for the classes in song and dance and some to take part in the constant math and science tutoring, which ran every evening. No one thought it strange that a big, young teenage boy should be in the same tutorial as, and occasionally helped by, a tiny little girl who did not speak English well. Everyone knew and respected the fact that the Foundation children were different.

To her surprise, it turned out that she had a reasonably good singing voice, but not quite as good as the girl they called Arizona. She learned to play the Spanish guitar, as several of the children liked it, and Munro liked it when they played and sang mournful Spanish songs after their evening get-togethers. She began to dress like the others, in tight jeans and cowboy boots. They were never allowed to go into the sun without heavy sunscreen and wide-brim hats, either the Western Stetson or the Mexican flat hat. It was constantly emphasized to the children that they must protect their skin unless they wanted to look like a prune in later life.

She had not been there for long when she noticed that most people seemed to use one name only. She asked why. She was told that most of the children came from other cultures and their names were often difficult. It was easier if they simply picked some simple name for themselves. One evening, she asked Munro what she should call herself.

"Well, we already have an Arizona, an Idaho, and a Montana, so you can't call yourself that. You are ash-blond, so why not call yourself that."

She liked that name, so Ash she became. After six months, she thought she would like to go home for Christmas. "You will not like it," the other girls told her. "You have changed, and you cannot go home. You will find yourself a stranger in a strange land."

"Like Robert Heinlein."

"Yes, maybe, but more like Starship Trooper."

Since her arrival, she had been in contact with her parents through email and phone calls, but these slowly decreased in number and volume as she adapted to her new very high-pressure life. She did decide to go home for a visit. A visiting Japanese Praetorian accompanied her, again also acting as a Sky Marshal.

While standing in the gangway watching the passengers board, a marine in uniform spoke to the Praetorian in Japanese. It turned out he had been stationed in Okinawa and had heard Tomiko-san's now famous speech to the troops on a couple of occasions and had learned a little Japanese. He recognized the white obi with the purple lightning bolts as being the uniform of the Praetorians. While she was patrolling the aisle after takeoff, he spoke to her again. It turned out that he and three friends were actually on their way home from an exercise. The shooter knew that Tomiko always encouraged friendly relationships with anyone's military, especially the US Marines, so she stood and talked to them. They told her what a good time they had had in Okinawa and wanted to go back. They told of how much they had learned from Tomiko-san and how well they had been treated.

When the drinks cart came around, she bought them all beer. It turned out that another two men sitting close by were also military, so she bought them beer also. She told the surrounding passengers that she was a US Sky

Marshal, showing her identity badge. She asked their permission to speak to the soldiers, who she said were the defenders of America. She said if the conversation bothered anyone, she would go away.

Put like that, no one seemed to mind. Another man from further up the plane heard what she said and got up to join the party as he, too, was military. She went to the galley and brought back a case of beer and distributed it to the military men and the passengers sitting close by, who were likely being inconvenienced, although some joined in the conversation as they also had relatives in the armed forces. Ash came to join them to see what was happening. The Praetorian introduced her as a genius, the cleverest woman they would ever meet. Ash loved the compliment, being called clever and a woman, not a girl. The men complimented her.

After thirty minutes or so, the Praetorian broke off and returned to first class. There were no further incidents. Ash asked her who paid for the beer. The Praetorian said she had, but that her pay as Sky Marshal would easily cover it.

At home, Ash greeted her parents. The Praetorian, who was a senior police officer, had already made arrangements to have a dinner meeting with the local chief of police, who had met Tomiko at one of her police lectures in the US. He had invited Tomiko to visit if she was ever nearby. Tomiko always kept these invitations as, after all, she had equipment to sell, and having secured a large contract for boots for Japanese female police, she was trying to interest various police forces in the US to sign something similar for their own policewomen.

The Praetorian had brought samples of the equipment that Tomiko and Manon were selling and was wearing the boots herself, so she was quite happy to host the police chief, his wife, and several others under his command. She had given Ash her phone number in case any problems arose. They had a pretty good meeting. The policewomen all preferred Tomiko's line of boots, for style and comfort. It helped that the boots for sale in the US were made in Texas, and the silver on the pointed toe came in stainless steel for work boots and was a very useful, if undeclared, weapon. Once they knew their size and width, the women could order boots of any material and design, a few of which the Praetorian had brought with her as samples.

They were halfway through the dinner when Ash called. She was deeply unhappy. Things had turned out exactly as the other children had told her they would. She had changed and no longer fitted in with her former friends. They mocked her neatly pressed jeans, her Western shirt, and her cowboy boots. They thought it was old-people music when she played her Spanish guitar and sang. They talked about the doings of celebrities she had never heard of. She told them about her shooting. They told her that that was gross and that guns should be banned.

They went to a house party where there were no adults. Her parents went out for the evening, being assured that she would take a taxi home. She talked to some of the boys she had grown up with. Ash—now being accustomed to men and boys at the ranch, many of whom were Deputy Border Patrol, who worked out, and who danced and treated females with exaggerated courtesy—found little or nothing to say to these boys. She told one of them that she knew three world champions, Munro, Miguel, and Archie Moore. The boy recognized the name of Moore but was completely uninterested. She told another she knew Isis and Little Sister. He had no idea who they were.

Ash realized she no longer had anything in common with these children, as she now thought of them. She had no desire to spend more time with them. The Foundation kids had been correct. There was no going back. She was different. Her parents could come and visit her if they wished, but the place where she had grown up was no longer home.

She phoned her parents, but they were out at a party, as it was that season. So she phoned the Praetorian, who picked up her call. She said where she was and wanted to go home. By "home," the Praetorian asked, did she mean Arizona? Ash said she had better spend the night with her parents, but they were out, and she did not know when they would be back. The Praetorian promised to pick her up.

She told the chief of police about the problem. He, his wife, and his senior staff, by now several bottles of excellent wine to the good, did not want to disrupt the dinner, so he instead sent one of his police cars to pick up Ash to bring her to the restaurant. Ash's friends were surprised when a knock at the door revealed a uniformed police officer come to take Ash with him. She had been alerted by her guard and was ready and anxious to leave.

At the restaurant, she sat with the adults and found she had far more in common with them than with her childhood friends. The Praetorian had told her dinner companions about this girl's extraordinary promise. They were not only interested in that but even more so when they found out Ash actually knew these legendary heavyweight fighters. The policewomen liked to talk to someone who had danced with Miguel and Archie Moore. They were amazed that she had seen videos of the great Tomiko-san in action and the videos of Elizabeth's gunfights in South America. They were awed by the fact she knew Little Sister, the Nobel Prize winner and one of the greatest scientists the world had ever seen.

Ash had a wonderful time being the center of attention. She was in no hurry to get back to her parents. The Praetorian also had a good time, securing a contract as the preferred supplier of boots to the policewomen of that town and leaving them considering the extendable club for the policewomen.

The next morning, Ash hugged her parents and flew back to Arizona. She never went home after that. There was nothing there for her. Her parents would visit her, but she preferred to meet them on neutral ground, like Rome or Paris. She took her father fly fishing in the Yellowstone River and hunting in Alaska with some of the Indian guides she knew, having spent some time with Running Bear, the Athabascan chief who was associated with the Prometheus Group. For her, home was the ranch, and her friends, the other hard-driving children.

At age fifteen, she had had all the education she wanted. She had her engineering degree but did not want to be a full-time scientist. After discussing the issues with some of the other Foundation girls, she decided she would like an internship in Europe working for Manon and Teresa. She talked to Maria Martens, who did not see any difficulties and who told her that Munro was going to Europe in a couple of weeks and she could go with him. She would arrange accommodation, and Ash should just take with her what she immediately needed.

A couple of days before she was due to leave, Munro asked her to speak to him in his office after their evening durbar.

"Sorry, Ash, change of plans. I cannot go to Europe this week. Maria Martens tells me that there is something I will have to be here for. As you know, normally she handles everything, but if she says I have to be here, I have to be here. We will make arrangements for you to fly commercial. One of the Praetorians can go with you. You have never met Manon, have you?"

"I have been in Europe, but I have never met her, no."

"Working is different from visiting. People are different, the customs are different, and expectations are different. Any ideas about what you want to do?"

"Unlike most of the girls, I don't think I want to be a scientist or an engineer, but other than that, I don't know."

"You have your engineering degree, so do whatever you want. The field is wide open. Takes all kinds. Like Maria, who could easily manage the whole world, or Star and Hinchcliffe, who want to be warriors. La Contessa became a politician. We will certainly need protectors."

"Protection? From what?"

"The wolves are always just beyond the light of the campfire. The myrmidons of chaos are out there, circling the walls, looking for a way in."

"You think? Mostly I see a bunch of silly children in universities, like the kids I grew up with, and the socialist idiots in the media, but who else?"

"The mountain of bureaucrats. Their name is 'Legion', and they hate success in all and every form. Look at you, bright, beautiful, and wealthy. They will hate you for all of these reasons, especially your brains and your beauty. All socialism, postmodernism, and every other *ism* in the final analysis is simply envy. 'All the conspirators save only he, did what they did in envy of great Caesar.' And I think Brutus also did it for envy. All your life, people will envy you and hate you."

"That does not sound very good."

"That's why you need to spend time with Manon. I try to come across as the slightly brain-damaged baffled buffoon, so I am not seen as much of a challenge, and so I am not hated too much. But Manon is different. All her life, she has faced down these people. It is not the people you think, the monsters like Putin. He is easy to understand. He has other things to do, and God help you if you get in his way. But he will only do things for a reason. It is the greasy little bureaucrat. That woman who wrote *The Banality of Evil* knew exactly the type."

"Hannah Arendt, wasn't it?"

"I think so, about Eichmann, the little bureaucrat who had all the Jews killed. That banal little man who failed at everything in his whole life. These are the people who will come after you. Manon will teach you how to face these people, and you must learn to never apologize and never surrender."

"That does not sound good."

"You are only what? Fifteen? But you must grow up. Look at what Isis says she came from, 'married at nine, grandmother by midtwenties, dead by thirty."

"I don't want that!"

"Sure. But don't forget to have babies before it is too late. What was it Shakespeare wrote? 'Die single and thine image dies with thee.' But not just yet. You have a few more years."

"Yes, sir! What a relief. A few more years."

"Stay in touch, Ash, let me know what you are thinking and what you are doing."

A couple of days later, Ash was able to board the plane with the crew, as it was a US-based carrier, so her Praetorian was acting as a Sky Marshall and wished to take up position at the end of the gangway so she could observe the boarding passengers. When the Praetorian boarded, she stood looking for a while and then walked the length of the plane before sitting down. As usual, they were sitting in the last row in first class so that she could see those ahead, and anyone trying to rush the cockpit from the back of the plane would have to pass her. Ash thought she seemed uneasy.

"What is it?"

"Probably nothing."

"Nothing?"

"I should not tell you, but I have a bad feeling about one of the passengers. I wanted to take him back and search him, but the loading officer overruled me, saying that he had gone through security. She thought I was overreacting."

"Well, that's true. Except for us, all the passengers have to go through security."

"Yes, but! A gun or a knife can easily be smuggled in by those working in security, and there are so many of them, that airport security really is a joke. How thoroughly the investigators are investigated is unclear."

"So what are you going to do?"

"Nothing! Nothing I can do except be worried the whole trip. I can see the man sitting halfway up in first class, so maybe she is right and I am overreacting, as most terrorists fly economy."

The takeoff was uneventful. They had been in the air for about four hours. As it was an overnight flight, the lights were dimmed. The pilot came out, opening the cockpit door. The man the Praetorian had been watching was on his feet in an instant, running for the door with a knife in his hand. The Praetorian, who had hardly sat at all during the flight, was actually on her feet and reacted immediately, pulling out her 22 mm and shooting him three times in the back. He staggered, grasping a seat back. Running swiftly, she was on top of him, jammed her gun into the back of his head and shot him another three times, the soft bullets bouncing around inside his skull.

She took him down so quickly and the gun was so quiet that most sleeping passengers hardly registered the event. The curtains to first class remained closed, and a stewardess made sure no economy passengers came forward. The Praetorian stood, waving her Sky Marshal's badge in one hand and holding the ceramic knife she had taken from the terrorist between finger and thumb in the other, and motioned the passengers who had reacted to sit down, and with her finger to her lips, she made the universal sign for quiet, pointing to the back of the plane. The first-class passengers fortunately recognized the need for quiet so as not to panic the other passengers on the plane. .

The Praetorian and a stewardess dragged the body into an empty seat and covered it with a blanket. As they were well over halfway across the Atlantic by then, and as the Praetorian could not identify any other terrorist, the pilot carried on, and the plane landed uneventfully in Luxembourg. No announcements were made on board, so most passengers never knew of the disturbance. In keeping with airline policy to reduce the incidence of copycats, the media were not informed. Eventually, some passengers did talk, but the airline made no official statement.

The day she arrived in Luxembourg; Ash met Manon for the first time. Manon had heard of the affair.

"An exciting trip?"

"Yes. I have never seen one of the Praetorians in action up close and personal before."

"They are pretty good at their job. I only wish more airlines would use them. More importantly, I wish that Western government would use the Israeli technique of identifying the potential terrorist rather than wasting their resources searching elderly nuns. Luxembourg is still pretty safe, but if you are going to go to some places like Paris, I want a bodyguard with you. Other places just be careful. I don't want a bodyguard preventing you from having some fun."

"Fun?"

"Oh yes. Life is not all work. Just mostly. And most of the people you will do business with will be men, so you must learn how to handle them."

"Handle men?"

"Yes. Handle men. When they sent you to the mining camps to be teacher, nurse, cook, and whatnot and to spend time with the Indian chief in Alaska, it was to teach you how to handle the salt-of-the-earth men, but there are others. Handling them is a skill to be learned like any other, and you will learn it here."

"Who should my protector be?"

"We will use one of the female Praetorians, but not in fancy dress. If we use a male Praetorian, his presence will frighten off other men and cramp your style. Rules are different in Europe than the US. You will spend most of your time with Teresa and me and maybe a bit with Sheila MacDonald in Paris. But there are other interesting things that you should learn that your mother never taught you."

"I wait with interest."

CHAPTER 9

President Moore

Moore had been the world heavyweight boxing champion by now for five years. He had done his best to avoid brutal punishment, but head shots are inevitable in boxing, despite all protective maneuvers. The effect of repeated head trauma was likely cumulative, although no one knew for certain. Munro had insisted Moore have brain MRIs after every fight; and to date, neither hemosiderin deposits, indicative of bleeding, or demyelination, indicative of other damage, had been seen. Nevertheless, there were concerns.

It was not as if Moore needed any more money from fighting. His winnings, carefully protected by Manon and invested widely among other things, especially with Elizabeth's son, the Buccaneer's hedge fund, were more than enough to keep him in comfort for the rest of his life. The advertising dollars continued to roll in, not only from English-speaking countries, but also from Japan and the Hispanic world, as he had learned to speak both of these languages. Additionally, he had avoided the ridiculous expenses that had bankrupted so many of his fighting colleagues.

He had bought property close to the Foundation ranch and continued to train there, his familiar surroundings. His cars consisted of vehicles that he had been given for advertising dollars and which he mainly kept at the ranch for general use. The vehicle he mostly drove himself was one of Sandra's trucks, an SWD, the Sandra Desert Wagon, as he knew he could survive almost any crash unhurt in that monster truck. Women were plentiful, but he remained very careful, often preferring to use

Manon's bordello chain, which she had franchised in the US in states where prostitution was legal. In those states where it remained illegal, she had opened robot sex doll brothels, which were very popular and very lucrative, much more so than employing live people. When he was on the road, Yaeko, his favorite Praetorian bodyguard, protected him from any me-too accusations.

On Munro's advice, he had stood for and won the position of mayor of Flagstaff. Using the brilliant girls of the Foundation, the actual management work involved was not onerous and allowed him to learn and hone his people skills one-on-one at meetings and with the media. After doing that for a couple of years, the concept of the world heavyweight champion being a serious politician became less foreign, and Munro felt he should run for the US senate.

The existing Republican senator had weakly, if at all, supported Elizabeth and Sandra, so both these women would be happy to see him replaced. A bruising battle ensued, as the existing senator had many favors that could be called in. Moore was attacked as a vicious unpredictable thug who used and abused women, and therefore, no matter how well he had run Flagstaff, he was unfit to be a senator. Moore, the worst of his wildness long behind him, had been thinking of settling down anyway, and after discussing things with Tomiko and Munro, had come to a decision. He planned to make his decision known in a blaze of publicity.

At a large campaign meeting, during the question-and-answer session, someone, a planted questioner, indicated that they would not vote for a single man who was known to have numerous girlfriends. Moore asked the audience how many more would vote for him if he had a stable, happy marriage. There were loud shouts of approval.

"All right," said Moore, "I hear you. The people have spoken. It is time to make a commitment."

Yaeko, his Japanese bodyguard, dressed in her kimono with the Praetorian's white obi with the purple lightning bolts, was standing behind him. He turned and gestured to her to come forward and went down on one knee before her.

"I, James Moore, born in New York, citizen of America, current heavyweight champion of the world and mayor of Flagstaff, ask for the hand of Yaeko Yamaguchi in marriage. I promise to love and protect her and her children as long as I shall live."

Yaeko, who had known this was coming, responded, "I, Yaeko Yamaguchi, born in Hiroshima, citizen of Japan and America, currently a captain in the Tokyo police and member of the Praetorian Guard, accept the offer of marriage from James Moore. I promise to bear his children and to love and honor him all the days of my life."

Still kneeling, he took a ring from his pocket and put it on her finger. She leaned over and kissed him on the forehead. He stood, and they embraced to the thunderous applause of the crowd.

The wedding took place at the Shinto shrine on the hill above the ranch in Arizona. The bride wore the classic white kimono, but no headdress, as she was definitely not promising submission. As Moore spoke Japanese, as did many in the crowd, the first part of the marriage was conducted by a Shinto priest in that language. That was followed immediately by a Judeo-Christian ceremony in English, conducted by the old ninja priest who was well-known to the group, who came over from Japan for the ceremony.

The crowd walking up the hill to the torii gate was memorable in the number of dignitaries who were present as personal friends. The bridesmaids were Tomiko and La Marquesa, and the best men were Miguel and Munro. The Foundation girls came from all over. Sandra, the president, surrounded by all the Praetorians, put in an appearance. La Contessa came up from Mexico, as did Little Sister. Don Pedro accompanied La Marquesa, who had come from Spain.

The video of the wedding was seen worldwide, especially in Japan, since, in Japanese, Moore thanked the people of Japan for providing him with such a wonderful, brave, and beautiful wife. They held a huge fiesta in Flagstaff. The roads into the main square were closed, and multiple grilling stations were set up. All the bar and restaurant owners were encouraged to set up booths and patios.

To the delight of the crowd, Yaeko and Moore danced the flamenco to start the proceedings while Maria and Arizona sang the songs of Andalusia to accompany the Spanish guitar. The celebration lasted long into the night.

He had been confirmed as senator for four months when his next fight was scheduled. He had given no indication as to when he would stop professional fighting. During the election process, he had released brain MRI images so that it could be seen that he had no brain damage. This, of course, did not help much as his opponents simply got a physician to say, quite correctly, that it proved nothing. For this fight, which he and Munro had talked about maybe being his last, he chose a European, hoping to go out on a high note.

Fighting is always risky, and there are no guarantees, so he did not want to make a big spectacle of this one. He trained very hard for the fight, as he always did, and they studied all the videos available of his opponent, looking for a point of weakness. The fight took place in Caesar's Palace in Las Vegas. His seconds as usual were Yaeko and Munro.

Early on, the fight did not go well for Moore. He did not appear quite as sharp as usual, absorbing an unusual amount of punishment. He did not seem to have the same snap to his punches. They rocked his opponent, but they did not floor him. In his corner between rounds, Munro did not have anything to say, and Yaeko, kneeling in front of him, looking into his eyes, did not see anything wrong. It simply seemed as if the fire had gone out. She became increasingly worried as the fight went on.

Fortunately, in the seventh round, Moore connected with a big right hand to the other fighter's head, which rocked him. The sleeping tiger finally awoke, and three smashing hooks put the challenger down and out. Yaeko and Munro heaved a sigh of relief. When he returned to his corner, waiting for the referee to finish his tally, Munro cut his gloves off.

"Archie. Archie, this is enough. Go out on top."

Munro, having done it himself, knew how difficult, how terribly difficult, it is for a champion to step down while he is still triumphant. There is always the thought of just one more fight, to be king of the world for just another six months. Moore looked him in the eye for a few long seconds, and at Yaeko, who was looking at him with mute appeal. He took a deep breath and then nodded. Yaeko breathed a sigh of relief. When the referee raised his hand in victory, Moore motioned to Yaeko to join him in the center of the ring.

"Ladies and gentlemen, my wife, Yaeko, is pregnant. That was my last fight. From now on, my role and my goal is to cherish my wife and child-to-be and to serve America to the best of my ability."

The audience rose to their feet and cheered. Moore raised his arms in a salute, pivoted, and bowed to the crowd. He never fought again. He devoted most of his time to the senate, where his wisdom and solid common sense were appreciated.

Sandra was looking for a successor. The upcoming election was going to be difficult, as the last three presidents had been Republican, and people would want a change, no matter how terrible the Democrat platform would be. It was liable to be awful, as the Democratic Party seemed to have been taken over by doctrinaire socialists and the identity politics crowd, who had fomented a deep divide in the US. She was concerned that if she ran Moore now and he lost, he would not be in a position to run the next time. Therefore, she resigned herself to a probable loss and four disastrous years for America.

Munro and Running Bear had the same feeling—that loss was inevitable. All that Munro asked was that Sandra try to protect the Prometheus Project as best as possible from destruction at the hands of the Democrats. Anticipating for several years the inevitability of Democrat interference, she had made very large grants to the space project years before and topped these up. The number of emigrants going into space was quietly ramped up with minimal fanfare.

In the end, Sandra was correct. Any political machine that has been in power for any length of time inevitably becomes corrupt, complacent, and incompetent. The people who had kept the party honest for a long time had gone.

Takes Away Clouds Woman had returned to Alaska, where she was preparing to run for the position of governor. Sweet Wolf was now back in Japan, where she had dropped that name and any suggestion of American citizenship and was high in the rankings of the leading political party. Her brief marriage of convenience to Munro was over, and her child was safely tucked away at the ranch in Arizona, where the Japanese public took no notice of its existence. She was free to devote her considerable intellect and energy to scheming for a higher position in Japan. Her only residual contact was that she quietly remained CFO of the Apache nation, and occasionally, when she would visit her child and felt that no one was about, she would dress as she had as a girl in her buckskins and ride with the young men of the tribe who enjoyed being with her. Other than that, she was now outwardly a staid Japanese lady.

The new American president was everything any thinking person in the free world dreaded. Munro could never decide if the left wing actually believed in their lunatic policies or if it was all just some cynical show to fool the useful idiots, bribing people with their own money. This one was an elderly Marxist who called himself a Democratic socialist. He actually made little attempt to disguise his Marxist views, ignored the awful human cost of the history of Marxism, and simply left the obfuscation and misrepresentation to the media, the universities, and the public service unions.

The real reason for his almost inevitable success was that Oswald Spengler's winter of civilization had begun with all institutions failing. American education at all public schools had been taken over by the so-called Social Justice Warriors, a code name for a Marxist blend of postmodernists who had been educated—or really, indoctrinated—by the departments of education, who had been gradually taken over by ideologues from the Frankfurt school since the seventies. These were international socialists rescued by America from the national socialists. Instead of showing any gratitude, they began to deliberately corrupt America in the thirties.

Virtually all the humanities in universities had been corrupted and even faculties of law. STEM fields were under attack but so far had resisted, at least to some extent, although the green movement and the global warming cabal had destroyed the competence of and corrupted so many fields that the general public came to regard many scientific pronouncements as fake news. The efforts of Sandra and Elizabeth at the federal level had resulted in some university departments being saved, but even these were under severe attack. They had done their best to reverse the tide of useless studies, which simply left poor, foolish young people with no usable skills and deeply in debt to these corrupt universities.

In the states run by Munro, the schools and universities were radically different. State schools had largely disappeared and had been replaced by charter and voucher schools, where the money followed the child and where all parents were expected to contribute a small amount to ensure their continued interest in their own children's education. Humanities at universities had been defunded where possible, and alumni had been made aware of the fact that they could direct every dollar they donated and that it should not go to a bloated administration to hire more administrators, whose only interest was in increasing their own benefits.

Periodically, he would bring in time and motion students to examine the workings of his and every other administration over which he had any political power. Financial rewards were given to those students who could produce reduction in the number of administrators with consequent significant administrative savings. This was a popular program, which he encouraged with prizes and constant feedback and suggestions from the citizens. The results were widely publicized. Military cadets, Deputy Border Patrols, and other similar organizations were encouraged. The

Boy Scouts of America, which had been under relentless attack for years and sadly had finally been politically corrupted beyond all recognition or reconstitution, was defunded. All the states he ran were now right-to-work states.

To his shock and dismay, he found that the people moving into his states from failed states like California or the northeast wanted to vote for the same policies that had bankrupted the state they had come from. When the data on this lunatic phenomenon was actually published, he mounted a loud, noisy, and very public campaign asking the Californians and others to stay in California and out of his states. He pointed out that if they stayed in California, they could practice their socialism to their tiny heart's desire and give one another all the free stuff they wanted, as long as they paid for it themselves.

As sure as night follows day, Billy, the new president, reintroduced all the old, tired, failed policies of the past. Elizabeth and Sandra, who had been followers of Milton Friedman, had reduced taxes as soon and as much as possible. They had believed his dictum—that if they concentrated on balancing the budget and reducing the debt, the next spendthrift government would simply ramp it up again. If taxes were reduced first, the economy would improve, leading to more tax revenues, and then the debt could be paid down. Billy, using the tried and failed socialist policies, raised the taxes on the rich and big business, who responded by either stopping work or moving offshore, leading to a huge increase in unemployment and a reduction in overall tax revenues. To compensate for this inevitable increase in unemployment in the private sector, Billy did a new deal, expanding the public sector and increasing unemployment benefits and proposed spending huge sums of money on infrastructure, which seldom got built, and when it did, it was often simply numerous bridges to nowhere. He also attempted to institute free health care, that never-ending money pit, and partially forgave student loans, which resulted in every young person in the US, with no ideas and no ambition, going to school to have a good time forever, as there was no end date and no necessity to study anything of any practical value.

The universities naturally ramped up their social justice programs, which had been held in check by the last two administrations. To fund this, Billy did not raise taxes except, of course, the ineffectual and punitive ones on the wealth generators. Instead, he borrowed money, reasoning, as all socialists do, that it is the children and their children's children who will have to eventually pay the debt, and they do not get to vote in the next election.

Within a short time, Billy succeeded in raising debt to levels unheard of previously. When warned about this monumental folly, he deployed the media talking heads, who spoke learnedly on the wisdom of John Maynard Keynes, who believed that a government could spend its way to prosperity. They did not point out that this had been tried and failed numerous times before and was not quite what Keynes said. They certainly did not tell the uninformed that Keynes last statement was that "in the long run, we are all dead," or by the time their folly catches up with them, the politicians have departed, either to their rich indexed pensions or through the gates of death.

Like all true socialists, they regarded their progeny, when they could be bothered to have any, as not worthy of concern. The fact that their children's children would be grubbing around in the ruins of civilization was of no significance. Munro pointed out these depressing thoughts at the evening meetings he had with the Foundation children. There was really nothing that could be done, other than patiently wait for the next election. He encouraged people to hunker down, fight what rearguard action they could against this monstrous, malevolent, and callous stupidity, and for the young, outside the genius class, to avoid universities and go to technical colleges, learn a skill, and escape into space as soon as they could.

Fortunately, Billy had no interest in space and, in spite of the urging of his supporters, largely left the Prometheus Group alone. Issues of racial and sexual discrimination in the Space Academy were raised, but fortunately, the fact that the Prometheus children were girls and the opacity under which the selection process took place protected them for a while. Eventually, a lawsuit was launched about exclusionary policies. The last thing they wanted were students whose families were trapped in totalitarian regimes and could therefore be coerced into stealing intellectual property. Manon and all other manufacturers had all seen the massive stealing of intellectual property over the last twenty years in spite of the efforts of Elizabeth and Sandra to prevent it and had no wish to facilitate it. They simply delayed the lawsuits in the hope that Billy would only last one term.

Massive quantities of money were given to the usual totally corrupt and ineffective international organizations like the UN. Virtue-signaling speakers were everywhere to make Billy's supporters feel good. With no grasp at all of history, as none of his younger people in the states not controlled by Munro had been taught any in school, and if Billy had personally ever known any history, he ignored it. He gradually got sucked into regional conflicts, which Elizabeth and Sandra had avoided. After all, if one group had been raping, murdering and crucifying an almost identical group for more than a thousand years on the basis of tiny differences in dogma, it makes no sense for onlookers to get involved in the carnage. If, however, one knows nothing about history and is given lavish praise by sycophants who know no better, it is easy to get involved. The old saying that "fools rush in where the wise fear to tread" has not changed in all human history.

Billy and his ranks of ill-informed advisers did just that. They rushed in to "save the children" in an unstable country in the Middle East. The fact that it was the unspeakable in pursuit of the uneatable never seemed to occur to Billy or his European counterparts, who egged him on. At least the existing regime, foul though it may have been to its own people, did not export terror. The insurgents that Billy decided to assist were well-known worldwide terrorists. Even more foolishly than simply throwing treasure down the toilet, he put boots on the ground, sacrificing young American lives to help those who, as all involved in the conflict knew, hated America, and attacked Americans wherever and whenever possible.

The usual cast of idiots around the world, like Beaupre in Canada and the chancellor of Germany and whatever moron was currently running Britain, flooded their own countries with refugees. Few seemed to notice that these refugees were all young single men of fighting age, with no education, no skills, and no concept of Western culture. Most had no connection with the area of conflict, coming from failed states in North Africa. These were people who looked on all unveiled women as prostitutes, who could be assaulted with impunity, and thought that young boys were there to be raped. The Western governments and police forces and especially the judiciary did nothing to counteract these beliefs and, if anything, appeared to pander to it.

Even the women so assaulted did not seem to object. There was the famous story of the German social worker who was raped by three refugees and who apologized publicly to the rapists. There was another famous case in Canada where a Middle Eastern man beat his wife to a pulp with a hockey stick and simply received a caution from the judge, as that was held to be the cultural norm in his own country. Under the guidance and help of Billy, the USA began to go down the same destructive European path; and areas of Chicago, New York, and other northern cities developed the same no-go zones. San Francisco and Los Angeles followed, although in these cities, the Hispanic gangs put up some resistance to that encroachment.

In the states run by Munro, there were no no-go zones. Sexual violence against women and children was taken seriously, despite screams of racial and religious prejudice by the media, universities, and media-talking heads. In his states, women and children were encouraged to defend themselves. The influx of Californian socialists made things difficult, but the local people did their best to fend off these foolish interlopers who, having destroyed their own state, made strenuous efforts to destroy the states they had fled to. "Three strikes and you are out" remained the law, and people were not only allowed to but encouraged to defend themselves.

Various well-known foundations funded by those countries whose finances depended on oil exports were generous donors to some politicians. These, in turn, pushed for vast areas of the US to be designated as wilderness areas, where oil and gas exploration were forbidden. Billy began to close coal and nuclear plants. All plans for new ones were shelved. Federal money for fusion generation ceased. Fortunately, Isis and the bulk of the research on fusion was now being done on Mars, which remained beyond Billy's grasp. No one spoke about this research, and if asked, they simply said that basic research continued.

Fortunately—or unfortunately, depending on one's viewpoint— the "peacekeeping," as Billy liked to call it, or the "save the children" intervention, did not do well. The European allies declined to risk any of their own people or their own funds. Those with newfound military capability, such as Poland and Hungary, refused to take part in what they saw as a pointless exercise in nation building in places where family and tribal loyalties were supreme, with no actual nation to build, no objectives, and no exit strategy. The number of young US men and women killed and mutilated in this pointless exercise continued to grow.

A few observers pointed out that more sexual slavery, rape, murder, and genocide were carried out by the people Billy said they were helping than the so-called enemy. By now, Slavery, for the first time since it was suppressed by the British navy, was openly rather than covertly practiced in the Middle East. Open slavery also came roaring back in North Africa, after Billy's ludicrous so-called Arab Spring, where he did his best to destabilize every state run by the usual dictator. By destroying the dictator running Libya, he opened the gates for all of North and sub-Saharan Africa to flood across the Mediterranean into Europe.

Billy also managed to thrust himself into the turmoil of the Caucasus. Another Chechen war had begun in which Putin, his patience finally exhausted, was pursuing with extreme vigor virtually a scorched-earth policy, and refugees—or what was left of them—were flooding out. As usual, none of the neighboring countries or the major sources of terrorist funding wanted anything to do with these refugees, so by a very circuitous route, they ended up in Europe. Billy began to threaten Putin and moved US troops back into Europe, as the Europeans were simply doing their usual virtue posturing without spending any treasure at all on their own defense. NATO had been abolished as worthless by previous US administrations, but the European version still existed, really on paper only, a superfluity of generals, but there were no troops or warplanes that were capable of flying or pilots who had sufficient training hours in to fly them, even if they had they been available.

This, of course, was hugely expensive. To cover the cost, Billy simply borrowed more money. What was worse was that the US troops who had been moved back into Europe began to experience the same roadside bombing around their main camps in Germany that they had been subjected to in Middle East conflicts, as after all, the same people were now in Germany.

Billy also began to make threats against Hinchcliffe's Legion, who had been progressively freeing Central and South America from one socialist dictatorship after another. Since Billy had entered the scene, Hinchcliffe had carefully done nothing, other than a few cleanup operations against recrudescent socialist terrorists, such as the communist Sender Luminoso, who continued to be funded by various ideological groups in the US, Europe, and the Middle East.

Sweden became the first European country to adopt Sharia law as its primary legal system. The Swedish ideologues had been able to open their borders to such an extent that the refugees had become a flood. The same ideologues managed to change the law such that refugees could vote, which led to a further refugee influx. As these were completely unskilled and usually functionally illiterate, there was no work for them. To pay social benefits, the taxes were raised so high that the few young Swedes who had not been corrupted by decades of socialism, tried to emigrate. The few remaining Swedes who worked only did so out of habit because it no longer actually made any sense to work. The leaders of the country were warned that their borrowing had reached unsupportable levels. Only the EU bureaucrats would lend them money. Thus, the EU became the de facto rulers of Sweden, and all the Chechen refugees were sent there.

Polygamy became the accepted Swedish law. Some Swedish men had banded together to try to protect their women from sexual mistreatment and rape, which was by now customary for any woman found uncovered outside her home. This group gave themselves the fanciful name of the Sons of Thor. The Swedish government was not amused and declared them a terrorist organization, and they were hunted down and jailed by the police. As the normal prisons filled up with migrant criminals and Swedes charged with newly formulated "hate crimes," Swedish nationals were eventually transported to work camps in the north of Sweden, along with all those who objected to the government policies. Like the police in Scotland, the Swedish police put up signs in every public area encouraging people to inform on anyone who said anything that anyone, including the police themselves, could construe as hate speech. As the gulags gradually filled, the populace quickly adapted, learning to say nothing. The migrant religious police also became increasingly active outside their own no-go areas, acting against those who had not yet converted and even against those who had.

In the US, given Billy's copy of the European model of no convictions, all terrorists were labeled as having mental problems and were placed in minimum security facilities until they were "cured," which usually took a very short time. As there were no reprisals, the attacks on Americans abroad continued to escalate, as did the terror attacks at home. All major cities in the US began to sprout bollards to prevent vehicles from being driven into pedestrians on sidewalks. These, of course, were completely ineffectual. The only industry that grew under Billy's regime was the all but useless strip-and-search of anyone but a government official entering a federal building. Following the Swedish and German model in many major cities, it became dangerous for women and children to walk outside after dark. Complaints about this state of affairs were treated as hate speech and were not allowed.

After three years of increasing misery in America, Archie Moore announced that he was running for the presidency. His goal was to reclaim America so that anyone could walk the streets in peace and stop the waste of American life and treasure in a war in the Middle East, which had no beginning, no point, and no end and where all combatants and indeed onlookers cheered on the deaths and mutilations of young Americans.

As the US had a volunteer army, the returning veterans were called baby killers by the Social Justice Warriors, egged on by the media and their university professors. One small collection of troops, who had been caught in an ambush, fought their way out with surprisingly little loss of their own lives. In a major public relations coup, the ambushers then killed numerous women and children from adjacent villages, brought the bodies, and dumped them at the site of the ambush and invited in the world's press to see just how despicable the Americans were. The press failed to mention that some of them had actually been on standby, waiting to be transported to such an event, which they had been promised would occur. Billy made sure that the whole troop was prosecuted and jailed. The media applauded, while Middle America despaired.

Archie Moore had fought Billy on every ill-fated and stupid move down every useless dangerous path, usually to no avail. Mainstream media was dying as a result of their extreme collectivist twisting and warping of all news. As few would accept anything they said seriously, their advertising revenues were falling off, and one newspaper after another closed. In their death spiral, the media became shriller and shriller, espousing one ludicrous position after another. It had reached the stage where the media had effectively declared war on the US.

When Moore stood for president, he was attacked as "this phobe" and "that phobe." He was also attacked by women who accused him of sexual improprieties. Fortunately, Tomiko had foreseen that this was likely to happen and could produce a Praetorian to answer each of these false charges. Eventually, totally fed up, Middle America rose up and elected him president to the anger and despair of the media, the universities, and the political class.

During the campaign, the so-called deep state comprising the FBI, CIA, DOJ, and the rest went to war against Moore, with wiretaps, fraudulent accusations, and all the other machinations of a corrupt government. The favorite trick of the justice department was to accuse one of his supporters of something, anything, and then pile on the charges such that if the judge was not absolutely scrupulously honest, the accused would be jailed for twenty years. Faced with this travesty of justice, there were very few brave souls who tried to fight back, and most admitted to some minor misdemeanors, for which they were jailed.

The mess that Moore faced after the election was monumental and mind-numbing. Fortunately, things had deteriorated to such an extent that the public had given him control of both Houses. He moved swiftly. He began by issuing pardons to those who had been pursued and unjustly convicted by his opponents. He fired the heads of all these utterly corrupt organizations and encouraged criminal charges to be brought against all those involved. He again immediately cut funding to all the corrupt UN and other bodies Billy had supported. Foreign aid stopped immediately. He cut taxes to the income generators and cut corporate tax so that people began to go back to work. Anticipating the demise of Billy, many companies had shipped all their income offshore to prevent it from being stolen by insane taxation. That money came back to the US, and in a surprisingly short time, people began to go back to work.

Moore was still left with the unenviable task of bringing the troops home. He asked his staff for solutions. They came up with the standard US retreat, abandoning all equipment and rescuing the personnel. This had been done before relatively successfully. The despairing photograph of the last helicopter leaving Saigon remained seared into the minds of all who saw it, emblematic of America's failure in that futile venture. Moore, however, did not want to abandon equipment, which had cost millions of dollars and would either be used against the US directly or be sold to the enemies of the US to copy.

The other question was how to get out geographically? There were three choices, none of which were desirable: the Persian Gulf, the Mediterranean Sea, or the Black Sea. Xenophon, in a similar situation more than two thousand years ago, had taken his ten thousand Greeks out via the Black Sea. But given the current hostility of Turkey due to the rise of the Caliph Ardogan with potential problems getting through the Bosporus, which was possible, but a dangerously unpredictable option. Going through the Gulf left them vulnerable to Iran, who had numerous small motorboats staffed by shaheeds or suicide bombers. The navy was equipped for a major sea battle but had little defenses against such mosquito-bite attacks, in spite of the success of such an attack years before. The wrangling among the staff went on and on until Moore became fed up with the pessimism and indecision. He called in Star, who was the one person he knew personally, who was by now a brigadier.

She put the situation succinctly. Going any other way but the Gulf meant crossing many miles of terrain not only filled with hostiles, who were manageable, but the terrain itself, which was so difficult they would inevitably lose vehicles to attrition breakdown. Unless they were prepared to accept a considerable loss of life and ships to the Iranian suicide bombers, they would have to stop Iran.

This would effectively mean war. She pointed out what Moore knew to be true that one cannot sign any sort of treaty with a country whose whole political and religious belief system is predicated on lying to people not of their group. Treaties with people like that, as always, had no meaning and would be ignored the moment they were signed. Star talked to Hinchliffe, who had been studying the situation with interest, as it was one of the classic war games. Hinchcliffe reinforced the obvious: the Persian Gulf made most sense, but the munitions would have to be assembled for an all-out strike against Iran when the first suicide motorboat hit an American ship. All shipping other than tankers would have to be warned to stay out of the Gulf on pain of immediate destruction. Recognizing that the mullahs in Iran would ignore warnings and simply assume Western posturing, nonetheless, they would have to be warned that there would be serious consequences if they failed to keep their suicide bombers in check.

Faced with a no-win situation, Moore agreed to give Star authority to do whatever she felt necessary, short of nuclear warfare. As this was simply a retreat, he did not feel any need to discuss it with Congress, as that would be a meaningless and futile exercise. He ignored Europe. After taking over, Star began to consolidate the forces for retreat and build backup. With the first troop ships and transports and aircraft, she repatriated all noncombatants and all nonmilitary equipment. She then began to fall back on Kuwait. Her troops were harassed by a ragtag bunch of terrorists. After the first suicide bomber ran into a vehicle on the road, she announced that any civilian seen near the road she was retreating down would be shot on sight. Of course, this meant that the Iranian clerics made sure that there were women and children strapped into suicide vests and forced onto the road, and the media were encouraged to view the carnage. Where American troops did not kill enough women and children, the clerics ordered their own troops to do it and blame the Americans.

Some of the so-called insurgents producing harassing fire were captured. They turned out to be regular Iranian troops, specifically Artesh. Star had about a third of her forces embarked when the Iranians released their suicide boats. Most were blown out of the water, as the order was to destroy on sight, and patrolling aircraft and satellites identified many.

Some, however, were able to go through to damage the transports. Star knew if she did nothing, her losses would be horrendous, with attacks not only from the suicide boats but also from the regular Iranian army disguised as insurgents. She felt she had no alternative but to pull a Sir John Moore, the commander of a British Expeditionary Force who had been retreating to Corunna in Spain, pursued by the French army. He had turned back and inflicted a defeat on the French of sufficient magnitude that his own troops had time to escape by sea.

Star turned back and unleashed the US forces. Since the WWII, the US troops had been hamstrung by rules of engagement, increasingly overseen by lawyers sitting in comfortable air-conditioned offices in the US. Star indicated her only rule was to kill all combatants. She set in motion a lightning attack that outflanked the Iranian army and swept in behind them. She then closed in on the doomed forces and annihilated them. An even wider encircling sweep carried out by Special Forces in the desert trapped the remaining insurgents. Surrender was not an option. The suicide boats were taken out by US warships, shelling the boats in every town and village along the sea route, and flying gunships destroyed all inshore shipping.

The clerics responded by sending more troops to close the Gulf. These clerics, to whom human life meant nothing, were the same people who had sent in children to run over the minefields during the Iranian war with Saddam. Star knew that there was no sense in talking to these people. She bombed Tehran using daisy cutters, enormous fuel air bombs, which almost completely annihilated the clerics in command. Not all, of course, as some, who had less interest in meeting their allotted virgins in Paradise, had felt that this might happen and had hidden away in some spider hole until the conflict was over. She also bombed the Quds Forces in their barracks. Their air force was destroyed. She used bunker busters to get down to and destroy their nuclear lairs hidden deep underground. This required repeated bombing of the same craters to get deep enough. She bombed every seaport that showed activity. Any sign of significant military aggregation brought a cruise missile.

The clerics had been accustomed to cheating, lying, and twisting the tiger's tail. It never seemed to have occurred to them that the tiger would unleash his full force against them. Having smashed them flat, in the ensuing shocked stillness, Star quietly embarked all her remaining troops and material and sailed back into the expected storm of criticism from the mainstream media. The European governments, now run by the EU, of course demanded punishment for what had been done. Moore, in a press conference, simply told the Europeans that from now on, they could defend themselves and brought home all the US forces that Billy had placed in Europe.

Disdainfully, he refused to throw Star to the wolves and instead made her head of the Joint Chiefs of Staff. He met with Putin and reinstated Sandra's doctrine that Russia should leave the Baltic states—Hungary, Czech Republic, and Poland—alone. The US had no other interest in Europe. By simply facing down the domestic opposition and apologizing for nothing, he made criticism go away.

Of course, the Iranian problem was not solved. Individual freedom, or the concept of the individual as an individual, as always seemed and was a completely alien concept not just in Iran but throughout the whole Middle East. The clerics, whose numbers seemed inexhaustible, remained in control. They commanded the women to have more babies to make up for their crippled military. The docile population responded. Moore maintained strict sanctions, but the Europeans made strenuous attempts to circumvent these. The Iranian nuclear program was reactivated, in spite of the desperate economic situation of the populace. The clerics would rather fund foreign terrorism and nuclear weapons than feed their own children. Star pointed out to Moore that given the size of the country and the openness of the population to brainwashing, nuclear war, with the complete annihilation of Iran, would likely eventually be necessary, as the populace gave no sign that they would ever voluntarily throw off the yoke of the clerics or even that they saw it as a yoke.

CHAPTER 10

Sweet Wolf

She lay there, trying to get herself into the mood as he pounded away on top of her. She had initially welcomed his stroking and his kissing and his penetration, but then it had inexplicably gone away, and she just wished it was over. He grunted, crammed himself deep into her, and spasmed. She let him lay there for a minute and then rolled him off.

"That was good," she said, "but now I have to get some work done. We will get together some other time." *Like never again,* she thought.

Understanding dismissal when he heard it, he dressed and left, thanking her as he did so and expressing hope that she had had a good time. After showering, she donned a robe and sat down at her computer. She turned it on and then simply stared at it. Then she got up, found a bottle, and poured herself a shot of Suntory, and sat and looked at the screen without actually seeing anything.

What am I going to do? she thought. *My life is over.*

She closed her eyes, leaned back in her chair, and thought of the road she had traveled. Sweet Wolf's term of office as prime minister of Japan was coming to a close. She was somewhat sad, but all things come to an end. She had done what she had plotted to do when she was very young. Clawing her way up the ladder to the pinnacle was exhilarating. The time she had spent in Alaska with that old man, Running Bear, had been crucial. He had seen through her and had seen the wolf under the sweetness, but he had loved her anyway and had helped smooth the way for her success.

Her drive had pushed her into assistant secretary of state of the US, the most powerful country in the world. Being Japanese-born, she could never be president, but it was clear to all that had she been native born, she would have been a contender. She wanted it all, and she had married Munro, not for love; about that, they had never been under any illusion, but for a child. She wanted the experience of having a child but did not want the responsibility of looking after it, of being a full-time mother. She knew Munro could and would, had been doing so for years with the genius girls they had found for the Prometheus Project. And he was great breeding stock, as she had joked with Don Pedro, who had bred his own daughter with Munro for the same reason. All it had taken was a few months out of her life, and she actually quite liked her daughter, who was growing up and was very respectful of her. Munro had seen to that. He encouraged Sweet Wolf's child to admire, respect, and love her as much as she could, given her mother's infrequent visits.

She found it strange that these gaijin men of the Prometheus Project knew her for what she was and were under no illusions but liked her anyway. They not only recognized it—the hardness, the thrusting ambition—but they applauded it. They encouraged her individuality and her single-minded drive. They had given her all she had asked. Was that love? What was love? *Who knows, who cares? I am turning into some idiot philosopher.*

Munro had admired her ferocity and her driving ambition and never laughed at her. He had guided her in tamping down her fires, keeping them hidden. Sex with him had been good, but their pillow talk was of things other than love. She had never felt the fierce longing for a man, which possessed Tomiko, who had given Munro to her in a fit of black despair, which had since passed; and now Tomiko and Munro continued to spend as much time together as their jobs allowed. Sweet Wolf really did not understand that attraction. It was not as if they had not played around with other people over the years. *Maybe I should look for another serious man,* she thought. *Or maybe not. Maybe there is someone out there waiting to be found.*

Japan had always been her goal. Those who laughed at her as a child did not laugh now. She had shown them all. She was so far above she could not remember the names of her tormentors. For six years now, she had associated with the rulers of the world and had despised almost all of them. She thought they were mostly sleazy, self-important charlatans. But it was not clear what she should do now. If she stayed in Japan, she would be subordinate to the next prime minister, but where to go? Maybe space.

Mars was opening up, but that was still hard grunt work for pioneers. Perhaps if she were twenty years younger, carving out an empire in the new world might have been appealing, and maybe it still was. Whatever she did, or wherever she went, she wanted to be in charge.

Munro had suggested that maybe she could take over as the head of what they grandiloquently called Earth Base One. It was still fairly primitive, really only a launching and landing pad for shuttles taking those leaving for the moon or Mars up to orbit, where they would load onto the ships that would take them onward. If she could build it into a true Earth base, then maybe it would become semiautonomous. To date, the Prometheus Group had been able to avoid takeover by the US government, but Munro and the others were getting old, and young blood would be necessary to fight off these useless grasping politicians, who would inevitably ruin everything.

She could always accept some job at the UN but had no desire whatsoever to spend time with those greasy buffoons, wandering around with their hands out, looking for bribes. Eventually, she could think of nothing else that currently interested her, so she accepted Munro's offer. The base was reasonably close to the Apache reservation, with which she still had this childhood romantic fantasy. All through her other accomplishments, including being prime minister of Japan, she had remained, through various means, their chief financial officer; and in consequence, they had done extremely well. Earth Base One was fenced, but the fence was very extensive. She had secured employment for some of the young Apache men to provide casual security for the base with long-range patrols in the surrounding desert to discourage strangers, who could be identified by circling drones. If there were any concerns, the strangers were really discouraged.

Anyway, she would try Earth Base for a while. Munro, she was certain, ultimately wanted her to run Mars Base, as he did not want Isis, the brilliant physicist, burdened with administration. Ryoko knew Munro's mind, and what he really wanted was having the Wolf in charge. He wanted Mars protected from what he assumed would be the panic-stricken flood of earthlings when the West fell apart and civilization collapsed. It was not something she liked to think about, but he was obviously correct that the light was dying out in the West. Even in her own Japan, the lack of babies was a concern for the future. The Dark Ages were returning.

She had never asked but was pretty certain that Mars was already weaponized as Quiet Bear, President Sandra's former head of security, had been there for some time and continued to oversee things from the twin moons, where he preferred to live with reduced gravity. She could not imagine that someone as security conscious as Quiet Bear would not be prepared. Even Moon Base One, with its monstrous maglev rail gun, which was used to send materials and shuttles into Earth and Mars orbit, could handle anything Earth could throw at it simply with kinetic weapons. She toyed with the idea of taking over Moon Base. Two or three fairly large rocks dropped from space on a couple of Middle East cities would give Earth peace for a few generations. It surprised her that no one seemed to have the will to do so. If she got bored, maybe she would do that. If she did, how would history define her? Saint or sinner? That would be up to future generations to decide.

For her successor, she really did not want anyone mismanaging the economy she had labored over. Japan was out of its malaise, and she wanted it to stay that way. She had made it much more affordable to have children, and she did not want that changed. Her best option was Tomiko-san, who was not any sort of idealist or even a truly creative thinker, and therefore would not reverse any of the policies she had brought in, which had finally overcome the so-called lost decade, which was a lot longer than a decade. Japan was doing well, and Sweet Wolf wanted it to stay that way so that her legacy would, in the future, be looked back on as being crucial. If she controlled Earth Base, she could push more Japanese into space. Expand or die, she believed. Tomiko-san was no economist, and Sweet Wolf was sure that her advice would be taken, if she felt it necessary to offer it. The path she had charted for the future would be fairly easy to follow. The problem would be to get Tomiko-san accepted by the Japanese people.

A significant drawback was Tomiko's numerous non-Japanese activities. On the plus side, she had been Olympic pistol champion, and the teams she had led had dominated the 25m pistol shot, and still did, a source of considerable pride for the Japanese people. She was the only Japanese woman recognized as being a movie star in the West, albeit now a somewhat senior one. That was maybe a plus with the women and maybe a negative with the men. There were very few country leaders who had multiple movies showing her body. But it was a good body and never completely naked, so perhaps that was a plus, as how many other country leaders could say that?

She had been chief of police for many years, with no scandals at all and no terrorist attacks, which plagued the West; and for the last few years, she had occupied a respectable position in politics, being foreign minister, among other roles, so she knew the outside world. On the negative side, she was still one of the leaders of the Praetorian Protection Agency, although she herself had not been active for some time. But there were all these videos going about of Tomiko-san shooting people. On the plus side, the people she had killed were regarded by the Japanese as terrorists, so nobody really cared.

The main problem that Ryoko saw was that she was still seen as being the girlfriend of her own ex-husband, Munro. This was a sticking point. She did not see the people of Japan, especially the men, voting for a woman who was openly consorting with a Western man. That would have to stop. She thought that Tomiko-san had enough sense of duty and self-sacrifice to recognize this and terminate the relationship. Having thought things through, she gave Tomiko an ultimatum. She would have to speak to Munro. That relationship would have to end. She was sure that both Tomiko and Munro, being realists, had always known that; and she was sure they would accept it, however reluctantly. Her assessment was correct.

Ryoko did succeed in getting Tomiko elected as prime minister of Japan, against considerable opposition. After that triumph, she reluctantly accepted the job of running Earth Base One. At least everyone would be calling her Sweet Wolf again, the name that Running Bear had given her years ago when he had secretly adopted her. In Japan, she had always been called by her birth name, Ryoko.

Earth Base Two would have to be built, as they would ultimately become too busy for one base to handle everything, and she was concerned about a sneak attack from the terrorist-supporting countries, who were in the process of and would progressively lose their financial importance. Maybe China would fund a slap at them, although she felt this was not a big risk, as unlike the ideologically driven Middle East, the Chinese government could work out how much they would lose if it came to a nuclear war. Sweet Wolf, when she was president, anticipating potential trouble from China, had heavily armed Japan with nuclear weapons, the possession of which she and her government had always halfheartedly denied. The two terrorist-funding countries really did not seem to care how much of their own population would die in a war, as they felt they could rebreed quickly enough.

Maybe she could build a base in Mexico, but how stable that would be after La Contessa inevitably stepped down was not clear. Maybe the corruption was gone permanently, or maybe it would creep back in again. From the physics of the shuttle launch viewpoint, the optimal place would be North Africa, close to the equator, but those countries were all disaster areas, mired in the Dark Ages to which their clerics had returned them after a very brief flowering of their civilization. Almost one thousand years ago, they turned their backs on Averroes and the enlightenment. This medieval madness, which she had had to educate herself about when she was president of Japan, was not likely to change. Incomprehensible as that might be to anyone capable of independent thought, but it was reality. The bushmen in Australia had had a static Stone Age culture for several thousand years, and the Middle East culture itself had produced no significant advances since Ibn Rushd had been proscribed and his books burned in 1195, when they decided to abandon reason for faith. Thank God for Thomas Aquinas, Duns Scotus, and Martin Luther, who had taken Christianity in the other direction. Faith-based encouragement of familial inbreeding also likely played a significant role in the intellectual stasis or decline.

Egypt was coming out of its long nightmare. Perhaps, she thought, it was not a nightmare for those who lived inside it. She had heard the average IQ in the Middle East was only 85, so perhaps stagnation and absence of independent thought was what the people really wanted. Perhaps the lack of any necessity to think in an abstract sense or indeed to think any independent thought at all was deeply satisfying. Whatever the cause, building a base amid such a population was unthinkable. Even the current genetics of Egypt, despite its long and illustrious history, made it not likely that the country could be used as a base, at least in the near future.

Maybe she could build a base on an equatorial island in the Pacific, but there were real drawbacks, including isolation, humidity, and submarines. Pro tem, she decided to accept the position at Earth Base One. Maybe if she got bored, Mars Base might be acceptable, recognizing that with present technology and cost, it was still a one-way trip.

Following the handover of power to Tomiko, Ryoko moved to the US to live on the base. The hustle and bustle of busy, clever, driving people going places enthralled her. Cadets from the Space Academy and girls from the Prometheus Group were a constant feature as they sought and did internships. The emigrants were still mostly from the Academy, but there was an increasing demand from Mars for various specialists. They were constantly building more shuttles to lift people into Earth orbit on a regular basis, to be loaded onto ships traveling out to the moon and Mars. The numbers made it more difficult to ensure really deep background checks of the emigrants. She was sure the psychologists were catching the absolutely crazed ideologues and psychopaths and, the Prometheus Group hoped, most of the less suitable overly empathetic.

Munro's belief was that when the civilization on Earth collapsed; the various government officials would try to flee to space. Feelings of empathy or not, that could not be allowed to happen, as the colonies would be overrun and fail. He would quote the inevitable poem,

> Here is neither hate, nor haste, nor anger
> Peal the trumpets.
> Pardon for their penitence
> Or pity for their fall.

The thoughtless buffoons who had destroyed the most glorious civilization the world had ever seen could not be allowed to destroy a new one.

Every employee at the base was also screened carefully, but this had to be done to some extent surreptitiously, due to the increasing political pressure for equity and inclusivity. There was always the worry about someone being tempted by money or ideology to steal intellectual property or plant a bomb. Sweet Wolf was not at all keen on secret police and constant surveillance, but to some extent, she had little option.

Once in a while, as it had been from the start, they would find a traitor. Maybe *traitor* was not exactly the correct name, but it was an accurate enough description. The question was what to do with them when they were identified? It made little sense to simply dismiss them, as there would be complaints about wrongful dismissal and discrimination. Criminal charges would be even worse.

The judges in Texas, Arizona, and New Mexico were probably not too bad, but no one could guarantee that some judicial ideologue would not be found hiding further up the legal appeals chain. There would be endless negative publicity from the legacy media, which would encourage and lead to increased demands for political and bureaucratic oversight.

She faced the problem realistically. Ultimately, there was one answer, an accident or a disappearance. Any accident could not be around or associated with the Base, as they wanted no possible connection to be drawn. Sometimes a quiet investigation of the family or acquaintances found terrorist cells. Again, the question about what to do about that remained unclear. Given the current political climate, such cells were usually passed over by the police, with the media colluding, arguing that the potential or actual terrorist was mentally disturbed and the family and friends had no idea about the planned destruction. That anyone could swallow that nonsense without laughing out loud seemed absurd. Reporting it to the deep state, such as Homeland Security, the FBI, and other organizations, was also a worthless exercise, considering the number of terrorist attacks carried out by those who had already been reported to but ignored by these authorities. The upper levels of these bureaucracies were completely worthless, as had been discovered by both Elizabeth and Sandra. This, of course, was or should be no surprise. They were, after all, the same people who ran the post office and selected people who thought and acted just as they did.

Producing a secret police force was not what she wanted to do. An evaluating branch already existed and would have to be expanded somewhat, but what to do about a wet division? She knew that the Praetorian organization did not want to be involved in this, and Hinchcliffe pointed out that her Legion were soldiers, not executioners. There were other questions, not only operational, but also the scope of action, whether it would be purely national or international.

None of these deliberations could be written down or communicated by anything other than word of mouth, and to whom? Sweet Wolf recognized that while everyone saw the problem, they would really prefer to avoid being involved in the solution. Reluctantly, therefore she realized that, as base commander, it was her problem; and she would have to solve it without much help—in fact, in secret. If she did this and if it were found out, she would be an outlaw and probably have to flee to Mars or else commit seppuku. The only ones she felt she could talk this over with were Manon and Munro. So she flew to Luxembourg.

She had known Manon when she was growing up and had always enjoyed spending time with that hard, cynical woman. Manon's advice was always appreciated on a range of issues. Once when she was very young and not too clear about Western values, she had told Manon that the Christian Bible had said to "return good for evil." Manon, quoting someone named Vanbrugh, sniffed and said that that must have been a mistake in translation. When she became the prime minister of Japan, she had had to distance herself, at least publicly, from Manon; but now that burden had been lifted from her shoulders.

Manon was waiting for her in her office, pleased to see one of her very successful protégés. As Sweet Wolf would not tell her on the telephone why she was visiting, Manon was fairly certain she already knew. After greeting her, she raised her eyebrows in questioning, "Security issues?"

"*Hai!* Can we speak safely?"

Manon rose and opened a door to an adjacent room. Inside was a very large metal box structure. They entered a door in the metal mesh box, and as they stepped into it, the floor moved slightly.

"A Faraday room?"

"Yes, no electronic transmissions. Also, on a rubber bumper to prevent vibration detection. One of the visiting Foundation girls built it for me. It is far more security than I need, but it certainly mightily impresses visitors. This is as secure as it gets."

"But it cannot be that secure. The people would have to be naked."

"Even then, I am sure you could put a recording bug in a tooth, so nothing is completely safe, ever."

"As you know, I have accepted the job as head of Earth Base One. I have some security, but I have the problem of enforcement. Dismissal of suspects leaves them free, charges mean an open trial—"

"So they must disappear?"

"Yes, but how and who, and who funds? I must ensure that nothing can be traced back to the Base. Whoever does it, must be prepared to leave for Mars or commit seppuku. No stories, no memoirs. The Foundation girls have always whispered about Manon not being someone to annoy."

"Yes, whispered, rumored, but not a trace of evidence. *Rien de rien.* Initially, I did it myself, but years ago, when Munro married Kodama, her father sent two wolves with her to protect her. One wolf turned out to be a man of God. The other was Joshi, the ninja, who took care of my little problems when they came along. He is now too old, and I am concerned about facial recognition technology in Europe, so he must not come back here. He recruits people for me when required. They are mostly young Japanese policewoman."

"No, surely not the Praetorians?"

"You do not need to know the details of this. The Praetorian leaders, especially Tomiko-san, do not know of this activity, and must not know, at least officially. Most girls do just one or two executions, and then never again. Perhaps for them, it is a rite of passage, an initiation into a secret subgroup of the Praetorians. One girl, who has been involved several times, does it to overcome her fear, as she was shot once. In reality, there are very few cases. I have it done only for business reasons. Many of these awful European politicians should perhaps be executed, but that is not my role, and no matter how tempting, it should not be your role. If Tomiko wants to get rid of some dreadful world leader, then she should use Japanese security. You are no longer the leader of Japan. You, we, must remain separate from issues of state."

"I agree. How do we coordinate?"

"You identify. Then have someone bring me the file or, better still, bring it yourself, so there is no chain to follow, nothing to back-check. Nothing on paper. Nothing on email. I will make the arrangements and bury the costs. You never need know. Tell only me. Teresa, my deputy, of course suspects, but does not ask. She will have to know when I die or become incapacitated, but not before. She already has enough on her shoulders, without taking the guilt of this."

"So this will be between us?"

"Yes, but you will have to tell Munro. He has been worried about this since the inception of the Prometheus Project. Maybe he has his own enforcer. I sometimes wonder about Pedro Morales, the border security man who has had a very close relationship with Munro for a very long time. Or maybe one of the other young Mexicans who work for him. It is not likely he has secrets from me, but one never knows."

Having resolved the issue as well as she could, Sweet Wolf flew back to Arizona and met Munro at the ranch. To ensure their conversation was absolutely private, they walked up the hill behind the ranch to the Shinto shrine, which Munro had built years ago for Tomiko. Sweet Wolf had once been married to Munro for a couple of years and had a child with him while she was assistant secretary of state for the US, before returning to Japan to begin a political career. She had climbed that path with him many times before.

This time, she noted at the start of the path a couple of white marble pillars bearing a large, polished black-and-white marble ball made into the

Daoist symbol, with the white serpent of order with the black eye of chaos embracing the black serpent of chaos with the white eye of order.

"This is new since I was last here, yin and yang."

"Yes. I think it is good for the children, for all of us, to consider the Daoist way, to walk the line between order and chaos."

"And you think these kids understand?"

"Understand? These kids are so smart they probably have a mathematical formula for it."

"You are still bringing in these little kids from all over the world?"

"Yes. We could do with finding a lot more, as we are losing them to space as soon as they grow up. Now that we also have all these incredibly bright boys at the Space Academy, the girls find intellectually equal soulmates pretty quickly. They are mostly very pessimistic about the future of Earth. They see nothing but impending catastrophe and want out of it."

"They really all feel that way?"

"Not all. Some little kids think like Hinchcliffe, that they can slay the dragon of chaos. But these kids are a little scary. They are not talking about peace on earth and good will toward all men. Anyway, was your meeting with Manon satisfactory?"

"You knew?"

"We talk. Not as much as I would like. I wish she was here, but there is no way she is going to move, and even with Maria Martens and the girls running things here for me, I can only spend so much time in Europe."

"She always was your mistress? For years, wasn't it?"

"For years, yes. She was my rock in hard times, my Roxelana, my Theodora. I was dependent on her. But you have the relationship wrong. I was her suitor. I would have married her if she had let me."

"You asked?"

"Several times, but she always said no, that the age difference was too much and too many people knew too much about her."

"So you married Kodama instead?"

"Not instead. I don't think of Kodama that way. 'Tread softly, for you tread on my dreams.'" His voice suddenly turned hoarse. "God, Sweet Wolf, I still miss Kodama. Jesus, I miss her so much. The empty years." There were tears in his eyes and a catch in his voice. "She promised that we would meet again, another time, another place."

His voice was breaking. "'I trace the rainbow through the rain, and feel the promise is not vain, that morn shall tearless be.' Some part of me hopes to waken up some morning and find she is beside me again." He sniffed and wiped his eyes. "I am sorry, Sweet Wolf. I don't think of it often, but the hurt has never gone away."

"You still have Elizabeth and Tomiko."

"God, life is so complicated. Tomiko is such a traditional woman of duty and honor that I will have to stay away from her while she runs Japan. And Elizabeth. Well, what you see is what you get. 'Whiskey, cigarettes and wild, wild women.' But you," he said in Japanese, "how about you, Ryoko?"

They continued walking up the hill, talking. They went through the torii gate at the top and both prayed at the Shinto shrine.

"You are Shinto now?"

"I admire God in many forms. Shinto is good enough. But come and see what is new."

He led her down a path that wound around the crown of the hill to where it overlooked the valley. Looking west, a shallow cave had been hollowed out of the side of the hill. It had a platform with a large seated Buddha on one side and a bench beside it.

"Because I cannot go to the big Buddha at Kamakura, I have brought Kamakura here. I sometimes bring some of the little kids up here. Some of them like to sit on Buddha's lap while we talk. They are so clever and so much fun. Hinchcliffe thought that I made too tempting a target sitting beside the torii gate at the top of the hill. She felt that even a poor sniper could make that shot. Here, it is a little more difficult."

He opened the door to a small cupboard high up on the back wall of the cave.

"A drink? Some sake? I have not found it to spoil much, but it is not the best quality. Or some scotch or Jack or Suntory. They keep forever."

"No, nothing. Well, I am in America, so maybe a little Jack."

He opened a bottle and wiped two shot glasses, stored the wall cupboard, filled them, and sat on the bench beside her.

"*Kanpai* or, better, *otsukaresama desu.*"

They clicked glasses and drank.

"To the future, I suppose. What is your future, Sweet Wolf?"

"I don't know. I am unsettled. I will stay and run Earth Base One for a while. I know you want me to take over Mars, and someday, maybe I will, but not just yet. I have never felt at a loose end before. Maybe I am depressed since my time as prime minister of Japan is over. Maybe you should cheer me up."

"Me? There are lots of young strong men out there who would give their eye teeth to cheer you up, Sweet Wolf."

"I know. When I wear a short skirt, guys still notice. The last one I had on top of me was giving it to me as hard as he could, poor man, when I just lost interest. That's pretty unusual for me."

"The poor chap. That would probably make him impotent for life."

"Oh, no. I made some appropriate noises of appreciation."

"That was awfully kind of you, Sweet Wolf. We men need so little approval, which is good, because the average guy gets almost none. As Robert Service said about how men think of women,

> 'And they were so far above,
> But I'd gladly have gone to the gallows
> For one little look of love.'"

"You feeling underappreciated, Munro? Do I need to tell you that you are a big, strong man and I want you? We used to have fun together. I still remember the first night I seduced you. Hinchcliffe was so jealous."

"Hinchcliffe jealous? She was only a child."

"Blind man! Hinchcliffe was never a child. Where is she now? Off conquering some other part of South America and raising the Munro banner?"

"Jesus, Sweet Wolf. Don't ever even think that. My job is to save civilization. The West is only part of that. Buddhism, Hinduism, that's all fine. There are only two foul ideologies that threaten this world."

"Yes, and I know what they are. Give me Hinchcliffe and that other woman, the colored girl who won the Medal of Honor, and I'll save the world, or at least Mars."

"Star! Yes, you three could hold The Wall."

"What is this wall you keep talking about? That ineffectual Wall of China?"

"No. I mean the wall the Romans built to keep my people out of their empire."

"So you were savages. I have seen videos of your fights, Munro. You still are a savage. Beating up on these poor guys in the ring"

"Just trying to stay alive."

"Anyway, Munro, I remember that first night with you. In fact, I am getting horny just remembering. I have been telling Tomiko that she must marry a Japanese man to make the people happy so she will not be coming for you for about another six years. That is a long time to wait. So come to bed. Take a Viagra or two, and let's remember old times. Tell me I am still the youngest, smartest, most beautiful woman in all the world."

"Sweet Wolf, this was not intended to be a seduction."

"I know. I did not plan it either, but it has happened. Finish that drink and come with me now, former husband." She leaned over and kissed him. She was, as always, irresistible. He took her in his arms, stroking her hair. She was as slim, vibrant, and desirable as ever.

"Sweet Wolf, you are that young and smart and beautiful and utterly ruthless, as you have always been. I only hope that age and nature will allow me to give you what you want."

"Viagra, and I will see to that. Prepare for a long night."

"If you stay here, there will be ample young guys in the Space Academy. As they are almost all destined for space, it would be largely *ave atque vale*—hail and farewell."

"Unless I go to Mars."

"There would be suitors lined up around the planet."

"Perhaps I should have one more kid before I go?"

"Jesus, if it were to be known that I was the father, it would embarrass Tomiko. She would look like an abandoned woman. I could not do that to her."

Mindful that Tomiko was the woman he longed for, Sweet Wolf avoided any emotional involvement with Munro, as she did not want to produce any animosity. In any case, while she liked Munro, she was not in love with him, whatever that meant, or indeed with anyone else. Running Earth Base One gave her ample exposure to young, single, vibrant men who were moving on, so she did not lack for male companionship.

She was at her desk one day when one of her not-so-undercover policemen brought her a disturbing file. A young scientist, more of a technician than a scientist, had been quite vocal about various social ills he perceived. He had begun to voice these attitudes about six months after he arrived. No one thought much about it, other than thinking he was not too smart and needed to grow up. Then he suddenly stopped talking about the things he had been very vocal about. Everyone in EB1, as they called Earth Base, knew and was concerned about possible suicide bombers and fanatic assassins, which was increasingly in the news from Europe. One of his coworkers thought such a change of heart unusual, and while he was having a drink at a bar, he happened to casually mention it to a security woman he knew.

Security had casually investigated it, initially thinking nothing, but then noticing trips to the big city, which was not usual behavior of the EB1 scientists. They put a tracer on him and found a cell of presumed radicals. They then put a bug on him and listened. They found the usual extremely vocal threats of violence and unworkable plans to blow up the Statue of Liberty, planes, etc. Clearly, they were dealing with mostly upper-middle class, somewhat radicalized university useful idiots, but even idiots can do real damage; and there was one in the group who maybe was serious. No acts of terror had actually been committed, but they were certainly being talked about, especially putting a bomb on one of the space shuttles.

Sweet Wolf thought about it for a while. This was exactly the situation she had known she would eventually have to face. Nothing illegal had been done. A report to the deep state like the FBI would produce no response from these utter incompetents. Even if they wanted to do something, the bumbling bureaucrat lawyers looking over their shoulders would not allow any action. She had not found her own people in Japan much better, as evidenced by the failure to follow up on tips, leading to the nerve gas attack on the Tokyo subway.

She saw no alternative, so she took the file, flew to Europe, and talked to Manon. While in Europe, she took the opportunity to visit Sheila MacDonald in Paris and La Marquesa in Madrid to encourage them to encourage more bright young men and women to consider emigrating to Mars—the high frontier, as the Prometheus Group called it. They wanted more genetic diversity in space.

She heard nothing further, but a few weeks later, she got the sad news that her problem had been the tragic fatal victim of a mugging in New York. The mugger was never identified. A person, perhaps a woman, had been seen leaving the scene. A few months after that, there was an obscure report of an explosion in the basement of a house on the outskirts of New York. There had been a meeting or a party of some sort. There were no survivors. Sweet Wolf sighed. That was one problem solved, but inevitably, there would be others. She just hoped that any attack could be forestalled.

CHAPTER 11

Think of Me Now and Then

Munro had never been under any illusion. He knew if Tomiko was to run for prime minister of Japan that they would have to say goodbye. He had, after all, briefly been married to Ryoko, who had been called Sweet Wolf for a reason by Running Bear years ago. She had never made any secret of her ambition or his role in her life. He was to be the father and caregiver of the child she wanted but would always remain on the periphery, never central.

This had never bothered Munro. He enjoyed the company of hard, driven women like Sweet Wolf. Time with them might be short, but it was usually intense. To expect a deep emotional attachment from someone like that was completely unrealistic. Occasionally it could happen. He felt a strange, elastic but unbreakable bond with his former wife, Elizabeth. The fact that she showed her reciprocal love only intermittently came with the territory. That was part of the package. Either accept it or reject it, but don't expect it to metamorphose into a new package.

But on this issue, history and culture were clear. There was no way the Japanese people would elect someone who was emotionally involved with and therefore potentially influenced by a non-Japanese. The interests and values of Japan must remain paramount, and to ensure that, it must remain in the hands of Japanese. There was no desire whatsoever to dilute their own culture, which they found perfectly acceptable.

The Japanese regarded the West's fascination with multiculturalism with horror as slow-motion cultural suicide. Like carrying out a life-or-death experiment on your own child without a clue as to the final outcome. It was obvious, therefore, that at a reasonable time before the election date, Tomiko would have to publicly separate from him. The most obvious way for her to do that was to marry a Japanese man. He himself could always marry another woman, but then Tomiko might be seen as a weak victim, and who would want to be led by a victim? He had been hinting these thoughts to Tomiko when it became obvious she would enter political life, but she did not seem to want to think about it.

After the meeting with Sweet Wolf, Tomiko phoned him and asked him to come to Japan to meet with her. He slipped into Japan with no fanfare, and they met at his son Tall Bear's house in Tokyo. She led him to the small exquisite garden where they walked and talked.

"Sweet Wolf has given me an ultimatum."

"That you must stop seeing me. I have been expecting that."

She stopped and looked up at him. "You knew?"

"I always knew. I was married to Sweet Wolf. You cannot be associated with a gaijin and expect to run Japan. The people will not accept it."

"This bothers you?"

"It breaks my heart. But I knew, when a determined young woman came to me and gave me the children she loved, that she would pursue her dreams. The end of that road was inevitable."

"All these years, you knew?"

"Yes. Heidegger may be right that we should ignore what others think of us, but not in Japanese politics."

"And that did not bother you?"

"We don't get out of this life alive. Two thousand five hundred years ago, Heraclitus said, 'All things flow, nothing abides.' Nothing is forever. The best you can hope for are hours of happiness and moments of bliss." He put his hands on her shoulders, looking down at her. There were tears in his eyes. "The times we spent together were magical and will live in my dreams forever."

"Like the times with Kodama, Manon, and Elizabeth?"

"The three loves of my life. Yes. My loves and my sorrow."

"And me?"

"You know how I feel for you, how I have felt for you all these years. We are one blood, you and me. But I cannot and will not ask you to sacrifice your manifest destiny for my hurt feelings. You were born to be one of the great ones of this world. There may be pain and suffering, but it is your duty to take your country in your strong hands and guide it through the bad times that are coming."

"Bad times?"

"Europe is dying. A power struggle is inevitable. Civil war will come. How bad it will get, I do not know, and it is not at all clear who will win."

"And you want me?"

"To stay out of it. The foolishness of Europe is their problem, not that of Japan."

"And us?"

"Tomiko, thirty years or more ago, I watched a Japanese woman whom I thought I loved more than life itself walk away from me, and my heart broke. I am now about to watch another." His voice was hoarse. "God help us, we have no other choice. You will have to find a Japanese man for a husband."

She put her arms around him. There were tears in her eyes.

"Do you remember the song from that very old Dr. Zhivago movie?" she said and put her head on his chest. She quoted softly to him,

"'Someday my love, out of the long ago,
Sweet as the wind, soft as the kiss of snow,
Till then my love think of me now and then,
Godspeed my love till you are mine again.'"

He started to say, "'Ah Love, could thou and I with fate conspire to—'"

She looked up and put a finger to his lips to stop him. "No, you and I, we have said all there is to say. I cannot bear to hear anything else. Leave me now. *Sayonara*, I will love you forever."

He turned and walked away, through the door, into his son's house, and out of her life. She stood there alone.

She took a deep breath and held herself erect and her head high. "I am Tomiko. I am unbreakable."

Munro flew back to Arizona. A few days later, when he was sure that the state business was under control, he left everything in the capable hands of his assistant, Maria Martens, and flew to Luxembourg. He timed his arrival as Manon's workday was winding down and appeared at her office at 7:00 p.m. As he entered her office, she put down her phone and looked up from her desk, calm and beautiful as ever.

"Bonsoir, monsieur. I have been expecting you. Les misérables, eh? Tomiko-san is going to try for the presidency of Japan, *n'est-ce pas*? I always thought that was her goal."

"Yes, *une affaire de coeur* with a gaijin would not be acceptable to the Japanese people."

"*Bien sûr*, of course. *Mais toujour*, but you always knew that."

"Knowing does not make it easier. But assuming she wins, it is only for six years, unless she changes the rules. We have had separations before, but 'darkness falls, and pain is all around.'"

"So you come to see me. You know I still have the record of that song and have played it for you before when Kodama left. You have not seen Elizabeth?"

"She is not so big with the triste, that one, with the sadness. She would say, 'Man up, Munro, have a drink and come to bed with me.' You have a softer heart."

"Only you would think that, monsieur," said Manon softly and sadly. "Only you in *tout le monde*, the whole world, and I am too old."

"All I see is the woman who entered my gym and my heart when I was *le champion du monde* I first came to Luxembourg. As it is written,

> 'In robe and crown the king stepped down
> To meet and greet her on her way.
> It is no wonder said the lords
> She is more beautiful than day.'

And something else, Manon, 'Age shall not weary, nor the years condemn.'" He crossed to her side of the desk and knelt before her, taking her hands in his. "I loved you, Manon, from the day I saw you. Always have, always will."

She bent forward and kissed him on the mouth. "Ah, *cheri*, I miss you when you are not here, the sweet words. The gentle lies you tell me. Where would you like to go?"

"*Ce soir*, this evening, I don't know, somewhere quiet, just to be with you, to hold you in my arms. But tomorrow, if you can make the time, I was thinking on the plane coming over that I have not danced with you in forever. I dream of a ballroom, waltzing with you, the doors open onto a balcony and the moon shining."

"Many people? Bright lights? Full orchestra?"

"A few, maybe just us, a few instruments. A gypsy violin. Shadowy, a spotlight. You in a ball gown. Maybe a red rose in your hair."

"Where?"

"Maybe Spain. Don Pedro will have a place like that."

"Yes. I would like to see *mon vieux*, my old friend, the Don, again, and his wife. I will phone him, and we shall see. *Maintenant*." She rose from her seat holding his face in her hands. "I want you to hold me and tell me again how much you love me, how much you have always loved me. Je ne regrette rien, rien de rien."

CHAPTER 12

Space Exodus

Elizabeth was quietly happy when her presidency was finally over. She had no regrets at having taken on that burden, as she felt it had been necessary to assist in moving her country forward, away from the evil of Marxism, postmodernism, and the rot of decadence and identity politics. She recognized that all organisms die eventually, but if she had assisted America in standing for freedom for a while, like the Eastern Roman Empire, she would be well satisfied. The Eastern Empire, based on Constantinople—or Istanbul—as it was now called, had for a thousand years held back the tide of barbarism.

Her hope was that by the time America eventually collapsed, the colonies, which were by now established on Mars and the moon, would be able to survive the Dark Ages, which would eventually sweep through Earth with wars, famines, and the return to the inevitable slave states. When Earth was reduced to rubble, a peon culture, with a few brutalized survivors scrambling about in the ruins of civilization, maybe in a few hundred years, La Reconquista, the reconquest, could be led from space.

She gloried in the fact that for a few weeks after the close of her presidency that she was footloose and fancy-free. Tall Bear continued to run their mining company. She no longer needed anyone's vote and therefore no one's approval, so the divorce from Munro was finalized that first week, as they had planned. Their remarriage had occurred because she had been pregnant with their third child and was planning a run at the presidency.

Neither wanted to or would ever be free of each other. She was certain that Munro would always have a place in his heart for her, and he would always be a safe haven, no matter what her problem was. She loved him, even after all these years, knowing that he was her rock in the wild stream of her life. When they were together, she found sex with him alternately comforting and exciting, as he was still the same hard, dangerous man she had met years ago. She came to the ranch in Arizona, as she had many times before, to celebrate their divorce. For a short time, they frolicked and had fun, trail riding up in the mountains, dancing, laughing, and joking with the children, who she oversaw at the evening meetings.

After that intermission, it was time for the open road, time to get back to what she loved. Tall Bear's geologists had found a promising site in Argentina. As usual, the government there was completely corrupt, the standard mixture of doctrinaire socialism, corruption, and utter incompetence. If she mined the actual area she wanted, once the mine was up and running, the useless central government would inevitably nationalize it. Anticipating that, she developed a plan.

Tall Bear believed he had found a large deposit of consolidated rare earth minerals. They already had one small mine in Alaska producing them, but the bulk came from China or the mines in Africa controlled by the Chinese, who had no difficulties with their mines, as their agreements with the various corrupt governments allowed them to protect their mines with the Chinese Red Army, who were not in the least shy about killing any interloper on their property. They operated on the famous three S principle: shoot, shovel, and shut up.

Elizabeth or Tall Bear, who had run the company when she was president, did not have the same luxury because so-called investigative journalists would hang about and report any suppression of crime as brutal tyranny or genocide. The number of these media pests was reduced by "accidental" deaths or the finding that unprecedented numbers were pedophiles. Nonetheless, they kept coming, and Elizabeth was fairly certain that it was the Chinese government who, through intermediaries controlling the media, was paying to have them snoop around. She found it hard to believe people with such reportedly stupid, contorted worldviews could cross a street safely, let alone find their way to another country. She used mercenaries from other paramilitary forces for protection at her mines, not Hinchcliffe's Legion, as she did not want their name tarnished by any trumped-up charges.

They picked a place in Argentina and, after obtaining mining leases, salted the samples, and glowing data was leaked. Munro Mines remained private, so with no shares to buy or sell, no one was affected by this false data. They began to drive a shaft and brought in the usual equipment. The place chosen was in the middle of nowhere, so few could see what was happening. Those in the business wondered why the equipment they bought was so old and if it was still functioning. The contract that Elizabeth had signed with the Argentinian government had very large penalty clauses if the mine was nationalized, and these contracts were enforceable in the US.

The reports of wealth beyond dreams from the mine continued to be leaked. None of these reports were official and all were halfheartedly denied. Six months after mining had begun, a new election was held in Argentina; and as expected, one of the first things the new socialist government did was nationalized the mine, assuming that it would be the new El Dorado. The government began hinting that negotiations would be in order, with payoffs to the newly elected politicians and their families, with discreet give backs and foreign banks and offshore accounts and all. That did not happen, so the government made arrangements to take over the mine. The day the nationalization papers became legal, the mine closed. The power was switched off, and the workers trucked to a primitive airport that had been built for the mine. Transportation flew in to airlift them out. Everything, including vehicles, the camp, kitchens, and refrigerators were abandoned, as these were now property of the state. Within twenty-four hours, no one remained.

Elizabeth, expecting that to happen, had lawyers and papers ready and moved swiftly, and a court order was obtained to freeze all the Argentinian funds in the US, amounting to several billion dollars. The contracts she had signed were clear and ironclad, and the monies were therefore transferred to her company before the Argentinian government knew what was happening. In retaliation, the government moved to seize everything left at the mine site, only to find that it was mostly old and coming to the end of its working life. Some of it clearly did not work at all and had not for some time. In other words, what had been abandoned was obsolete, useless junk.

The party leaders took some time to realize that for their efforts to steal the mine, they were left with worthless equipment and a hole in the ground, which did not seem to contain any ore at all, for which they had paid immense sums of money from their holdings in the US. What Elizabeth had done was all perfectly legal. They opened negotiations with Elizabeth, as there was no other recourse. She, via her lawyers, agreed to negotiate with them but wanted to negotiate with the new president in person. She agreed to reopen mining operations in Argentina, but the old mine was history and finished. There was nothing to negotiate about; it was the property of the government, and the compensation was hers. A new mining venture could be embarked on, but as before, cast-iron guarantees would be required with assets being deposited in the US, which could be seized if some new government came in and again nationalized her property. As no one else appeared to have any interest in negotiating with them, because of their propensity to nationalize private holdings, they eventually agreed. She also planned on possibly building a new road through the Andes to Chile. All or any part of that road would belong to her, including mineral rights below and air rights above, for the next century.

Having achieved the objectives, she and Tall Bear began work. The mine was so far from any town that it was felt stealing would not be a problem, at least initially. Wells were drilled for water and camps set up. The area leased was so large that it was felt that interlopers could be kept at a safe distance. The Legion was hired to provide security and logistics. A start was also made on making a road through the Cordilleras.

The establishment of a new mine was routine for Elizabeth. Tall Bear's geologists had been right; it did contain a significant concentrated deposit of rare earth materials. The road through the Andes was, for her, a new and glorious experience; and she had great fun blowing the tops off mountains and driving tunnels. She made sure that she owned the land on either side of where the road would enter or exit the mountain range. The route was planned with the help of Isis, who was developing transportation both on Mars and the moon. Don Pedro's company, based in Spain, was the main contractor.

Much of the funds obtained from the Argentinian government went into the Prometheus Project. The moon base and a growing Mars base were open for business, and it was hoped that soon, they would be independently viable. In the early days, the main problem on the moon had been water. Plentiful water in the form of ice had been found on Mars, as expected.

Quiet Bear, one of the Prometheus children adopted years ago by Running Bear, the Athabascan Indian chief, who was also associated with the group, had been badly wounded protecting Sandra while she was running for the presidency. In spite of what medical science could do for him, he remained in pain when he walked. He never complained, but it was obvious. Munro and others wondered if the reduced gravity would help him.

There was a problem with the shooting of an interloper, for which Tall Bear was blamed. He became despondent following that, to such an extent that Arizona, another of the Prometheus children, who had fallen in love with him, took his place as Sandra's chief of security, allowing him to go into space. His work at university had been in the field of propulsion, so he was perfectly capable of captaining a moon or Mars shuttle.

While he was Sandra's head of security, he had been studying asteroid mining, as he saw that it was going to become very important, as the space shuttles would have to be built either on the moon or on Phobos or Deimos, the moons of Mars, due to gravity issues. Metals would have to be brought to them as the chances of finding enough metals locally was not high, although titanium, which they would use to build most of the space ships, was plentiful on the moon.

There had been much talk about this. Their biggest need for Moon Base was water, and their secondary need was minerals. All their telescopes and other devices had been set for years now to find a dusty snowball within approachable distance. The other problem was who was going to man the ships? Sex was a potential problem. There did not seem to be any way to have a mixed sex crew. Emotions would inevitably lead to problems, which could not be resolved in a cramped space on board a ship, which would have to be endured for years. The sex bots that Manon's engineers had been working on had been a reality for years now, and the unexpected finding was that, in her franchised brothel chain, a large percentage of men preferred the sex bots to actual women. The initial ships therefore would be men only. Perhaps later, female crews could be considered, but initially, women were very precious as a baby-making commodity, as the artificial uterus had yet to be adequately developed. The sex bots could now be programmed to produce variable looks and body shapes and had an endless number of interchangeable personalities, which the user could select depending on his mood.

What also was not known was how humans would respond to cosmic radiation. There was no way of completely shielding a mining ship, so the crew would get a significant dose of radiation for a long time. Maybe they would die rapidly, maybe slowly, or maybe live forever. The radiation was unlikely to produce a quick death but maybe result in cancer in a decade or so. No one knew. The hope was the Hiroshima paradox.

After the atomic explosion in Hiroshima, three groups were identified. The group within the blast zone died immediately. The group inside the high radiation zone died within a few years due to various forms of cancer.

The people within the low radiation zone, who got much more radiation than normal, experienced less cancer than those completely outside the radiation zone. Maybe therefore, the combination of some radiation and low gravity would prolong rather than shorten life. The simple answer was no one knew. They felt that until they did, the best choice was elderly miners and engineers prepared to take the risk that this was a one-way journey, with potentially a computer-driven ship full of dead men returning to base. The payoff would be that their families would be well looked after, no matter what, and if they made it back alive, they would be wealthy.

With no particular fanfare, the first mining ship, named Cecil Rhodes, had been launched years before. For their first try, they got extremely lucky. They rendezvoused with a small comet three years out, and after transferring and locking on the ion drive engines they had brought with them, within six months, they had developed enough power for a course correction, which would bring it back into moon orbit within four years. Once they were certain of the trajectory and that enough robotically controlled power was available for any minor corrections necessary, they cut loose and netted a small metal asteroid. Space mining was not necessary as the whole asteroid could simply be harnessed. On the way back to base, they were able to capture another very small, very dense asteroid.

The ship arrived back at Moon Base shortly ahead of the comet. When that was firmly captured in moon orbit, there were sighs of relief, as whatever happened on Earth, the moon maybe could survive as an independent entity. The transfer of ice from the comet to the caverns dug deep in the moon would occupy at least the next couple of decades. The Hiroshima paradox had proved to be accurate. The miners had not aged. There had been no major problems, and in most cases, the men had become fond of their sex bots, which as pioneers, they were allowed to keep. A few of the miners, after a decade in space, felt happy to retire and remain on the moon, as there was no way they could ever return to Earth due to the thinning of their bones from lack of gravity. Several had become so accustomed to space and their dolls that after a few months, they shipped out again.

Other asteroid mining ships had been sent out, and the amount of metal now available meant that the moon had become a major shipyard, and the number of workers continued to rise. Robotics had improved dramatically as Manon and others had been spending massively on that for years. So much of the work was now done by machines.

Anticipating that there would be water on Mars, the first Mars expedition had been launched soon after the first asteroid miner. The ship was called the Christopher Columbus. It was billed as a scientific exploration only, with no fanfare at all. Even the name of the ship was not released. It was only mentioned if there were direct questions and was dismissed as nothing of much note, an engineering exercise only. The ship however was large enough to establish possibly the first colony, with nuclear power, hydroponics, and all the rest that went along with that. Water was found in a frozen state underground so that the planet was definitely capable of supporting a colony.

The colonists had been landed by shuttle, which remained behind when the ship returned to the moon. Geologists, engineers, and food processors went on the second voyage. The shuttles were one way initially, but at 40 percent earth gravity, it was anticipated that in fairly short order, they could build adequate facilities to relaunch them up into orbit to meet the spaceship. The numbers coming from Earth increased fairly dramatically as new habitations were built and power sources delivered. As on the moon, until metals were discovered in mineable quantities, the building material used was glass, as all that was required for it was power and silica, both of which were readily available.

The asteroid mining ships continued to be built and manned. As word slowly got out that asteroid mining appeared to be the fountain of youth, more and younger men signed up. The miners were making enough money that they felt that they could support a family in space as well as the one left behind on Earth, and therefore they began to freeze their sperm before shipping out. Some of the space women were prevailed upon or liked the idea of donating their eggs. Thought had been given to designing incubators to produce children, from sperm and eggs, but a study of the world's literature on the subject contained the cautionary tale of the babies in Romania who, denied human contact, sickened, and died. There was no immediate desire to repeat that experiment, although research would have to be done on it eventually, as current theory would not allow travel back from a wormhole, even if it could be identified. In the absence of two-way wormhole access, with existing technology, it would take so many light years to reach out into the galaxy, that either sperm and eggs or a Mars moon-size ship would be required.

Some women with huge maternal instincts were happy being surrogates for a large number of children. These women were flown to the moon and Mars, where their maternal instincts and the desires of men coincided. The women space pioneers thus had the option of having their own babies or using surrogates. The female multiple surrogates were greatly honored and rewarded by the space pioneers as being essential to the viability of the colonies.

As the number of colonists grew, a second Mars base was established. Emigration from Earth continued, handpicking those who would go. Bulk emigration was not yet possible due to the expense. Skills were required, and very few outside the STEM fields or some trade schools were even remotely considered. The only ones who qualified had initially come through the Space Academy. Entrance into that was supervised by the psychologists, who they hoped were able to weed out undesirable traits.

As the graduates from the Space Academy were disappearing into space as soon as they graduated, the Space Academy kept expanding, and more ships became available for transportation. Most of the original asteroid miners had come from Elizabeth's organization, but it soon became obvious that while it was a slower process, it was easier to bring the asteroid to the orbit where it was needed than actually mine in deep space. Low moon orbit mining meant that it made increasing economic sense to ship some of the rarer materials back to Earth in empty shuttles, and the whole exercise began slowly to cover its own costs. They did not want mining carried out in low earth orbit, as any debris would be hazardous in the extreme. The Prometheus Group even had a small branch in the business of collecting the deadly space junk from Earth's orbit. Earth orbital tourism also contributed to balancing the budget.

Munro kept pushing his three geniuses—Little Sister, Helga, and Isis—now helped by the bright young people from the Space Academy, who increasingly were recruited from all over the world, for sustainable fusion, as clearly unlimited energy would ultimately be necessary for space travel. Producing enough propellant to get a reusable rocket off the surface of Mars to rendezvous with the earth or moon shuttle was initially difficult. Going up empty meant less fuel was required as the payloads were being delivered down to the surface of Mars, not yet off it. The problem was not producing fusion but sustaining and—on the very odd occasion—containing it; and explosions from failed containment, while exceedingly uncommon, occasionally rocked the deserts of America and Mexico. The Prometheus Group found that increasing pressure was being brought to bear, as those with no knowledge became increasingly alarmed that these experiments could somehow destroy the world. Some segments of the media seemed to be mounting a fear-mongering whisper campaign that these experiments might produce a black hole that would swallow the earth.

Sandra and La Contessa kept the authorities at bay, but the negative publicity was growing, produced by media disinformation, probably or almost certainly promoted by funding from the oil-producing states, who would lose everything if fusion became a reality. The whole Middle East would become again simply an irrelevant backwater, ignored by the world.

The last thing the Prometheus Group wanted was to have any public attention drawn to their activities, let alone negative publicity. They had always wanted to fly under the radar. Their preferred news was no news. This unwanted publicity was such that it became a priority to move the bulk of the physical experiments on fusion off Earth to the moon or, better, to Mars.

Little Sister was married with children, and Helga, the longtime sufferer of Asperger's syndrome, did not feel she could manage in a new environment. The one thing Helga did was donate a few of her own eggs to be taken into space in place of herself. That left Isis. But she was a free spirit, turning her incredible agile mind to whatever took her fancy. As a result, she had spearheaded numerous advances in many fields and, with the backing of Manon and the Keiretsu, was able to monetize her findings. In consequence, she was extremely wealthy and could have anything she wanted on Earth. Would she give that up for the hard, gritty life of a pioneer on a new planet?

Outside on Mars still meant a survival suit and would be for the foreseeable future, although the pioneers had begun to melt the ice caps of Mars to produce an atmosphere. There were lots of young clever men who adored Isis, and Isis liked clever men. There would be boundless opportunities for these people in space in the future, but they and she would have to make that future. The decision was not easy, and no one could blame her if she decided that it was too much to give up the sybaritic pleasures of Earth.

Isis had known Munro's feelings for a long time, and she had known deep in herself that eventually, her destiny lay in space. To give up the present for the dream of the future was not easy for a young woman. The initial asteroid miners were old men, and the emigrants were what emigrants had always been—the young and the restless who wanted more than their current situation could ever give them. They were tough, hard people dreaming dreams, not only for themselves, but also for their children. As a group, they had no time for the effete Western culture, which had given up on life, with no ambition, no children, and no future. But Isis was different. She already had everything.

There was, however, a further complicating factor. It was obvious to all that if fusion became a reality, there would be little value in Big Oil. Its sole function would be to provide hydrocarbons. Anticipating this, the Buccaneer—one of Elizabeth's sons who ran two huge hedge funds based in Luxembourg—and Manon's people had already or were in the process of unloading energy holdings. Elizabeth's father, whose company was public, had, on his daughter's advice, reduced his own family involvement in his company to the bare bones, which allowed him to maintain control. Elizabeth's second son, who, with numerous others, was still fracking like mad, was finally producing sufficient fuel that the US finally was fuel independent and actually exporting energy.

Governments are generally not led by people with any useful education. Most are lawyers or have been in government or public service–type jobs. This means that almost none have ever had to meet a payroll and the concept of cost benefit analysis is virtually unknown. Furthermore, the time focus is simply the next election.

This means that the spending horizon is only the next election. Children do not vote, and grandchildren are not born, so have no voice. Shifting debt onto their shoulders therefore has no downside at all for a politician. What was worse was that public education was now controlled by the ideologically possessed who wanted to try Marxism again, ignoring the 100 million dead people already produced by that attractive but utterly failed ideology. "That was not true Marxism," they would parrot, in spite of the repeated examples from numerous countries producing the same litany of poverty, enslavement, and death.

Given this level of ignorance, it is little wonder that any scam imaginable can be sold to politicians, as after all, it is not their money, and the existing generation will not have to pay the full cost. Green energy or renewable resources was an incredible scam. Most agreed that this particular scam originated in Sweden initially as the acid rain or lake-acidification scam because one politician wanted to bring in more nuclear power, and to do that, he had to demonize coal.

The scam itself went nowhere until China realized that it could be weaponized, and it was popularized via the United Nations to damage the West economically, especially the US. To everyone's surprise, in spite of the obviously ludicrous nature of the claims, it became an overwhelming force. The money to be made in this fraudulent exercise was so great that no sensible person could ignore it. Manon was no exception. The various semi-fraudulent green energy scams, such as windmills and solar they had involved themselves in, were so protected by promises and failure avoidance clauses that even when it all went bankrupt, the instigators could walk away and still realize huge profits.

Operators in America were well aware of the coming replacement of Big Oil and were preparing for it, and the other Big Oil producer, Russia, had secured so many long-term agreements with the moronic EU bureaucrats and others for pipeline oil that they would be cushioned for the next couple of decades.

The situation in the Middle East was quite different. These countries had never been able to overcome their total dependence on their sole products, oil, and ideology. They had spent huge sums of money on international proselytizing, terrorism, and paying welfare for their rapidly increasing young and essentially unskilled and functionally illiterate populace, who never had worked and had no prospect of work. They had also spent hugely on arms, which they used to fight one another over miniscule differences in ideology. The demise of Big Oil would for them be a disaster, as they had absolutely no fallback position, with nothing except oil, which no one needed, and local conflict. Some of the more intelligent of them realized that, and they felt that they had to make it their business to stop the unlimited energy fusion would provide.

There were two obvious ways of doing this. The first was the tried-and-true technique of convincing young students and all Lenin's standard useful idiots in the media, politics, and universities that fusion was evil and would destroy the world. This technique had been used in the past to stop plant genetic research, which could easily have cured the world of hunger. They had even been able to stop the cultivation of Golden Rice, which was genetically modified to be high in vitamin A and thus would prevent night blindness in affected children in areas of the world where the diet was deficient in vitamin A. Blind children meant nothing to these ideologues, a mere bagatelle of no significance.

It had been used to ban DDT, which led to the greatest mass slaughter in all of human history, with millions upon millions of children dying of malaria. It had been used to stop the development of nuclear fission power such as breeder reactors, which could have supplied the world with energy, as well as burning the residual waste from less efficient nuclear plants. It had been used to bankrupt Canada by blocking pipelines, thus preventing tar sands oil from being exported. It had been used to ban coal-power plants in the West, which increased dependency on the oil-producing Middle East countries. It had been used to limit fish farming, which would have supplied the world with protein.

The various "charitable" foundations with considerable experience in organizing protests and many of the radicalized university departments suddenly received very large donations, and all the usual suspects were ordered to ramp up their protests. In order to demonstrate how dangerous atom bomb or nuclear research was, one obvious move would be to create nuclear power–plant disasters, which really would stir up the populace to ban all nuclear research. Germany, after all, had begun to decommission nuclear power plants after a tidal wave damaged some nuclear plants in Japan. No one died of any radiation in that disaster, and just how a tidal wave was going to get near to a nuclear plant in Germany was never made clear to anyone.

The instigators assumed correctly that the scientific illiterates in the media and politics and universities would never understand the difference between nuclear fission and fusion that if anything happened to a nuclear fusion plant, it would likely just stop, not blow up. State-funded terrorism was therefore redirected from random lone-wolf acts of terrorism or destruction, such as the burning of Notre Dame Cathedral in Paris, to nuclear plants. The first strike was at a nuclear power plant in France, a country that seemed to lack the political willpower to protect itself.

A number of terrorists invaded one nuclear plant in a carefully coordinated strike. They shot their way in and managed to damage the intake coolant system and several backup systems, which led to a nuclear meltdown. Fortunately, the meltdown was largely held within the containment walls of the plant, so the escape of radiation was limited. Certain members of the media were paid to write stories suggesting that there had been no terror attack at all, and it was simply an expected disaster, which could occur anywhere, anytime at any nuclear power facility. The French government, who had issued the usual "We will stand firm," "We will not change our way of life," and "There will be no persecution of minorities" had little to say to disprove this disinformation, because, as usual, there had been little or no investigation; and what little information had been found had been covered up to prevent the populace from finding out who was financing these attacks.

So the movement grew, especially in Europe, to close nuclear plants and rely solely on imported oil and the chimera of green energy. Following this attack, Chancellor Merkel announced that she was going to close all remaining nuclear plants in Germany and rely purely on oil imported from Russia. The threat to nuclear power plants led other countries to enhance security arrangements around their existing plants and, more importantly, to cancel the building of new ones.

The second approach was to eliminate those involved in the development of fusion. Munro and Sandra had always been aware that ultimately, a terrorist strike against their research facilities would come, unless they were prepared to declare such a strike an act of war and strike back at the heartland of the originators. Sandra, of course, was quite prepared to do that, but there was no political will in Washington to do so. The people, she felt, would support her, but the political class, the media, and the chattering class would do their best to impeach her.

Munro an old friend, at an official function shortly after her inauguration, had whispered to her in congratulation a couple of lines from Kit Marlowe,

"Is it not passing brave to be a king,
And ride in triumph through Persepolis."

"Sure," she said. "Yes. But in order to do that, I would have to drop a couple of nukes on Tehran, one on Qum, and another on that town, what's it called? Mashhad?"

"I know. How could the Persians, with their two- or three-thousand-year history of civilization, let themselves be taken over by a band of semiliterate theological thugs spouting Arab claptrap?"

"Courtesy of Jimmy Carter. He thought he was doing God's work getting rid of the Shah, and this is what he got instead. What an utter moron!"

Munro had grimaced in agreement and drifted off. He thought her summation of the situation was entirely accurate.

Sandra privately warned the funders of terror that any major assassination would be met by force, but as usual, they simply smirked and denied any involvement. She brought in the military to surround and protect all nuclear facilities in America and also the Space Academy and the fusion laboratories. She considered also protecting the University of Arizona and the ranch, but felt that politically, she could not do so overtly with the military. Nonetheless, covert moves were made.

Munro was reasonably happy with the level of protection around Helga, who, due to her Asperger's, almost never left her windowless room. She had no interest in the outdoors, so to shield her from rocket or kamikaze plane attacks, she was moved to the deepest floor of the ranch building. Those who had laughed at Munro's initial plans now understood why the building had been constructed that way.

Little Sister was a problem. She was married and had children and moved between her research facilities in Arizona and Mexico. La Contessa had no difficulty in surrounding her homes in Mexico and her research labs with men and women of the Legion. She also had installed surface-to-air missiles and had a no-fly zone over the desert lab where testing was carried out. Munro would have liked to have the same thing at the ranch. Surface-to-air missiles could be installed and manned, but a no-fly zone would be impossible to establish legally.

Miguel was officially constrained in what he could say or do, but unofficially, he was the same fierce, hard man who had been the world heavyweight boxing champion. He did speak to the ambassadors of the countries sponsoring terrorism, and in private, he told them that if his wife or children were injured, he personally would ensure that the leaders and their families would not survive. One ambassador laughed in his face. A few weeks later, that ambassador's brother, who was in England, was killed in a drive-by shooting. The same day in Monte Carlo, a large, very expensive boat containing a number of relatives of the ruling family and their friends unexpectedly blew up, with few survivors. Miguel again saw the ambassador. He said nothing, but simply dropped a couple of newspapers on the ambassador's desk, detailing the brother's unfortunate demise and the unexplained explosion aboard the yacht. He looked at the ambassador for a long minute, tapped the newspaper article with his forefinger, bared his teeth at him with a smile, and left.

Munro had warned Isis that he was afraid she would be a target for assassination by those who would seek to prevent the development of the unlimited energy supplied by fusion generators. Isis intellectually understood this. She had previously been a target in Toronto, where Jock MacGregor had almost lost his life in the aftermath of that event. She was still unsure if this was due to stupidity or malfeasance on the part of the authorities. By contrast, Sheila MacDonald, who had also been attacked in Canada, had no doubt at all. Isis, however, was a blithe spirit, and she did not want to be protected behind walls, either masonry or people. "If I had wanted that, I could have stayed in my village in Egypt, hidden inside a burka."

In major cities, she would accept bodyguards and wear body armor, but it was not something she did willingly. Around the ranch, she felt safe. Walking in the streets of Flagstaff, where she was well-known to all the school children, as she would sometimes lecture to them, she also felt safe. The school children, who had been warned of possible assassins, were all immensely protective and proud of her, as she always emphasized when she talked that she had been one of them.

In Munro's world, or the world where he was governor, an armed society was viewed as a polite, safe society, so many children, especially those who had joined the Deputy Border Patrol organization, which had replaced the tragically politicized Boy Scouts of America, had a license for open carry of firearms. The photos of teenagers walking around wearing guns would horrify those who felt that only the police and criminals should be armed. Of course, there were accidents, but on the whole, these areas were very safe, and housebreaking was virtually unknown.

Unfortunately, that feeling of safety was illusionary. One day, Isis was walking down the sidewalk in Flagstaff, in earnest conversation with one of the young scientists from the Space Academy. He was propounding a theory that she found interesting and was concentrating on and was unaware of her surroundings. A nondescript man, who had been sitting at an outdoor café, drinking coffee, pulled out a knife hidden inside his shirt, rose, and attacked her without warning. She saw him coming out of the corner of her eye and flung herself sideways, scrambling away. She fell but kept her right arm upraised. The young scientist, without thinking, turned to face the assassin and was knifed in the chest, dying immediately. The assassin pulled out his knife, brushed him aside, and loomed over Isis; and she watched in horror as the knife was raised.

He was blown sideways as three bullets hit his chest. More shots hit the falling man. Isis looked up to see a teenage girl with a pistol in her hand. The girl stepped forward and emptied her gun into the face of the assassin she had just shot. Feeling numb, Isis got to her feet shakily and hugged the girl who had saved her life. The girl seemed herself shocked by the suddenness of it and almost afraid because she had just killed someone. A crowd rapidly formed around them. Isis, a recognizable figure in Flagstaff, lifted the girl's hand above her head. "My savior!" she said. "This girl saved my life." The crowd applauded. The applause calmed the girl down, as no one cared at all about the dead body lying in the street.

A policeman searched him. Ominously, no ID was found, which meant someone had brought the assassin to Flagstaff, had sheltered him, had given him money and the knife, and had pointed out Isis to him.

Munro went on local TV with the girl, whom he congratulated and gave a substantial reward. He pointed out that without her swift action, Isis, one of the greatest minds of her generation, would have been assassinated. He asked for assistance from everyone, including the children, in monitoring all strangers in Flagstaff. He pointed out that as the assassin carried no ID, it clearly was a planned attack, and the helpers remained in Flagstaff, so there were likely to be others, and that all the clever children of the Foundation were at risk.

"Much as I would like to, I cannot ask everyone to carry ID at all times, but if you guys, especially you Deputy Border Patrol guys, see a stranger loitering about, ask him who he is."

After that, no one wanted Isis flying or traveling commercially. In Japan, she felt reasonably free but loathed being trapped in the ranch when she was in the US. She pointed out that she could work all day at mechanical-type problems, which did not require much thought on her part, such as transportation up on the moon and on Mars. Fusion and some of the spaceship drives she was thinking of required pure thought, which she said she could do for only one or two hours a day, as she was walking in the subatomic territory. No one other than Little Sister and Helga and a few men knew what she was talking about.

Short of bombing the two main terror-exporting states, Munro could not think of a way to keep her safe. He was really unhappy knowing that all this terrorist activity that plagued the world could be solved swiftly with a couple of big nukes in the appropriate places. Or a couple of large rocks dropped from space.

At one of the fiestas, which they held regularly in Flagstaff; another attempt was made. On this occasion, fortunately Isis was wearing body armor. The assassin appeared so suddenly no one had time to stop him. The first knife thrust hit her on her chest but failed to penetrate. Munro, who was with her, still had the hand speed of the fighter he had been. He caught the arm as the assassin drew back for the second strike, twisted it up behind his back, breaking the arm and dislocating the shoulder. Enraged, Munro, holding him by the back of the head, took him down so hard people heard the assassin's teeth break as his face hit the ground. Munro stifled the screams by holding his hair and smashing his face several times into the paving stones of the plaza. A gag was quickly inserted, and the man hustled away. The attack had been so quick and the response so overwhelmingly violent that few saw what had happened. The assassin succumbed on his way to jail, which took a surprising time, considering how close the jail was. Unfortunately, little of the information extracted was of much value. The terrorist cell members had skipped town immediately before the attack and were being hidden by others.

They were pretty certain where the orders and the money had originated, but that was hardly enough to launch a war on a country, especially given the fact that the media seemed to be largely in the camp, if not the pay, of the perpetrators. Munro seethed with anger. There was no doubt who was ultimately responsible for the attacks, but the West seemed to have lost its will to protect itself. Sandra agreed, but the useless, tiresome, greedy, and incompetent Houses were only interested in virtue signaling and refused to support her. By this time, Europe was simply a basket case. Space was indeed the only viable option.

This was obvious to Isis also, that if she stayed on Earth, she would either have to live like a mole or accept the fact that someday, an assassin would get to her. Reluctantly, she agreed, and a few weeks later, with no fanfare and somewhat tearfully, she lifted off on a shuttle to take her into orbit. There she connected with one of the shuttles that would take her onward to Mars to continue her research. As many technicians as possible went with her and the focus of the macro-research occurred there, where there was no opposition and no assassins. The new fusion generators were to be built there rather than on Earth.

Munro felt ashamed and sad that he had been unable to protect her and that her only hope of living out her days unmolested was in exile in space. That solved one fear, but the other was that the terrorist masters would try to smuggle one of their followers on board a shuttle to create mayhem. The screening of pioneers therefore remained as rigorous as possible.

The other concern that they had was screening those infected with the twin horrors of Marxism and postmodernism, as these ideologies—or brain worms, as they had been described—had between them effectively, in less than a century, destroyed the West. Inevitably, differences of opinion would arise when the number of settlers reached a critical mass, but as long as they taught the children the lessons of history, the hope was that progress would continue. Eventually, the solar system would not be enough, and to ensure the survival of the human race, they would have to expand into the galaxy.

The colonies in the high frontier were by now almost self-sustaining, and it was hoped that within a year or two, contact with Earth could rapidly be severed when the final cataclysm of collapse and war occurred, with the realistic hope of the colony's survival. If they did, a century or so later, they could recolonize Earth. They did recognize that when Earth reached its final precollapse, there would be a mad scramble to escape into space. It would be the same worthless political class responsible for the destruction of civilization on Earth who would demand the loudest to be rescued and would likely use the threat of weapons to back their demands. All governments after all, unknown to the general public, had plans for self-preservation of themselves and the bureaucrats. It had various names, but the commonest was COG, which stood for continuity of government. At its most basic, it meant that politicians and civil servants live, and everyone else dies.

With a heavy heart, therefore, the Prometheus Group decided that defensive weaponizing of space was necessary to keep out these parasites. Nothing was said about this. Fortunately, the political class, who in general have little or no practical education, did not understand how easy this weaponizing was simply using kinetic objects. One very large rock coming down from space packs a lot more energy than a nuclear bomb. Munro was fairly certain that Sandra's former head of security, Quiet Bear, who had been in space now for years, likely had put such measures in place a long time ago. The group fervently hoped that open conflict with Earth would not occur in their lifetime.

CHAPTER 13

Mayday, Mayday

An incoming message reached several TV stations, including Manon's network. An astute programmer contacted the show host, who aired it immediately. A voice was speaking. The screen flickered then stabilized. It was a shot of what seemed to be the inside of a plane. A woman was speaking.

"Mayday. Mayday. This is Elizabeth Munro, former president of the USA. We are trying to contact anyone. We are in a plane over the Andes. An engine has blown, and a wing has gone. We are in a spin, going down. Girls, try to bail out or speak to your parents."

The camera cut to a young Japanese woman in a kimono strapped into her seat. Her face was serene. She spoke, "I and camera woman Katsomo love our parents, and we love and honor Japan and the emperor. We are samurai. We will die with you, shogun."

The camera cut back to the original woman.

"My children, I love you. Tall Bear, you have been my strong right arm, my shield, and my protector all these years. I have loved you deeply and always. Neil Munro. I have loved you since the day I saw you. I love you with all my heart and my soul and my body. My absences made my love deeper and our lovemaking sweeter. We are going down in the jungle. Do not bother looking for us. Build me a monument in the Andes. I will meet you again in the hereafter. Tomiko, look after him."

She glanced away from the camera. "I see the jungle coming up. We are going in. Hold your guns in your hand's girls. We will see you in Valhalla—"

The feed cut off abruptly.

Munro did not see the original broadcast, but one of his aides contacted him immediately. They managed to locate a replay. He knew it was real. He felt numb, nothing. He had last seen her about two months before when she flew into Flagstaff on her way south, and they had had a few days together, filled as always with fun, romance, and reminiscences. She was the same wild woman he had met years ago now that she was freed of the duties of the presidency. She still had the tumbling golden-blond hair, the toned body, the fierceness, the urgency, and the unexpected tenderness. She was the Texas woman who, decades ago, had stolen his heart. Like the old song of El Paso, the diamond in the desert.

He always looked forward to her visits, even if they were usually fleeting. She phoned him when she landed, and he was waiting for her at the door of the ranch when she was driven up in the limo. He opened the car door for her, and she stepped out and embraced him. They went into the building arm in arm.

"Do you remember when I first saw you? I called you Elizabeth of Bohemia, the Winter Queen?"

"Yes, and then by rights, we should have called our first son Rupert. But I guess the Buccaneer suits his temperament better."

"I found a poem the other day, written by Sir Henry Wotton in about 1600 addressed to the original Elizabeth of Bohemia."

"Munro, sometimes I think that you are trying to be Sir Walter Raleigh, spreading your cloak in front of me to keep my dainty feet dry."

"That was always my wish, my lady!"

"Then tell me this lugubrious poem you have found."

> "'So when my mistress shall be seen
> In form and beauty of her mind,
> By virtue first, then choice, a queen,
> Tell me, if she were not designed
> The eclipse and glory of her kind?'"

"Not up to Shakespeare's standard, but for something written six hundred years ago, it is OK."

"'Oh mistress mine where are you roaming?'"

"I'm about to roam into your bedroom, Munro."

Later that night, after the evening durbar where Elizabeth had chaired the female's session and Munro the male, they walked arm in arm up the hill to the Shinto shrine. Munro bowed his head.

She laughed at him. "You and your gods, Munro."

"Might as well believe in something," he said peaceably.

They stood under the torii gate, looking out over the moonlit valley below them. Munro felt a sense of peace, that he was with the woman of his dreams.

Now the news had come that she was gone; that wild, bold beauty was gone forever. He knew there was no hope, but he had to find her.

Going down in a spin would have prevented any attempt to parachute out, which was why the Japanese girls had not even tried. Finding them in the jungle would be difficult. They would have to parachute in, and he had never parachuted in his life. He would have to skydive in tandem, which he had seen done but had never had any desire to try. It had looked terrifying. Hinchcliffe's Legion stationed in Mexico was probably his best bet. They would have paratroopers. Tall Bear was working down in South America. He phoned his son. Tall Bear had not had word of the crash.

As always, his son was calm and in control. "If she went down in the jungle in a spin, there is no way she could survive that, but I need to look. I need a location. Maybe see if any of the military satellites can help. There will be no place for a fixed wing plane to land. We are way south of her probable crash site. I will bolt some extra fuel tanks on and will bring up the longest range helicopters I have and establish a base somewhere closer to the site in anticipation of you locating it.

Munro's people called in all favors to get satellite data to see if they could locate the crash site. They thought they had some ideas simply following the plane's prior trajectory. He phoned La Contessa in Mexico, and she sent some planes to fly over. Hinchcliffe's military planes had look-down/shoot-down radar capacity, but that was Doppler dependent, requiring movement. They expected no movement at the crash site. The mining look-down radar was different, but very difficult to use to locate something as small as a downed plane. Tall Bear knew the best people in the business and hired them for as much money as it took to break their existing contracts.

By the time they thought they had located the approximate area, Tall Bear had brought his helicopters up to the nearest fixed wing airfield and was looking for a forward base. The approximate area of the crash site was too far for a single flight. He would have to stop and refuel, probably twice. He had taken two helicopters from the fixed wing airfield, and they set off laden with fuel. He established a forward base where they could refuel and pressed on. Over the valley where they thought the plane had gone down, there was nothing to see but dense jungle. The surrounding mountains were steep, with no visible flat areas for a helicopter to land.

He had brought some explosives, so he rappelled down to a small ledge he could see on a mountain face that looked down on the valley. Even this was perilous, as updrafts threatened to push the helicopter against the mountain. He pushed the explosives into a crack in the rock and took off. When clear, he set them off and blew off part of the mountain face. The ledge he established was still too small, but with further controlled blasting, a potential landing area could be blown out of the mountain. He flew back to his forward base, phoning for necessary supplies to be brought up and drillers who could direct the blasting.

Meantime, Munro had flown to Hinchcliffe's nearest military base, where she had paratroopers. They were still trying to narrow down the coordinates. If they dropped ten miles away in heavy jungle, it might take a week to get there, if ever.

Little Sister contacted her astrophysicist friends, and they were analyzing satellite data. Tall Bear had hired the people with the most experience with look-down radar, and they were flying a grid pattern with whatever planes were available.

Tall Bear was making the most progress. His hover time in the area was still limited by fuel in spite of the extra fuel tanks bolted to his helicopters. A second survey found where he had blown off the cliff face, and the ledge was still visible. This time, he winched down with a drill and used shaped charges and was able to really blow off a large amount of overhanging cliff face. The resulting rubble field was almost enough to land. A third blast did give enough room to get down some professional drillers, and the fourth blast brought down enough of the cliff face to give enough space to land a helicopter The larger boulders were blown apart to level the area to the extent that it became workable and establish a base for refueling and bring in the other equipment necessary.

The look-down radar people announced that they had pinpointed the location, so Munro was set to go with Hinchcliffe's paratroopers. Tomiko, the current prime minister of Japan, had seen the video of the Japanese woman praising Japan and contemplating their death with equanimity. She experienced an intense feeling of nationalistic pride for those brave women.

In consequence, she felt she should be part of the rescue attempt too, so she got permission from La Contessa to bring her own aircraft and Japanese paratroopers. Like Munro, she had never parachuted, so she would need a tandem drop. They had been on hold, and on day 2, and when the location was announced, bombers went over to blow the jungle canopy to create a clearing near the crash site. Parachuting into the dense jungle canopy would have made no sense.

Once a clearing was established, a few of the best parachutists could direct their drop into that site. With explosives and chainsaws, they rapidly expanded the clearing. A video journalist also jumped in tandem with the first troopers so that she was ready to video the main drop. She got some videos of the huge explosions on the cliff face looking down into the valley, where Tall Bear and his men were rushing to establish the helicopter base. Munro came down in a tandem drop with the second wave of parachutists from the Legion, and Tomiko in the third, with her own Japanese troops.

The landing party made their way through the thick jungle to the coordinates given. After an exhausting trek, they found the downed aircraft. At the last moment, the pilots had managed to flatten out the angle of entry so the plane was not completely concertinaed. No one had survived, but there had been no fire.

As they got to the plane, they heard the helicopters. After filling their tanks at the new base, the first helicopter came and hovered over the crash site. The paratroopers were cutting down trees with chain saws they had brought to create a clearing for the helicopter to land. Tall Bear did not want to wait for the landing area to be large enough and rappelled down a long rope to the clearing being created.

As a group, they approached the plane. The front part had been flattened and torn off, leaving the back two-thirds of the plane still a partial cylinder. The pilots' bodies in the detached front part of the plane were missing. The bulk of the fuselage was intact but severely crumpled. Munro was able to access the plane from the front. The bodies of three people were present but smashed. One wore a kimono, and one had long golden hair. The others were dark-haired. The seat belts had given way, and the seats had come off the floor, and they were all crammed together against the bulkhead.

He picked out the body with the long golden hair and carried it outside in his arms. The legs were missing from the knees down, chopped off by the sliding seats as they detached from the floor. The face was barely recognizable. He wrapped the body in a blanket. Tomiko and Tall Bear were with him. His face was stone. The others swarmed into the remnants of the plane and carried out what was left of the other two women.

As he held the smashed corpse in his arms, they heard him murmuring to himself. "She is a little thing now, but I loved her. Oh, Elizabeth, *gra mo chroi*, my darling, my darling."

He carried her off a little way and sat on a felled tree with the body in his arms. They could hear his vague words...

"Now the carnival is over. I will love you till I die. Our tears were sweet as wine, but the carnival is over. We will never meet again." There were other snatches, which were occasionally audible. "Till all the seas gang dry," and eventually, "Eloi eloi, lama sabachthani."

Tall Bear stood silent, tears in his eyes, witnessing his father's grief. His own heart was breaking. Here was all that was left of the woman he had loved and protected since he was a child. At age twelve, he had followed her into the bush and had largely been the muscle at her shoulder ever since, other than her time as president of the USA, when he had to run the company they co-owned. He had always known that she loved his father in her own way. Even when she had been with other men, he knew that that love had never changed, and because of that constancy, she had never let him touch her.

Tomiko, dressed in a paratrooper's uniform for the sky dive, stood still, also expressionless. Her heart was full of mixed emotions. The reason she could never fully have the man she wanted was gone. Elizabeth had known for years how Munro felt about Tomiko. The other women in Munro's life, Don Pedro's daughter and Sweet Wolf, were simply meaningless interludes; but Elizabeth had always known that with Tomiko, it was serious. In dying, she had told the world of this recognition and had given Tomiko what she had long wanted. Munro was finally free, but she, Tomiko, was trapped. She had begun her second term as prime minister of Japan. It would be another two years before she was free. In spite of the urgings of Munro and Sweet Wolf, the former Japanese prime minister whom she was replacing, she had not married; and in spite of that, she had been elected.

Maybe she should ask the people of Japan if she could marry a gaijin or if she should resign, or maybe she should just go ahead anyway. She had been waiting twenty-five years for this. It was not an easy decision.

Eventually, Munro stood, turned around, and came to them. They came forward and helped him place the broken body in a body bag. Tall Bear stroked the golden hair and said his own farewell silently to the woman whom he had devoted almost all his life. Tomiko had helped place the other two women in body bags. The bags lay in the middle of the clearing. The search for the pilots had failed to find anything, as the nose cone had been completely destroyed.

Tall Bear called the helicopter in, and they winched up the body bags and then Tomiko and the others. A crash expert, whom Munro had brought with them, took samples. Munro had been fairly certain it had been sabotaged by enemies unknown, as engines usually do not just blow up and take part of a wing off. It took three trips to lift the personnel onto the plateau that Tall Bear had blown into the mountain.

As they refueled, Tall Bear, Munro, and Tomiko stood at the edge of the plateau, looking out on the jungle below. Tomiko and Munro stood together, and she had her arm around Munro's waist as they stood silent, lost in their own thoughts. Tall Bear was alone. He glanced at the couple. They had always seemed to him a little incongruous. His father was by now in late middle age and probably not as tall as he had been, but still he had the massive shoulders of a fighter. Tomiko was so small in comparison; she was more like Kodama, his own mother, Munro's first wife. He looked at the ground at his feet and, with a miner's eye, saw something. There was a streak of ore. He picked up samples. Gold! He had blown his way into what looked like a very high-purity gold seam. Elizabeth Munro's last mine, he thought. The greatest miner in the world, even in death. There was no doubt they would call this Elizabeth's Last Mine.

He would have to establish which country he was actually in, which he was fairly certain was Peru, and then request mining leases. This would have to be done as soon as the samples he had picked up had been analyzed, in the unlikely chance that some reporter or disaster video operator would want to visit the crash site to make a macabre video of Elizabeth's life.

They flew back to the nearest airfield and Elizabeth's remains were placed in cold storage, until the funeral arrangements could be determined. From there they were transferred to Hinchcliffe's base and then the ranch.

The bodies of the Japanese girls were flown with Tomiko back to Tokyo. Tomiko had decided that the video of their last moments was compelling enough to give them official recognition. The families had been contacted and had agreed to an official lying in, which was organized in an official building, and the bodies were protected by Japanese soldiers in full dress uniform. They had been so badly damaged that the coffins were closed.

Munro and Tall Bear were part of the group, paying tribute to the courage of these women. One of the women had been a Praetorian and a Japanese policewoman, and the other, a video journalist, so the Japanese police and Jacques video school people also were part of the cortege, making it a huge funeral. Munro said a few words in Japanese about the courage and dignity shown by these women and how their behavior had allowed the world to see the nobility of the women of Japan.

Back in America, the president had decided that Elizabeth should lie in state. A state funeral followed. She joined other famous Americans in her final resting place.

Munro and Tall Bear commissioned a statue of Elizabeth after the height and style of the Christ of Corcovado, the statue on the hill overlooking Rio de Janeiro, except at her feet were bas-relief statues of the Japanese girls who had died with her. She was dressed as a miner with her gun holstered at her hip. Her head was tilted back with her left hand shielding her eyes, which were fixed on the sky, where her money and drive had enabled the space colonies to be established, first on the moon and then on Mars. Her geologist's hammer was in her right hand. The statue was sited at the Chilean entrance to the pass which she and Tall Bear had blown through the Andes, where the new road and rail ran through to Buenos Aires. The statue took about four months to complete, and when it was finished, there were many who took the long journey to pay their respects to a great woman.

Tomiko, unusual for her, was uncertain about her future. She had waited more than twenty-five years for this moment, ever since she, as a young woman in her twenties, had met Munro. From the start, they had been hungry for each other. She had been the epitome of the Orient, being small, graceful, and beautiful. He was the West, tall and rugged. They always looked like an incongruous couple. He liked to play the simple friendly giant, and she, the quiet submissive woman. In reality, they were both the same, fierce and deadly.

She had not only seen the videos of him beating other men unmercifully in the ring but had watched him cave in the skull of a rapist when they had rescued Leda. She herself, acting as a Praetorian, had killed so many evil people she had lost count. Neither of them gave a second's thought to the violence inherent in the other. Tomiko never forgot the spasms of rage she had felt shaking Munro while he carried her after she had been beaten by the Japanese sword master. It had only been with difficulty that she had stopped him then from extreme violence. She felt it comforting to know that she was with a man who would kill for her without a second's hesitation.

They endlessly delighted in being with each other, either in silence or when he quoted poetry to her, which for her was sometimes a murmuring background and sometimes made her heart overflow with feelings, entranced by the beauty of the words. As he always said, the greatest thoughts had already been spoken by other men. She had heard so many of them so many times that she could say some lines with him when she desired. They shared many memories, from the thrill of battle when they had rescued Leda from a gang rape in Germany, to the quietness and peace of some of the great gardens of the world or on hilltops, where they loved looking out on the valley below, or cliffs looking at the wild ocean. She liked it when he would pick her up in his arms and carry her like a baby. She loved dancing with him, the feel of his body when she aroused him, and the quickness and the coordination of the dance, and the flamenco, when she swirled and swooped around him as he strutted with his arms crossed. She reveled in the gentleness or fierce passion of physical love with him, much more so than any of the other men she had been with. He cared deeply that she should have the same fulfilment that she gave him.

But there always had been the shadow of Elizabeth. He would never be free of her as long as she was alive, and when Tomiko wanted something, she wanted it to be hers and hers alone. And now there was another dark cloud. She had given him up to be prime minister of Japan. *The people would not like it if I married a gaijin. Maybe I should resign, but it is only two more years, and I have waited more than thirty already. But I want to give him a child of my own body, and I am already too old. But what no one knows is that I froze some of my eggs.*

The techniques of doing so had been perfected for the space people, and she had taken advantage of the technology. She would need all sorts of hormone balancing, but that was not out of the question. After all, the

Italian surgeon Antinori had managed to help a woman in her sixties give birth in 1994, and there had been others since. Her pelvic joints would be too stiff to allow a natural delivery, but there should be no problems with a C-section.

She thought about these things. She thought of talking to Running Bear, the old Athabascan Indian chief, but he was long gone to his final rest. He would have told her that he had no insight worth giving. The only other one she could talk to was Sweet Wolf, and she already knew what that one would say—"Tell them to go to hell, and do what you want, and stand for a third term." She thought some more. *Sweet Wolf is right. This life is not a dress rehearsal. Go for it. If the hormones make me irritable, well, my assistants will just have to live with it.* Her irritability might help her push through some government measures that she and Sweet Wolf had discussed.

A month had passed since the funeral of Elizabeth. The immediate agonizing heartbreak had passed, but Munro still felt the darkness and lingering sorrow. He tried to comfort himself by considering that it had been a life lived to the full, so where was the regret in that?

> The hand of the reaper takes the ears that are hoary
> But the voice of the weeper wails manhood in glory.
> The autumn winds rushing waft the leaves that are seerest.

She had done more in her life than almost anyone who had ever lived. Without her, there would be no colonies in space, and the future of mankind would look bleak. Because of her consummate skill and fierce drive the human race might have a future. So her requiem might be,

> Achievements manifold and happiness untold,
> And bade you spring to death as to a bride
> In all your ripeness power and pride
> And on you sandals the strong wings of youth.

It is not likely she would have wanted anything else.

Manon, concerned about his inaction, flew over from Europe to be with him, which she almost never did. She had not felt it would be proper for her to attend the funeral. She spent a day and a night with him. She was as gracious, brilliant, and pragmatic as always.

"We are getting old. I doubt that my body is much fun for you anymore. As you would say, I am like a misty dream, a faded scent of your youth, the last rose of summer. But there is one who has waited for you all these years. You must go to her now, without delay. Carpe diem! If she decides to wait until her presidency is over, *tant pis*, but you must make the offer now. I have brought you the ring for her."

She showed it to him. It was a central ruby set in white gold with radiating ruby crystals.

"The Rising Sun," he said, marveling.

"*Mais oui.* A fitting emblem for her to wear as she has never been anything but Japanese and has never wanted to be anything but Japanese, except for this strange liking for a certain gaijin man. Meet her in that garden you always talk about in Hirosaki or, better still, have her wait at the foot of the statue of the big Buddha surrounded by her people so that they can see that it is you who is coming as the supplicant, not her. And when you do, dress like the barbarian you are to show her people that while you are of the West, you are different from an island, like her."

Munro, who all his life had been in love with, been guided by, and had listened to Manon, did what she recommended. Tomiko, dressed in a classic kimono, with a few of her senior government people on either hand, stood in front of the big Buddha at Kamakura. He walked across the immense plaza on his own, dressed in his Gaelic finery, and went down on one knee before her. With both hands, he offered her a silver thistle of Scotland clamshell and sprung it open to reveal the ring that Manon had given him. She picked it up and put it on her finger.

He spoke to her in Japanese, "Tomiko-san, we were born for each other. Will you marry me?"

"I will. With all my heart."

She placed her hands on his shoulders, leaned over, and kissed him on the forehead. The crowd parted, and they walked hand in hand to the foot of the Buddha, where they both knelt in silence for a long moment.

They had a traditional Japanese wedding. Tomiko wore a white kimono but did not wear the *uchikake*, or white headdress, the symbol of submission, as she was not submitting to anyone. They married in a Shinto shrine and sipped from the three-stacked cups of sake.

Tomiko had discussed her possible resignation with her cabinet, but no one thought it was necessary. Her life, after all, had been an open book for years and very few did not know that her children had been brought up by Munro. One of them had remained in the West, mostly based in South America, working for Tall Bear. The other had joined Kodama's father and subsequently Munro's second son John, who was now running the keiretsu.

When they were alone the night of the wedding, he picked her up, stood her on the bed, and undressed her. He found it hard to believe that he had been so graced by this one, who was one of the most powerful women in the world. She stood before him as slim and sleek as the first time he had seen her. The ageless classic Japanese face, the same beautiful legs, and flat belly. Her arms were muscular, as after all, one does not get to be the best pistol shooter in the world for years without it showing. A couple of hundred pushups and hours of dry firing per day for thirty years leaves evidence.

"You are so wondrously beautiful, Tomiko."

"We are no longer young, gaijin," she said, holding his shoulders and looking seriously down into his eyes.

Looking up at her, he said, "You are *gra mo chroi*, the love of my heart."

She opened her legs and pulled him to her to start a long night, which he hoped would last the rest of their lives.

News of her pregnancy was initially kept quiet as they were worried that at their age, genetic problems would arise. It was not difficult to conceal as she had always worn a kimono at official meetings. It had always been her position that she was Japanese and intensely proud of it and was quite happy to wear traditional robes and stand out among the other heads of state at official meetings.

After the flamboyant dress at their engagement and marriage, Munro adopted the standard Japanese male dress of conservative black suit and white shirt when she felt he should be present at official functions with her. As the long-time governor of three states, Munro spent most of his time in the US but would fly to Japan when he could. In the last few weeks before the planned delivery, he was with her constantly. He knew his senior assistant, Maria Martens, was perfectly capable of overseeing all his positions and fulfilling the bulk of his duties in the US.

By this time, it was common knowledge that Tomiko was pregnant. She was roundly criticized in some quarters for having a child at her age. Her answer was quite simple, that if a woman marries a man, she should try her best to give him a child. She also pointed out that if the women in Japan and the West didn't start having more babies, their culture would die out eventually. She quoted the writer Mark Steyn that "the future belongs to those who show up." She felt she was young enough that she would still be around to watch the infant grow. The child was delivered uneventfully by C-section, and there were soon official photographs of the happy couple and their little boy.

Munro, when interviewed, said that he did have six children already from four different women, but to have a son from Tomiko was a gift from God. The child remained with her for the rest of her term in office. When that was up and her replacement installed, she flew to the US, where she took over as head of the Space Academy. That, and motherhood, was enough to occupy her time at present. What the future would bring was unclear, but she looked forward to it with interest.

CHAPTER 14

The Silk One

She was crouched in a corner, bleeding, and weeping. The woman came in and struck her across the shoulders with a stick. "Be quiet. Stop crying. This is your life. Get used to it."

She had no idea of her age, perhaps seven or eight. She had grown up in a poverty-stricken village. She was never sure where, perhaps Kyrgyzstan. She never subsequently had any interest in finding out. She was one of several girls in the family. The family had no money and no prospects, and in that culture, girls were useless, an encumbrance. She was sold to a commercial traveler who took her to a small town where she was sold to a brothel. She was a pretty little thing, with very almond eyes and a round face, which gave her a Chinese look. The brothel owner kept her as a servant for a year or so until she was felt to be worth something sexually and, at that time, sold her on to an acquaintance in a larger town.

That day was the first time she had served her destined role in life. She had known this was coming for years, but the reality was just as bad as she had feared. The man had a huge belly and was poorly endowed sexually, so he had difficulty entering her, but he had paid a lot for her and so beat her until he could manage it. Her face hurt as much from his beating as her body did from his penetration.

Her life continued in much the same fashion for the next couple of years. She was clever and learned her trade, so fortunately, there were relatively few beatings, and her face remained undamaged. One reasonably wealthy passing merchant had her and liked her looks and her skill, so he bought her to take home with him, to the larger city where he lived. He treated her well. To his surprise, he found the little thing was not only decorative, sexually inventive, and experienced but was clever and could do arithmetic. He then taught her how to read and write, which again surprised him, as she learned with consummate ease. He showed her some accounting and started to use her for his business and found her extraordinarily capable. His wives, of whom he had three, felt she was different, so they forced her to do the worst chores around the house and beat her every chance they got.

The merchant found them doing that one day and did his best to put a stop to it, so they no longer beat her in visible areas. He heard from another traveling merchant that someone in Afghanistan, or maybe it was Pakistan, was looking for girls who could do mathematics. He felt sorry for the little girl in his house and was sure his wives would maim or kill her if she stayed. He knew she was good at figures, so he prevailed on another traveling merchant he knew to buy her. That one took her over the border into Tajikistan. She was to his taste sexually, but eventually, he found someone else who had heard the rumor, so he sold her to a merchant who brought her into Pakistan, where someone had a phone number. This contact contacted another, and eventually, the merchant had a visitor.

The visitor wished to test the girl before he bought her. The girl found it very strange to sit down with the man. He showed her a book of puzzles and asked her to identify patterns. She found the first ones easy to do, so he produced another book, which again gave her no problems. The visitor and the merchant then haggled for a while, and he bought her. She had had to sexually satisfy the merchant, and now this new purchaser also, which she expected, as being normal male behavior. She was taken south and tested again and sold on.

She eventually ended up in one of these awful dreary towns in the north of England, living in a house with some other little girls, but these were white girls, which she had never seen before. She had to sexually service her new owner but was not placed on the general market like the other girls. Some of the youngest of these, who looked younger than she, were servicing up to fifteen clients a day, and they moved in and out as some were sold and others bought. The younger they were, the more they were in demand. Her new owner contacted a telephone number, and a meeting was arranged.

A psychologist came to see the child and tested her. By this time, she was well aware of Raven's matrices, having been tested often, and flew through the books he showed her. The psychologist scored her as at least 200, recognizing that at that level, testing was unreliable. He also did some personality testing but found that very unreliable as she had been brought up to lie about everything and was so clever that she could twist her answers to whatever she thought he wanted. The psychologist contacted one of Manon's London-based assistants, who came to see the owner to buy the child.

The negotiations lasted an hour or so as the seller wanted more than the buyer was prepared to pay, as this might set a precedent. The buyer gave up and had actually entered a taxi and was preparing to depart for the train station when the seller realized that she was serious and came running out of the house and knocked on the taxi window. Disgusted and fed up with this heartless pimp, as she had seen the other children in that foul place—and everyone in Britain knew what was happening to these poor children, with no police or official interference either at the state or federal level—the buyer opened the window and offered 30 percent less than she had previously been prepared to pay. The seller balked so she told the driver to take her to the station and began to close the window. Frantic, the seller agreed. The buyer remained in the car, while the seller brought the child out. When she was safely in the taxi, money changed hands, and the taxi left.

From London, the girl was moved to Luxembourg. As most illegals were going the opposite direction, from Europe to the UK, reverse smuggling was not difficult. She ended up in the same house Isis had been in several years before. The woman supervisor was different, but the doctor and the old professor were the same. He had, by this time, a number of brilliant children pass through his hands and relished the thought of another.

Isis, the brilliant Egyptian theoretical physicist, had been one of his early pupils and had contacted him when she was older and had thanked him for his help. He basked in the reflected glory of her achievements when she sent him speeches she had given and research papers written, where his name was mentioned.

He never asked where these incredible children were from, and some were not even sure themselves as their language, when they first met him, was not good enough and their general knowledge often nonexistent.

They were simply in transit, waiting until their various medical afflictions were cured so that they could be passed on up the line to America. He knew that their ultimate destination was the Munro Foundation School in Arizona. His role was to teach them as much math as possible, as quickly as possible. Some were quiet, frightened children, but some were almost preternaturally calm.

This one was different. She was strikingly beautiful and knew it. She had a round face, almond eyes, and long, black hair, which she frequently plaited into a long pigtail that would almost extend to her waist. She was very knowing and very confident in herself. She set about seducing him as soon as they were alone, stroking him as they sat together. In spite of his age, she aroused him. For a fleeting moment, he considered allowing her to carry on, but then his sense of morality and reality kicked in, and he put her hand away and told her no. He waved his finger in front of her and said, "No, no, no!"

She simply grinned at him and reached again for his obvious arousal. He grabbed her hand and lightly smacked the back of it, again saying, "No!"

"No?" she said disbelievingly. "No?"

"No!" he said firmly and pointed to the math book.

Like the other girls he had coached, in spite of her rudimentary English, he found her grasp of math principles quite extraordinary. This girl had the same blazing genius he had seen in Isis. It took two doses of medicine to clean out her intestinal parasites. The private jet, which had to be used to avoid official scrutiny, was unavailable for some time, so she was with him longer than most. Therefore, her grasp of English became such that he could converse with her before she flew off to the US.

She told him her story of child prostitution and indicated that she had been married many times. When he asked how that could be, she told him that some conservative men made the pretense of marriage before they would have her. Apparently, this was because of some custom she did not understand. It was meaningless, so she did not care one way or another, as it always ended up with a man on top of her. She tried to seduce him several times, but he had the strength to refuse. He told her she had been brought to him for her mind, not her body. She had some difficulty understanding that anyone was interested in her for her mind. She had known she was clever because she had done some accounting for the original merchant, but this world of symbols and concepts and praise when she understood and mastered new intricacies was totally alien and foreign to her. She loved it and loved the lavish praise given to her by the old math professor.

The woman who brought her over from England had shown her how to use the language-teaching machine, and the lady who ran the house showed her the various other wonders she had never seen or used. The food was quite different from anything she had known, and when she was allowed outside, which she had never been in Pakistan or England, the weather was also. It rained, which she had seldom experienced, and everything was green. Eventually, the word came that the plane had arrived, and she would be leaving the next day. She hugged the old man and made one last halfhearted attempt to seduce him, which he gently stopped. He knelt down before her and hugged her.

"I think you will be one of the great ones," he said. "I have been honored to teach several girls of genius, but I think you may be the greatest of them all. Do not forget this old man who loves you."

She looked at him to see if he was making fun of her, but he seemed to be serious. She hugged him in return.

The only plane she had been on before was the flight from Pakistan, jammed in economy, overflowing with people, bags, and smells. A private jet with wide seats and its own galley was a revelation. Her female escort took her to the plane, where she met the two pilots. She had been given a computer, which she took with her on the plane. The guide showed her numerous memory sticks that she could use, as well as her math and English lessons. While they waited for the passengers, the guide showed her some maps of the world, of where she thought she was from, where she was, and where she was going to in America.

The main passenger was a Western woman, with an Oriental female companion dressed in a kimono. The Western woman introduced herself as Teresa.

"Happy you have come to join us," she said. "You will find things very different, and you're going to like it."

They strapped in, and the plane took off immediately. When they were in the air, Teresa made sure the girl had enough to keep her amused, and the two women got down to work on their own computers. After an hour or so, the Oriental woman brought some tea and snacks for the girl and sat with her, talking to her about who she was and where she was from. The Oriental woman was struck by the fact that the girl looked like her. She told the girl that she was from a country called Japan and showed her on a map. The girl did not know where she came from.

The girl was excited about this new place she was being taken. Her time in Luxembourg had been totally different from anything she had experienced in her short life. There had been no beatings, no sex, and no housework. She had had a room of her own, with a bathroom. She had been taught things she had never known. People were interested in her learning things. She was valued for her mind, not her body. It all seemed like a dream. And now this incredibly luxurious plane. She hoped it would not end. She found unbelievable the range of memory sticks available for her to review. By now, she could understand enough English that she watched a couple of movies. Eventually, she fell asleep and woke up as the plane was coming in to land.

No officials accosted them at the airport when they landed. A limo with a young dark-haired woman was there waiting to pick her up. Teresa introduced the girl to the young woman, who called herself Maria, and then after speaking to Maria for a short time, she got back on the plane, which was refueling, as she said she had a meeting she had to attend on the Coast. Maria escorted the girl with her few belongings to the vehicle. She made sure she was strapped in, and they drove off. Maria chatted to her as they drove. They eventually left the main road and entered a compound through a gate, which was opened after they were checked by an armed guard at the gatehouse. She could see, stretching out on either side from the gate, a high fence of multistranded barbed wire. The limo drove up to a large house, where a man and woman were standing at the door, waiting for her. He opened the car door for her and helped her out. She stood in front of him, looking up as he was very tall. He looked down at her, then went on one knee in front of her. He held her arms.

"Welcome to your new home, princess, I am Munro, and this is Marine, who is a nurse and who will look after you."

The nurse showed her around the building, including the dining room, gymnasium, and piazza, where they held their evening meetings. She then showed her to a room, which would be her own. The room had its own facilities, which by now the girl knew how to use. She opened a door in the wall, which opened into an office where the man who called himself Munro sat at a desk with Maria, the young woman who had escorted her from the airport. He indicated that if she needed anything, she could ask him.

The girl soon fitted in with the others, who appeared to be from all over the world. Her English was already understandable. She found herself woefully behind the other children in math, but she understood the concepts easily and, with the help of tutors, caught up with astonishing rapidity. Within a few weeks or months, her math was outstanding, as the old European professor had predicted. She had been with them for a few weeks, and no one had propositioned her, so she was not clear about the protocol. She fearlessly entered Munro's office one evening after the meeting in the piazza and asked him when he wanted to have sex with her. He was behind his desk, working on some papers. He looked up.

"You are here for your brains, not for sex."

"You mean I don't have to spread my legs for you?"

"This is America. It is against the law for you to have sex with a man until you are seventeen years old."

"That makes no sense. I have had sex many times before. Since you are the master here, I would like to make you happy and to thank you for bringing me to this place where I am no longer beaten. I am very good at sex. Why do you want to wait until I am seventeen before you have sex with me?"

"Child, it will never be necessary for you to have sex with me. This is America. You are free."

"Even after seventeen?"

"Even after seventeen. It is your body. You decide. You can say no."

"This is fantasy. It cannot be true. Even if the man insists?"

"This is America. If you say no and he tries to force you, you shoot him. That is why we are teaching you to shoot."

"You mean I, as a woman, can kill a man?"

"Yes, of course. In this culture a woman's body is her own. If you kill a man who forces you, we don't beat you or stone you to death or throw acid on you. You are an individual whose name I unfortunately can't pronounce."

He told her she was from one of the "stans." He was not sure which one, but he suspected somewhere up near the Chinese border, around Kashgar, given her oriental appearance. The only woman he had ever heard of from that area was called the Silk One, so maybe she would like to be called that, as he liked the name. She went off and got one of the other girls to help her look up the name. She found it in one of George MacDonald Fraser's books.

She went back to confront Munro.

"I will consent to be called the Silk One, but she was Ko Dali's daughter. I want nothing to do with my biological father. So will you be Ko Dali, my father?"

"I will, if you keep it a secret between us."

"I promise. Also, if I am the Silk One, then I want to wear silk."

"Wait till you are a little older, then you may."

A few days later, she again spoke to him. "I read that book. I do not like the man the Silk One was in love with. I loathe and despise these people. I will never fall in love with one of them, and I will never go back."

"No one here will ever make you go back, Silk One. Stay with us as long as you like. I know you know how to seduce men, but please don't until you are a lot older."

The Silk One had been trained, and it showed. "If I do not entice men, what will you give me in exchange?"

"Silk One, if you keep your mind pure, someday I will find a man worthy of you."

"Will he ride up on a white horse to take me away?"

"If that is your wish, Silk One. I will arrange that. You have my promise."

The Silk One blossomed. Little Sister, the first theoretical physicist the Prometheus Group had found, recognized her incandescent brilliance and took her under her wing; but like Isis, the Silk One remained a wild one. All the girls could wear what they wanted, but most conformed to jeans and Western shirts. The Silk One took to wearing silk, as she was happy to stand out, and on occasion, she would wear the Chinese Chong Sang dress. She did all the things the other girls did, including horseback riding, shooting, and dancing. Her main goal, however, was quantum physics, and she soon could describe in words what the other geniuses could only hint at.

She described it as sinking into matter and seeing the patterns of atoms and electrons. Even Munro could visualize that. It was when she sank in deeper that only a few could follow. She described it as walking down and sometimes up glittering canyons where stars on shining strings appeared and vanished, moved, and shifted, joining, and separating, sometimes purposefully and sometimes random. Isis had described a similar eerie landscape to Munro. Isis had been afraid of getting lost in these canyons and not being able to find her way home. She had wanted someone at the entrance to the maze, calling her name, so that she could find her way out. Little Sister and Helga had never really been able to describe it, although they did not argue with the picture painted by the Silk One. Some of the boys who had joined the Space Academy knew what she was talking about and could walk with her through the same canyons of the mind.

Like a few of the others, by age fifteen, she had significant theorems, theories and equations, and principles to her name and was a full professor in both Arizona, Tokyo, and Madrid; and people were talking about a Nobel Prize in the near future. Before Isis was forced into space by repeated assassination attempts, the Silk One spent time with her. The pair were equally wild and far-ranging in their interests and imagination and, in consequence, took some interest in geopolitics. The obvious collapse of the West fascinated her, with eloquent descriptions by authors Mark Steyn and Douglas Murray. She had difficulty understanding why such a successful culture should voluntarily submit to the violent primitive culture she had come from or try again the failed experiment of socialism. She thought that the history of 100 million corpses as a result of multiple previous socialist attempts should be enough, with the ongoing disasters in South America and Africa.

She began to consider the root cause of the decline, as it had happened to all successful states and empires. It seemed obvious that there had to be social telomeres in the same way that there were biological telomeres so that life was not and could never be immortal. The telomere perhaps was that a society simply got so comfortable that individual life span began to matter, and if it did, why throw away one's own life or the life of one's children if you could hire no-account foreigners instead? She had read somewhere that civilization rises on hobnail boots and falls on silk slippers.

The strange concept of welfare also seemed universal that "all men are paid for existing and no man must pay for his sins." As someone once said, "All democracies eventually vote themselves more stuff than they can afford and in consequence go bankrupt." Before that happens, with sufficient wealth, utopian dreams could in theory become possible, and in an ideal world, Epicurus and his beliefs could function for a time. She pointed out to her friends, however, that in reality, theoretical utopia was, as someone else had said, "approached across a sea of blood and no one ever got there." Welfare or bread and circuses were as old as time itself. Marcus Aurelius fought all his life to preserve the Roman Empire, but when his son Commodus took over, he signed useless peace treaties and retreated to a sybaritic life in Rome. Similarly, the empires in the Far East would rise and fall as they were weakened internally by corruption. Therefore, logically, the West was doomed.

As she dreaded the thought of being thrown back into the brutal theocratic medieval culture, which had so abused her as a child, she wondered if the West could be resurrected. Her conclusion was quite simply that to do so, the Calvinist Protestant work ethic would have to be reintroduced. This would require some concept of God. It did not matter if God existed or not; it mattered that people lived and acted as if he did. The slave religion of Judeo-Christianity did help to further that role. Isis preferred the gods of Egypt, whom she was busy reinventing. Munro, when she questioned him about God, admitted to the Silk One that he had a sneaking admiration for the Norse gods and thought Valhalla sounded like a pretty good place to end up while waiting for Ragnarok, the battle at the end of time. That seemed much more attractive than Nirvana.

As far as the Silk One could see, the loss of basic religious principles led to acceptance of jealousy, fake compassion, and resentment, which currently was ruining everything in the West. It meant that the political leaders ultimately had no morals, as if there was no higher being to answer to and no judgment after death, there were no long-term consequences to lies and corruption. The absence of any future penalties meant continuous expansion of lies and corruption. Education had been taken over by collectivist ideologues who had and continued to corrupt the naive and not-too-bright young people who entered universities, the media, and politics. Why young people, many of whom never had and never would have an original idea in their whole life, should attend a university in the first place was a great mystery to the Silk One. And why would anyone pick such a dead-end profession as a humanities professor if one could do anything valuable, useful, and intellectually or physically satisfying, such as build a wall or dig a well? The old saying was perfectly accurate—"Those who can, do, and those who can't, teach," and it could be added currently that those who are morons, preach. Eighteen-year-olds rushing about, waving placards about changing the world about which they knew nothing, egged on by their idiot professors, were simply a sign of the times. The fact that the global warming scam could persist for twenty years or more was simply an indication of the level of corruption in the higher orders and idiocy in the lower.

The current Judeo-Christian clergy, at least in Europe, were worse than useless, with some English bishops loudly proclaiming that God did not exist. How such hypocrisy could be acceptable and not be laughed out of existence was stunning. Even the most corrupt must surely have a few qualms about preaching something in which they had no belief. Outside America, with its Constitution, free speech was no longer allowed. These silly snowflakes bellowing about hate speech had no idea what was waiting for them in the wings.

The Silk One would giggle with her intellectual equals about the foolishness and stupidity of the Western world imbeciles encouraging and helping prepare the boot that would stamp on their face forever. One of her friends, in a somber mood, described these fools as parasites feeding off the remnants of those who had fought for freedom. She felt sorry for Munro, whom most of the girls regarded as their savior, as he seemed to hope that the situation could be salvaged. It was obvious to her that if one wished to turn things around, a wholesale house cleaning would be necessary. A few nukes or a couple of big rocks coming down from space onto the Middle East would take care of outside enemies. The fifth column within was much more difficult. Closing down all universities, other than STEM departments, would only be a start. All educational colleges would have to go. Governments consisting of useless bureaucrats and politicians would have to be downsized almost out of existence.

This was such a great task that she did not think any Western country would be prepared even remotely to carry out such a program. Without some major changes however, nothing would be left but a slowly progressive slide into a dystopian hell. Likely eventually a tipping point would be reached where it would happen overnight. The Silk One felt it very important therefore to keep an eye on the approach of the tipping point so that she and her friends could hastily leave and go into space and pull up the drawbridge behind them for a century or two.

Munro regretfully agreed with the analysis of the Silk One and her friends. The only question really was whether the tipping point would be gradual or occur suddenly. At the back of his mind was always the possibility that maybe there would be a terrorist airstrike. For some reason, no one seemed to know, or they had forgotten, that a single high-level air-burst nuclear explosion could knock out all electronics under the blast area. If that were to occur, civilization under the area of the explosion would collapse in days. A major Carrington effect or sunspot coronal mass ejection could do the same thing.

Meantime, as an intellectual game with Isis, she played with Martin Luther's edicts. To reactivate Judeo-Christianity, new rules would be required and enforced socially, in the same way that cigarette smoking had been largely stamped out. She constructed her tentative new rules, but apart from showing them to Munro and the Foundation people, she made no attempt to publicize them, especially in her own name. Isis, after all, was driven off Earth essentially by relentless suicide attacks a short time later, more for her work on fusion rather than her apostasy, although that was given as the main reason for the attacks. The Silk One had no wish to follow just yet. She was having too much fun.

In view of the attacks on Isis and crazed calls to violence by idiot university students and more sinister forces, the Silk One had always avoided conferences, to the great dismay of her senior colleagues. She would video conference but only with a pixelated face. She never spoke to the media and never went near universities. A few of the more brilliant men in her field were allowed to visit her in Arizona, as she preferred to meet them at the ranch or the Space Academy, where she was surrounded by multiple layers of protection. Having kept her face out of the media, no one knew what she looked like, so Munro felt that it was relatively safe for her to fool around in Japan, where she was just another anonymous oriental beauty, with a couple of friends. No one needed to know that her friends happened to be heavily armed world-class shooters.

As well as Isis, La Contessa was interested in the Silk One's views on reactivating religion as a way of curtailing the pervasive corruption that Catholicism did not seem able to prevent. Hinchcliffe was looking for a bleak, stern warrior religion. Something to inspire her soldiers before battle and comfort them in the long watches of the night. She wanted a version of Mithras from Silk One.

> Mithras, God of the morning
> Our trumpets waken the wall
> Rome is above all nations
> But thou are over all.

and

Mithras god of the midnight,
Here where the great bull dies
Look on your children in darkness and
Take our sacrifice.
Many roads hast thou fashioned,
All of them lead to the light
Mithras, also a soldier
Teach us to die alright.

The Silk One did eventually produce a version of religion that Hinchcliffe approved.

The three heavyweight boxing champions Munro, Miguel, and Archie Moore—or the three stooges, as some unkind people called them—liked to get together and share war stories. Usually, they did so privately. Once, however, when Moore was visiting Japan, they had a dinner meeting at a semi-traditional restaurant. Miguel and Moore were with their wives, Little Sister and Yaeko, and Munro accompanied Tomiko. One of the video journalists was also there and shot some footage. They never did that again, as they were not sure the publicity was good, as it looked too strange for a Western audience.

The women were all dressed in kimonos, and the men were relaxing in the traditional Japanese male robe. They sat around a table, drinking sake from tiny cups, and eating food brought to them by a traditionally dressed waitress, who knelt to serve them. The only concession was that there were foot wells, as none of the Western men could tolerate a kneeling position for more than a few minutes. The shoji screens were open onto a small perfect Japanese garden. There were complaints in the US media that Moore was getting too friendly with the Japanese. As the media complained about him all the time, he largely ignored them.

After the birth of her child, Tomiko agreed to a short holiday in the Caribbean, so Munro rented a place on one of the islands and his friends joined him. Most Oriental women loathe the sun due to the damage it would do to their skin, which was why so many of them remained flawless even in old age. The Caribbean therefore was not somewhere they actually enjoyed. A video journalist did record them on a small boat. It was festooned with awnings to keep the sun off the women, who were covered in sunscreen. Munro realized fairly quickly that it was a mistake, especially as the boat had to be followed by a couple of boats full of Praetorians and other grim-faced gunmen. The Silk One, who accompanied them, did seem to enjoy it.

The men, all former fighters and physically fit, were recorded as doing pushups with their women kneeling on their backs. Munro said he was too old to compete with the younger men, but Tomiko protested that she was the smallest and, in spite of her recent pregnancy, the lightest, so that was cancelled out. Moore, of course, won the competition, which ended up with the men throwing the women overboard.

The Silk One was laughing at the women being thrown into the sea, so the men picked her up by her arms and legs, swung her, and pitched her high in the air. She had spent time on a trampoline, so she was lithe, flexible, and beautiful as she touched her toes at the top of the arc before going vertical for a perfect dive. Everyone was very impressed, so they threw her in again. The gunmen in the accompanying boat applauded loudly.

The men in the accompanying boats began to throw the female Praetorians into the water. In retaliation, the women swam to the main boat and helped throw the men in. The video of President Moore being thrown into the sea by four women, each holding a limb, was not terribly dignified.

When they returned to the harbor, they found a very large traditional three-mast sailing ship had arrived. As few had seen such an old-fashioned beauty, the women asked permission to climb the rigging, as it was something they had never done before and would likely never do again. None of the men did. Munro told them about how in the old days of the sailing ships, some of the more intrepid men would dance the "High Level Hornpipe," a sailor's dance, on the highest cable between the masts. He regretted doing so because the Silk One immediately wanted to try to do it.

Much against her wishes, Munro insisted that she be tied on with a rope through a belt he forced her to wear, attached to the cable with a slipknot. Being fearless, she performed, dancing heel and toe, forty feet above the deck. The video of her hair-raising exploit produced some copycats, but as far as anyone knew, fortunately there were no deaths. Her name was never mentioned and the face blurred, as the policy of the Foundation was to keep her under the terrorist radar.

In fact, while there had been a great deal of publicity about Little Sister, the committee of the Foundation recognized that when she began to work on sustained fusion power, which would put the finances of the terrorist funders in the Middle East under pressure, assassination attempts were likely. They had to find the brilliant children, and to do that, they had to publicize the Foundation; but they did not wish the individuals to be easily identified, as it was too difficult to guard them all. The only truly safe place for these geniuses was in space, where assassins had yet to penetrate. So they avoided public forums such as lectures at universities, outside a small very select number, such as Arizona, Tokyo, and Madrid; and even there, the talks were only to highly selected STEM students, as the rest were not likely to understand concepts or outcomes. Bodyguards were always present. At such meetings, the Silk One wore a mask to avoid or interfere with facial recognition technology.

The Foundation had always been ambivalent about publicity. They needed some to attract the children, and they needed publications in the appropriate journals to attract the best and the brightest young minds to the Space Academy, but they did not want the individuals to become well recognized or be household names. This had not been clear initially so Little Sister was world famous. Helga had always kept herself in her own Asperger's prison and so was safe. Isis, the flamboyant one, had attracted extremely unwelcome attention, as the repeated assassination attempts had shown.

In the older, simpler days of the War of Jenkins' Ear, such threats were usually eliminated at source. Even the world's most famous assassination program, the hashishim, run by Hassan the Assassin, the Old Man of the Mountains, had been stamped flat by the Mongols Jebe Noyan and Subotai, when they overran the Middle East and climbed up and literally threw the Old Man off his mountain.

Rather than walking toward the fire, however, the cowardice, the lack of Western response to the fatwa declared on Rushdie had changed the world. The constraints of today, at least at present, prevented measures being taken against current hashishim or shaheeds. For these reasons, the Silk One was kept as hidden as possible. All those in the field of theoretical physics were well aware of her incandescent genius, but that was a fairly tight-knit international community.

Munro hoped that her relative anonymity would give her cover, but he still wanted someone to keep a close eye on her. He would have preferred someone as cold and quiet and deadly as the ninja, but the ninja was already protecting La Contessa. When he spoke to him, fortunately, the ninja felt his job in Mexico was done, that La Contessa was now adequately surrounded by enough people with adequate skill and loyalty.

He was quite happy to return to the ranch, where he would serve as the silent shield on her shoulder. The Praetorian girls, dressed anonymously, also served as bodyguards, but she wanted more freedom, so his fear for her safety never fully went away. He would have preferred to have her in the safety of space, but the Silk One had no desire to leave Earth. Her foul childhood had not destroyed her love of life, the gaiety, and the wonder.

CHAPTER 15

Out of a Misty Dream

Munro knew that Manon was not long for this world. The last time he had been with her, he was shocked as she looked old and tired. Never before had he seen her like that. She herself felt her decline. For a hard, competent, supremely confident woman, her physical appearance and her weakness were distressing. Being exceedingly wealthy, she had more than enough staff to look after all her needs, and she still had biweekly meetings with Teresa, who now handled her business empire.

For years, Manon had acted as a mentor to many of the genius girls of the Foundation, teaching them how to navigate through the difficult political, personal, and emotional side of life. Her earthy cynicism was a source of great amusement to these girls. The boys who grew up at the ranch also looked forward to getting to know someone whom the Foundation girls regarded with a mixture of gratitude, awe, and affection. She found these fierce, bright, often totally independent young minds a source of pleasure, and in spite of her increasing frailty, they still came to spend time with her in Luxembourg.

She had an episode of pneumonia and feeling really unwell, she phoned Munro. He immediately flew to Luxembourg to look after her. With antibiotics and some chest physiotherapy, she recovered, but the illness left her weakened and clearly aware of her own mortality. Munro was in a quandary. She had never had any desire to leave Europe, but she had by now outlived all her old friends. Edith, a former employee in her first bordello and with whom she had started her fashion empire, had passed on.

The madams who had run her entertainment division had retired and had been replaced. The politicians and police chiefs she had worked with for years were all now replaced with younger people who knew Teresa better than her. Her secretive main enforcer was now a middle-aged Japanese American housewife with several almost-adult children, who was married to the head of US Border Patrol. This man, Pedro Morales, suspected but preferred not to know of his wife's unorthodox activities, which she undertook as an antidote to her own post-traumatic stress disorder, which had arisen as a result of injuries sustained in a gunfight years ago when she had been guarding Munro.

Manon took pleasure in lunching once a week with Munro's eldest son with Elizabeth, the former president of the US. She had long ago, when he first worked for her, nicknamed him the Buccaneer for his numerous financial exploits. He ran two huge hedge funds based in Luxembourg. They would reminisce over past coups, and he was still interested in her views on affairs and felt comfortable telling her about his recent exploits, about which he was usually very reticent. Young Pedro, Munro's son by the Don's daughter, now in a very senior position in running that large international construction company, would visit her when he was in Luxembourg consulting with the firm's bankers. She knew it would not be long before young Pedro would take over the whole company.

Munro was worried that Manon was becoming isolated. Of course, people still danced around her, but Munro begged her to come and live in Arizona, where he would be closer to her and she would be surrounded by all the admiring children. She could continue her business connections, and she could teach the children there and hold seminars for the young people at the Academy who were going into space. The colonies on Mars were quietly beginning to reach a degree of sophistication, but the moon still resembled a combination of a sprawling, brawling wide-open STEM university and shipbuilding yard. Deimos and Phobos, the moons of Mars, were also developing into engineering and shipbuilding centers and repair shops.

Knowing that it is never a good idea to uproot an elderly person from their familiar surroundings, as this can lead to confusion and rapid deterioration, Manon was very uncertain about accepting Munro's offer. She eventually decided to do so, with the proviso that if she did not feel at home within a short time, she would return to Luxembourg.

She had what she felt she needed packed and came across on the company jet. Munro was waiting for her on the apron as the plane taxied up and the stairs were lowered. Maria Martens, Tomiko—now head of the Space Academy—and several of the children were with him. He boarded to help her deplane.

"Welcome to America," he said, as he enfolded her in his arms.

She descended the stairs and met the others with smiles and embraces. At the ranch, her new apartment had been remodeled to match her own in Luxembourg. She found chaotic mealtimes with the children milling around and adults dropping in and out and very different from her usual quiet, calm existence. She initially liked the evening meetings, where she would often chair the sessions for the girls, who either knew her or knew off her and questioned her about the numerous facets of her life and her views on some issues.

But it was different. It was a little noisy. The muted gunfire from the range where visiting Praetorians and others taught the children to shoot was a background noise, and there was the music from the singing and the dance lessons. There was constant intellectual conflict among the girls of the Foundation, which had been muted when she first came, and the obvious adulation when Little Sister or the Silk One was present. Manon was used to being the center of attention and being ignored by the girls as they would fight and argue over points and theories about which she did not understand a word unsettled her. Whiteboards and computer screens would come out, and flip charts with little children drawing unintelligible formulae.

Munro apologized for this intellectual ferment and pointed out that he did not understand much about quantum physics either, but this was the whole basis for the school. They wanted ideas—the wilder, the better—and no one was more off the wall than the Silk One—with her *qipao*, a Chinese-style dress, and long pigtail—occasionally rushing off to share a concept with Helga, who was worshipped by the girls, but who remained trapped in her room in the basement of the ranch by her Asperger's.

Manon found this intellectual hothouse just too much. She had handled numerous girls from the Foundation over the years, but that had been one-on-one, not in an overwhelming mass—or a pack of ravening young wolves, as she described it ruefully to Munro. Besides, Tomiko was there, and while the two women got on with each other, as they knew each other's history, there was a certain tension. After a couple of weeks,

Manon realized that this was not going to work and decided to return to Luxembourg. It was with a sad heart that Munro saw her off.

Teresa was there to meet her at the other end. It was a reversal of their original encounter decades before, when Teresa—the lonely, unhappy waif from an American trailer park, a stranger to Europe—first met Manon. Munro, deeply concerned at her increasing frailty, tried to call her several times a week to speak to her, even if only a few words.

About six months later, Manon called unexpectedly at midday. This was unusual, as it was usually him who called her, and she would have known that at that time of day, he would be at work, likely at some sort of meeting. Alarmed, he excused himself, leaving Maria to chair the meeting, and took the call in his office.

"Manon, are you well?"

"No. I feel very tired—very, very tired. Come to me now."

She was not peremptory. She just sounded utterly weary. He had been dreading this call from the woman he had loved since he first met her in Luxembourg many decades before. He had been young, unsophisticated, and full of raw power and savagery, the newly crowned heavyweight champion of the world; and she was the most elegant, beautiful woman he had ever seen. She was at least fifteen years older than he was, and her early years had been hard, very hard, so this phone call had been inevitable. No one lives forever, and she was getting old, "on the way to dusty death." He left Maria Martens to finish the meeting, and as usual, she assumed control of his affairs in the US. He called an assistant to get him a private jet and have a bag packed for him, caught a cab to the airport, and within a little over an hour, was in the air.

One of the Japanese policewoman Praetorians happened to be visiting the ranch prior to returning to Japan, having just finished a shooting competition in America. When asked, she signed on and came along as Munro's bodyguard. People were waiting for him at the private airport they used in Luxembourg, and he was rushed to Manon's apartment. Aware of his impending arrival, Manon, ever a fighter, had her nurse get her out of bed and smarten her up, and she met him sitting in a chair. Munro went on his knees before her, picking up and kissing her hands.

"Manon, l'amour de ma vie. How good it is to see you."

"*Merci beaucoup*, thank you for coming so quickly. I was afraid. I thought I was slipping away and would never see you again."

"Manon, you will live forever."

"Liar, *toujours*, always the gentle liar. *Mais peut etre*, perhaps in your heart. But now, *je suis fatigue'* and would pass on. I have done everything I set out to do. My only regret is that perhaps we should have had a child. *Mais, c'est la vie*, that's life. We can't have everything. I have been thinking about that Roman Centurion."

"The one in Libya? What was it? 'I Lucius, Centurion of the Ninth, have found that in life you can have love or power, but not both.' Manon, you have always had my love. You were my Theodora, my Roxelana, all my life."

"I know, I have always known. A lifetime ago. That big, terrible young man walking with me, arm in arm down the Champs-Élysées, telling me he loved me and wanting to marry me. I loved it. I never told you, but I loved it when you hammered these other men into the ground, the savagery you hid from the world. My man, *le champion du monde*, who would protect me from anyone who would harm me. I never forgot that night you snarled like a wolf, 'I am the man on the pale horse. Who would dare insult you?' I felt safe in your arms. I had arrived, and no one would ever hurt me again. I loved it and loved you then, but my heart was breaking because I knew it could never be. *Quelle dommage.*"

"Manon, you know that I have loved you all my life, *toujour*, and will, until the stars fall."

"I know. I have always known, but the song ends eventually, the Carnival is over and evening falls around. I would like one more time, *encore une fois*, to wear the purple, to dress up, wear my jewelry, and drink some champagne with you, maybe at La Tour D'Argent in Paris. *Mais non*, that would be too exhausting. Maybe your old restaurant, Munro's, *ce soir*, this evening."

"That, we can manage. Who would you like to invite Teresa, Leda, La Marquesa, Sheila, and the Buccaneer?"

"Local people would be fine. No country's president. That would result in too much publicity, and we still do not want to draw too much attention to the company, as I think civil war in Europe is not so far away. Sheila MacDonald would be good. I have not seen her for some time. She has been busy with her kids and with Madeleine de St Exupery's growing party in France. But now, *cheri*, I am exhausted and must lie down. Perhaps you could get me a stimulant, maybe some cocaine for my weariness, or some other chemical boost to see me through the evening."

"I am sure I can, but there will be a big letdown afterward."

"I would like one more good evening, then perhaps I could go to sleep tonight, go to sleep forever. I do not want to die alone. Maybe you could hold me."

"Oh, Manon, *gra mo chroi*, love of my heart." There were tears in his eyes. "You know what you are asking?"

"I know. I have discussed it with my doctor and Teresa. There will be no difficulty with a death certificate or the will."

"And after, do you have any wishes?"

"A grave here, a monument there? Who cares, who would visit? Who would remember?"

"Maybe your ashes and a plaque on the wall of honor on the moon and on Mars, as you were the one who got the human race there. Without your money, it would not have been possible. Maybe a statue in the Andes, beside Elizabeth, as the Prometheus Group could not have existed without you."

"Sounds interesting. That would be far enough away that no protester is likely to throw paint on it."

"How would you like the statue dressed? A mini skirt? Or a ball gown with a décolleté and gloves to the elbow, looking up at the stars?"

"Why not? A ball gown sounds good. Maybe the ninja priest could say a mass for me when you dedicate the statue."

"He is now a cardinal. Do you want me to bring him now?"

"No. I am not that religious, and he is far away in Japan."

As she was clearly failing and knew it, delay was not an option. An elaborate dinner was held that evening in Munro's old restaurant in Luxembourg City, filled with masses of flowers and numerous guests in formal dress. Teresa and the Buccaneer had sent out word, and when they asked, people responded. A gypsy band with strolling violinists, which they had both loved, played quietly in the background. Manon came walking in on the arm of Munro, with the Buccaneer close by her other side, in case of weakness. A table had been set on a raised dais at the back of the room, and Teresa and Sheila rose to greet her.

Manon looked almost like her old self, with her hair and makeup professionally done, wearing a diamond-studded tiara and pendant and a gorgeous ball gown, with a mink stole on her shoulders. As she ascended the dais, leaning heavily on Munro's arm, which was around her, she turned and waved to the patrons, who stood to applaud. She inclined her head and was seated. The table was arranged so that she sat at the head, with Munro at her right hand and close friends around them.

Sheila MacDonald, sitting close to the couple, was fascinated by them. She had known Manon and Munro almost all her life. Manon had always been calm and in control, and he was the hard, physical man she had looked up to, the protector. She had seen them together on many occasions, but it seemed as if for the first time, they were not hiding their true relationship. Munro hardly looked at anyone else. He had eyes only for Manon and touched her constantly—her hand, her arm, her shoulder. They talked and laughed quietly, reminiscing with the others who had known them both for a very long time.

They had a good evening. Munro gave her a couple of surreptitious chemical boosts when she flagged, so she was bright, cheerful, and engaging, the center of attention. She eventually whispered that she was tired. She stood to leave. Munro held up his hands. The audience quieted, then applauded again as she descended the dais and left with Munro's arm around her. She had asked him not to make a speech. The waiting limo took her home. She was exhausted. She was helped out of the limo. Munro was still a strong man, and she was now very frail, a shadow of her former self. He picked her up in his arms. A maid opened the doors, and Munro carried her into her bedroom. The doors closed behind them, and Munro kissed her, tears in his eyes.

"Don't cry for me, Argentina," she said, arms around his neck, with a sad little smile, looking up at him.

He sat on a sofa, and she rested in his arms, her head on his shoulder, and they murmured quietly to each other.

"I love you. I always have. From the moment I saw you."

"When I was a little girl, like Roxelana, in poverty and misery, I dreamed of a prince, a strong man who would rescue me. I eventually found one."

"You were the most beautiful woman I ever saw."

"Tell me something. Tell me one of your poems."

"'They are not long the days of wine and roses,
   Out of a misty dream our path emerges for a while,
   Then closes, within a dream.'"

"I followed my dream. Take me to the bathroom so there will be no accidents." When he did so, and they were back on the sofa, she said, "Give me the pill now. Share a glass of Dom Pérignon with me."

He got up, uncorked a bottle, which had been resting in an ice bucket, poured two glasses, and gave her the pill he had had prepared. Without ceremony, she swallowed it; they clicked glasses and drank. She gave him her glass, which he put down. He sat down again on the sofa, and she lay comfortably in his arms.

"Je ne regrette rien," she said softly, "rien de rien."

He began to recite softly to her, his voice a hoarse rumble,

> "Oh love that will not let me go
> I rest my weary soul on thee
> I give thee back the life I owe
> That in thine ocean depths its flow
> May richer, fuller be."

Her eyes closed, and she said, "I like it. We had good times. Tell me some more."

He continued in a whisper, his voice breaking,

> "Oh joy that seekest me through pain
> I cannot close my heart to thee
> I trace the rainbow through rain
> And feel the promise is not vain
> that morn shall tearless be."

"That is good. One more. Do not be sad."

> "Oh cross that liftest up my head."

His voice strengthened as the glory and the peace of the lyrics he had known all his life calmed his grief.

> "I dare not ask to fly from thee.
> I lay in dust life's glory dead
> And from the ground where blossoms red
> Life that shall endless be."

"Love you," she said, and her breathing slowed, became intermittent, and then stopped; and she grew still. Munro held her for a long time. She had been the rock on which he had built his young life, a cynical certainty in a sea of doubt. *Sic transit Gloria mundi*, he thought. *A great life and a good death, but oh Jesus, I miss her so.*

Eventually, he rose, carried her over, placed her on her bed, and opened the door. Sheila and her doctor, who knew what had been planned, were seated outside, waiting. He nodded to the doctor, who went in, examined the body, signed the death certificate, and left. An undertaker was called. While they waited, they talked.

"Any regrets?" asked Sheila, pouring him a glass of scotch.

He took the glass she offered. "Aye," he sighed. "Aye, there are always regrets. I loved her so much. Maybe if I had tried harder to get her to marry me, we could have had a child. I wish we had had a child. What is it Shakespeare said? 'Die single, and thine image dies with thee.' But now she is gone, and future generations will never know what role she played in saving mankind by getting us into space. I want a plaque on the wall of honor on the moon and Mars and maybe a hologram at the Space Academy and a statue in the Andes, far enough away from those who would deface it, both the statue and her memory."

"I think she would like that."

"Ah god, Sheila," he said, lifting his hands helplessly. "I miss her so much. She was my rock, and now gone, gone with the wind."

Taking his arms, she looked up into his face. "There are others, Bruadarach, dreamer. *Gra mo chroi*, love of my heart. I am here."

"You were my child, Sheila Neach-Gaoil."

"Children grow up. But you are right, now is not the time," she said, releasing him and turning away.

"Oh Christ, Sheila, what am I going to do without her? How can I go on?" He caught himself and shook his head. "Man up! I want to wash her and dress her, and I must hold a vigil tonight for her brave soul. Teresa will arrange to have her funeral in the cathedral, then we will cremate, and I will take the ashes in three urns back to the US."

"I will come back for the funeral, but after that, come with me to Paris, where we can walk down the Champs-Élysées, and you can dream a little of things past."

After the cremation, as the company jet would not be available to take him back to the US until the next day, he took up Sheila's offer. He and his Praetorian Guard took the company's SUV stretch limo to Paris. The vehicle was much bigger than they needed, but Munro liked the space.

They both had their computers and so both could work undisturbed, the Praetorian at her university studies and Munro reading reports and answering questions from Maria in Arizona.

Sheila had told him that Paris was no longer the city of his youth, where he had preferred to fight when he was a professional boxer. Then, it had been the city of stunning architecture, clean streets, and beautiful women. She warned him of the dirt, the squatters, the feces, the tents on the streets, and the women, either covered or scurrying by, trying to avoid the attention of the groups of young migrants standing around with nothing to do, no jobs, and no prospects of there ever being jobs.

At Sheila's house, on a very expensive and fashionable street in the heart of Paris, he met her children, who knew him from visits to the ranch in Arizona. Her husband, a wealthy, extremely hardworking businessman in his own right, was out of town on business. An amah was looking after the children, along with another Praetorian, whom Sheila used to protect herself and the children. The two Praetorians knew each other, so Sheila and Munro left them exchanging information while they went for a stroll along Avenue Foch. They only meant to go a short way, but the sun was shining and the sky was blue. It had been a long time since Munro had been in Paris, so they walked down the Champs-Élysées, across the Place de la Concorde, and onto the bridge across the Seine.

There were numerous tourists walking by, although due to its unfortunate current reputation as a city of terrorism, there were far fewer than there used to be. The Eiffel Tower was visible. The tent cities, the bazaars, and the filth were not very obvious, unless one looked closely. They were sharing reminiscences of how, as a little girl, she had come from poverty and despair in Scotland to join his residential school in Luxembourg, eventually ending up in the US. How she had returned to Europe to work for Manon, Munro's long-term lover and business partner, and had fallen in love with Paris.

Arm in arm, they were a striking couple. He was still tall, broad in the shoulders, and slim in the waist. She was a pale-skinned, green-eyed beauty with flaming red hair. When he had been asked by Sandra, the former US president, to pull Canada out of its economic disaster, Sheila had run one of the biggest provinces for him. They reminisced about how she had been set up for assassination by a treacherous official and how she had managed to fight off the assassin. She had returned to Europe after that and had a spectacularly successful business career.

"You seem happy."

"Content, certainly. Hard to believe how my life has unfolded. Working in the country of my dreams, a couple of healthy little children, and an OK husband."

"OK?"

"Well, better than OK. What woman is ever totally satisfied? I don't think it is in our nature. The grass is always greener."

"Maybe. But grass is just grass."

"I know that intellectually. But we women are emotional creatures. With five wives and other lovers, you know that."

"Mea culpa, or mea maxima culpa. The women I married were maybe just not the marrying kind. Or maybe I was just another dull, boring guy who would rather stay at home and look after the children."

"Yeah, yeah. And the governor of three states."

"I really don't do that. I am just a figurehead. It is Maria Martens who actually does the job."

"You should get her a country to run, like Brazil or Portugal, and get her a husband. Her biological clock is ticking."

"You are probably right. But she is so smart she has probably frozen some eggs already. If she were running either of these countries, they certainly would be much better off. But what is going to happen here? It looks like Paris is turning into a third-world Middle East cesspool."

"I know, but the French keep voting for these anti- or post-nationalist EU-type globalists."

"Do they? Or is the voting rigged?"

"Maybe it is. But I suspect it is a combination of the unions, the universities, and the terrible media bias, which is making the difference."

They were halfway across the bridge over the Seine when an overwhelming sense of loss suddenly overcame Munro. Tears came into his eyes, and he groaned, turning into Sheila, who held him in her arms.

"Oh Christ, Sheila, I canna stand it. She is gone. Manon, the love of my heart. I will never see her again. Manon is gone, Kodama is gone, Elizabeth is gone. What can I do? What can I do?"

She held the man in her arms. She had known him for years but had never seen him like this. She had been a child when she first met him, and he had been the one who protected her and all those around her. She knew he was a man of violence, a fighter who had beaten a man to death with his bare hands in the boxing ring. She remembered the story that Tomiko had once told her laughingly, how she had been beaten in a training dojo and the difficulty she had had holding an enraged Munro back from killing those who had hurt her.

Some years ago, when he was waiting for her return to Toronto after the attempted assassination, she had loved him when felt his strong, comforting arms around her. She had called him then what she thought he was, Ard Riach, which meant the high king in the old language. He had corrected her by calling himself Bruadarach, the dreamer. She had thought he was mocking himself, but now she thought that he was not. That was indeed how he saw himself.

As a child, she had asked him what it felt like to be in the boxing ring. He had been curiously inarticulate. But then, so had the other great fighters she had known, Miguel and Archie Moore, both world champions. They had described the sense of calm, of peace, of invincibility. There was, of course, the dopamine rush, which she understood, but this was different. Maybe men just cannot explain their feelings. Maybe the inexplicable calm before battle is just hardwired into the male psyche.

And then she thought of the women he had always been with, Manon and Elizabeth, hard, joking, utterly cynical. There was the deeply hidden cold ferocity of Tomiko and the often naked aggression of the one they called Sweet Wolf. Until this moment, she had never quite realized how much he depended on and deeply loved Manon and maybe Elizabeth too. These were dominating, domineering women. *Well, I am also,* she thought. She had always wanted him, but he would never touch the girls of the Foundation. He was now in extremis of pain and loss. *Maybe now she is gone,* she thought.

"Oh, Sheila," he said, his voice hoarse with pain. "My cousin wrote her epitaph, 'Heart of a rose, *gra mo chroi*, bird song at the lip, star eye and wisdom, yet woman to the core.' Oh Jesus, I wish I were as young as I then was when first I met her, but *ochanee*, what would avail my teens if the one woman who ever understood me were but dust and ashes. She is gone and has taken my heart with her. Sheila, my heart was in that coffin with her."

The attack happened suddenly. Sheila was listening quietly, looking over his shoulder while she held him. She saw three bearded men with drawn knives suddenly rushing at them from the crowds of passing pedestrians, shouting the death slogan, now so well-known to all Europeans. In retrospect, Sheila never knew if they were targeted by the Kingdom, the Mullahs, or the Caliph, or if it was a random act, as the police claimed. For years, no one in Europe believed any police statement about anything to do with migrants, as truth had long since disappeared from those corrupted and politicized arms of the state. Having been attacked before and having the scars to prove it, Sheila had never completely lost her vigilance. She glimpsed the movement and instantly came alert. "Attack! Knives behind you!" she shouted, releasing him, and stepping back.

Munro had never lost the old professional fighter's lightning reflexes. He spun round, pushing her away behind him. They were on him. There was no time to draw the gun he had in his shoulder holster. His trained fighter's brain locked on and instinct took over. The dopamine hit came immediately. Everything went into slow motion as the visual frames-per-second processing speed went sky high from the standard sixty, and the light got brighter. They were on top of him. He was going to get cut. There was no way of avoiding that. He stepped into them. Both arms went up, crossed in front of his face, and came down and out. He could feel the knife from the right-hand man open up his left arm as he pushed him away. His right arm, which he had been concentrating on, backhanded the middle man in the face, driving him into the third one, which broke up their charge.

The right-hand man again had his knife raised. Munro got his left arm under it, forcing it up, and hooked him in the belly with his right fist. The assassin, who had never been hit by a trained boxer, began to double over. Munro was able to get his left hand around the assassin's knife hand. At the same time, his right hand was coming up for another backhand strike on the middle man's knife arm, forcing it sideways. The years of training gave him the strength to hold the right-hand man by the wrist, in spite of the defensive cut on his upper arm, while he stepped in and hooked the middle man in the kidney with his right fist.

He had pushed Sheila backward as he surged forward. In a move she had practiced repeatedly after her previous attack, as she stepped back further, she snapped open her purse where her gun was held firmly and prominently, took a further step back, and gut shot the left-hand man as he was recovering from the stumble of having the middle man knocked against him. Munro's kidney punch twisted the middle man around, and Sheila shot him initially in the chest, then twice in the face. Seeing Munro had caught the assassin on the right of the group, she shot the left-hand man a couple of times in the face.

The dopamine surge let him ignore the pain of his left arm, and still holding the last assassin's knife hand with his own left hand, Munro hit him in the head with his right hand and immediately wished he had not done so. He had never in his life hit anyone on the skull with an unprotected fist, and he felt his fifth metacarpal give way, the boxer's fracture. This assassin, who was not a big man, was floored by the head strike. Enraged, Munro picked up the stunned assassin by the ankles. Pivoting, he spun him around in the air and, in a move reminiscent of throwing a Scottish hammer, smashed his head against the edge of a bridge pillar. The head exploded in a spray of blood and brains.

Munro and Sheila, with good reason, were so distrustful of all European police forces that their first thought was of escape. They knew the immediate police response would be to charge them with murder, and they would be placed in a jail, likely filled with migrant inmates. That was the way the British government and others took care of those they disliked. A death in prison was just a death in prison. No matter who it was, no state media took any interest in it, and the official reports were always so contradictory that no one believed them. Even asking for an enquiry was a waste of time as these enquiries were run by suborned judges, looking for awards such as a British knighthood to be awarded if they made the correct government-approved findings.

Munro picked up one of the dead terrorists and threw him onto the road in front of a car, which screeched to stop. He leaped at it and grabbed the door handle, pulling it open. Fortunately, the car doors were unlocked. He reached over and seized the driver by the collar and shouted to Sheila to jump in, which she did, sliding over into the left rear seat, holding her gun at the driver's head. Munro got in the front seat.

"Drive to the hospital," said Sheila, giving the driver directions while holding her gun at his right ear so the driver could see it in the mirror. He swerved around the corpse and drove off. Munro had his jacket off and wrapped it as tightly as he could around his left arm to slow the bleeding. With one hand, he got out his wallet and gave it to Sheila. She added money from her own wallet and gave it to the driver, telling him there was no reason to concern the police with this matter unless they asked. He nodded in understanding, knowing, as most Europeans by now knew, that the police were not there to help citizens—rather the reverse.

Munro indicated to her that he did not need immediate hospitalization, so Sheila directed the driver to another intersection a fair way from her house and called her own Praetorian to get the limo and meet them at that intersection as soon as possible. She spoke in Japanese so that the driver would not understand, although he seemed a reasonable man when she explained to him that they had just killed three terrorists. The problem was that the police would likely not recognize that her gun, and the gun Munro was obviously wearing in a shoulder holster were legal and would jail them. The driver agreed with their jaundiced view of European justice. Sheila asked for his name card and promised a few thousand Euro on top of what she had given him if they got away. Having had altercations with the police himself while demonstrating against the EU friendly central government running France, the driver agreed to say nothing unless the police identified him and he was questioned.

Within minutes, the driver of the limo was alerted. He had been waiting in the vehicle anyway, and Sheila's Praetorian came with him, directing him to the chosen intersection, telephoning Sheila that they were approaching. Sheila and Munro got out of their car, thanked the driver, and walked around the corner so the driver could not see their vehicle. Munro had his arm wrapped in his jacket to conceal the injury and the gun he wore in the shoulder holster. The stretch limo drew up almost immediately. They entered and set off for Luxembourg. In case they had been noticed and perhaps the police informed, Sheila made arrangements to exchange cars on the way. She also contacted Teresa in Luxembourg City, telling her of the affair so she would make sure that the company jet was fueled and cleared for immediate departure when they got to the private airport they usually used.

Meantime, in the back of the stretch limo, Sheila and the Praetorian got Munro's shirt off to look at the wound. Sheila remarked that it was much the same as the one she had sustained when she was attacked in Canada. The whole upper arm was laid open by the defensive cut, through the muscle, down to the bone.

"These terrorists must all be trained in the same school," she said.

Munro laughed. He was able to move his wrist and fingers, so he was not terribly concerned about nerve damage. As usual, given the constant threat of terrorism, they had a large medical kit in the limo, which the Praetorian, apprised of the attack and Munro's injury, had brought inside the vehicle.

"Just pour some hydrogen peroxide on it and put in a few sutures," said Munro.

"Me?" said Sheila. "I haven't stitched up anybody since I was in a mining camp more than twenty years ago."

"Nothing has changed. Just use one of these big needles to get it down deep. Four or five retention sutures should be enough."

"Do you want local anesthetic?"

"The cut is too long. You girls can just hold me down and pay no attention to the screams."

"Jesus, Munro. Are you sure?"

"What I am sure of is that I do not want to stop in France, and I need to slow or stop the bleeding. So no choice, Sheila."

He lay face-down on the seat with his arm out to give her easy access to the cut on the back of his arm, and she laid drapes around it, preparing to close the wound. She marveled as he only grunted and did not move as she poured peroxide on the wound, and then he encouraged her as she pushed the big three-inch needle in one side and out through the cut and then back in and out the other side to get it deep enough to close the wide-open muscle. She put in six huge retention sutures, and after she tied them tightly, the arm looked quite presentable.

She cleaned it, took off her gloves, and with the help of the Praetorian, applied a pressure dressing to stop the bleeding. He sat up and moved his fingers.

"Good job, Sheila. That should keep until we get to the US."

Within a little over one hour and a half after clearing the outskirts of Paris, they approached the pickup point where they exchanged vehicles into a different make and color, as Sheila was deeply concerned that their original vehicle had been identified. When they were settled in the new limo and beginning to feel somewhat more confident that they would avoid being picked up by the police, Sheila opened a bottle of a single malt scotch from the bar in the limo, took a slug herself straight from the bottle, and gave it to Munro, who also took a drink. He offered it to the Praetorian, who looked at it doubtfully, took a small sip, and made a face, at which Sheila and Munro laughed.

"Islay malts are an acquired taste. I am going back to the US immediately. But how about you, Sheila?"

"I think it would be safer if I came too, until we can find out how the French police are going to handle this."

"And you?" he asked the Praetorian, who was dressed in Western clothes and was not at all conspicuous.

"My contract is for another two months, and I am not involved, so I should go back to look after the children. If you drop me off somewhere, I can get a train back to Paris. Your own Praetorian can fly back commercial. She has most of her stuff with her, and the rest can be shipped, so she can simply fly back to Kansai. She is due to return to duty in a day or so anyway."

"That would make sense," said Sheila. "We should probably know within a week or so if there is going to be a problem for me. If there is, then I will get my kids across to the US, but I would rather not disturb them if it is not necessary."

A couple of hours later, they boarded the waiting plane. Thankfully, it was at a private airfield, which very few international flights used. Munro, who had seldom actually seen an official, never asked what flight plan they filed. Even when he had seen an official, nothing was ever said, as they recognized him as a former prime minister of Luxembourg and seldom, if ever, asked about his business. As soon as they were strapped in, as they were the only passengers, the plane lifted off. As usual, there were two pilots up front, but no cabin crew. When they reached cruising altitude, Sheila unbuckled, went to the bar, opened a bottle of scotch, and took a slug. She offered him the bottle, and he joined her.

"God, Munro, that was close! That is twice now these bearded animals almost killed me. If you had not been there, I would be dead. I owe you my life. Just thinking about it, look at my hands, I am still shaking. How does it go?

'The flesh is bruckle, the fiend is slee,
Timor mortis conturbat me.'

The fear of death disturbs me." She took another drink. "And you?"

"The realization comes later when the dopamine drains out. But I used to face that in the boxing ring. The defensive cut comes with the territory, but I feel a real idiot breaking my right hand. A fighter hitting a man full power to the skull with his unprotected fist. What a moron."

"But you have hit people before?"

"Not without padding. It's OK to hit someone in the face. The facial bones are soft, like the crumple zone in a car. But the skull, that's like hitting a bowling ball. What an idiot."

"How long will it take to heal? Will you need surgery?"

Munro flexed his fingers and looked at the angle of the nails. "A boxer's fracture. No, the fingernails lineup. There is no malrotation. It will not need treatment and will heal in six weeks. But what an idiot. This is the first time I have ever significantly hurt my hands, and it still hurts, so pass the bottle along, Sheila. Give me another dram."

"Here, Bruadarach," she said, holding out the bottle. "But not such a dreamer when I shouted 'Knife!'"

"An old fighter's reflexes."

"*Gra mo chroi*, Bruadarach. Funny, it is easier to speak one's heart in the old language."

"You know that Manon was and Tomiko is a *cuishle mo chroi*."

"Goddamn it, Munro, you learned more Irish Gaelic than Scottish. And 'the thread of your heart,' indeed? But anyway, she is not here, and I am, and I know my John Donne. 'I swear, no where, lives a woman true and fair.'"

"You demean your sex, Sheila. Besides when I was in the limo half asleep, dreaming of Manon, some Milton crossed my mind.

'She inclined to me. I waked, she fled
And day brought back my night.'
Oh, Sheila, she is gone."

"I hear you, Munro. 'When darkness falls, and pain is all around.' Enough, enough, Bruadarach. I am going to get shit-faced drunk, seduce you, and be your bridge over troubled water. With two hands busted, you can't resist. If you want to be poetic, just stop talking and listen to Marvell,

'Had we but world enough and time
This coyness were no crime.
But at my back, I always hear
Time's winged chariot hurrying near.
The grave's a fine and private place,
But none I think do there embrace.
So let us sport us while we may.'

And have another drink and look at me. Am I not worth it?

'What fool is not so wise,

To lose an oath and win a paradise.'"

"I did not know you knew so much Shakespeare. Kit Marlowe was obviously thinking of you?

'Was this the face that launched a thousand ships
And dashed the topless towers of Ilium?'

What are you doing?"

"I am getting undressed. I was not kidding. There is a bed in the back of the plane. It is not every day that a woman escapes death by a hair's breadth. I know with your busted hands, you can't hold me, but just come to the back of the plane and lie still and watch."

"Jesus, Sheila. 'Frailty, thy name is woman!' Or is your name Greensleeves to match your green eyes? What about your husband? Probably sitting at some boring business meeting somewhere thinking of you, and here you are,

'Alas my love you do me wrong
To cast me off discourteously
For I have loved you for so long
Delighting in your company.
Greensleeves was my delight
Greensleeves was all my joy.'"

"We are doing OK, my husband and me. He is a good guy and a reasonably good father, as good as anyone who is running a major corporation can be. I like him, maybe I love him, but we are French, and a Frenchwoman can love more than one man."

"Since when did the daughter of Og become French?"

"A long time ago, in my heart. But enough of that. I have survived. I live another day 'to dance at dawn with death.' I want you now. I have always wanted you. Remember when I was a child, 'I was a stranger and you took me in, naked and you clothed me. I was sick and you visited me. I was in prison and you came to me.' Look at me, dreamer. Am I not a thing of beauty?" And she slipped off her clothes.

"Ah, Sheila. I always suspected that pale, pale face of yours and those green eyes were not of this world. Out of the mists, a child from Avalon, the faerie place of our dreams in the Western ocean. 'I was hearing a woman singing, on dark Dunvegan shore.'"

"Hush now and come with me *a cuishle*."

They went to the bed at the back of the plane and closed the door. She helped him undress, and after a time, being careful of his left arm, she straddled and sank down on him.

"*Gra mo chroi*," she said. "I have been waiting for this since I was a girl, especially when you were waiting for me when I came back from the hospital in the US. It has been a long time. I read all the poetry books in your library and have copies in Paris. 'Quia amore langueo.' Oh jeez, Munro, that feels good. When your arm is better, I want you on top of me. I want to feel your weight. God, Munro, I have been hungry for this."

Later, Munro jerked awake as the pain in his arm hit when he rolled on it. He sat up and looked down at Sheila, asleep beside him. *Just buried one woman, and so help me God, falling in love with another.* And then the sadness hit.

> O Western wind, when wilt thou blow,
> That the small rain down can rain?
> Christ, if my love were in my arms
> And I in my bed again.

He picked up the glass, swallowed the scotch, and felt the burn all the way down. He reached for the bottle, then set it down. Manon would not have approved. "Too easy to get to like that stuff. Real life was to be lived, not found in the bottom of a bottle." He got up, dressed painfully, and with another look at the sleeping Sheila, went back to the main cabin and picked up his constant companion, an anthology of poems and parts of poems he and one of the Japanese shooters had published years ago. The first line as always was William Dunbar's,

> Done is a battle on the dragon black,
> Our champion Christ confounded has his force.

And then he thought sadly, *Manon is gone, another of our champion's dead and the battle scarcely begun.*

> On loft is gone Apollo radiant and bright.

I hope she has, to some heaven, some Elysian fields. Again, the sorrow overwhelmed him, tears in his eyes. *Wait for me, Manon, wait for me,* gra mo chroi. *Someday, I will come and find you.*

Still mourning, he fell into an uneasy sleep where later Sheila found him, the book open on his lap.

They had kept telephone silence themselves on their way across the Atlantic, but the people in Luxembourg had contacted Tomiko in Arizona, telling her that they were on the way. Half an hour out, Munro had spoken to her, telling her of his wounded arm and that he would need to see a surgeon at the hospital. Tomiko was waiting for him on the apron as the plane taxied in, and Munro disembarked. Sheila was with him. Tomiko embraced Munro gingerly.

"Glad to have you back in one piece. The first videos of the affair have just surfaced. Everything gets videoed nowadays. You can't escape. You are both recognizable, at least to me. So far, there is no word out, although I am sure it will soon be. But the European governments go to such an extent to cover up any terror attacks, they may not investigate, or if they do, if you say nothing, they may not either. Busting that terrorist's head in such a spectacular fashion may stir up unusual interest. Next time, just break his neck quietly."

"Now Manon is gone, I have no immediate reason to ever go back to Europe, but Sheila, you may be at risk."

"We will have to wait and see. After what that French government scum did to Madeleine, removing government protection and allowing that slimy little judge to force her to undergo psychiatric evaluation, who knows what they will do to me. I need to see Hinchcliffe anyway."

"Hinchcliffe?" said Tomiko. "You are thinking of open conflict? 'Red war,' as Hinchcliffe calls it?"

"I don't know, Tomiko, but I think an explosion is coming. Leda may be calling you."

"Me? What about?"

"She does not trust her officials, especially the police. But more than that, I do not know or should not say. Anyway, if I can borrow the plane, I will go on to Mexico. Good luck with the arm, Munro."

"I will see you when I see you," said Munro, and she walked over to where the plane was being refueled and boarded.

"She thinks Leda may be calling me. Interesting. Maybe they are all thinking the crisis, civil war is coming."

"I think so too. Leda has been hinting about a problem you possibly might be interested in. But now I need to get a doc to look at this arm. Sheila sewed it up. It looks OK, but I should have it seen, as we could see bone in the base of the cut, and I need to have my hand x-rayed."

"What happened to that?"

"I am almost too embarrassed to say. A trained boxer hitting a man on the skull with his unprotected fist. What an idiot. What a moron."

"Better a broken hand than dead. I would have missed you. Where were your Praetorians anyway?"

"We left them at home with Sheila's kids while we went for a short walk. Not too smart. Still thinking thirty years ago. Maurice Chevalier, Gene Kelly, and me strolling down the Champs-Élysées with Debbie Reynolds, Catherine Deneuve, and Sheila, singing in the rain or something. Ah, well, I'll never do that again."

Tomiko took him in her arms and looked up at him. "There are safer places to walk. Underneath the cherry blossom."

"Sakura time with the woman of my heart and my soul, who just happens to be the best shooter in the world."

A few days later, a call came from Leda as Sheila had suspected.

"Leda really wants me in Germany. I should stay with you until you are better."

"I will be fine, my love. Things are healing up OK. There is no sign of infection. I know what Leda will ask of you."

"I do too, but do I want to?"

"Shakespeare said, 'There is a tide in the affairs of men, which taken at the flood, leads on to fortune.'"

"I already have my fortune. I have our child, and I am with you."

"Ah, Tomiko," he said, taking her in his arms and kissing her. "'One moment in annihilation's waste. One moment of the well of life to taste.' Did I ever tell you I love you?"

"I think you did, but tell me again, man of my dreams."

CHAPTER 16

Crossing the Rubicon

Following in the footsteps of La Contessa, Leda had made herself very wealthy, initially largely working for Manon, and then she had married an equally wealthy German many years her senior, picked out by Manon and La Marquesa. She had two children shortly after marriage and then entered politics. Initially, she was in the back rooms of the main centrist party, although even that was fairly Far Left. The Merkel insanity so destabilized Germany, especially when, as in Sweden, she insisted on giving the so-called refugees the vote. This resulted in the main parties moving even further Left. Ardogan, the caliph of Turkey, began to insist that all Turkish Germans vote as a bloc, even those who had been in Germany for a couple of generations, and largely, they complied with his wishes.

It became completely unsafe for women to be out of doors on their own after dark. Even during daylight hours, women who were not covered were sexually attacked on the streets. The police appeared completely paralyzed and unwilling to intervene, perhaps because if they did so, it was they, the rank-and-file police, who were criticized and disciplined, not the sexual predators. None of this, of course, was reported in the media. Being unaware of or completely uninterested in the level of despair sweeping over the vast number of non-politicized Germans, at her lunatic policies, Merkel proposed bringing in a parallel legal system of Sharia law as they effectively had in Britain. Leda mobilized her own party, planning on taking it back to the center by organizing a coup against her worthless party leaders and then making a common cause with the fragmented right-wing parties. She phoned Munro.

"Come to Europe. I need to speak to you urgently."

"No phone talk?"

"No. Private. Teresa will set it up."

He knew she would not ask unless there was a good reason, and she was concerned about information leaks. He thought he knew what was going on. Teresa, who now ran Manon's companies, sent the company jet to pick him up to make tracing difficult, as clearly Leda did not want to be seen talking to him. He landed with no fanfare at a private airport in Luxembourg. A limo was waiting for him, which drove him to an isolated house in the countryside. The driver indicated he would wait.

The house looked familiar. He realized it was the one to which he and Tomiko had taken Leda after her rescue years ago. When he went inside, it was empty, but obviously freshly cleaned and provisioned. He did not know that this was the house where the little girls who had been accepted into the Foundation were brought for treatment prior to transfer to the US. With nothing to do, he checked the refrigerator in the kitchen. Of interest, he found a chilled bottle of very light Federweisser, which he opened, poured a glass, and went into the garden at the back of the house. Awaiting developments, he strolled around, enjoying the unaccustomed quiet, the greenery, and softness of the air.

Leda arrived shortly thereafter on her own, as her people stayed in the limo that brought her. They had not seen each other for a year or more, but the desire was still there. She came to him with open arms and embraced him.

"Kiss me," she said.

"Christ, Leda, you know I am married to Tomiko."

"I don't care. You are always getting married to someone. Kiss me anyway." And she put a hand behind his head and pulled him down, opening her mouth. "Call me *gra mo chroi*."

"Ah, you have learned some Gaelic. *Gra mo chroi*, love of my heart, indeed. The Irish say it better. A *chuisle mo chroi*, pulse of my heart. You are hard to resist, Leda."

"Then don't."

Later, he brought her a glass of wine as she lay on her side on the bed, covered with a sheet, propped up with pillows. He sat down beside her.

"I need to talk to you."

"I presume you are going to make a run. 'Du kannst, denn du sollst.'"

"Goethe! Yes. I must. Merkel the moron, or the anti-German globalist—I can never decide which—has finally overreached trying to bring in Sharia law. But the current leader of my party is such a wimp. He says nothing but platitudes and is afraid to stake out a position much different from hers, so the right will not coalesce behind him."

"You think you have enough votes to topple him?"

"If I am going to try, it will have to be soon to give me time to unite the right. If I go too early, I will fail in my own party, but if I go too late, I will fail in the general election."

"And if you fail?"

"If I fail at the party level, they will throw me out, and I will be out of politics, at least at a significant level. But if I lose at the federal level, will there still be a Germany in five or six years?"

"Exactly! Even if you win in five or six years, the migrant demographics for the tipping point are said to be 20 percent, from where there is no return. The way it is going, in six years, it will likely be over the tipping point, so it will be a civil war, which you will lose, or a voluntary return to the Middle Ages. I guess we could call it an Aquinas/Averroes inflexion. So there would not be much point in even trying, and you might as well bring your kids and come to the US."

"Aquinas, I know, but Averroes?"

"Ibn Rushd, the Muslim theologist. In about 1150, they turned their back on reason, burned his books, and all progress stopped, and they retreated into medievalism. If you do nothing, that is what you will be looking at."

"I know, I know. But I am afraid. There will be riots. I will be called a Nazi bitch. Maybe I was born afraid. That is why I need you here. Tell me not to be afraid."

"What would you have me say? To quote the great Julius, 'Cowards die many times before their deaths, the valiant never taste of death but once. So why should men fear death, which being the necessary end, will come when it will come.' Or how about this one. I have always liked Kit Marlowe,

'Is it not passing brave to be a king,
And ride in triumph through Persepolis.'"

"Munro, you know that is not what I want. I wish someone else would."

"I apologize. I was joking. This is you,

'Hear the wolves across the snow
Someone has to kill them so—'"

"I know that poem," said Leda.

"'Someone has to kill them so,
Makes me it.'
'Lord, let this cup pass.'"

"You will have to drink that cup, although it may be a bitter one. 'That is the cup of the old world's hate, cruel and strained and strong.' If Kierkegaard is right, life sucks and then you die. Heidegger says you were thrown into this world not of your own making. But think of it, the redemption if you succeed.

'Wassail to the kingly stranger
Born and cradled in a manger.
King like David, priest like Aaron,
Christ was born to set us free.'

Maybe you were born to set Germany free. 'Sie macht sich nur durch Blut und Essen.'"

Leda sat up. "Blut und essen. So you learned a little Bismarck for me, 'it can only be done by blood and iron.'" She took a long, shuddering breath. "There will be blood on the streets. If I die, will you look after my kids?"

"Get the chancellorship, then get one of these hard women, Hinchcliffe or Carmenlita, and then martial law."

"I have no choice. 'I can do none other, so help me God.' Take me again now. We will not be able to meet when I am chancellor. There will be no privacy."

Leda did what she set out to do. She led a revolt and overturned the leadership of her own party and, against all the media opposition, turned it dramatically back to the political center. She was able to unite the other smaller parties behind her and won the federal election, becoming chancellor.

Her first move was to close the borders to so-called refugees and attempt to close all so-called refugee camps and deport the young men who inhabited these camps back to Turkey, the Middle East, and North Africa. These moves were blocked whenever possible by the opposition parties. She found her police force useless in controlling the crime on the streets, as they had been under instructions for years to ignore it. She interviewed the police chiefs of the major cities. All had been appointed by followers of Merkel and appeared to believe, or stated that they believed, that it was immoral to judge migrants by Western standards, as all cultures were equally acceptable and therefore refugees were not in general to be prosecuted for rape of women and children, which was acceptable in their own culture. Stalemated and appalled by this invincible stupidity, but not at all surprised, Leda thought of Tomiko. She phoned Munro and again arranged a meeting at the house in Luxembourg.

Leda's husband had a secret desire. All his life, he had wanted to drive in Formula One race cars like the great drivers Lada and Shoemaker. He had made enough money that he could afford a spin on these famous tracks like the Nürburgring. When Leda became a serious politician, he had been advised to get her a driver and a bulletproof Mercedes. He listened and bought one for her, but he preferred to drive his own Mercedes sports car.

The pressure to get a driver became worse when she became chancellor, but he resisted. "It's not living, being driven around by someone else," he told her. "I don't want to hide away like a coward."

On the odd weekend Leda had free, he liked to drive her up to the mountains, where he had a chalet. There were car loads of security following them. Her husband had no objections to security surrounding the chalet or shadowing the couple, as they delighted in walks through the forested mountains on their own. At least the security men were far enough away to give them the illusion they were on their own. When he drove, he became competitive and would delight in outdriving her security. After years of marriage, she had begun to relax and trust his skill, but the journey with him was occasionally a white-knuckle experience.

The meeting with Munro was again kept as secret as possible. He met Leda with a glass of light white wine, and they sat down to talk. She skirted around the subject for a while, mentioning her somewhat hair-raising drive to their chalet with her husband last weekend.

"It is a guy thing. Boys like their toys," said Munro, commiserating.

"It could be a lot worse," said Leda. "He could be off chasing women in public. He is still young enough, virile enough, and wealthy enough that there must be real temptations. I really respect that there has been no breath of scandal. Whatever women he is using, he keeps it very well covered, and he looks after our two children very well. You know my kids, as they go to the ranch in Arizona every summer. I would like them to stay longer, but I have to be very careful as the media are already accusing me of being too pro-American. Anyway, why are we still sitting here and not in bed? It is not like we have many opportunities. Are you going all moral on me? Is Tomiko exhausting you?"

"'Tread softly, for you tread on my dreams.' Being married to Tomiko is something we waited for most of our lives. I would love if Tomiko had another child, but she said the hormones the doc filled her with last time made her crazy, and she does not want to go through that again,"

"I don't blame her. It was hard enough for me, and I was twenty years younger than her."

"I know, it must have been so difficult. What a woman! I don't know how she does it, but once the kid gets a bit older, I am not sure what she will do. Being head of the Space Academy is unlikely to be enough to keep her fully occupied."

"This is what I wanted to talk to you about. Maybe I should give her the job of chief of police in Germany. What I have right now is so politicized that the whole bunch of them are useless. If I try to radically change things, they might actually conspire against me actively, or more likely passively. Tomiko is ruthless enough to do what is necessary."

"Maybe. Probably. That would be interesting. A Japanese woman head of the police in Germany? Would the public accept it?"

"The public, the real public—not that awful media—are so fed up with our useless police that they would accept anyone who promised any real policing. Maybe just initially as my adviser. She is a woman, and she is not German, so she could serve as a foil, a scapegoat. I can offload everything bad onto her. You would know what I am doing and might resent me making her the sacrificial goat. Which is why I have to talk to you to see if she would be prepared to do it. I know she said years ago that she would never return to Germany, but I would like you to convince her otherwise. I know it is asking a lot from her, but who else is there? Hinchcliffe is already too well-known as a war lord. That fierce little one, Carmenlita, has never done any policing. Tomiko has already done everything, so there is nothing anyone can take away from her, and her background is impeccable. That is my message, my request."

"You ask a lot, Leda. I don't know that Tomiko will agree to potentially sacrifice herself for a country she cares nothing about, for a culture she is indifferent to. But I am pretty sure she is getting bored, or if not now, soon. Simply being a mother and running the Space Academy will not be enough for her, so she may look favorably on the challenge. It is a winner-takes-all situation. If you succeed, you get to write history. If you lose, you are a bloodthirsty tyrant. I think I will put your proposition to her. She is not stupid. She will know exactly what the implications for her are. But she is samurai, or really a Ronin, and may relish the challenge to risk it all. We will have to discuss what to do if it all falls apart."

"Not to be too melodramatic, but if I fail, the West is doomed, and the end of European history is in sight. It will then be America and Japan alone versus the twin tigers of China and Islam. Canada and Australia are already so seriously compromised as to be irrelevant, and La Contessa has not yet had enough time to rescue South America, so they also are irrelevant. She has closed the southern border, but given Canada's post-nationalist policies, the Americans will have to build a northern wall to keep those flooding into Canada out of the US. So we really are talking about the Götterdämmerung, the Twilight of the Gods, the end of civilization as we know it. And so, *faut de mieux*, the outcome rests on the shoulders of two women, me and Tomiko. Who would have thought it would come to this?"

"I did, years ago, when I thought you would have to go back to Germany with fire and sword. Either the West runs away until it falls off the edge of the world, or someone has to turn and face Goliath of Gath. Someone has to be David, William Tell, or Martin Luther."

"More likely Leonidas at Thermopylae. Ach, *mein Gott*, let this cup pass from me."

"The three weird women are sitting under Yggdrasil, the tree of life, spinning our fate."

"I was not born to be crucified for the Western world. Hold me in your arms this day. Make me feel loved because I am going to be hated. Tomorrow then, I will raise my banner and let fate run its course. Ah God, why me?"

By this time, Tomiko was running the Space Academy. She had the help of many extraordinary clever people, both men and women. The men were entering the Space Academy at age fifteen, occasionally younger.

Things ran so smoothly that in some ways, she felt she was simply a den mother or a figurehead, whose duty it was to put out fires. Her child with Munro was now of an age where there was plenty of help raising her at the ranch. She did not really want to admit to herself that she was getting a little bored.

There was an episode that somewhat shocked Tomiko. For the first few years after the birth of her child, Tomiko was content as there was so much to do. She was still prime minister of Japan, and she was with the man for whom she had been waiting most of her life. After her term of office, she made the occasional movie, and she ran the Space Academy, which was interesting, watching these clever young people mature and disappear into space. The new Elizabethans, Munro called them. She no longer shot competitively, as the younger women were now better than she was, simply due to the march of time. She no longer acted as a Praetorian, other than when she was with Munro. She seldom wore a kimono at work, finding Western dress easier and more comfortable.

She had always been an independent woman, having been widowed at a young age. She had taken and used men as she needed. Munro had been there, but there had been long periods of absence, especially when she ran for the office and became prime minister of Japan, when she could not be seen with a Western man. During these absences, she had found pleasure with other men, as he had with women.

Sitting at her desk one day, she was daydreaming about nothing in particular when a young man came to see her. He had made an appointment with her secretary. This was not unusual, as some of these very clever young men, whom Munro affectionately called geeks, often had little experience with life and needed advice. She saw this as part of her job. He came in with some routine papers for her to sign. Tomiko was not sure why he felt the need to see her, but he seemed to want to talk. As she was not busy, and as she had a tea-making machine in her office because she liked Japanese green tea, she got up and made one for herself and offered him a cup, which he gratefully accepted. Rather than returning to her chair behind her desk, she perched on the corner almost in front of him.

She was wearing a short skirt, which rode up. She watched with some amusement as his eyes dropped immediately to look at her thighs. She crossed her legs to give him a better look and saw the telltale bulge at his crotch. He gulped.

Jesus wept, she thought, using one of Munro's favorite oaths. *I am getting wet. What is happening to me?* "You are going into space soon?" she asked.

"Yes, in the next two weeks. I take the shuttle up to orbit to rendezvous with a ship going to Mars."

Two weeks, she thought. *Munro will not mind if I have a little fun, and the boy will be gone and never come back.* She wriggled, and her skirt slid higher. His bulge became more pronounced. "You will have a good time on Mars. I hear some of the girls up there are pretty wild."

He gulped again. "I have seen all your movies."

"Oh yes? Including the ones where I am undressed?"

"Especially those."

"And you liked what you saw?"

"Tomiko-san, you are the most beautiful woman in the world."

"Quite a compliment," she said, standing up, almost in front of him, and pulled her skirt higher. "You like? You can touch."

"I can?"

"Why not? You are leaving soon. Ships that pass in the night. Stand up."

He stood, and she stroked him. "Do you want me?"

He goggled and gulped. "More than anything."

She pressed a button on her desk to illuminate the sign outside her office that indicated she was busy.

"Welcome aboard, spaceman," she said, opening her arms.

In spite of her injunction to "slow down, spaceman, there is no hurry," there was a few minutes of frenzied activity, then he climaxed and softened.

"I am sorry. I could not help myself. I have been in love with you since I first saw your movies years ago."

She cleaned him with a handful of tissue from a box on her desk. "It's OK. Don't say anything about this to anyone. This is our secret, and my going-away present. Do not come and see me again. Find a good girl on Mars and have lots of babies. Have a good life. Think of me now and then."

"Tomiko-san. What can I say? I love you."

"No. You want me. That is different. I love my husband. You are a good man. You will find a woman to love and spend the rest of your life with. She is out there, waiting for you. Sayonara, and good luck."

When he had gone, she thought, *My God, I must be getting bored. I can't do this too often so close to home. I need to start lecturing more to be on the open road and meet more guys, or there may be trouble. All my life, the man I wanted was with other women, and I thought it natural. I have been with so many men that the thought of keeping my body for one only sounds and feels a bit silly. But still, why do I feel this is not right? This must be the fate of an independent woman I suppose.*

That evening, still feeling a little emotionally disturbed, she dressed in a kimono, which she knew Munro loved. After the durbar, they walked hand in hand up the hill to the Shinto shrine.

"I never asked, why do you love women dressed in a kimono so much?"

"I don't know, but I have always have. It makes women so feminine, alluring, and desirable, at least to me. But why? I don't know. One of life's mysteries. I don't think it needs an answer. Maybe it was because you and Kodama liked to dress that way."

Later that night, she made love to Munro. *God, I love sex,* she thought. *And I could probably do with more of it, but I will not hurt or embarrass him. If I am on the road, he will not mind. I had better set up a lecture tour or write a new book.* She was still thinking about it when, a few days later, Leda phoned her and asked her to come to Berlin. She spoke to Munro about the call. He said that Leda had talked to him and had been thinking about offering her a job as chief of police or as an adviser in Germany. He outlined the problems and the potentially disastrous implications. Whatever she decided, he would support her.

Tomiko was not sure what she thought. She had never planned on returning to Germany. It would be very challenging, but perhaps a challenge was what she needed, so she had no hesitation about taking time off. Her assistants would have no difficulty running the Academy while she was away. Her child was growing up, and there was lots of help around the ranch. *I am not much of a mother,* thought Tomiko regretfully, *considering abandoning my second family.*

The decision made to at least discuss the situation, Tomiko flew to Berlin dressed very conservatively and almost incognito. A curious sense of relief came over her when she boarded the plane, leaving the ranch behind. She celebrated with a little champagne on the way over and thought long and hard about what she knew Leda was going to offer her.

At the Reichstag, Leda told her of the problems she was having with her senior officials, especially in the police and courts. Even truly egregious cases when malefactors were arrested were seldom convicted, as evidence was deemed inadmissible, extenuating circumstances were present, and on and on. In spite of that, the jails were full of migrants who had committed so many crimes that even the most ideological judges could not avoid giving them some jail time. After several decades of this conditioned foolishness, the rot went all the way to the top, so Leda had no hope of changing things by any constitutional methods. She would have to declare martial law, and she would need some pretext to do so. The only pretext would be a crisis with dead bodies piling up on the streets.

Tomiko raised her eyebrows but said nothing, as she knew that what Leda was saying about the bureaucrats was true. Elizabeth had faced the same problem when she first entered office as president of the US. She had found most agencies like finance, taxation, the foreign office, and especially the intelligence community—the so-called deep states—being run almost as independent governments; and they had strenuously opposed her wishes. She had had to fire or retire almost every department head and all senior officials. Sandra, when she was elected, had found the same thing. The bureaucrats were like cancer and had replicated themselves. Munro had quoted a poem that Tomiko remembered, "How softly but how swiftly they have sidled back in power, through the help and the connivance of their kind." Sandra had used Sweet Wolf and Takes Away Clouds Woman to clean house, but Tomiko was certain that they had all oozed back in when the silly Billie became president.

Leda pointed out that given Germany's past, the world would look with suspicion on any move to martial law. The precipitating affair therefore could not be led by a German man, as the immediate reaction would be to brand him a Nazi. It would have to be a woman, certainly not a blond German woman and preferably a non-European. "A non-European," she emphasized, looking at Tomiko.

"Obviously, that's what needs to be done," said Tomiko, "but don't look at me. Why would I want to get involved with this rat's nest? Every globalist and every brainwashed media ideologue and every university idiot would hate me. I would immediately be branded as the worst criminal in the world."

"Suppose we bring you in as police chief, say in Cologne, to restore order, and if things get out of hand, as they will, then you call in the army, and then that gives me the excuse to bring in martial law?"

"But your senior police authorities and senior military authorities are probably all infected with this brain worm, as Munro calls it. So even if I brought the army in, the number of arrests would be so small that it would be hard to justify anything. I would also need to have some military command to ensure enough numbers. A Japanese woman head of the German police and military. How is that going to happen?"

"I could do it, I think, by simply appointing you, but only for a short time. Very soon, you would be able to find good young men who could take over from you, and what happens then is not your concern."

"In theory, I suppose, but why me? I don't speak German, and I really have no interest in Europe. I care about Japan, and Japan has no pony in this race, as the Americans say."

"If Europe goes down, several things will happen. Putin must retake a large part of the Ukraine, as that is like America taking back Texas. He has begun to already and will reconquer the Caucasus. The Poles will stop him from taking Mittel Europe, but they have no interest in protecting the Scandinavians, who are so weak they don't have the will to protect themselves. So Putin may take Scandinavia. There is no one to stop him. The US won't care. Of much more concern, China is buying Portugal right now, and may buy other bankrupt European countries like Sweden and will take all the Far East, leaving Japan and the US isolated."

"Europe is not going to stop any of that from happening. It has no military, and its men have no balls."

"It might help if it ever became Europe again."

"Fallen empires historically have never risen again."

"Poland is rising, and that is a country that has not really existed for a long time."

"I think you forget Marshal Pilsudski, who led the Poles who whipped the Red Army at the Pripet Marsh. Poland was defeated militarily. It never defeated itself, unlike Rome or current Europe. But again, why me?"

"You have done everything. You won the Olympics. You ran a national police force. You ran a major country. You are a movie star. You have just had another baby. Running the Space Academy will not be enough for you. You will get bored. And besides, you owe me."

"I owe you?"

"You rescued me years ago. If you had not, I would not be here wrestling with these problems. I would have been the standard childless, mindless, obese, unhappy European woman living in a tiny apartment on my own, smelling of my cat's piss. It is your fault I am here."

"I did not rescue you. I would have left you. I only got involved to protect Munro, my naive and sentimental lover."

"Yes. He and a small, fierce woman saved me. He said I would return with fire and sword to rescue Germany."

"He is a mad dreamer, full of other men's poems."

"His dreams have taken humans to the moon and Mars. Help me with this dream of Europe resurgent."

"Oh god. Not another dreamer. One is quite enough. Let me talk it over with him again."

Back at the ranch, Tomiko and Munro again discussed the issue. He had felt Europe was a lost cause and had taken little interest in that continent for several years, although Don Pedro in Spain had been fighting a rearguard action against the steady erosion of civilization, and La Marquesa was now doing her best to follow his lead. Leda's potential revolt had produced a glimmer of hope. To confirm his belief that it likely was too late to save Europe, the news came through that Sweden had accepted Sharia law.

What was interesting was that many in Sweden, especially the political class, seemed to think that this was a good thing, a noble thing, in its rush to egalitarianism and every other *ism* known to man. Or what? Mankind—or personkind, as that fool Beapre in Canada had said. Sweden had imported very large numbers of so-called refugees, supposedly from various civil wars in the Middle East. No one actually checked who they were and where they were from, and the vast majority had actually come from failed North African states, such as Somalia and Sudan, along with large numbers of Afghans. Many were supposed to be children, but on the very odd occasion when one was checked, these "children" were found in fact to be single men of fighting age. They were illiterate and could not speak the local language, so there were no jobs available.

Jobs had actually become increasingly unavailable for the lower echelon of European citizens long before the migrants came. This made their importation so inexplicable. Various estimates were available, which had suggested that about 15 percent or more of the indigenous population would likely be permanently unemployable. Manon had pointed this out to Munro years before, when she began to automate and use robots for manufacture, as European Union rules had made it too difficult and expensive to use European labor. Finland, recognizing that problem, had already tried a guaranteed income for its own unemployed. This program had failed in its goals and had been cancelled.

Because they were on welfare with nothing to do to pass the time, these refugees congregated in a few areas, where they set up new mosques. These areas became centers of harassment and petty crime. The fire trucks could not even enter these areas, as their equipment would be stolen. No-go areas developed, as they had in the rest of the major cities in Europe. Being sexually deprived, as no young women had come with the migrants, and being told by their leaders that uncovered women were women of loose morals, the local Swedish women became sexual targets, as did the rape of male children, as that was apparently a custom in some of these countries. An interesting phenomenon developed of blond women dying their hair black so that they were less obvious sexual targets. To the world's surprise, or at least surprise outside of Northern Europe, where strangely such behavior seemed to be accepted or ignored, there was no push back by anyone.

The few men who objected were prosecuted and ultimately jailed for hate speech or hate crimes if there was a physical altercation. A few defiant nationalist groups arose, but they were widely condemned and mocked by the European media. Unbelievably, the majority of the population of Sweden continued to vote for the party who celebrated open borders. YouTube commentators warned that there was a tipping point, which seemed to come when about 20 percent of the population became nonnative. These Cassandras were ignored or maligned.

For some time, the only question had been which European country would be the first one to become non-European. To no one's surprise, it was Sweden. The refugees or rather migrants, as none of them were truly refugees, were given the vote, so all local town councils were taken over by nonnatives or by locals so desperate to be in charge of something, as was happening in Belgium and Britain, that they followed all the migrant's requests. The mayor of Molenbeek in Belgium typified this appalling attitude, as she appeared to feel no guilt that she had protected the murderers of Parisiennes.

Sharia law was introduced into all major cities in Sweden. No one objected, or those who did were silenced by job loss and threats of prison terms, which rapidly became a reality. Migrant criminals were released from jail on so-called supervision by their communities. The native Swedes very quickly learned to keep their mouths shut. As there were no objections at a local level, the federal government saw no reason why Sharia law should not become the law of Sweden initially as a parallel legal system, as in Britain; but soon it took control of all civil and, shortly thereafter, criminal cases.

The police force had slowly been converted to a largely migrant force, and again those who objected ended up in their own jails. The Swedish military had long since been gender neutral, so it was an easy matter for this to be also taken over by migrants. Sweden cheered this multicult approach and remarkably kept cheering when laws were passed that initially all women working for the government, and subsequently all women in government buildings, must be covered. Again, there was no pushback.

Those few who objected were simply jailed for hate speech, with no publicity. The numbers in jail were now so large that regular jails were overwhelmed, so temporary camps were built in northern Sweden to house the prisoners who were undergoing implicit bias training, where they were taught to accept and believe the various *isms* in current practice.

Latterly, anyone accused of a hate crime had their property and goods expropriated and given to new migrants who continued to flood in. Throughout this whole process, the Swedish central government continued to announce that everything was going to plan. The next rule passed was that Swedish natives who wished to leave had to acquire exit visas, and if they were thought to be trying to emigrate, their property was confiscated, and if they objected, they joined their fellow countrymen in the northern reeducation camps.

It became increasingly difficult to feed the prisoners in these camps, and when winter came, it turned out there was little or no heating, and winter clothes did not seem to be available. News of these camps eventually leaked out, but the Swedish central government denied their existence. The visitors who insisted were shown around a Potemkin village, where all was sweetness and light.

Sweden's economy had been in decline for years, and the collapse accelerated. The central government tried the standard socialist technique of printing money, as there were few lenders. Putin, the czar of Russia, offered asylum. He had already done so for the South African farmers who were being dispossessed and slaughtered. The South Africans fled by the thousands to the newly liberated areas of the Caucasus, where they were given new land. In a few years, they turned agriculture around in these areas, which had never before experienced modern productive farming. In offering asylum to the beleaguered Swedes, Putin hoped that it would equally spur development.

For those who were unable to legally escape their own country, he simply ignored the spineless Swedish central government and sent in a well-publicized armada to pick up those who could make it to the coast. The Swedish military, their original leaders having by now been retired or demoted, were led principally by migrants and secondarily by women. They dithered but made no move to stop the Russian boats. The US looked on but did nothing. The Swedes had stayed out of the First and Second World War, as they did not see it as their problem. Moore, the US president, did not feel what was happening in Sweden was America's problem. The rest of the Western world offered the standard platitudes and did nothing.

Moore, the current US president, had a healthy distrust of his own deep state people, such as the CIA and foreign affairs, and liked to have occasional meetings with his old friend Munro. Moore felt that having grown up in Europe and with continued contacts and interests there, Munro's views on that subject were interesting. Munro, in private meetings, felt it likely that Belgium would follow the path of Islamization. Soon France as well, as they had just elected another globalist president who, against all common sense, was rapidly increasing the number of migrants. That, Munro felt, might lead to a civil war in France, as he did not think that the French would crawl into history without a fight. Britain, he felt would simply sink into meaningless mediocrity and, in a few years, would no longer be a player in world politics.

Moore had no plans to intervene in Europe. America had spent its youth and treasure in two essentially European wars and had no interest in another. They could sort out their problems themselves. He was much more concerned about the Chinese presence in Portugal rather than anything that was or was not happening in Europe. If Portugal became a Chinese naval base, there would be problems controlling the Atlantic Ocean.

Tomiko pointed out to Munro that if she decided to return to Germany to take over their police force, what backup would she have? A bunch of useless testosterone-challenged bureaucrats who seemed to actively dislike the Western world and a police force so politicized that they were almost as ineffective as the British police? The German police were probably not yet trafficking little girls forced into sexual slavery as the police in Northern England were suspected of almost certainly doing, or were they?

Inevitably, military backup would be necessary, and who in Germany would give her that authority? Even if she were given it, would any of these half men, these beta males, these soy boys, be capable of helping her? Munro was dubious in the extreme. For a moment, he could not think of any civilization who had come back from the brink. Then he remembered Belisarius. Maybe Tomiko and Hinchcliffe could again defeat the Vandals and rewrite history, at least for a time.

"Let us drop the dreams and think practically about this," Tomiko said. "If I want to do it, Leda will have to move almost immediately to declare martial law, but will they listen to her? She has been stroking the nationalists and may have enough of a power base to get away with it, but it would be a close-run thing."

"Germany is still stable," said Munro. "But that cannot last for long. Fifty percent of Germany's GNP comes from exports mostly to other EU countries. That cannot last. All the southern EU countries are in effect bankrupt, with 25 percent or more unemployment, worse than the US during the Great Depression. The only reason there are no soup kitchens is that their central governments are borrowing money for welfare payments. As long as they are part of the EU and use the Euro, these bankrupt countries have no way out, as they cannot devalue to make their products competitive. Brexit is the first attempt at a breakup, but the rest will have to follow. That will give rise to huge unemployment in Germany, as their costs are way too high, and factories will have to close or go offshore. Significant unemployment will produce social unrest, as paying for welfare and all the other problems with their stupid EU programs will become an intolerable burden."

"So how long before the breakdown? Six months, nine months, years?"

"Who knows? Jeez. I am sorry, I was daydreaming, Tomiko. Cui bono? As the Romans say, who benefits? Someone always benefits from a disaster, so someone made money from the collapse of Sweden, but who and how?"

Then he shrugged his shoulders. "God! It is obvious. Who was the one spending millions and millions of dollars to flood Europe with these so-called refugees? If you actually think about it, they are agents provocateur, designed to speed the collapse of the EU."

"Oh, him? Yes. Yes, of course, but how could he have made money?"

"I don't know. Maybe he is waiting for the collapse of the EU itself. Or maybe he is just an old man who hates Europe. Maybe he has always hated Europe. I will have to ask my son, the Buccaneer, as his hedge funds made money from that one's forays into destabilizing countries. Teresa and Ash are running multinational conglomerates, so they will likely know just how money could be made from this disaster. If money could be made, then I am sure they are doing it. And I will have to speak to some of the political leaders, including Sheila MacDonald."

"Why her?"

"As you know, she made a lot of money and got married to a lot of money in France, which is where she has always wanted to be. They had a couple of kids. She is still married, and the marriage seems OK, as far as I know. She's a French citizen and has joined Madeleine de Saint Exupery's party, and I think she is pretty well connected in the back room. So she must have some idea."

"About this immigration, I heard another interesting theory from that Canadian YouTube guy Molyneux, which sort of makes sense. That they were bringing in immigrants who, by forming ghettos, would force the local people out of their existing houses into newer, higher-cost ones to prop up the real estate market, which would otherwise have collapsed because of population collapse, because European women are not having children. So these policies were actually being dictated by the central bankers."

"That makes sense in a weird way. Teresa will know." Arm in arm, they walked up the hill to the torii gate outside the Shinto shrine; and after praying quietly, they sat on a bench beside the statue of the Buddha in the little cave hollowed out of the western side of the hill, looking out at the sun setting over the valley beneath them. The scene was calm and, as always, breathtakingly beautiful. He put his arm around her. She rested her head on his chest.

"You want to leave this, Tomiko?"

"I don't, but I feel restless."

"Et tu Brute!"

"You feel it?"

"It is my destiny to fall in love with women who have heard the 'Song of the Open Road'—'something missing, something lost behind the ranges.'"

"I don't think I have heard that one before."

> "'Came the whisper, came the vision,
> Came the power with the need
> And the soul that is not man's soul
> Was sent us to lead.'"

"So you think I am going to try?"

"I don't think that the ronin, the samurai in you, could resist a challenge like that."

"So where does that leave you?"

"I sometimes feel I am living the 'Ballad of Grey Weather' that 'makes a man sick all the days of his life for something he cannot name.' But that is not really true. That is just me feeling sorry for myself. The reality is an overwhelming sense of pride. No, not that, it is gratitude—no, maybe humility—that it has been my good fortune to have known the great ones of this world."

Putting down the glass of scotch he had been twirling in his fingers, he turned and took her in his arms.

"I could say about you, Tomiko,

'That you were born a king's child.
Born and nursed a crowned king's child.
King of a land ayont the sea
When the gaijin he first kissed you.'

Doesn't quite rhyme, but you get the idea."

"So I am going to try?"

"I don't know, Tomiko. But yes, yes of course you will. In our bible, it says, 'To everything there is a season, and a time to every purpose under heaven. A time to be born and a time to die. A time to love and a time to hate, a time of war and a time of peace.' 'That those who have sown the wind will reap the whirlwind.'"

"Me? Kamikaze? The divine wind!"

"Who else?"

CHAPTER 17

Decision Time

That evening, Tomiko and Munro were side by side on a sofa in his apartment at the ranch. She lay with her head resting on his chest. One of the new Foundation girls they had recently found, a little lost one from Burma, was asleep on a blanket on the floor at their feet. The child still found everything so strange that she clung to Munro as the one constant in her new life. Munro picked her up and carried her to her own room next door and put her in her bed. He then returned and sat down beside Tomiko. He looked seriously at her.

"You are going to go back to Germany?"

Tomiko sighed. "Yes. I think so. I have done everything else, the Olympics, chief of police, leader of Japan. Married two men I loved and had their children. I hoped we could sit back and relax for the rest of our lives, but now it is obvious we cannot. That scary poem you talk about, 'the beast slouching towards Bethlehem.'"

"So sad, isn't it, and so prophetic,

> 'Things fall apart, the center cannot hold.
> Mere anarchy is loosed upon the world.
> The best have lost all conviction.
> The worst are full of passionate intensity.
> The darkness drops again.
> The rough beast, its hour come at last
> Slouches towards Bethlehem to be born.'"

"Yes, that awful prophetic poem. Japan is safe for a while, but if the beast is not stopped, it will take Europe. It pretty much has already. China will collapse into civil war as it always does, and Russia is tied up in the Caucuses, so it will be Japan and the US alone, and maybe the US will fall too. There are so many traitors in Washington. Why is it that the people who hate their country end up running it? And that foul deep state bunch, every country collects the same creatures. For me, I don't care about Europe. These idiots gave up on their own countries. But it is my duty to protect Japan, the code of Bushido, the way of the warrior. I would rather stop the beast in Europe than on the beaches of the Home Islands."

"You know if you go, you will be alone, facing the hate of the fifth column inside the West and the barbarians they have already imported and the hordes who are waiting to be imported."

"Not entirely alone. I will have Leda, La Marquesa, Sheila MacDonald, and Hinchcliffe at my side."

"We few—"

"Yes, we few. What is that one I have heard you say about Prince Henry?"

"We few? Yes! Agincourt,

'We few, we happy few. We band of brothers.
For he today who sheds his blood with me
Shall be my brother.
Be he ne'er so vile this day will gentle his ambition.
And gentlemen in England now abed
Shall think themselves accursed they were not here
And hold their manhood cheap
While any speak that fought with us
Upon St Crispin's day.'"

Tomiko sighed. "Hope it will not come to that."

"Me too. But Europe can either surrender as that clever man Malcolm Muggeridge said it would decades ago, or bloody civil war. I don't really see any other choice. And other than these few women, who will back you? As King Henry said, 'We would not live in that man's company that fears his fellowship to die with us.' What will you do if it all goes bad? As my own people of Scotland said after another futile war,

'Now all is done that men can do
And all is done in vain.
My love and native land farewell
For I must cross the main my love,
For I must cross the main.'

The main was the ocean, but what will your main be? If it all goes bad, we can always commit hara-kiri together and go into the future hand in hand. That has its attractions. 'Hotly we stormed Valhalla, a million years ago.'"

"Traditional, yes. But no! If I become tainted, you must somehow avoid the taint, otherwise it taints your Prometheus Project, and you have, what is it? That poem, 'Miles to go before you sleep.' If I go, we must publicly dissociate."

"Not again, Tomiko! We seem to have been doing this off and on for the last thirty years."

"Well, we have had lots of practice. If I win, I get to write history. If I lose, I lose quickly, then space or the grave."

"To fly with you to the stars. That would be acceptable."

"You will need another woman to make our split obvious."

"And you, another man—just not someone I already know, otherwise I would have this atavistic urge and not be able to stop myself from killing him with my bare hands."

"What are your plans here?"

"Just more of the same. Try to keep politicians and bureaucrats from writing new laws to make life more difficult for people. Maria Martens runs the states for me while I play around with the students, giving prizes for the Lunatic Law of the Month competition. And keep looking for brilliant kids, like this little one who we just found in Rangoon."

"So the die is cast. I will cross the Rubicon. Give me a few months to learn German, and then I will take over the police and suborn the army."

"'Once more into the breach, dear friends.' High noon, Tomiko-san. I love the ronin in you. I remember when I first saw a young woman who brought her children for me to look after." Gently stroking her hair, he said, "I fell in love with that combination of boldness, brains, and beauty."

"And I remember a hard, violent giant whom I knew wanted me the moment he saw me. I have waited for that man most of my life. I will love you forever with my heart and my body."

"Oh, Tomiko, I wish the world were different, but I suppose people have always been saying goodbye.

> 'What can the grave against us Oh my Heart,
> Comfort and light and reason in all things visible and
> invisible.
> Thou that wast I these barren unyoked years of trifling
> now at end.'"

"This is not sayonara," she said, turning and taking him in her arms. "We have survived before. We will do so again. Germany is not so far from the private airport in Luxembourg, and there is not much that Teresa can't make happen."

CHAPTER 18

The Gathering Storm

Having mourned the recent passing of his old friend Manon, whose funeral he had attended, and not being sure how long he was for this world himself, Don Pedro, feeling unwell, contacted Munro, who had been his friend and confidant for more than thirty years. Concerned that the episode in Paris, where he and Sheila had killed a group of assassins sent to execute them, might lead to criminal charges in France, Munro had been uncertain about returning to Europe. That affair had been hushed up however, and no charges were laid, so Munro felt it safe to return, at least to Spain. Without fanfare, he slipped into a private airport close to Madrid to visit the man who was one of his oldest friends.

Fortunately, by the time Munro got there, the Don, who by now was very elderly, was feeling much better. He was happy in the twilight of his days that his young wife, La Marquesa, a former Japanese police officer and Praetorian, had been recently elected as prime minister of Spain. She was steering that country as best she could through the turbulent times of the visibly failing Western Europe.

The Don and Munro spent a leisurely afternoon talking and laughing quietly over the times and events they had shared, such as Munro's arranged temporary marriage to the Don's lesbian daughter to produce the Don's grandson, now running the huge international construction company, and his own unexpected marriage to the Japanese Praetorian, who had after that marriage gained the title of La Marquesa and had slowly climbed the political system to her current position. The Don acknowledged that his wealth and influence had helped that climb a little. But he felt she had common sense, which so many of the idiots running Europe did not.

He totally agreed with Munro that Spain could not remain within the EU indefinitely, as its economy had never recovered and never would, unless they dropped the Euro and all concepts of a central currency. He also agreed that it would precipitate turmoil in Germany, which depended on exports, largely to EU countries, for almost 60 percent of its GDP. He also noted that once the EU bureaucracy was gone and borders no longer porous, Spain would have to have another Reconquista, as the level of lawlessness among the unemployed and unemployable migrants was becoming an extremely serious problem, and Spain simply could not afford the required welfare payments to support these completely unproductive people.

La Marquesa was busy with internal state affairs that afternoon, but Munro was invited to meet her at an official reception that evening. Upon entering the hall, he joined the reception line of ambassadors and the usual high-profile people who like to attend such soirees. He was accompanied by a Praetorian Guard he had brought with him from Arizona. She was dressed as a European woman, wearing a Hinchcliffe's shoulder holster covered by a wrap, not a kimono, as Munro did not wish to draw attention to his presence in Spain. The Don was not there, as he loathed these affairs and used the excuse of his age to avoid them if he could. The staff were aware that Munro was coming and were keeping an eye out for him.

They noticed his entrance and moved him up to the head of the reception line. He had known La Marquesa for many years, as Don Pedro had actually met her when she was training to be a Praetorian at the ranch in Arizona, but the protocol had to be followed. When he was formally introduced, to her amusement, he bowed and kissed the proffered hand. Looking quizzically down her cleavage, he said quietly with a little smile, "You have misplaced your gun this evening, Marquesa."

"I have my protection here," she said, smiling, indicating another young Praetorian standing behind her, dressed in a colorful kimono with a white obi decorated with purple lightning bolts. She pulled Munro forward and put her hand inside his jacket and felt the gun butt in the shoulder holster, which he now always wore when he was in Europe. "I see I have additional protection," she said. "Since the Don is not here, might I request that you stand at my shoulder as my oldest friend and confidant."

"I would be honored to do so, Marquesa." He took his place to the right and behind her, standing silently while the remaining introductions were being carried out. His own bodyguard took her place behind him.

At the tail end of the receiving line, there was an ambassador from a Middle East country with his entourage, grouped together, all wearing Middle East robes. As the ambassador approached to be introduced, one of the group to the left of the ambassador suddenly pulled out a long knife and flung himself at La Marquesa. It is said in the business that old fighters lose their legs, but their hand speed remains the same. Munro, the former heavyweight champion of the world, was no exception.

With his left hand, he swept La Marquesa, who was quite petite, backward off her feet out of the way of the knife. With his right, he pulled the ambassador into the path of the onrushing assassin who, without thinking, as he was doubtless in his hashish-induced Shaheed trance, stabbed the ambassador. This gave Munro a chance to grab the knife hand with his left as the attacker attempted to pull the knife free from the ambassador's body. With his right, he hit the assassin in the face, smashing his nose. Holding the assassin's wrist, he jerked the assassin forward, exposing him from behind the ambassador, who was falling to the ground. Munro hooked the assassin to the belly with his right fist.

Most people have no idea just how hard a trained boxer can hit. Munro's blow to the abdomen doubled the assassin up, almost lifting his feet off the floor. Then dropping his right shoulder, he hooked the assassin in the face with an uppercut, throwing him up and back. These hits stunned the attacker. Munro took the knife from the assassin's hand and holding him by the throat, rammed it up to the hilt in the man's left eye, based on the theory that a dead assassin is less of a problem than a wounded one, as subsequent governments have a distressing habit of freeing murderers. No one ever forgot the stench of corruption that surrounded the Libyan Lockerbie bomber who blew up the American plane and who was subsequently released from jail by a Scottish judiciary for very, very dubious reasons.

The ambassador was on the ground, writhing in pain from the knife wound to his shoulder. Munro looked on him with utter contempt. This pathetic excuse for a human being had just broken every law regarding an ambassador's duties, respected by even the most primitive society. Munro stamped very hard on the ambassador's face a couple of times, breaking his upper jaw, and crushing his facial bones. He knew that this attempted assassination of La Marquesa had been arranged by that country, but it would never be proved, and that country would simply deny all knowledge with a smirk and a shrug of the shoulders. Western culture demanded that an ambassador be inviolate.

By this time, the two Praetorians had their own guns out and were menacing the ambassador's staff. Munro pulled out his gun and, the anger still hot in him, pistol whipped the nearest one, knocking him to the floor.

"On the floor pigs!" he shouted, backhanding the next one with another strike of his gun. Cowering back, they complied, and while the Praetorians held their guns on the ambassador's retinue, Munro began to pull up their robes, looking for weapons. He had the robes pulled up over the heads of two of them by the time La Marquesa's own security burst through the onlookers and took over. The emergency medical people arrived shortly and took away the wounded ambassador and the dead assassin.

Giving the appearance of complete imperturbability, La Marquesa got to her feet from where Munro had thrown her, ignored the people on the floor, and gestured for the group to move to the next room. The soiree carried on as if there had been no interruption. Munro, his gun having disappeared back into his holster, remained silent at her shoulder.

"I owe you my life, Munro."

"It was my privilege, Marquesa. But it would be better if it were reported to be a soldier of Spain who protected you."

"Yes. What you say is true. But I will remember."

"With your permission, Marquesa, I will withdraw. If I am back in the US, there is no one for the media to question."

"Vaya con Dios, Munro. Come again soon."

"As your Excellency wishes."

This attack gave La Marquesa an opportunity to move against the violent in Spanish society. For some time now, it had been obvious that one day, it would be necessary to remove all the illegal migrants and fake refugees from the whole of Europe, but it was only in Spain that La Marquesa had any influence; and even there, she had to be very careful, as the collectivists/globalists among the media, the political classes, and the universities were very strong.

A decade of unemployment and steady reduction in standard of living with an equally steady increase in taxes to pay for benefits to illegals had produced widespread dissatisfaction. The rising crime rates, especially against women and children, had resulted in simmering discontent among the working class, who, unlike the elites, were exposed to this on a daily basis. Their very real grievances had been heard by La Marquesa, and she had pointed out on numerous occasions in the media that the only way to solve this problem was to control their own borders and their own destiny and that the EU was ruining them. She had been, and continued to be, roundly criticized by the media and the ruling class for these views; but they were being expressed more and more vocally by those affected.

Seeing the inevitable road she would have to follow; she had considered where these unassimilated migrants and criminals could go after their expulsion from Spain. Many of their countries of origin were failed states, and the others barely functioning. As remittances from the welfare recipients in the EU as more or less their sole source of foreign currency other than foreign aid, no country wanted them back. She had been in quiet negotiations with Mauritania, as the ruler there was prepared to accept them. With a per capita income of less than $5,000 per year, she was able to get an agreement that he would take them for $3,000 per head, paid directly to him. Once they arrived in that country, she would accept no further responsibility. All their EU documents were taken from them prior to deportation, as this was a tiny fraction of what these welfare recipients and jailbirds were costing Spain per year. La Marquesa thought that was a good deal and would have gone higher if necessary.

After the attack on herself, when she went on television and pointed out the crime statistics to the people, she was able to get a consensus to deport to Mauritania the nonrefugees, whom she defined very loosely and those noncitizens currently in jail. The NGOs who were importing these people across the Mediterranean were accused and held in jail on charges of people smuggling, and the military were dispersed along the coast to interdict the boats. The NGO boats were impounded and put to use interdicting the people smugglers approaching Spain. The smuggler's boats were towed back to North African countries they had come from, unloaded in the surf, pulled out to sea, and sunk. The coyotes or people smugglers were taken back to Spain and jailed. There was an international furor, but La Marquesa and the people of Spain ignored it.

President Moore in the US refused to comment, stating that it was an internal matter for Spain and he had no opinion on the issue. The number of illegals arriving in Spain vanished almost overnight, and thousands and thousands of migrants, taking advantage of the open borders, simply left for other countries in the EU or, sensing the change in Europe, simply went home.

After her spell of working in Canada bringing the bankrupt province of Ontario back to life, Sheila MacDonald returned to work for Manon and Teresa before taking over a subdivision of the conglomerate and subsequently starting her own company based mostly in France. France had always been her favorite country, although she could never say exactly why.

After all, taxes were terrible, the bumbling bureaucracy was unhelpful in the extreme, and the widespread trade unions were dreadful. Je ne sais quoi was all she was left with. She even agreed with Munro that the poets had been poor quality and no longer existed, the writers unreadable, and their attempts at philosophy in the last hundred years simply an unintelligible mixture of envy, gobbledygook, and a desperate need to justify an ongoing belief in Marxism by whatever means necessary. The proletariat actually liked capitalism, so the Marxists had found it necessary to convince some other groups that they were oppressed. Given all that, or in spite of that, not only did she love France but she managed to find a Frenchman she fell in love with, and he with her.

Her husband was a wealthy businessman. He had come from money, his father having built the business, but he had expanded it and done very well for himself. He and Sheila had been lovers for some time, but after her return from Canada, they got married and settled down together. They tried to keep their businesses separate as much as possible to avoid any clash between two strong-willed individuals. After she had her first child, Sheila reduced her business activities, bringing in some of the senior Prometheus Foundation girls to oversee the international wing while she concentrated on the domestic.

She wanted her child to have a mother, unlike her own miserable childhood. The second child, which she had in quick succession, further reinforced this belief. The lifestyle of Sheila and her husband was fairly sybaritic, with a house in Paris, a country house in Provence, and an apartment in Monte Carlo and Martinique. Both were running large companies, so life was not quite as opulent as it appeared on the outside, as the commitments were very time-consuming, with meetings with customers, advertisers, lawyers, government bureaucrats, and all the other myriad of activities necessary. Nonetheless, they were looked on by the paparazzi as a newsworthy couple worth pursuing.

As the children got a little older, Sheila, money no longer being a problem, as both she and her husband were independently wealthy, began to look more at the world she would be leaving for her children. Having run a major province in Canada, she was well aware of the difficulty with Democracy, especially the entitlement Democracy, which had arisen in the West, where those who had less, for whatever reason, felt entitled to take from those who had more, in effect robbing selective Peter to pay for collective Paul.

She also saw that this entitlement mentality of those who did not generate significant wealth themselves also spilled over into the lunatic concept that a country could import large numbers of those who would never produce wealth and could support them financially indefinitely. The political class, the media, and academics, having never ever had to meet a payroll, seemed blissfully unaware that in the long run, this was financially impossible. Sheila never ceased to be amazed by this breathtaking inability to do the simplest math. The problem was compounded by the fact that the new migrants had no skills and were young men who brought no young women with them and therefore had no prospect of ever getting a woman. What was even more lunatic was that these young men of fighting age came from a culture totally inimical to the West.

For some strange reason, no one seemed to question why underdeveloped countries were underdeveloped. It was hardly likely that it was because of some cosmic accident that the culture of Australia had not changed for thousands of years. Or that Islam had voluntarily retreated from science and reason almost eight hundred years before when they rejected the teachings of Ibn Rushd and, in the hundred or more years after the development of the printing press, had managed to print four books. It was the old chicken and egg. Countries were underdeveloped as a result of their culture. Their culture had not arisen as a result of their underdevelopment. To expect that representatives of a culture that had been static or regressed since the Averroes inflection in AD 1100 would suddenly embrace Western values was beyond all comprehension. As someone said, "Only an academic who had never had a real job could argue such foolishness."

Looking at the way her beloved France was changing; Sheila became very worried. The only hope she could see short of a civil war was political change, and the only politician in France who had any sense was Madeleine de Saint Exupery, who had slowly created a centrist party from what was left of the Gaullists and had combined with the daughter of the former paratrooper who had established a political party he called the National Front many years ago. The intelligentsia had laughed at the initial founder, and the media had mocked him, but the future had turned out to be infinitely worse than his worst predictions. In that he had joined Enoch Powell, the brilliant English member of Parliament who gave his infamous but prescient "Rivers of Blood" speech decades previously, predicting the outcome of the disastrous immigration policy with absolute accuracy.

This combined party, now led by Madeleine, had for years been a lone voice crying in the wilderness, but now people were beginning to look beyond the reflexive socialist jargon spouted by the media and grasp the underlying truth—that these policies were altering France beyond all recognition. Sheila sought and obtained a meeting with Madeleine. They shared views and found that they did have significant similarities. Perfectly aware of her own outstanding abilities, Sheila realized that if she wished to save the France, which she had known and loved, it would be necessary for her to join and support Madeleine. From Madeleine's viewpoint, the addition to her staff of someone who was widely recognized as being brilliant and being a foreigner could never seek to depose her, and that was a very large plus. She was gaining a woman of business who was independently wealthy, who was married into the moneyed class, who had had the experience of running a large turbulent Canadian province, and who was well connected with those running America. It would be difficult to paint Sheila MacDonald as some crazed right-wing lunatic.

They got on well together as Sheila avoided the limelight. She eventually became in effect the éminence grise. As she was a citizen of France, Madeleine did not really see it as a problem, and Sheila became the deputy head of the National Party. When it came to international affairs, Sheila became the party's spokesperson, as she was quite at home in the halls of power in Washington and Europe.

The National Party grew slowly over the years. Sheila's recommendation was always to try to get control of school boards, local politics, and entertainment. The people who did these usually thankless tasks, she made sure were honored by the party, with recognition in newsletters, frequent little conferences, and networking little soirees, to encourage not only the party faithful but also the energetic youth. The bigger the grassroots movement, the more difficult it was for the globalists and leftists to brand them as crazed Nazis.

While her children were small, Sheila was quite happy with her role. She made sure that they spent time in Arizona, as she wanted them to avoid the reflexive anti Americanism that dominated Europe. Her children were clever, but she wanted them exposed to the incredible brain power of the Foundation girls and, increasingly, the brilliance of the young boys who were being invited to join the residential Space Academy. The thought that they would grow up surrounded by her wealth was never far from her mind. She wanted her children to know just how hard the world could be and the incredible intellects that were out there. If civilization fell apart, she wanted them to have a shot at escaping the surly bonds of earth, and to get that chance, they would need degrees in STEM, as the Prometheus Group wanted no one else in space.

The National Party slowly expanded its base, becoming more of a force in French politics, especially as the situation in the larger towns grew ever more chaotic. The mainstream media, as was happening throughout the whole Western world, had fallen under the sway of ideologues who had sought and slowly gained control of the teaching of journalism. They were therefore complicit with the political class in concealing the disaster that mass migration had become, with the incredible rise in welfare payments, as naturally there were no jobs for migrants and no prospects of there ever being jobs. The huge increase in crime, especially against women, went unreported and ignored, not only by the media, which was expected, but also by other radical groups. The torching of famous old cathedrals were dismissed as "accidents."

The catastrophic destruction of Europe was so self-evident that how anyone could have thought that these policies would have a different outcome was beyond comprehension. Merkel herself had, years before, pointed out that these policies simply did not work. Normal people were eventually faced with the unenviable conclusion that they were being run by the incompetent or the malevolent, and it was hard to decide which was worse as the eventual outcome would be the same.

For the first few years, Sheila and her husband had a great relationship, but with the passage of time, they grew apart. There was no vitriol and no great arguments over politics, religion, or indeed anything that frequently divides couples. It was not even infidelity. After all, this was France, where lovers were condoned, if not encouraged, and a mistress was not a source of shame or even major concern. It was simply that Sheila gradually became more interested in the future of the world. She never put it that way herself as she felt it was ridiculously grandiose, but she was increasingly part of the inner circle of the Prometheus Group, to which she provided significant financial contributions and encouraged her friends to do likewise.

The apocalyptic view of the future of the world espoused by the Prometheus Group had initially seemed unnecessarily gloomy, but the course of events was actually following their predictions and a lot sooner than anyone would have credited. Who would have thought twenty years previously that Sweden would voluntarily give over sovereignty to an alien culture and effectively vote to no longer be part of the Western world?

Sheila became increasingly worried about her children's future. She and Manon had agreed that living in the fin de siècle, or the end of time, was reasonably pleasurable, if one did not think of the future. Rome, after all, survived a long time after the death of Marcus Aurelius sealed its doom. Belisarius, striking back from the Eastern Roman Empire, had even been able to revigorated it for a while. Unfortunately, it seemed that the grace and glory of Europe, which began with the Renaissance or even earlier at Runnymede, with the establishment of the Magna Carta, was to be but the blink of an eye in the long history of tyranny and barbarism. It looked as if Hobbes's view of the world was correct—that the natural state of man had been, and always would be, nasty, brutish, and short. Quite where the seemingly intractable longing for chaos came from was never clear to Sheila.

Tomiko, anything but a philosopher, had suggested to Sheila when they met while Sheila was visiting Arizona, and occasionally in Tokyo, that perhaps it was part of the endless cycle of Daoism, that chaos and order were cyclical and lay at the heart of all existence, which would explain why Earth had never been visited by beings from another planet. If that were a universal law, perhaps no civilization had ever evolved in any planet or any galaxy that was stable over a long enough period of time to develop the knowledge that would allow space exploration. If so, perhaps the moon and Mars colonies might be the eye of order in the Daoist serpent of chaos.

It was obvious to Sheila that America alone would be the last refuge for the Western world. But even that was failing with the ship of responsibility adrift and sinking in the sea of rights and cynical or thoughtless politicians bribing people with their own money. Japan would defend Japan, but they did not feel that honor required them to protect the foolish gaijin from themselves. China was building hegemony but given the fact that their prosperity was dependent on their exports to the West and the fact that the vast majority of their population lived in abject poverty, civil war was the likely outcome, as it had been for several thousand years. India would remain India, as chaotic as always. The Himalayas would protect them from the Chinese, but perhaps the Moguls would come back with further wars with Pakistan, possibly nuclear, as that country grew increasingly lawless and desperate.

Sheila wanted US citizenship for her own children, but if she obtained that, someone would inevitably leak the information, and it would not look good if the deputy head of a political party did not believe in her country's future. So she approached La Contessa and got them Mexican passports, as this was much easier to conceal. Similarly, she made sure that a fair percentage of her wealth was now in America and Mexico.

As a businesswoman, she had always been acutely aware of the economic rise of countries such as Poland and Turkey. She became convinced that Turkey was going to become again a major political player. She saw it supporting the demands for a greater Albania and Kosovo, with the gradual expulsion of the Serbians. Ardogan no longer bothered to correct anyone who called him the caliph. When he began to dictate how the German Turks should vote in their internal elections in Germany, the writing on the wall seemed clear. Jan Sobieski may have stopped the Turks at the gates of Vienna centuries ago, but there were now more mosques than churches in that city, and clearly it was being conquered from within, the assault from without having failed.

After the fall of Sweden, it was obvious that other states would follow. Western women were no longer interested in having children, unless they converted, and migrant women were, in large numbers, funded by welfare. Simple demographics alone would ensure that in a few decades, the migrants would outnumber the local inhabitants. The West, as it had been, would no longer exist in twenty or thirty years. This, however, would not occur in Caliph Ardogan's lifetime, and he was not likely to simply await events. He likely wanted to be remembered forever as the conqueror of the West, the sword of Islam. Fireworks were therefore likely to happen soon.

While Silly Billie ran the US, Hinchcliffe and her Legion had kept a very low profile, simply consolidating and training for the future. They all breathed a sigh of relief when that fool lost the election and was replaced by Moore as president. Moore, however, had no intention of getting involved in European internal affairs. America had twice spent her treasure and young lives to save what, exactly? For what and from what? Europe had never shown any gratitude and had consistently mocked and vilified the US. As far as he was concerned, Europe could look after itself if it wished.

Sheila had communicated her fears to Madeleine and La Marquesa and had also been speaking to Hinchcliffe. She found that Hinchcliffe and Munro had seen this coming years ago, and Munro had suggested to Hinchliffe, while she was a little girl, that this was her destiny—to be the savior of the West. Anticipating what would very soon become a civil war in Europe, Hinchcliffe began slowly, and without drawing any attention to the fact, transporting a fair amount of the Legion's equipment to Spain. Troops and planes could be moved swiftly, but it would take time to build up the armor, stores, and munitions. Colin, one of her senior leaders who had been reduced to an administrative role after the loss of an arm in combat years before, had been war-gaming the likely events in Europe for some time.

They saw no reason to speak to the current president of France as he was an avid EU and globalist supporter. Like Beaupre in Canada, he no longer believed in any national identity. France was simply a piece of real estate who could be occupied by anyone and everyone. The cry "Vive la France" was, for him and his coterie, simply a foolish symbol of the past, something to be ignored or surveyed with eye rolling and sneers.

CHAPTER 19

Götterdämmerung

Leda, when she was elected chancellor of Germany, put forward a motion that the mayor of Cologne had shown complete inability and unwillingness to protect the people of that city. She moved that given the civil chaos, the central government take control. In protest, the mayor resigned. A replacement could not be decided by the existing elected groups of city politicians, and new elections were proposed. Eventually, this activist apologist was replaced by a supporter of Leda, someone who was more in tune with the wishes of the people, who were becoming increasingly shocked and despairing by the unchecked, ever-increasing migrant violence.

Watching this play out, it became obvious to Leda and the newly elected mayor that the existing chief of police was utterly incompetent and could not remain in office. As his senior officials were equally complicit in the cover-up of the Cologne rape fest, or the Tahrir game, as the affair had become known worldwide. An experienced senior police officer with absolutely no connection with the existing power structure, either in the police force or in local politics, would have to be brought in to radically change the system.

The new mayor announced on national TV that they would have to look internationally for such an individual. Leda then pointed out that the logical choice was Tomiko-san, whose book on the techniques of policing had long been available in German and who was potentially available, having retired from Japanese politics and was currently running the Space

Academy. Not only was she very experienced in policing, but she was not German and therefore was in a position to bring in changes more aligned to world policing. Leda pointed out the very low crime statistics in Japan while Tomiko was chief of police and subsequently prime minister. Raucous discussions were held, but clearly the German policing model had become totally nonfunctional and required significant changes. Tomiko was offered the job for a year with possible reappointment, and she accepted the position on the understanding that she was answerable to the central government, specifically Leda, and not the Cologne town council or any other local government.

The first step that Tomiko took on her arrival in Germany was to evaluate all her senior officers. She found that almost all of them were political ideological appointees, so she forced their retirement or moved them sideways into meaningless jobs. This approach had been pioneered by the board of education in New York to deal with utterly incompetent teachers who, by union rules, essentially could not be fired. The job consisted of simply showing up, sitting in a room together, and reading the newspapers, with nothing else to do. After a few months of that, many, but unfortunately not all, preferred an early retirement.

She also set about organizing a fighting force as opposed to the weak, effectively helpless, politicized force whose sole goal seemed to be oppression of their own citizens who dared to protest the takeover of their country. Crime and punishment had largely disappeared from the lexicon of policing, not only in Germany, but across the whole of Europe, especially in the UK.

The Rapid Response Team, the equivalent of a SWAT team, was interviewed first. This was not easy, as Tomiko was still learning to speak German. Tomiko had the sense that these still were men and not pathetic weasels, as someone had called the rest of the European police. Using the Cologne team as a core, she doubled then tripled their unit size. As she still did not know who was who, she essentially allowed the men of the rank and file to pick those with whom they would like to stand shoulder to shoulder.

She armed them with the club she had developed with Munro many years before, an extendable, semiflexible titanium shaft with interchangeable heads, depending on its prospective use. When she first demonstrated the club to the men, she showed them how it could be varied. There was a steel core covered in soft plastic designed to stun for general police use, and the man killer. That was a three-inch long, two-inch diameter heavy, lethal stainless steel head resembling the mace used by armored knights of the middle ages, being heavier at the tip and flaring out from the base into six wicked flanges.

She passed it around the group of men from the SWAT team. One, holding it and running his other hand over the head, looked at her and said, "Commander, this will kill a man if he is hit on the head with this."

"*Hai!* So?"

Tomiko had brought a thick, short wooden plank that she had placed on two supports. Saying nothing further, she swung the club, which smashed the plank in two. Via a translator, she explained to them, "If I as a small woman can do this, think what you men can do. Arresting these rapists is a waste of time. Either they will not be formally charged, like the tiny numbers after the rape of Cologne, or no witness will testify or some useless judge will release them or give them a derisory sentence. I have not come over from Japan to play catch and release. I want crime to stop. And if it takes a few bodies on the street to stop it, so be it. I am in charge, and the rules have changed. Anyone who does not feel that he can join us in restoring law and order can leave this meeting. I will find him a desk job somewhere."

She looked around at the assembled men. They looked at each other. The one holding the club asked her, "If I hit a criminal with this, and he dies, will you support me? Do you have the authority to make sure I am not charged with murder or excessive use of force?"

Tomiko took out a document and showed it to them. "I have been given authority by the chancellor to bring back law and order, using whatever force is required."

"So if I hit a criminal, and he dies?"

"Too bad. He obviously was violently resisting arrest. He was obviously a criminal, and he died. There is no reason to report to the Police Enquiry Board. Until this crisis is over, I am disbanding that Enquiry Board, and the members can return to regular policing."

The big man holding the club gave a savage grin and looked at his fellows. "So we can enforce the law, Commander?"

"Indeed you can. Forget these stupid arrests."

He looked around the group. They grinned and nodded. "Commander, we will be happy to follow you," they said in chorus.

Women police officers were also recruited into these teams, but only the ones approved by the men. She wanted no shrinking violets and none who were afraid of rough men or violence in the streets. She indicated to them that they were going to be the decoys, and they had better learn to trust the men who would be their protectors.

When she trained with them, which she did separately from the regular police force, she again emphasized that when the clashes began, she did not want prisoners, as she thought the courts were worse than useless. Her men quietly agreed with these sentiments. She promised to protect them against claims of excessive force, and they noted that she had already disbanded the police investigation unit. She indicated that she did not know what constituted excessive force when protecting themselves from armed migrants, who were known to carry knives, and she had the rules of engagement rewritten to protect her officers.

There were a few clashes and some rioters died, showing that the new clubs were effective and that the cover-up of information—or news blackout, which had been practiced by the Merkel government and the media—worked both ways. Knives, presumably carried by the dead migrants, were frequently found lying on the streets after such clashes. It was rumored often the same knives.

The members of the state media found that the techniques they had used against people they saw as their opponents were now being used against them. This resulted in a few of the most vocal being accused of various crimes. Suspected pedophilia, with the discovery of pedophilic files on home computers and memory sticks, was found to be common among the more radical media types. What was truly surprising was that much of it was actually real. Similar accusations of misconduct by media types against females also became common, and again, a surprising amount was actually true.

The first main opportunity occurred during a New Year's celebration. It was night, and the streets and squares of Cologne were crowded with large numbers of people having fun. The SWAT teams were hidden in closed vans parked around the central square, and spotters were in the high buildings, some with night-vision capability, and all were in radio contact with Tomiko and the teams. At about 10:00 p.m., the trouble began. After the infamous rape of Cologne, when the authorities had done nothing, these rape games, or the Tahrir experience—named after the sexual assault of the South African journalist in Cairo—had become commonplace. The regular police had previously been instructed by their superiors to ignore the happening, and senior officers ensured that they always had the excuse that there were not enough officers to police the unruly crowd.

As the evening progressed, the violence began. Women in the crowd were separated from their partners by large groups of migrants, who proceeded to strip and rape them on the street, with some of the group facing out to prevent interference while the rest looked in and participated in the fun.

The first rape group in the square outside the cathedral was identified by the spotters, and the information was transmitted to Tomiko. She wanted to be visible on the inevitable videos of the affair, as any movement needed a point man to take the blame, and Leda wanted that to be a woman and preferably a non-German citizen. So Tomiko wore a modified kimono, as an oriental woman in traditional dress could hardly be accused of being a Nazi bitch. She did consent to wear a helmet and the new thin, flexible body armor under her kimono, as many of the migrants carried knives.

Anticipating the inevitable videos, Tomiko led her men as they came piling out of the closed vans and forced their way through the crowds to get to the rape scene. She led the charge as several of her SWAT teams came smashing in around her into the rapist group. Two very large men, delighting in the attitude of their new commander, were on either side of her without being asked, towering over her, protecting her from any side assault. The new clubs were going like metronomes, and the crunching blows sent blood flying as skulls and faces were smashed. They knew she wanted broken heads, permanently broken heads.

While they were destroying the first rapist group, a second had been identified, and a smaller SWAT team attacked. The knives came, out and several of the police died before the first teams reached them with reinforcements. No one in that second rapist group survived. Four other groups and numerous individual acts were punished that night. In the vast crowds, the destruction of the Tahrir gangs happened quickly, quietly, and violently; and the bodies were hauled away without any fuss or flashing lights. The street party continued unchecked until early morning. One annual event was missing, the firing of rockets at the cathedral by the migrants. The SWAT team strongly discouraged that—with broken heads and broken arms. The ambulances, waiting in the side streets with no lights or sirens, quietly transported the bodies to the city morgue and the odd survivor to the hospitals.

When morning came, the unofficial tally, which never was made official, of what came to be called the Battle of Cologne had resulted in the death of more than sixty rapists and four policemen, with more than fifteen non–life threatening stabbings. There were no prisoners. Tomiko did not feel it was worthwhile charging the survivors who had broken limbs unless they made a fuss. The expected outcry occurred from the international media, with screams and accusations of white supremacists, Nazis, Islamophobes, and all the other run-of-the-mill name-calling. This was muted however by the lack of any official documentation.

In the inevitable interviews, Tomiko indicated that she had been appointed as the chief of police, and as a middle-aged Japanese woman, she could hardly be called either a white supremacist or a Nazi. She indicated that the law was the law, and as chief of police, she would enforce the law. That was what she had been hired to do, and she would do it. She pointed out that if people do not want to have a problem with the police, then they should not break the law. She also pointed out that she was not about to let her boys be killed by knife-wielding lawbreakers.

The outcry inside Germany was much less than anyone expected, including Leda, as even the university students were becoming a little alarmed at the level violence, which was beginning to pervade all aspects of German life. The average German man and woman felt relieved that someone was finally putting a stop to this madness of open season on German women and children, which had been allowed by Merkel and her law courts. All over Germany, men quietly raised their beer glasses in a toast that someone with testicles, albeit an oriental woman, finally seemed to be in charge.

The opposition political parties tried to insist on an inquiry, but Leda managed to block that move. The courts were not really involved as there were virtually no arrests, simply dead rapists, who elicited few tears, as all of them were young single men with no families in Germany. Leda used the affair as an excuse to close the borders to migrants and begin deporting all young men in so-called refugee camps. She initially had them put on a train to Turkey, but after the first few thousand were deported, the new caliph, Ardogan, refused to accept them, as did all other functioning countries they had come from. These countries were financially dependent on money being remitted by recipients of German welfare.

As Sweden had an open-border policy, Leda had them deported there. In Sweden, with the takeover of Sharia law and what military there was paralyzed, there was nothing to stop Leda dumping many of the unwanted into that country. Her new policy, however, resulted in very large numbers of migrants leaving through the open borders to other EU countries such as Belgium, Holland, and France. Many others, including Turkish people who had been there for a generation or more but who had never really integrated, sensing the change in the wind, simply went back to the countries they had come from. Immigrants ceased pouring into Germany within a very short period of time.

Tomiko sought and was now given police authority over the province. She used her female police operatives as decoys. She rewarded them handsomely for each exploit and developed an award system. The men of the SWAT team were also rewarded for each exploit, and these women, who put their lives on the line, were greatly respected by the men who protected them. SWAT teams in closed vans were ready for immediate and overwhelmingly violent activity.

The decoy activity was standard—one or two women walking alone down a street in the evening. Initially, that was all that was required. They would be swarmed by migrant's intent on raping the uncovered women. A SWAT team would then erupt from their concealment in the vans, and mayhem would ensue. If they were lucky, more migrants would be enticed to join the fray by the relatively few policemen in the initial SWAT team. Further, SWAT teams would then appear to join in the fun. No prisoners continued to be the unstated aim, as no prisoners meant no useless time-consuming counterproductive court appearances.

The men and women in these teams developed intense camaraderie, which combat brings out. Tomiko would go drinking with them in the beer halls, where they would celebrate after the violent activity. She made sure they were given bonuses, decorated, promoted, and relieved of routine police work so that there was significant competition to join their ranks.

As the news of rape attempts and their suppression was either not reported at all or vastly downplayed by the media, and as many migrants were illiterate, the news of the change in policing and therefore migrant behavior spread slowly. The policewomen began to dress more provocatively and venture into worse zones in numerous towns, so the number of events continued to rise. Tomiko insisted that these women wear some of the new flexible body armor, initially developed by one of the Foundation girls in cooperation with some of the Space Academy engineers.

When interviewed, which she very seldom agreed to, Tomiko made no mention about the use of decoys. She began to refer to these men and women as her Teutonic Knights, rather than a SWAT team, and had a uniform patch made of a black cross on a white background, resurrecting that ancient symbol. The recruitment into these teams increased as more personnel became available when Tomiko called a halt to and disbanded the hate speech and hate crime divisions and other silly modish divisions in the police forces she controlled. Leda appointed her chief of police for an additional region, and then another. There were several months of minimally reported but brutal violence with hundreds of deaths as the new clubs were indeed lethal weapons. These included the odd left-wing media agitator, apparently stabbed by a migrant, although charges of pedophilia and assisting pedophilia were more effective. Leda soon appointed Tomiko chief of police of Germany.

As the number of rapists and other violent thugs clubbed to death rose, so did the number of police knifings. She therefore bought the new flexible armor for her Teutonic Knights in such numbers that Teresa's factory ramped up production and began to work shifts. Some of the migrants began to coalesce into groups in their no-go areas to fight the police, and guns began to appear, with a few police shot dead. Cheap hand grenades from Eastern Europe also made their appearance, as they had for some time now in Sweden.

With the advent of gun violence and hand grenades, Tomiko pointed out that her men were police, not the army; and if it was a shooting war, she wanted military involvement. Leda gave her authority to co-opt the army, as necessary. She found the same situation with the military that she had found with the police—a defanged, politicized, disheartened, and despairing group of men and women. She adopted the same principle, displacing the senior officers by early retirement or sideways promotions into meaningless positions of no authority, and encouraged younger men. By this time, she could speak German, so she could rely increasingly on her own judgment, but she was still dependent on a small group of police whom she trusted to advise her as to a candidate's suitability.

She did meet a young man in the Wehrmacht. He was a tall, lean young *hauptmann*, or captain, who impressed her with his intelligence, knowledge of history, and grasp of the situation. She spoke to him privately and found that his reading of the situation was the same as her own and that the difficulties they faced were political, not military. She asked for and got him seconded to her, and young Kurt effectively became her second in command. Guarding Tomiko's back, he took part in a few violent attacks on group rapists. He recognized the initial necessity for her to be seen as leading the charge, but thought the time for that had passed and was unhappy at her personal exposure in violent situations; so he gathered a group of volunteers, mostly young men—but to be politically correct, young women also—to be her bodyguard. They all wore the increasingly obvious Teutonic knight uniform patch.

He felt justified when an assassination attempt was made. The bodyguards managed to block the attempt, but one young policewoman died, throwing herself in front of Tomiko as a gunman opened fire. There was an official police funeral for her, her coffin on a gun carriage with the family walking behind, flanked by Leda and Tomiko. For that, Tomiko had her new unit wear tunics similar to those worn by Hinchcliffe's Legion, except they were white with the black cross of the Teutonic Knights. Tomiko, very unofficially, had a song written about the courage of the young woman, which they sang in the beer halls. The other song she encouraged was the song of the Teutonic Knights, *Die Eisenfaust am Lanzenschaft*.

Ardogan had firmly established himself as the caliph of Turkey after an attempted coup. This was almost certainly a black flag operation, organized by himself, which allowed him to execute hundreds of those followers of Kemal Ataturk, the man who, in the 1930s, had modernized Turkey, bringing that country out of the Middle Ages. The Kemalists would have opposed his aim of removing the secular state and reestablishing not only the caliphate but also the jihad, the conquest of Europe. Ardogan felt that that goal had not really changed since before the fall of Constantinople.

He had initially been content to let demographics do its work for him. Women in the West had effectively stopped having children and instead had imported large numbers of migrants from North Africa and the Middle East. These groups were having children, a lot of children. Sweden had already fallen, and in a few years, Belgium and France would be overwhelmed by the migrant vote.

The migrants, allied with the inevitable group of useful idiots, as Lenin had called them, who hate their own people for whatever reason would vote in Sharia law, with eventually complete dominance of Islam. He had begun to accelerate that process by making sure that the Turks living in Germany, even after several generations, were still effectively under his authority and would vote as he directed. By doing so, he was gradually taking over the town councils in much of Germany.

The sudden appearance of Leda, followed by Tomiko, and the bodies in the street and the fact that, for the first time, Germany was not listening to the globalist ideologue bureaucrats in the EU indicated that there was still a slight risk of Europe resurgent. Ardogan came to the conclusion that he did not want to wait. He would surely be honored by future historians as the conqueror of the West, but he preferred to be honored in the present for having done what Suleyman the Magnificent failed to do.

He began to build up weapons caches, not only in the radical mosques, such as the one in Kinsbury in England, where it was an open secret that weapons were stored, but also all over Europe. Even when such knowledge became commonplace, no police force in Europe acted on it. He also decided that a series of targeted assassinations would thin his opposition, hence his failed attacks on La Marquesa and Tomiko. Knowing, or suspecting that that was his likely plan, Tomiko and Kurt had surrounded Leda with her new force of Teutonic Knights as well as her official security, which they saw as inadequate.

Ardogan saw no need to eliminate the current president of France, who was an EU globalist, who had long since stated that he hated nationalism, and who had agreed with Beaupre of Canada that it was time for nation states to vanish and that a nation was simply a piece of real estate. The target in France was Madeleine de Saint Exupery. Ardogan had arranged the assault on Sheila, whom his advisers had seen as a potential danger, but that unfortunately failed; and in spite of the manufactured fuss created by his allies in the media, either paid or simply ideologues, Sheila was now back in France with Madeleine.

For some time now, Sheila MacDonald had been Madeleine's deputy and senior adviser. She had been told by Theresa many months previously that her whisperers were hearing that things were happening in Turkey and that meetings were being held in numerous areas with people who urgently wished to see the downfall of the West. As she felt that affairs were reaching crisis point, she arranged for Madeleine to meet with those she felt would become necessary aides if France was to be rescued, as the existing military and police were likely too politicized to be of any value.

CHAPTER 20

Cry Havoc

Madeleine de Saint Exupery, the de facto leader of the opposition in France, had a meeting arranged in Paris one afternoon with Jock MacGregor, the deputy head of Hinchcliffe's Legion, and Miguel, who was La Contessa's deputy leader in Mexico. The subject, which was kept secret, was a discussion of possible military responses to the rapidly deteriorating state of affairs in Europe, mainly France. There was an official government reception that evening, which she had to attend, so she invited both men to accompany her.

As Europe was now so lawless and as Madeleine was the obvious target for assassination in France, both men were armed as usual with gun and knife. Sheila MacDonald, who was Madeleine's chief of staff, was with them. Since her own assassination attempt in Canada years ago, Sheila had always carried a gun. As she was not yet comfortable in Europe with a visible gun, she carried her pistol in her clutch bag. Knowing few people and not being particularly interested in the others attending the soiree, the men, who knew each other well, stayed close to Madeleine. They were wearing conservative suits, cut as always to conceal their ever-present weapons.

"I thought you men of Scotland wore skirts or, what do you call them, kilts?" joked Madeleine.

"Yes, my lady. But tonight, Miguel and I have no wish to be conspicuous."

"*Mais oui,* of course. But why do you wear skirts anyway? Surely it is an obsolete form of dress?"

"Well, my lady, if I may give a rough soldier's response, which I first heard from my father, it is because the kilt is the best piece of clothing for diarrhea and fornication, both activities being important to poor soldiers like us. It's also a bullfighter's muleta, the red rag for the bull. It is a symbol that we Scotts are different and happy to be different. It is a man thing, laugh at me or challenge me at your peril."

"You understand this?" said Madeleine, turning to Sheila, who was also close by.

"I left Scotland as a child and never went back. But the challenge thing, I do understand. The men I grew up with were professional fighters like Munro or Don Miguel here, or Jake, an Olympic shooter, who taught me. Or the hard guys from the southern Border Patrol. So, yes, I understand the male challenge concept."

She caught sight of a group of traditionally dressed men from a Middle East country approaching through the crowd. The ambassador was in front, clearly wishing to speak to Madeleine. Sheila was not happy and gave a warning. "Here comes an ambassador from the Middle East. Be careful, I have all sorts of reasons not to trust these men in nightshirts."

Knowing of the recent attack on La Marquesa, which clearly had been organized by the ambassador of another Middle East country, they had no faith at all that any other country from that part of the world would follow the rules of civilization. That had been true since the time of the Mongols. Western customs and culture, at least since the famous frosty reception to some servants of the caliph by Vlad the Impaler, prevented them from strip-searching these ambassadors and their entourage. At Sheila's warning, Jock on Madeleine's left was like a coiled spring, and Miguel to her right watched them coldly, like a snake. Madeleine did not think it likely that violence would occur, as it had been centuries since an ambassador in Europe had acted as an assassin. Indeed no one could remember such an unthinkable breakdown of protocol.

Sheila's fears were amply justified when one of the men on the periphery of the ambassador's group pulled a knife from his robes and rushed at Madeleine with his arm raised, poised to stab. It was not happenstance or luck that had made Miguel, a world champion boxer. He was quick cat, sweeping Madeleine aside with his left arm.

As the assassin was concentrating trying to reach Madeleine, torquing to the left to avoid the assassin's rush, Miguel hammered his right fist into the left side of the assassin's face, which stunned the man. This gave

Miguel an opportunity to grab the man's wrist with his left hand. With his immense strength from years of physical training, he held the assassin and again hammered him in the face with his right fist. The assassin's knees sagged. With a cross draw from under his jacket, Miguel pulled out his own knife, a razor-sharp Ka-bar, punched the knife through the man's robes, and gutted him, opening up his belly from pelvis to chest. The man screamed, dropped his knife and with one hand, clutched at his robes, trying to hold his own intestines in place as they slowly fell from his abdomen and, coil by coil, descended to the floor.

Seeing this, some of the more fragile onlookers fainted. Miguel gripped him by the throat and forced him to the ground, with his knife almost in the man's eye.

"Who sent you? Tell me who sent you?"

The man simply screamed incoherently.

Jock had also moved quickly. Confident that Miguel could handle the assassin, in a couple of strides, he reached the ambassador, to whose party the assassin obviously belonged and kicked him very hard in the groin. The ambassador screamed in pain, clutching himself and collapsed to his knees. With his left hand, Jock grabbed him by his beard and pulled his head back. He also pulled out his own Ka-bar, the fighting knife of the US marines, and like Miguel, he put the tip of the blade a fraction of an inch from the ambassador's eye.

"How many more assassins in your group, you fat pig?" He reversed the knife and hit the kneeling man hard on the forehead with the haft of the knife before returning the point to the ambassador's eye. Gripping the beard, he twisted his head back further, "How many more, pig?"

The ambassador, who had glanced at the assassin, saw Miguel, fed up with the screams, sink his knife deep into the man's eye, stopping the sound immediately. Terrified, the ambassador's bowels let go. Smelling the immediate stink, Jock released him.

"Not only a pig, but a coward as well. A fitting representative of your country."

He cocked his head to Miguel, who understood the gesture. He pulled up the assassin's robes and holding the corpse by the throat and one leg, Miguel, who was still immensely strong, lifted it up and dropped it so that the ambassador's head entered the body cavity of the assassin. There were muffled shrieks as the ambassador tried to extricate himself.

The audience was rooted to the spot because this whole violent action had taken less than a minute. Miguel put his knife point under the chin of the closest one of the ambassador's entourage. "Pick up this garbage and carry it from this place. We have had enough of you pigs here." As the man did not move quickly enough, Miguel hit him with a left hook to the belly, lifting him up on his toes, and doubling him over, so he fell face-down.

"Take off your nightshirt and wrap that scum in it and carry them out."

Jock was by now holding his gun on the group. Miguel bent over and pulled the man's dishdasha up over his head, leaving him in his underwear. At this point, security arrived in numbers. There was a little unpleasantness before Madeleine could sort things out, pointing to the fact that both Jock and Miguel had Mexican diplomatic passports and were immune to standard French law.

Jock apologized to Madeleine. "I am sorry for this attempt on your life, my lady. We should have anticipated better and avoided some of the unpleasantness."

"There is nothing to apologize about. You and Don Miguel saved my life. I would like to reward you somehow."

"Just being here with you is reward enough, my lady."

"You flatter me."

"Nay, my lady, not so. We know you put your life on the line for France every day. I would that I could be at your shoulder through these times of trial."

"You may be doing that sooner than you think. I do not know how much I trust the French military."

"The Saint-Cyr gang?" said Jock, shrugging his shoulders. "Who knows? But I know some of the boys in the French foreign Legion. I think that they are loyal to France. The others, especially the senior officers in the regular army, they are mostly political appointees, so I do not know."

"We may find that out soon. Can I rely on you?"

"Your servant, my lady. I await your call."

This attempted assassination of Madeleine was the last straw. The then president of France had a 13 percent positive rating only in the public polls, and there were daily riots in the streets by the Yellow Jackets, the normal people of France fed up with the tyranny of the globalists. The very name *yellow jacket* was an anathema, named for the fluorescent yellow jacket every motorist in France was forced to buy by government fiat and keep in his car.

Madeleine felt it was now or never; she had to make her move. At her request, Sheila had been seriously war-gaming for months with Colin, one of Hinchcliffe's Legion commanders; and the people they thought could and would help were in place. Hinchcliffe had many of her troops and equipment in Spain, ready to move. Madeleine made the decision that night. She planned a rally and a march on the Élysée Palace in two days. The likely outcome of that march was not clear to her or Sheila.

As soon as this decision was made, Sheila took her two children, rented a business jet, and flew directly to Arizona. She arrived unannounced, as she did not want anyone in Europe to know that her uncertainty about the outcome of this potential uprising had led her to taking her children to the safety of America. At the main ranch house, after the staff had found a suitable room for them from the many available, she left her children in the care of the amah she had brought with her. She was about to walk down to the evening durbar when the girls came straggling back to the main ranch house, indicating that it was over. The Silk One was with them. Sheila stopped her.

"Is Munro still there?"

"Yes. He said something about climbing the hill to spend a few minutes alone with the Buddha. I think he is missing Tomiko and worried about her and the coming war in Europe. I offered to go with him, but he said no."

"Were you trying to seduce him?"

"Not very hard. He keeps telling me to keep myself pure and he will find a man worthy of me someday."

"I think he means pure in heart, Silk One. He does not want you to fall in love with some idiot. So you also think war is coming?"

"I can't see how it can be avoided. Hegel was right, the Owl of Minerva only flies in the dusk. People only waken up when it is too late. Presumably that is why you are here, to leave your kids. I suppose, as your man Shakespeare says, you are 'going to take up arms against a sea of troubles.'"

Sheila nodded in agreement, not at all surprised that the Silk One knew instinctively what was happening. She turned toward the path leading up to the Shinto shrine.

"You are going to see him?"

"I must. We are of one blood, he and I."

"A strange thing to say."

"Yes, but true. I need to talk to him."

She made her way up the path to the torii gate. Munro was not there, so she walked round the summit and down the path to the little cave that looked out over the valley. Hinchcliffe had insisted that the cave be constructed, as she felt anyone sitting on the crown of the hill was too exposed to possible sniper fire. Sheila saw the glow of light and heard the clink of a glass and stopped. Standing unseen in the dark, she raised her voice,

> "'Harp and carp True Thomas, she said
> Harp and carp along with me
> If you dare kiss me on the lips
> Sure of your body I will be.'"

Munro recognized the voice and knew the quotation and, in the ensuing silence, replied without looking around.

> "'My lance is tipped of the hammered flame,
> My shield is beat of the moonlight cold,
> And I won my spurs in the nether world
> A thousand fathoms beneath the mould.'"

Sheila remained hidden in the darkness and said again,

> "'Harp and carp True Thomas, she said
> Harp and carp along with me
> If ye dare kiss me on the lips
> Sure of your body I will be.'"

Still looking out into the darkness of the valley below, Munro asked, "Daughter of Og, Daughter of the Isles, what brings ye here?"

"I have brought two bairns that need fostering. Will you do that for me, Bruadarach?"

"Right gladly, but why now?"

Sheila quoted another old poem they both knew,

> "'Come hither Evan Cameron, come stand beside my knee.
> I hear the river roaring down towards the wintry sea.

There's shouting on the mountainside—'"

"Aye," said Munro, cutting in. "So that is the way of it?" And he continued the poem,

> "'There's war within the blast.
> Old faces look upon me, old forms go trooping past.
> I hear the pibroch wailing amid the din of fight
> And my dim spirit wakes again upon the verge of night.'"

He turned to look into the shadows, where she remained hidden. "And so the harbinger. What else is your desire, Sheila MacDonald?"

"Wed me and bed me, Bruadarach."

"Nay, lass, I am already, and why the hurry?"

Again, she quoted from another old poem,

> "'The eldest to the youngest said
> Brother we must awa.
> The cock doth craw, the day doth daw
> The channering worm doth chide.
> If we be missed at our place,
> A sair pain we mun bide.'

Wed me and bed me this one night. Give me strength to do what I must do. One night is all I ask, Bruadarach. Give me your courage."

"You never lacked for that, Sheila MacDonald. Or is it a pale, pale McCrimmon of the green eyes come from the Isle of Skye to bewitch me with a faerie's spell?"

She entered the shallow cave where he was sitting. There was a large ceremonial candle, which he had lit in front of the huge statue of the seated Buddha. He put down his glass and stood, taking her arms in his hands.

"If that is indeed your desire, Sheila MacDonald, then the Buddha will listen to our pledge."

They stood in the candlelight looking at each other, holding each other's wrists. Sheila felt a strange atavistic sense that she was taking part in a ceremony of her people from the dawn of history. He said, "I will be your man for this night, and I will be a father to your children as long as I live, and I will honor you forever."

She said, "I will be your woman for this night, and I will honor you until I pass from this world."

He picked up the glass of scotch he had been sipping and offered it to her. She toasted him, drank, and gave the glass back to him. He did likewise, toasting her then tossing it back.

"Make me brave, Munro. Last night, I felt the gray goose walking over my grave, and I thought of Otterburn.

> 'For I have dreamed a dreary dream
> Beyond the Isles of Skye
> I saw a dead man win a fight
> And I think that man was I.'"

Munro also knew that poem. "'Douglas was buried by the bracken bush and Percy led the captive away.' Ah, Sheila, is it worth it? The best and the bravest, you and Tomiko, La Marquesa, Leda, and Hinchcliffe. Sacrificing yourselves for what? Europe is finished. The West is finished. It is not worth saving. These half men that are left, do you think that they will fight? That political class, that scum, those weaklings who hate their heritage? Better take your kids and escape to Mars."

"That's not what I came to hear, Munro. I came to listen to the fighter, the man in the square ring, Braveheart. Don't you feel it? The surge and thunder. Your blood heritage,

> 'Where are the hearts that beat beneath Scottish skies?
> Towering in gallant fame, Scotland my mountain hame,
> High may your Proud banner gloriously wave.'"

He sighed. "You are right as always, Sheila. 'Yet we endure, yet shall the morning find us, children of the tempest, all unshaken still.' 'Wild waves the eagle plume blended with heather.' I have to snap out of this sense of doom and try to support you guys, at least emotionally. Man up! Remember Horatius,

> 'And how can man die better
> Than facing fearful odds,
> For the ashes of his fathers,
> For the temples of his gods.'"

"That's more like it, Munro. Tell me more."

"Ah, Sheila, maybe one last attempt. 'Where the lean locked ranks go roaring down to die.' I fear it is 'the broken jaw of our lost kingdom,' and that maybe it will be 'with never a foot lagging or head bent, to the clash and clamor of dust and death they went.' But the West won, against all odds, at Marathon, Actium, Tours, Vienna, and Lepanto, so maybe again. Tomiko says she would rather fight them in Europe than on the beaches of her Home Islands. If you lose, Sheila, Thor's hammer is there, but I have not said that to anyone other than Sweet Wolf."

She put her finger to his lips.

"Shh. No words. So you are sending that Wolf to Mars. Do not tell me. Remember I am a Foundation girl who knows a little math and kinetics. I also know Isis is up there on Mars, and the moon has that monster rail gun. I don't want to think of a world in flames. Kiss me, Bruadarach, give me another drink and take me to bed. Give me the courage to do what I must do."

In silence, they held each other for a long time and then walked off into the darkness.

Very early in the morning, Sheila left Arizona and flew back to Paris to take her position in the march, which had been organized. Sheila felt she had no alternative but to stand at the side of Madeleine to face the rapidly approaching civil war.

Munro saw her off at the airport. It was still the dark of early morning. Standing on the apron beside the plane, he held her gently in his arms for a long minute and quietly quoted a poem.

"'How far is St. Helena from a fight in Paris Street?'" Sheila knew that poem and its grim warning. Knowing that, she still saw no alternative.

> "'I haven't time to answer now, the men are falling fast
> The guns begin to thunder and the drums begin to beat.
> If you take the first step you will take the last.'"

Munro held up his hands in resignation. "Vaya con Dios. Go with God, Sheila."

She boarded the plane, head held high, and left for what she knew to be an inevitable conflict.

For the march through Paris, Sheila insisted that a couple of Japanese Praetorians be in attendance as Madeleine would not hear of any American men acting as her bodyguards. The optics would have been unacceptable. She accepted the Japanese girls as long as they dressed in Western clothes. Sheila also insisted that Chest Doc, the Miami surgeon and the only doctor she really trusted, whom she had brought back in the plane with her from the US, be present in an armored stretch limo, following them closely. She also wanted a couple of units of cross-matched blood for Madeleine to be available, and Chest Doc had brought his own anesthetist and some emergency equipment. They would be hidden behind the darkened windows of the limo, so no one in the crowd would know they were there. Chest Doc also wanted and got a couple of assault rifles and his favorite shoulder-mounted rocket launcher. Anticipating real trouble at such an event, as had occurred years before when Sandra was running for the presidency of the US, he had practiced with that weapon on numerous occasions in the US but had never had an excuse to use it in the field. The last time he had been in Paris was with Elizabeth when she was president. He had requested these weapons at that time, but the authorities had refused. This time, he smuggled them in under the label of medical supplies.

The packed crowd was heaving as they marched along with Madeleine in the lead. Sheila was at her right shoulder and a pace behind. She had eventually accepted that the old peaceful Europe had been swept away by the flood of migrants and that frequent public violence was here to stay. The butt of Sheila's handgun was clearly visible under her left shoulder. Two Praetorians were on either side, a little behind. There was an outer ring of private security, but no police, as Madeleine had been denied an official position.

The event that Sheila dreaded happened. Two gunmen somehow managed to break through the cordon of security and opened fire. Madeleine was hit and went down. One of the Praetorians, who threw herself in front of Madeleine, was killed. Sheila managed to shoot one of the gunmen in the center of body mass, and the remaining Praetorian killed both attackers with head shots.

Just as the limo surged up to cover Madeleine, who was on the ground, a machine gun opened up from a window in a high building off to the right. Fortunately, the bullet proof limo was between Madeleine and the gunner, who killed several security men who were rushing in to cover her. Chest Doc hopped out of the limo almost before it stopped. He scanned the tops of the buildings on the right, saw from where the machine gun fire was coming, and ducked back into the limo, bringing out the rocket launcher. Leaning on the hood of the limo, he sighted on the window where the firing was coming from and let the rocket go. A couple of seconds later, the rocket entered the window and the top corner of the building blew off. The roar of the explosion temporarily silenced the crowd.

He threw the rocket launcher back inside the limo and dropped to his knees beside Madeleine. She was wearing a fairly tight skirt, so he cut it up to the waist to expose the gunshot, fortunately a single wound in her upper thigh. It was through and through and had not hit the bone, and while it was bleeding copiously, there was no arterial pumping. He plugged the wounds front and back and wrapped the thigh with a tensor bandage to apply pressure to slow the bleeding.

"Help me up," she demanded. He pulled her to her feet. She took a step on the injured left leg and almost fell as it partly gave way. He grabbed her and put her left arm over his shoulder, and with him supporting her, she could walk.

"March!" she said. "And break out the tricolor."

They had the flag of France in the limo. Sheila snapped the two pieces of the flagpole together and stepped behind Madeleine so that she was walking with the national flag over her head. Her people closed ranks behind her, and they marched on as the ambulances came to take away the dead. It made a stirring video of Madeleine, head held high, limping forward under the tricolor of France, supported by Chest Doc. Her skirt, split open to the waist, showed her bandaged thigh with blood dripping down her leg.

The crowd began to sing the "La Marseillaise," the anthem of France, and surged in behind her, filling the whole street as they took a right-hand turn toward the Élysées Palace, where the president of France was cowering. This man, who felt and had stated many times that France was no longer a nation, but simply a piece of real estate, hid in the palace and refused to face the crowd, who obviously did not share in his nihilistic vision of themselves and their country.

The patience of France was finally exhausted with this man, who had openly sneered at them and their country on numerous occasions. Hundreds of furious young men in the crowd broke into the Élysées Palace, swept the guards aside, and hauled out the quaking and trembling leader. Without more ado, they slung a rope over a lamp post, put the noose around his neck, and hanged him high. His equally fed-up guards and the ever-present police simply stood by and made a token effort only to keep the young men out of the palace or protect this man, whom they all thoroughly despised.

Sheila knew the torch was finally lit. The long-expected rebellion had begun. "Cry havoc and let slip the dogs of war."

THE FUTURE OF EUROPE

It had been clear to all but the most obtuse that Europe was going to be plunged into a civil war, brought on by the apparently thoughtless policies of the political class. This had been predicted in the 1960s by the English politician Enoch Powell. He was scorned and dismissed at that time as a needless alarmist, but wishful thinking and a lack of knowledge of history does not change it. History is cyclical and repeats. Every civilization seems to be born with its telomeres, the death genes.

But this cataclysm will be more important than the collapse of a single empire. The Western world, which was not just a physical empire but a way of regarding civilization itself, is reaching the Aquinas/Averroes (Ibn Rushd) point of inflexion. On one side, there will be an exponential increase in knowledge leading to the artificial intelligence transfiguration, with eventual expansion into and beyond the galaxy; and on the other, the reversion to medievalism, with progressive loss of IQ, the burning of books, the banning of immunization, and a retreat into poverty, diseases, and numb acceptance of life. Chained in place forever until the sun goes nova, the whole sorry excuse for the human race will vanish in the fire. The lack of visitors from space suggests that this is actually an immutable fact of all civilizations in all times and all places and all universes.

In the short term, what would trigger the onset of civil war was not clear, as the West had passively absorbed one assault after another over the last two decades—in reality, since the end of WWI—with no significant response at all. Emboldened by this passivity, the demands were becoming more strident. Some countries were clearly going to cease to exist as a nation and simply become a piece of real estate, as the president of France and the prime minister of Canada openly supported the doctrine of post-nationalism. If their lead were to be followed, the West would simply disappear step wise as the tipping point of each state was reached.

But there are others who regarded this passivity as shameful, and there are some left who refuse to go gently into that good night. There are people who still believe that humanity can arise above all its frailties, retain the unlikely Western concept of individual value, and become a multi-planet species. For them "reach for the stars" is not a dream but a reality to be pursued at all costs, before the Hobbesian nightmare occurs, with the collapse of civilization on Earth.

The ominous words from the past resound like a clarion call: "you have been weighed in the balances and found wanting."

ACKNOWLEDGMENTS

In this book, there are extensive quotations from especially Rudyard Kipling. Also frequently quoted are William Shakespeare, Kit Marlowe, Robert Service, George Bernard Shaw, Lord Byron, Oscar Wilde, T. S. Elliot, G. K. Chesterton, Neil Munro, Sir Henry Newbolt, Francis Thompson, Immanuel Kant, Schopenhauer, Thomas Jefferson, Edward Fitzgerald, William Henley, Lord Tennyson, Wilfred Owen, John Donne, Ernest Dowson, Dylan Thomas, the King James Version of the Bible, Nancy Sinatra, the Seekers, Simon and Garfunkel, and numerous others. Any memorable phrase is probably a quotation, and efforts have been made to put all such in quotation marks. Intentionally, not all the quotations are entirely accurate, as a few have been modified to fit the narrative.

Published Books by the Author

The Technique of Total Hip Replacement
The Bone Implant Interface
Have Knife Will Travel
To Slip the Surly Bonds of Earth
    Book 1: About the Breaking of the Day
    Book 2: Upon the Further Shore
With Edna Quammie
    The Big House
    Rainbow through the Rain